Edited by Martin H. Greenberg, Jon Lellenberg, Daniel Stashower

Murder
in Baker Street

New Tales of
Sherlock Holmes

MJF BOOKS
NEW YORK

Published by MJF Books
Fine Communications
322 Eighth Avenue
New York, NY 10001

Murder in Baker Street
LC Control Number 2006931459
ISBN-13: 978-1-56731-805-0
ISBN-10: 1-56731-805-3

CONTENTS

INTRODUCTION

"THIS I AM sure of," Arthur Conan Doyle once remarked, "that there are far fewer supremely good short stories than there are supremely good long books. It takes more exquisite skill to carve the cameo than the statue."

The author was speaking from long experience. Some years earlier, in April 1891, Conan Doyle's career as a medical practitioner had reached its lowest point. He had recently abandoned a modestly successful practice in Southsea, near Portsmouth, to study diseases of the eye. Now, having moved his family to London, the 31-year-old physician declared himself ready to "put up my plate as an oculist."

Eager to establish himself, Conan Doyle set up a consulting room at 2 Upper Wimpole Street, a short distance from Harley Street, where the more established medical men plied their trade. "I was aware that many of the big men did not find time to work out refractions," he wrote. "I was capable in this work and liked it, so I hoped that some of it might drift my way."

None did. The young doctor's lease entitled him to a consulting room and a share of a waiting room, but, as Conan Doyle ruefully admitted, "I was soon to find that they were both waiting rooms."

Undeterred, Conan Doyle set out each morning from his flat in Montague Place and walked the fifteen minutes or so to Upper Wimpole Street. There, he sat at his desk until late afternoon— "with never a ring to disturb my serenity."

As he had already enjoyed some success as an author by this stage, Conan Doyle's thoughts naturally turned to literature. Sitting alone in his consulting room, he hit on an idea which may well have been the single greatest inspiration of his career.

For some time, Conan Doyle had poured most of his literary energies into novels, because the disjointed collection of short stories from his early days had done nothing to advance his career. Now, with his financial reserves dwindling, he decided on a new direction. It struck him that there might be some benefit in writing a series of stories featuring a single, continuing character. This offered an advantage over the more conventional serialized novel, because the reader would not lose interest if one installment or another was missed. Conan Doyle realized, of course, that the serialization of novels had done no harm to Charles Dickens, but there were now far more magazines on the stands, and a far greater number of literate people to read them, not all of whom would have the patience or the means to follow a continuing saga.

"Looking round for my central character," he wrote, "I felt that Sherlock Holmes, whom I had already handled in two little books, would easily lend himself to a succession of short stories."

The importance of this decision cannot be overstated. Not only had Conan Doyle made a very canny marketing decision, but he had also found an especially good showcase for the talents of Sherlock Holmes. In the two previously published Holmes novellas—"A Study in Scarlet" and "The Sign of the Four"—the detective had been obliged to trundle offstage for long patches of exposition. The short story format offered a compact execution and brisk pace, and highlighted Conan Doyle's singular talent for puzzle plots. Of the sixty tales comprising the complete Sherlock Holmes adventures, fifty-six are short stories. Sherlock Holmes was a sprinter, not a distance runner.

Having charted this new course, Conan Doyle needed only to find a magazine receptive to the idea. For ten years, a journal called *Tit-bits* had been a fixture at every corner newsstand. Made up of nuggets, or "tit-bits," of informative material, humor and stories, the magazine made a fortune for its founder, George Newnes, who parlayed the success into an entire stable of periodicals. The latest of these, as Conan Doyle set to work on his Sherlock Holmes short stories, was *The Strand* magazine, which began publication in January of that year under the editorship of H. Greenhough Smith.

Within weeks, Conan Doyle began sending the first of his Sherlock Holmes short stories to *The Strand.* In later years, Greenhough Smith would often speak of the day when those stories crossed his desk: "What a God-send to an editor jaded with wading through reams of impossible stuff! The ingenuity of plot, the limpid clearness of style, the perfect art of telling a story! The very handwriting, full of character, and clear as print."

And the rest—in a cliche that the good Dr. Watson would have abhorred—is history.

The editors of the present volume, though not overly concerned with handwriting, share Mr. Smith's concern for plot, style and the art of storytelling. It is a particular pleasure, therefore, to present this collection of new stories in the great tradition of Sherlock Holmes by eleven of today's best crime writers. In addition, we have the honor to present three pieces of nonfiction on the subject of the Great Detective and his world, including a series of entertaining reminiscences from Conan Doyle himself.

Once again, the game's afoot.

Daniel Stashower

THE MAN FROM CAPETOWN

Stuart M. Kaminsky

IT WAS RAINING. It was not the usual slow, cold gray London rain that spattered on umbrellas and broad brimmed hats but the heavy relentless downpour that came several times a year jungle drumming on the rooftops of cabs reminding me of the more mild monsoons I had witnessed in my years in India.

Time in India always moved slowly. Time in the apartment I shared with Sherlock Holmes had moved at the pace of a torpid Bombay cat during the past two weeks.

I kept myself busy trying to write an article for *The Lancet* based on Holmes' findings about the differences he had discovered between blood from people native to varying climates. At first Holmes had entered into the endeavor with vigor and interest, pacing, smoking his pipe, pausing to remind me of subtle differences and the implications of his discovery both for criminology and medicine.

Several days into the enterprise, however, Holmes had taken to standing at the window for hours at a time, staring into the rain-swept street, thinking thoughts he chose not to share with me.

Twice he picked up the violin. The first time he woke me at five in the morning with something that may have been Liszt. The second time was at one in the afternoon when he repeatedly played a particularly mournful tune I did not recognize.

On this particular morning, Holmes was sitting in his armchair, pipe in hand, looking at the coal scuttle.

"Rather interesting item in this morning's *Times*," I ventured as I sat at the table in our sitting room with the last of my morning tea and toast before me.

Holmes made a sound somewhere between a grunt and a sigh.

"A Mr. Morgan Fitchmore of Leeds," he said. "Found in a cemetery on his back with a railroad spike plunged into his heart. He was gripping the spike, apparently in an attempt to remove it. The night had been damp and the police found no footprints in the mud other than those of the deceased. About twenty feet from the body a hammer was found. The police are baffled."

Holmes grunted again and looked toward the window where the rain beat heavily on the glass.

"Yes," I said. "That is the story. I thought it might interest you."

"Minimally," said Holmes. "Read the rest of the story, Watson, as I have. Fitchmore was a petty thief. He was found lying on his back. The dead man appears to have left no signs that he attempted to defend himself."

"Yes, I see," I said reading further.

"What was a petty thief doing in a graveyard on a rainy night?" Holmes said drawing on his pipe. "Why would someone attack him with a railroad spike? Why were there no other footprints? Why did he not struggle?"

"I couldn't say," I said.

"Railroad spikes make passable chisels, Watson. A thief might well go into a graveyard at night with a spike and hammer to chisel away some cameo or small crucifix or other item he might sell for a slight sum. Such assaults on the resting place of the dead are not uncommon. A rainy night would ensure a lack of intrusion."

"I fail to see . . ."

"It is not a matter of seeing, Watson. It is a matter of putting together what has been seen with simple logic. Fitchmore went to the graveyard to rob the dead. He slipped in the mud flinging his hammer away as he fell forward on the spike he held in his hand. He rolled over on his back, probably in great agony, and attempted to pull the spike from his chest, but he was already dying. There is no mystery, Watson. It was an accidental if, perhaps, ironically apropos end for a man who would steal from the dead."

"Perhaps we should inform the police in Leeds," I said.

"If you wish," said Holmes indifferently.

"May I pour you a cup of tea? You haven't touched your breakfast."

"I am not hungry," he said his eyes now turned to the fireplace where flames crackled and formed kaleidoscope patterns which seemed to mesmerize Holmes who had not bothered to fully dress. He wore his gray trousers, a shirt with no tie and a purple silk smoking jacket that had been given to him by a grateful client several years earlier.

In the past month, Holmes had been offered three cases. One involved a purloined pearl necklace. The second focused on an apparent attempt to defraud a dealer in Russian furs and the third a leopard missing from the London zoo. Holmes had abruptly refused all three entreaties for his help and had directed the potential clients to the police.

"If the imagination is not engaged," he had said when the zoo director had left, "and there is no worthy adversary, I see no point in expending energy and spending time on work that could be done by a reasonably trained Scotland Yard junior inspector."

Holmes suddenly looked up at me.

"Do you have that letter readily at hand?"

I knew the letter of which he spoke and in the hope of engaging his interest I retrieved it from the portmanteaus near the fireplace which crackled with flames which cast unsettling morning shadows across the sitting room.

The letter had arrived several weeks ago and aside from the fact that it bore a Capetown postmark, it struck me as in no way singular or more interesting than any of a dozen missives that Holmes had done no more than glance at in the past several weeks.

"Would you read it aloud once more, Watson, if you please?"

"Mr. Sherlock Holmes," it read:

> I have a matter of the greatest importance to set before you. I have some business to attend to here in Capetown. It should take no more than a few days. I will then set forth for England in the hope of seeing you immediately upon my arrival. I must hurry now to get this letter on the next ship bound for Portsmouth. This is a matter of money, love and a palpable threat to my life. I beg you to give me a consultation. Cost is no object.

The letter was signed, *Alfred Donaberry*.

I folded the letter and looked at Holmes wondering why this particular correspondence, among the many so much like it he had received over the years, should draw his interest and why he had chosen this moment to return to it.

As he had done so many times before, Holmes answered my unspoken questions.

"Note the order in which our Mr. Donaberry lists his concerns," said Holmes looking in my direction and pointing his pipe at the missive in my hand. "Money, love and life. Mr. Donaberry lists the threat to his life last. Curious. As to why I am now interested in the letter, I ask a question. Did you hear a carriage stop in the street a moment ago?"

I had and I said so.

"If you check the arrival of ships in the paper from which you have just read you will note that the *Principia*, a cargo ship, arrived in Portsmouth from Capetown yesterday. If our Mr. Donaberry is as concerned as his letter indicates, he may well have been on that ship and braved the foul weather to make his way to us."

"It could be anyone," I said.

"The rig, judging from the sound of its wheels on the cobblestone, is a large one, not a common street cab and it is drawn by not one but two horses. I hear no other activity on the street save for this vehicle. The timing is right and, I must confess to a certain curiosity about a man who would venture from as far as Capetown to pay us a visit. No, Watson, if this man is as anxious to meet me as his letter indicates, he will have been off the boat and on his way catching the seven o'clock morning train."

A knock at the door and a small smile from Holmes accompanied by a raised eyebrow in satisfaction were aimed my way.

"Enter Mrs. Hudson," Holmes called.

Our landlady entered, looked at the plate of untouched food in front of Holmes and shook her head.

"A lady to see you," she said.

"A lady?" Holmes asked.

"Most definitely," Mrs. Hudson said.

"Please tell the lady that I am expecting a visitor and that she will have to make an appointment and return at a future time."

Mrs. Hudson was at the door with tray in hand. Over her shoulder she said, "The lady said to tell you that she knows you are expecting a visitor from South Africa. That is why she must see you immediately."

Holmes looked at me with arched eyebrows. I shrugged.

"Please show her in Mrs. Hudson and, if you would be so kind, please brew us a fresh pot of tea," Holmes said.

"You've eaten nothing Mr. Holmes," she said. "Perhaps I can bring you some fresh biscuits and jam?"

"Tea and biscuits will be perfect," Holmes said as she closed the door behind her, the tray balanced carefully in one hand.

"So our Mr. Donaberry is not the only one who would willingly venture out in a storm like this," I said pretending to return to the newspaper.

"So it would seem, Watson."

The knock at the door was gentle. A single knock. Holmes called out, "Come in" and Mrs. Hudson ushered in an exquisite dark creature with clear white skin and raven hair brushed back in a tight bun. She wore a prim black dress buttoned to the neck. The woman stepped in, looked from me to Holmes and stood silently for a moment till Mrs. Hudson had closed the door.

"Mr. Holmes," she said in a soft voice suggesting just the touch of an accent.

"I am he," said Holmes.

"My name is Elspeth Belknapp, Mrs. Elspeth Belknapp," she said. "May I sit?"

"By all means Mrs. Belknapp," Holmes said pointing to a chair near the one in which I was sitting.

"I have come . . . this is most delicate and embarrassing," she said as she sat. "I have come to . . ."

"First a few questions," said Holmes folding his hands in his lap. "How did you know Donaberry was coming to see me?"

"I . . . a friend in Capetown sent me a letter, the wife of a clerk in Alfred's office," she said. "May I have some water?"

I rose quickly and moved to the decanter Mrs. Hudson had left on the table. I poured a glass of water and handed it to her. She drank as I sat down and looked over at Holmes who seemed to be studying her carefully.

"Mr. Holmes," she said. "I was, until five months ago, Mrs. Alfred Donaberry. Alfred is a decent man. He took me in when my own parents died in a fire in Johannesburg. Alfred is considerably older than I. I was most grateful to him and he was most generous to me. And then, less than a year ago John Belknapp came to South Africa to conduct business with my then husband."

"And what business is that?" Holmes asked.

"The diamond trade," she said. "Alfred has amassed a fortune dealing in diamonds. Though I tried not to do so, I fell in love with John Belknapp and he with me. I behaved like a coward Mr. Holmes. John wanted to confront Alfred but I wanted no scene. I persuaded John that we should simply run away and that I would seek a divorce citing Alfred's abuse and infidelity."

"And was he abusive and unfaithful?" asked Holmes.

She shook her head.

"I am not proud of what I did. Alfred was neither abusive nor unfaithful. He loved me but I thought of him less as a husband than as a beloved uncle."

"And so," said Holmes, "you obtained a divorce."

"Yes, I came to London with John and obtained a divorce. John and I married the day after the divorce was approved by the Court. I thought that Alfred would read the note I had left for him when I fled with John and that Alfred would resign himself to the reality. But now I find . . ."

"I see," said Holmes. "And what would you have me do?"

"Persuade Alfred not to cause trouble, to leave England, to return to South Africa, to go on with his life. Should he confront John . . . John is a fine man, but he is somewhat on occasion and when provoked given to unconsidered reaction."

The woman removed a kerchief from her sleeve and dabbed at her eyes.

"He can be violent?" asked Holmes.

"Only when provoked, Mr. Holmes. Alfred Donaberry is a decent man, but were he to confront John . . ."

At this point Mrs. Hudson knocked and entered before she was bidden to do so. She placed biscuits and jam upon the table with three plates, knives and a fresh pot of tea. She looked at the tearful Elspeth Belknapp with sympathy and departed.

"Next question," Holmes said taking up a knife and using it to generously coat a biscuit with what appeared to be gooseberry jam. "You say your former husband is a man of considerable wealth?"

"Considerable," she said accepting a cup of tea from me.

"Describe him."

"Alfred? He is fifty-five years of age, pleasant enough looking though I have heard people describe him as homely. He is large, a bit, how shall I say this . . . Alfred is an uneducated, a self-made man, perhaps a bit rough around the edges, but a good, gentle man."

"I see," said Holmes, a large piece of biscuit and jam in his mouth. "And he has relatives, a mother, sister, brother, children?"

"None," she said.

"So, if he were to die, who would receive his inheritance?"

"Inheritance?"

"In his letter to me, he mentions that his visit is in part a matter of money."

"I suppose I might unless he has removed me from his will."

"And your new husband? He is a man of substance?"

"John is a dealer in fine gems. He has a secure and financially comfortable position with London Pembroke Gems Limited. If you are implying that John married me in the hope of getting Alfred's estate, I assure you you are quite wrong Mr. Holmes."

"I am merely trying to anticipate what direction Mr. Donaberry's concerns will take him when we meet. May I ask what you are willing to pay for my services in dissuading Mr. Donaberry from further pursuit of the issue?"

"I thought . . . Pay you? John and I are not wealthy," she said, "but I'll pay what you wish should you be successful in persuading Alfred to return to South Africa. I do not want to see him humiliated or hurt."

"Hurt?" asked Holmes.

"Emotionally," she said quickly.

"I see," said Holmes. "I'll take your case under advisement. Should I decide to take it, how shall I reach you?"

Elspeth Belknapp rose and removed a card from her small purse. She handed the card to Holmes.

"Your husband's business card," Holmes said.

"My home address is on the back."

She held out her hand to me. I took it. She was trembling.

"Holmes failed to introduce me," I said glancing reproachfully at my friend.

"You are Dr. Watson," she said. "I've read your accounts of Mr. Holmes' exploits and have remarked on your own humility and loyalty."

It was my turn to smile. She turned to Holmes who had risen from his chair. He took her hand and held it, his eyes on her wedding ring.

"A lovely diamond and setting," he said.

"Yes," she said looking at the ring. "It is far too valuable to be worn constantly. A simple band would please me as much but John insists and when John makes up his mind . . . Please Mr. Holmes, help us, John, me and Alfred."

The rain was still beating and the wind blowing even harder as she departed closing the door softly as she left.

"Charming woman," I said.

"Yes," said Holmes.

"Love is not always kind or reasonable," I observed.

"You are a hopeless romantic, Watson," he said moving to the window and parting the curtains.

"Not much of a challenge in this one," I observed.

"We shall see, Watson. We shall see. Ah, she wears a cape and carries an umbrella. Sensible."

I could hear the carriage door close and listened as it pulled away, horses clomping slowly into the distance.

Holmes remained at the window without speaking. He checked his watch from time to time but did not waver from his vigil till the sound of another carriage echoed down Baker Street.

"And this shall be our forlorn former husband," said Holmes looking back at me. "Ah yes, the carriage has stopped. He has gotten out. No umbrella. A big man. Let us move a chair near the fire. He will be drenched."

And indeed, when Mrs. Hudson announced and ushered Alfred Donaberry into the room, he was wet, thin hair matted against his scalp. His former wife had been kind in describing him as homely. He had sun darkened skin and a brooding countenance and bore a close resemblance to a bull terrier. In his left hand he carried a large and rather battered piece of luggage. His clothing, trousers, shirt and jacket were of good quality though decidedly rumpled and the man himself was quite disheveled and in need of a shave. His wrinkled suit was dark, a bit loose.

"Please forgive my appearance. I came here straightaway from the railway station," he said setting down his suitcase and holding out his hand. "Donaberry. Alfred Donaberry."

Holmes shook it. I did the same. Firm grip. Troubled face.

"I am Sherlock Holmes and this is my friend and colleague Dr. Watson. Won't you sit by the fire."

"I thank you, sir," Donaberry said moving to the chair I had moved next to the warmth of the hearth.

"I may as well get right to it," the man said holding his hands toward the fire.

"Your wife has left you," Holmes said. "Some three months ago. You recently discovered that she is in London and you've come in pursuit of her."

"How did you . . . ?"

"You missed her by but a few minutes," Holmes said.

"How did she know I . . . ?" Donaberry said perplexed.

"Let us lay that aside for the moment," said Holmes and, if you will, get to the heart of your problem."

"Heart of the problem. Ironical choice of words, Mr. Holmes," he said. "No, I am not pursuing Elspeth. If she wants no more of an old man, I can understand though I am broken of heart. The minute I read the note she had left me those months ago I accepted reality and removed my wedding ring."

He held up his left hand to show a distinct white band of skin where a ring had been.

"You do not want to find her or her new husband?" Holmes asked.

"No sir," he said. "I want nothing to do with him, the jackanapes who stole her from me and polluted her mind. I want you to find them and stop them before they succeed in murdering me within the next month."

I looked at Holmes with a sense of shock but Holmes simply popped yet another piece of biscuit and jam into his mouth.

"Why should they want to murder you Mr. Donaberry?" I asked.

He looked at me.

"I have entered my will for change in the courts," he said. "In one month time, Elspeth will be my heir no longer."

"Why a month?" I asked.

Donaberry shifted uncomfortably in his chair and looked down before speaking.

"When we married, because of my age and sometimes fragile health, I feared for Elspeth's future should I die. Though by law she would inherit, I have distant relatives in Cornwall who might well make claim on my estate or some part of it. Therefore, I entered specifically into my will that Elspeth should inherit everything and that there should be no revocation or challenge to my will and my desire. My solicitor now informs me, and Elspeth well knows and has certainly informed her new husband, that it will take a month longer to execute the changing of the will, so carefully has it been worded. For you see, the word 'wife' never appears in the will, only the name Elspeth Donaberry."

"But what," I asked, "makes you think they plan to kill you?"

"The two attempts which have already been made upon my life in South Africa," he answered with a deep sigh. "Once when I was in field a fortnight past. I spend much of my time when weather permits and the beating sun is tolerable, in the flats and mountains searching for gem deposits. It was a particularly blistering day when I was fired upon. Three shots from the cover of trees. One shot struck a rock only inches from my head. I was fortunate enough to escape with my life. In the second instance, an attempt was made to push me off a pier onto a trio of sharpened pilings. Only by the grace of God did I fall between the pilings."

"You have other enemies besides Belknapp and your wife?"

"None, and Mr. Holmes, I don't blame Elspeth necessarily, but that John Belknapp is a piece of work with friends of an unsavory bent and though he might have persuaded her otherwise, I know from my most reliable sources that John Belknapp is in serious financial trouble. He is a profligate, a speculator and a gambler. I think he wants not just my wife but my fortune."

"And you want me to protect you?" asked Holmes.

"I want you to do whatever it takes to keep Belknapp from killing me or having me killed. He's more than half a devil."

It sounded to me like the kind of case Holmes would have sent straightaway to Lestrade and the Yard.

"The price will be two hundred pounds payment in advance," said Holmes.

Donaberry did not hesitate. He stood up, took out his wallet and began placing bills on the table counting aloud as he did so.

"Thank you," said Holmes. "Dr. Watson and I will do our utmost to see to it that murder does not take place. Where will you be staying in London?"

"I have a room reserved at The Cadogan Hotel on Sloane Street," he said.

The Cadogan was a small hotel known to be the London residence of Lilly Langtree and rumored to be an occasional hideaway for the notorious playwright Oscar Wilde.

"You've told no one," said Holmes.

"Only you and Dr. Watson," he said.

"Very good," said Holmes. "Remain in your room. Eat in the hotel. We will contact you when we have news. And Mr. Donaberry, do not go out the front door and do not take the cab that is waiting for you. You may be watched. Dr. Watson will show you how to get out the back entrance. There is a low fence. I suggest you climb it and work your way out to the street beyond. Mrs. Hudson will provide you with an umbrella."

"My suitcase," he said.

"Dr. Watson or I will return it to you the moment it is safe to do so. I cannot see a man of your size and age climbing fences with the burden of this luggage."

Donaberry looked as if he were thinking deeply before deciding to nod his head in reluctant agreement.

"Then be off," Holmes said. "Remember, stay in the hotel. In your room as much as possible with the door locked. Take all your meals in the hotel dining room. The food is not the best but it is tolerable."

Donaberry nodded and I led him out the door and down to the back entrance after he had retrieved his coat and Mrs. Hudson had provided an umbrella.

Holmes was pacing the floor, hands behind his back when I returned to our rooms and said, "Holmes, while I sympathize with Mr. Donaberry's situation, I see nothing in it to capture your attention or make use of your skills."

"I'm sorry, Watson, what did you say? I was lost in a thought about this curious situation. There are so many questions."

"I see nothing curious about it," I said.

"We are dealing with potential murder here and a criminal mind that is worth confronting," he responded. "And we have no time to lose. Let us take Mr. Donaberry's waiting cab and pay a visit."

"To whom?" I asked.

In response, Holmes held up the card Elspeth Belknapp had handed him.

"To John Belknapp," he said. "Of course."

In the carriage, to the beating of the rain on the carriage roof and the jostling of the wheels along the cobblestones, Holmes said that he had examined the contents of Alfred Donaberry's luggage when I had ushered Donaberry to the rear entrance to Mrs. Hudson's.

"The suitcase was neatly packed, shirts and trousers, toiletries, underclothing and stockings, plus a pair of serviceable shoes."

"And what did you discover from that?" I asked as lightning cracked in the west.

"That Alfred Donaberry packs neatly and keeps his clothing and shoes clean," said Holmes.

"Most significant," I said trying to show no hint of sarcasm at this discovery.

"Perhaps," said Holmes looking out the window.

We arrived on a side street off of Portobello Road within twenty minutes. The rain had let up considerably and I negotiated with the cabby to await our return. Considering that we were now going to pay for Donaberry's trip plus our own, the slicker-shrouded driver readily agreed. Holmes and I moved quickly toward the entrance to the four-story office building which bore a bronze plate inscribed Pembroke Gems, Ltd., by Appointment of His Majesty, 1721.

Despite its history, the building was less than nondescript. It was decidedly shabby. We knocked at the heavy wooden door which dearly needed painting and were ushered inside by a very old man in a suit that seemed much too tight even for his frail frame.

"We are here to see Mr. John Belknapp," said Holmes.

"Mr. Belknapp is in," the frail old man said, "but . . . do you have an appointment?"

"Tell him it is Mr. Sherlock Holmes and that I have come about a matter concerning Alfred Donaberry."

"Sherlock Holmes, about Alfred Donaberry," the old man repeated. "Please wait here."

The man moved slowly up the dark wooden stairway in the small damp hallway.

"Why the urgency, Holmes?"

"Perhaps there is none, Watson, but I prefer to err on the side of caution in a situation such as this."

The frail old man reappeared in but a few minutes and turned to lead us up the stairs after saying, "Mr. Belknapp can see you now."

On the narrow second floor landing with creaking floorboards, we were ushered to a door with *John Belknapp* written in peeling black paint.

The frail man knocked and a voice called, "Come in."

We entered and the old man closed the door behind us as he left.

Our first look at Belknapp immediately provoked in me a sense of caution. He was, as we had been told, a handsome man of no more than forty, reasonably well dressed in a dark suit and vest. His hair, just beginning to show signs of distinguished gray at the temples, was brushed back. He was standing behind his desk in an office that showed no great distinction or style. Plain dark wooded furniture, several chairs, cabinets and a picture of the queen upon the wall. The view through his windows was really no view at all, simply a brick wall no more than half a dozen feet away. Prosperity did not leap from the surroundings.

Sensing my reaction perhaps, Belknapp in an impatient response said, "My office is modest. It is designed for work and not for entertaining clients. For that there is a conference space on the ground floor."

I nodded.

"I hope this will be brief," he said.

"Dr. Watson and I will take but a few minutes of your time," Holmes said. "We have no need to sit."

"Good," said Belknapp, "I have a client to meet if I can find a cab in this confounded rain. You said this is about Alfred Donaberry."

"Yes," said Holmes. "Perhaps you know why we have come."

"Alfred Donaberry is a fool so I assume you are on a fool's errand. He could not hold on to a beautiful wife, did not appreciate her. I rescued her from a life of potential waste in a barely civilized country torn by potential war. If he is in England or has commissioned you in some way to persuade or threaten me and my wife, I . . ."

"Mr. Donaberry is, indeed, in England."

"Money," said Belknapp as if coming to a sudden understanding. "It's about the money."

"In part," said Holmes. "If you answer but one question, we shall leave you to attend to your client."

"Ask," said Belknapp with distinct irritation.

"What would you say your business is worth?"

"That is of no concern to you," Belknapp responded angrily.

"Incorrect," said Holmes. "It is precisely my concern. You wish us to depart so that you can get on with your client, simply answer the question."

"My business is worth far less than I would like. The inevitable war with the Boers has already affected mining and my sources are threatened. My personal savings and holdings have dwindled. What has this to do with . . . ?"

"We shall leave now," said Holmes. "I have one suggestion before we do so."

"And what might that be?" asked Belknapp with a sneer that made it clear he was unlikely to take any suggestion made by a representative of Alfred Donaberry.

"Stay away from Mr. Donaberry," said Holmes. "Stay far away."

"A threat? You issue me a threat?" asked Belknapp, beginning to come around his desk, fists clenched.

"Let us say it is a warning," said Holmes standing his ground.

Belknapp was now in front of Holmes, his face pink with anger. I took a step forward to my friend's side. Holmes held up a hand to keep me back.

"You should learn to control your temper," said Holmes. "In fact I would say it is imperative that you do so."

I thought Belknapp was certainly about to strike Holmes but before he could do so, Holmes held his right hand up in front of the gem dealer's face.

"Were you to lose control," Holmes said. "It is likely that you would be the one injured. Would you like to explain a swollen eye or lip and a disheveled countenance to your expected client?"

Belknapp's fists were still tight but he hesitated.

"Good morning to you," said Holmes turning toward the door, "and remember my warning. Stay away from Alfred Donaberry."

I followed Holmes out the door and down the stairs. The rain had stopped and the streets were wet under a cloudy sky that showed no promise of sun.

When we were on the move again, I looked at Holmes who sat frowning.

"I don't see how your warning will stop Belknapp from his plan to do away with Donaberry. While your reputation proceeds you, he did not seem the kind who would be concerned about the consequences of any violence that might come to Donaberry."

"I'm afraid you are right, Watson," Holmes said with a sigh. "I'm afraid you are right."

We were no more than five minutes from Baker Street when Holmes suddenly said, "We must stop the carriage."

"Why?" I asked.

"No time to explain," he said, rapping at the hatchway in the roof. "We must get to Alfred Donaberry at once. It is a matter of life or death."

The driver opened the flap. Though the rain had now stopped a spray from the roof hit me through the open portal. Holmes rose and spoke to the driver. I did not clearly hear what he said beyond Holmes' order and statement that there was a full pound extra in it if he rode like the wind.

He did. Holmes and I were jostled back and forth holding tightly to the carriage straps. The noise of the panting horse and the wheels against the uneven cobblestones made it difficult to understand Holmes who seemed angry with himself. I thought I heard him say, "The audacity, Watson. Not even to wait a day. To use me for a fool."

"You think Belknapp is on his way to The Cadogan Hotel?" I asked.

"I'm convinced of it," Holmes said. "Pray we are not too late."

We arrived in, I am certain, record time. Holmes leaped out of the carriage before the horse had come to a complete halt.

"Wait," I called to the driver following Holmes past the doorman and into the hotel lobby.

As it turned out, we were too late.

The lobby was alive with people and two uniformed constables trying to keep them calm. Holmes moved through the crowd not worrying about who he might be elbowing out of the way.

"What has happened here?" Holmes demanded of a bushy mustached constable.

"Nothing you need concern yourself with sir," the constable said paying no attention to us.

"This," I said, "is Sherlock Holmes."

The constable turned toward us and said, "Yes, so it is. How did you get here so fast? I know you have a reputation for . . . but this happened no more than five minutes ago."

"This?" asked Holmes. "What is 'this'?"

"Man been shot dead in room upstairs, Room 116 I think. We have a man up there with the shooter and we're waiting for someone to show up from the yard. So . . ."

Holmes waited for no more. He moved past the constable who was guarding the steps with me in close pursuit. Holmes moved more rapidly up the stairs than did I. My old war wound allowed for limited speed, but I was right behind him when he made a turn at the first landing and headed for a young constable standing in front of a door, a pistol in his hand. The sight of a London constable holding a gun was something quite new to me.

"Where is he?" Holmes demanded.

The constable looked bewildered.

"Are you from the Yard?" the young man asked hopefully.

"We are well known at the Yard," I said. "I'm a doctor. I expect an Inspector will be right behind us."

"Is that the murder weapon?" Holmes asked.

"It is sir," the young man said, handing it to me. "He gave it up without a word. He's just sitting in there now as you can see."

I looked through the door. There was a man on his back in the middle of the floor, eyes open, a splay of blood on his white shirt. Another man sat at the edge of a sturdy armchair, head in hands.

The dead man was John Belknapp. The man in the chair was Alfred Donaberry.

"We are," said Holmes, "too late."

At the sound of Holmes' voice, Donaberry looked up. His eyes were red and teary. His mouth was open. A look of pale confusion covered his face.

"Mr. Holmes," he said. "He came here just minutes ago. He had a gun. I don't . . . He gave no warning. He fired."

Donaberry pointed toward the window. I could see that it was shattered.

"I grabbed at him and managed to partially wrest the gun away," Donaberry went on. "We struggled. I thought he had shot me, but he backed away and . . . and fell as you see him now. My God Mr. Holmes, I have killed a man."

Holmes said nothing as I moved to Donaberry and called for the constable at the door to bring a glass of water. Had I my medical bag there were several sedatives I could have administered but barring that, I could only minister to his grief, horror and confusion which I did to the best of my limited ability.

Holmes had now moved to and sat on a wooden chair near a small table on which rested a washing bowl and pitcher. He had made a bridge of his fingers and placed the edge of their roof against his pursed lips.

I know not how many minutes passed with me trying to calm Donaberry but it could not have been many before Elspeth Belknapp came rushing into the room. Her eyes took in the horror of the scene and she collapsed weeping at the side of her dead husband.

"I . . . Elspeth, believe me it was an accident," Donaberry said. "He came to . . ."

"We know why he came," Inspector Lestrade's voice came from the open door.

Lestrade looked around the room. I retrieved the gun from my pocket and handed it to him.

"Mrs. Belknapp came to Scotland Yard," said Lestrade looking at Holmes who showed no interest in his arrival or the distraught widow. "It seems Mr. Belknapp left a note which Mrs. Belknapp found no more than an hour ago. He told her he was going to see Alfred Donaberry and end his intrusion forever. Constable Owens has filled me in on what took place. We'll need a statement from Mr. Donaberry."

"May I see the note Inspector?" Holmes said.

Lestrade retrieved the missive from his pocket and handed it to Holmes who read it slowly and handed it back to the Inspector.

"Lady says her husband had quite a temper," Lestrade said. "He owned several weapons, protection from gem thieves."

"Yes," said the kneeling widow. "I asked him repeatedly to keep the weapons out of our house, but he insisted that they were essential."

"Temper, weapon, note, struggle," said Lestrade. "I'd say Mr. Donaberry is fortunate to be alive."

"Indeed," said Holmes. "But that danger has not yet passed."

Elspeth Belknapp turned to Holmes.

"I harbor no wishes of death for Alfred," she said. "I have had enough loss, Mr. Holmes."

"Well," said Lestrade with a sigh. "That pretty much takes care of this unfortunate situation. We'll need a detailed statement from you Mr. Donaberry when you're able."

Donaberry nodded.

"A very detailed statement," said Holmes. "Mr. Donaberry, would you agree that my part of our agreement has been fulfilled albeit not as we discussed it?"

"What?" asked the bewildered man.

"You paid me two hundred pounds to keep John Belknapp from killing you. You are not dead. He is."

"The money is yours," said Donaberry with a wave of his hand.

"Thank you," said Holmes. "Now, with that settled, we shall deal with the murder of John Belknapp, a murder which I foresaw but failed to act upon with sufficient haste to save his life. The audacity of the murderer took me, I admit, by surprise. I'll not let such a thing to again transpire."

"What the devil are you talking about Holmes?" Lestrade said.

Holmes rose from his chair and looking from Elspeth Belknapp to Alfred Donaberry said, "These two have conspired to commit murder which is bad enough, but what I find singularly outrageous is that they sought to use me to succeed in their enterprise."

"Use you?" asked Donaberry. "Mr. Holmes, have you gone mad? I went to you for help. Belknapp tried to kill me."

Holmes was shaking his head "no" even before Alfred Donaberry had finished.

"Can you prove this, Holmes?" Lestrade asked.

"Have I ever failed to do so in the past to your satisfaction?"

"Not that I recall," said Lestrade.

"Good, then hear me," said Holmes pacing the floor. "First, I thought it oddly coincidental that Mrs. Belknapp should visit me only minutes before her former husband. Ships are notoriously late and occasionally early. Yet the two visits were proximate."

"Which proves?" asked Lestrade.

"Nothing," said Holmes. "I accepted it as mere coincidence. As I accepted Mrs. Belknapp's statements about the basic goodness of her former spouse. She said she wanted to protect her husband. I now believe she came for the sole purpose of describing her former husband as a kind and decent man who would hurt no one and her now dead husband as a man of potentially uncontrollable passion."

"But that . . ." Lestrade began.

Holmes held up his hand and continued.

"And then Mr. Donaberry here arrived, rumpled, suitcase in hand showing us the finger from which he had supposedly removed his wedding ring three months earlier."

"Supposedly?" asked Lestrade.

"Mr. Donaberry told Watson and me that he worked almost daily with his hands in subtropical heat and sun. His skin is, indeed, deeply tanned. In three months, one would expect that the mark of the removed ring, though it might linger somewhat, would be covered by the effects of the sun. The band of skin where the ring had been is completely white. The band has been removed for no more than a few days."

"That's true," I said looking down at Donaberry's left hand.

"So, why lie? I asked myself," Holmes went on, "and so allowed my prospective client to continue as I observed that his clothes were badly rumpled and that he was in a disheveled state."

"I had hurried from the train, hadn't changed clothes since arriving in port yesterday," Donaberry said.

"Yet," said Holmes, "when I examined the contents of your suitcase when Dr. Watson led you out the rear of Mrs. Hudson's, I found everything neatly pressed and quite clean. You could have at least changed shirts and put on clean trousers in your travel to an appointment that meant life and death to you."

"I was distraught," said Donaberry.

"No doubt," said Holmes. "But I think you wanted to give the impression that you had not yet had time to check into this hotel."

"I had not," Donaberry said looking at me for support.

"I know," said Holmes, "but neither had you rushed to see me from the train station. I asked the cabby where he had picked you up. You had hailed him from the front of the Strathmore Hotel which is at least three miles from the railway station."

"I took a cab there and quarreled with the cabby who was taking advantage of my lack of familiarity with London," said Donaberry. "I got out at the Strathmore and hailed another cab."

"Possible," said Holmes, "not plausible. My guess is that you were staying at the Strathmore, probably under an assumed name."

"But why on earth would I want to kill Belknapp?" said Donaberry. "I was not jealous."

"On that I agree," said Holmes. "You were not. It was not jealousy that led you to murder. It was simple greed."

"Greed?" asked Elspeth Belknapp rising.

"Yes," said Holmes. "While John Belknapp's offices may seem shabby, the firm is an old and respected one and he supplied to my satisfaction that he was not only solvent but had an estate of some value. It will not be difficult to determine how valuable that estate might be."

"Not difficult at all," said Lestrade.

"And Mr. Donaberry, it should not be difficult to determine your financial status," Holmes went on. "You tell us you have a small fortune which Belknapp coveted. I doubt if that is the case."

"We can check that too," said Lestrade.

"Then, you counted on something that on the surface seemed to remove suspicion from you and your former wife. Mrs. Belknapp, even with tearful eyes, is a lovely young woman while you are, let us say, a man of less than handsome countenance. Belknapp, on the other hand, was decidedly younger than you and even as he lies there in death, he makes a handsome corpse."

"This is absurd," said Elspeth Belknapp.

"Indeed it is," said Holmes, "but easy for Inspector Lestrade to check. A final point, how did John Belknapp know that you were staying at The Cadogan?"

"He must have followed me from your apartment," said Donaberry.

"But you went out the rear," said Holmes. "However, even if we give you the benefit of the doubt, Watson and I went immediately to Belknapp's office after you departed. We were probably on our way before you found a cab in the rain. And he was in his office when we arrived."

"He could have had someone . . . ," Elspeth Belknapp said, and then stopped, realizing that she was now actively trying to protect the man who had shot her husband.

"No," said Holmes. "Mr. Donaberry made an appointment with your deceased husband, probably not giving his real name. John Belknapp went on the assumption that he was going to see a potential client. When he entered this room, he was murdered. We have only Mrs. Belknapp's word that her husband had many weapons and even if he did, we have no evidence that he brought a weapon with him. And then there is the note."

Holmes held up the note.

"I had a moment or two to glance at Belknapp's papers on his desk. There is definitely a similarity. However, I think careful scrutiny will show that it is at best a decent forgery. I suspect that Mrs. Belknapp wrote the note herself. Is that sufficient Inspector?"

"I think so, Mr. Holmes. Easy enough to check it all through."

"But Holmes," I interjected looking at the mismatched accused, "are you telling us that Donaberry and Mrs. Belknapp are lovers still, that he allowed his wife to not only marry but to enter into marital relations with another man?"

"I would suggest, Watson, that the white band on Mr. Donaberry's ring finger resulted from removing the wedding band from his marriage to Elspeth Belknapp's mother. I would suggest that she was not his wife but was and continues to be his daughter."

With that the woman ran into the arms of her father who took her in clear admission of their defeat.

"They made too many mistakes," Lestrade said motioning for the constable to take the pair into custody.

"Yes," said Holmes. "But the biggest of them was thinking they could make a dupe of Sherlock Holmes. I can sometimes forgive murder. It is their hubris which I find intolerable."

THE CASE OF THE BORDERLAND DANDELIONS

Howard Engel

I T WAS TOWARD the end of the fifth year of my acquaintance with the extraordinary consulting detective with whose name, he says, mine will forever be linked, that we found ourselves amid the smoke, steam, soot and noise of Paddington Station running to catch the departing train to Shrewsbury. Holmes had sent Billy around to my consulting rooms, with orders that I should bring my bag and meet him on Platform 7 in time for the 10:15. In the emergency, I could only pass on to my locum, Mr. Rankin, the obstinate stiff hip of Mrs. Caroline Fetherling, the complement of my waiting room that Friday morning. When Rankin went fishing in Scotland a few weeks earlier, I had seen to some two dozen of his patients and two of my own as well.

By some magical formula, known only to my friend, he found an empty compartment in the middle of the train. Immediately, he pulled up the window and attached a sticker reading "Home Office" to the window on the platform and another on the glass looking out on the corridor, before closing the curtain. I stowed my bag above my seat, while Holmes left his between us on the floor. Both of us collapsed in our seats, waiting to be off. My old war wound was giving me some pain as I tried to catch my breath.

Holmes paid no attention to the urban landscape moving past

us as we trespassed through the ugly back gardens of the city. I was impatient to know, of course, what I was doing in the middle of a July morning traveling into the unknown. The game was afoot, obviously, but what game, and where in the marches of Wales was it taking us?

By now I knew my friend well enough not to pester him with questions which time would answer soon enough. I had brought a medical article I was working on, and occupied myself in rereading what I had written so far before pressing on to a conclusion. Holmes lit his pipe with impatience at my apparent calmness and complete lack of curiosity.

"Have you ever seen a man hanged, Watson?"

"I wish I could say I hadn't, but you know what a shambles Afghanistan was for a time. Why do you ask?"

"I've accepted a challenge, Watson. If I succeed, I may be able to send the hangman packing. If not, Mr. Billington will add another statistic to his black ledger."

"Surely it's too late, if the hangman's been sent for?"

"He is sitting in the compartment next to ours."

"Billington? Scandalous. I thought he traveled Second."

"Usually Third to be precise. He customarily exchanges his free Second Class ticket for a Third and pockets the difference. I suspect that he has broken his customary habit because of the exalted rank of his client."

"Rank?"

"Yes, Watson. Unless I can do something about it, Billington will have Field Marshal Sir William Trotter dangling at the end of his rope in two days' time."

"Trotter! A much hated and feared man when I was in the service. But that was years ago."

"I understand that in mufti, he's quite civilized; domesticated you might say."

"Who is he supposed to have killed?" I asked. I had not been reading the papers recently, and was ashamed to say that I had no knowledge of the case. Holmes acknowledged that I must be part of a benighted minority to have missed hearing about it.

"But come," he said, rising to his feet and climbing over his bag, "let us ask these questions of the man who almost certainly has all the details at his fingertips."

"Whom do you mean? Surely *not* . . . ?"

"And why not Billington? Who better, my friend? James Billington is a professional in his trade. It goes without saying that he is well-acquainted with the facts of his client's case. He is a man of conscience, after all. You may be sure that he will know how to address the field marshal when they meet on Monday morning."

I followed Holmes from the compartment and into the corridor. Holmes braced his body against the windows as a passenger moved past us in the other direction. I did the same.

"Newspaper person," Holmes observed, indicating the now retreating figure heading to the far end of the car. "The death watch has begun!" I cocked my eye at Holmes. He turned away, muttering: "Fingers filthy from newsprint, rumpled clothes, that smell of too many nights sleeping rough and, of course, Watson, ink on his fingers. Since he's not a vagabond in a First Class car, it follows that he must have been sent out specially from a Metropolitan paper." Here Holmes rapped solidly on the neighboring compartment door, which was also adorned with a sign reading "Home Office." There was no immediate response. Holmes knocked a second time.

The man who slid the door back pushed a large, reddish face into the corridor. He'd been awakened from a nap, judging from his puffy eyes. "Yes?" he said with suspicion in a voice born and bred in the Midlands. Holmes introduced himself and then me to the hangman, who shot the door back so that it was completely open. A wave of his arm invited us to enter, which we did.

"There's newspaper persons aboard this train, sir. 'Have nowt to do wi' reporters, and you'll not go far wrong,' I always say." A whey-faced young man, wearing a suit a size or two too small for him, jumped to his feet. "This is my young assistant, Ned Willis. Ned, these are detectives from London traveling to Shrewsbury, I reckon." Ned pulled off his cap and rolled it out of shape as he made a place for us.

"I've heard you spoken of at the Bailey, Mr. Holmes. They say your name with respect, without a word of a lie they do." Billington had been eating nuts, by the look of the floor. He maneuvered his large form out of the way, back by the windows looking out on the lines. Holmes took a seat next to Billington, I sat facing them, with young Willis looking on from nearer the door.

After pleasantries were exchanged, Holmes asked Billington to rehearse for us the details of the case. I assumed that my friend knew the basic outline, but was hoping that the hangman might add an important detail omitted from the London papers. Billington took his face in a large bandanna and blew with all his might before trusting himself to speak. "It's a very sorry business, Mr. Holmes. I don't have to tell you I take no pleasure in Sir William's discomfort. I don't mind telling you that I would be relieved for once if there was a chance of the Royal prerogative being exercised. I'd sooner lose five pounds than execute a man of his standing."

"I see that you are well informed about the case at all events," Holmes said, pulling a sheaf of clippings from under the bag of nuts. "Capital! I wonder if you would mind giving my friend, here, the merest skeleton of the facts, Mr. Billington? It will pass the time." Holmes helped himself to a walnut, which he cracked between his palms. He offered the fragments to me, but so eager was I to hear what the hangman said, I shook my head. Holmes worked away at the kernels in his palm as he listened and helped himself to the bag when the need arose.

"As a fellow Mason, I would be honored, sir," I said. I had noticed the arc-and-compass breast pin on Billington's jacket, just above the blue ribbon of a total abstainer.

"Of course, of course," the executioner said, sitting back, pocketing his bandanna in an inner pocket and intertwining his fingers. "Where to begin? How to start?"

"Field Marshal Sir William Trotter left the army under protest, giving some relief to the government, I understand, when he retired," prompted Holmes.

"Oh, sir, that's not for me to say. But, no matter; it's his civilian life that's got him where he is in Shrewsbury gaol. You see, Mr. Watson, Sir William poisoned his Missus with arsenic he bought at the chemist's on High Street. He said at the trial that he bought the arsenic for killing dandelions in his lawn. It's true too. I mean arsenic's death on weeds like dandelions. No argument there. But Sir William gave it to his wife, who nobody in the town liked at all— she bossed Sir William around terrible. Then she ups and dies and Sir William appears to be heartbroken. Later on, he invites young Alister Cronin over for tea. Cronin was the *other* solicitor in town, you see. Cronin comes for tea, Sir William offers him a scone. 'Mind the fingers,' he says, and when Cronin gets home he's in horrible agony from his stomach. The doctor's called in. Dr. John Flanner. Flanner gets Cronin back on his feet again, but is just suspicious enough to save some of his urine and have it analyzed in London. Arsenic! The scone was laced with arsenic. That got Cronin, Mrs. Cronin and Mr. Rowan Styles, Cronin's father-in-law talking. Styles is the chemist and his daughter, Adelaide—that's Mrs. Cronin—is as good a chemist as her father. They got to talking. Soon after, Dr. Flanner wrote a letter to the Yard about Sir William trying to kill Alister Cronin and maybe, just *maybe*, somebody should have a look at Lady Edith's remains. You see, she was always sickly, but she fell into hysterics, convulsions with a lot of pain when she went."

"What animus did Sir William bear to Cronin?" I asked, feeling that a connection was missing.

"Ah, I should have mentioned that," Billington said, cracking another walnut between his great hands and sharing the kernel with Holmes. "You see, Dr. Watson, when Sir William came out of the army, he bought the law practice of an elderly solicitor named Greene and enjoyed a lively business. He had it all to himself until Alister Cronin moved to town and set up a law office across the street. Sir William wanted to get rid of his rival so he would have all the business to himself again."

"Was this the story that came out in the trial?"

"Yes, Mr. Holmes. That's what brings me and young Ned out, although I told them back in London I could handle the job by m'self."

"It's an impressive piece of work, isn't it?" This was addressed to me, and I answered as well as I could since I had no prior knowledge of the facts.

"I don't see why we've come all this way, Holmes. I can't see what you can possibly do to save him. The man has had a fair trial and he's been justly condemned. What is the point of our visit? You're not one to stand outside a prison gate in order to see the black flag raised any more than I am. And, by the by, who the deuce challenged you to uncover the true villains in so short a time?"

"What's this?" asked Billington, his small eyes wide open.

"Since coming to Shrewsbury, Sir William has lived in Maryfield, a large estate just outside town. He has two daughters who are devoted to their father and the memory of their dead mother. Eunice Trotter, the oldest of the girls wrote to me, pressing for me to interfere. What struck me about her letter was the fact that the letter seemed to come from a happy home."

" 'Happy home,' you say? That woman reduced Sir William to a milk sop. She repelled friendships, was always correcting his manners in public. She nagged him something terrible. I've got six or seven examples of her interfering behavior in that bunch of press cuttings."

"Mr. Billington, the fact that the town had no use for Lady Edith is no proof that Trotter wanted to murder his dear lady wife. No, the letter betrays equal love of both parents from at least the elder of the children."

"Was Sir William a dedicated gardener?" I asked. "This use of arsenic in horticulture seems innocent enough."

"At the trial, the court wanted to know why Sir William made small paper packets of the poison he bought."

"You mean the Crown asked this of him?" I asked, while Holmes sat back against the cushion on his seat, looking out of sorts and smug at the same time.

"No, Watson, it was the learned judge himself who asked Sir William this. Perhaps he's a gardener himself. I would have thought that Trotter's counsel might have done better at the appeal hearing had they mentioned this irregular questioning of the accused by the judge during cross-examination."

"That wouldn't 've saved 'im, Mr. Holmes. There was too much evidence: the poisoned scone, the poison in the exhumed body, the packet of poison found on Sir William when he was arrested. On top of that, Sir William kept inviting young Cronin to tea after his first attempt to kill him failed. Poor Cronin had the devil's own time thinking up excuses not to go, once they found out what was in the scones." Mr. Billington suppressed a yawn with his red bandanna. As a gesture to assuage his involuntary rudeness, he offered his bag of nuts again.

"You will excuse our bursting in on you, Mr. Billington. You can't have had much sleep this week. You have been a busy man, up and down the country: Liverpool, London, and York. I'm amazed at your energy." Holmes got to his feet, and I did the same.

"Very ordinary cases, Mr. Holmes, like the pair over in Dublin the week before. I've never had the, um, the duty to officiate at the execution of a high-ranking military officer before, and a knight into the bargain. I might retire after Monday. I'll not see his like again, if you know what I mean?" On our way out of the compartment, I could see the young Mr. Willis open a dozing eye to mark our passage.

Having regained our own seats, Holmes reminded me that I was no more a Mason than he was. "I was simply trying to establish a relationship on equitable terms with your friend, Billington," I said, somewhat jocularly.

"Billington a Mason? My boy, he doesn't even know the hand-clasp. That would have been a sight: watching the two of you trying to simulate funny handshakes. The *governor* at the prison is a master in the local lodge, Watson. Billington's simply currying favor."

For the rest of the journey, I tried to work on my medical article and make notes on how to complete it, while Holmes looked as though he wished to move the train, by pure force of will, more quickly than the engine could manage it. "On to Shrewsbury!" I could read it in his face.

When we did arrive, Holmes gave a cabby the name of the Lion Hotel at the top of Wyle Cop, and we crowded inside with our club bags. Through a window on my side, I saw a hansom loading Mr. Billington aboard, with the looming silhouette of the Castle in the background, and closer, a sleepy Mr. Willis passing luggage up to the driver.

The hotel was like a thousand other hotels in other small towns across the length and breadth of England: high-ceilinged, drafty rooms, threadbare livery and scant service. Holmes chided me for this observation as we climbed the stairs, blaming my gloomy view on the long journey. "The Lion's a Salopian institution, Watson. You'll feel better about it when we've found something to eat."

As usual, Holmes was right. With the world set right again, hunger satisfied, I set about to discover the town for myself. Holmes, he told me, had other business, upon which he neglected to enlarge in my hearing. When he returned some hours later, he discovered me with my feet in a basin of hot water. I had walked myself into foolishness up Pride Hill, to the Abbey, across both the English and the Welsh bridges, and was now paying for it. Suppressing a smile, Holmes attempted to cheer me up. "Take heart, old man. A good beef chop will put you in better humor." Holmes had already stretched out on the bed with the counterpane covering his closed eyes. The logic of a nap at this time of day and in my bed did little to improve my humor.

At dinner, my friend made good on his promise. It lacked the dimensions and tenderness I had imagined, but away from London, my standards change. I am once again an army surgeon in the field, attacking the available food scraps with gusto and happy to have them. Holmes said little during the meal, but consulted his pocket watch on three separate occasions. Promptly, as the dessert things were being cleared, we were joined by the ample form of Dr. John Flanner, the local doctor who had treated Mr. Cronin after he had been poisoned. Holmes made the introductions and the waiter brought us coffee. Once I got a good look at him, the doctor appeared to be an amiable man of fifty thereabouts, inclined to stoutness and shortness of breath.

"Well, sir, Mr. Holmes, there are not many who could make me forego my Friday chess game, but your reputation runs ahead of you. I also had a note from a most agreeable young lady, who arranged this meeting." Holmes pulled out a chair for our guest, while the waiter looked on, as though nothing more unusual had ever happened at the Lion in all his years there. When the doctor had made himself comfortable, Holmes asked: "You were acquainted with Sir William's family, Doctor?"

"I brought his girls into this world and saw their mother out of it, I'm sorry to say."

"Tell me about her last illness."

"You must understand, Mr. Holmes, Edith Trotter was a hypochondriac. I ministered to a dozen imagined ills to every real one. For some time she was actually confined in an asylum after being certified insane."

"But, I understood she died at home?"

"Indeed, she did: a most agonizing, dreadful, prolonged and painful death. At the time, I put it down to gastritis."

"Throughout history, Doctor, no one ever recognizes arsenic poisoning. How did Sir William take this?"

"He was solicitude itself during her illness and prostrate with grief after her passing. One night he fetched me in a blizzard to come to her bedside. He was a consummate actor, Mr. Holmes."

"Quite. During her last illness, you suspected foul play at no time?"

"Certainly not. He gave the appearance of a man stricken with grief."

"How long have you been the family doctor to the Cronin family?" Dr. Flanner seemed surprised at the sudden change of direction that the conversation had taken. I was surprised myself.

"I had occasionally been called in by Rowan Styles, the chemist, to look after his family. It was Adelaide, his daughter, who called me in to see her husband after he'd eaten scones at Maryfield. Until then, I was not their regular doctor. Dr. Arthur Hamilton Dixon has been associated with the family for a longer time."

"Was Dr. Dixon ill or away from Shrewsbury?"

"Not at all, sir. This is still a country where a body is entitled to call in whatever physician he chooses."

"Yes, of course, of course. Can you describe the scene at the chemist's when you arrived on the night of the 'poisoned scones'?"

"The Cronins live above the shop, you understand, Mr. Holmes. The table was still set for high tea. The cloth was disturbed and at Cronin's place the dishes were in some disorder. By the time I got there, Alister was in bed. Adelaide had covered him with heated blankets, and had provided an emetic, which I used after I inserted a soft rubber tube into his stomach. I washed out the organ with warm water. Adelaide even provided freshly precipitated ferric hydrate for me to give him in water. He was conscious most of the time, but in some pain when I arrived, I was certain that he was out of danger before I left."

"Who was it who first mentioned that the scones might have contained poison?"

"Why, Adelaide Cronin, of course. She was frantic with worry. Adelaide knows as much chemistry as her father does. She's been working in his shop since she was a girl. She got me a beaker for collecting Alister's specimen. It showed arsenic when tested."

"In lethal amounts?"

"Well, I don't just happen to know what a lethal amount of arsenic is, Mr. Holmes. I know an ounce will kill you, but where along the road from a scruple to an ounce, I couldn't say. I'm not a toxicologist, just a small town medical man with a good practice."

"I see. Yes. Of course. Two grains is conventionally thought to be a lethal dose, Doctor." Holmes took a sip of tepid coffee and replaced the cup with no sign of annoyance. I ordered a fresh pot from the waiter. "Returning to the illness of Lady Edith, Doctor: did you prescribe for her?"

"I did."

"What form did these prescriptions take?"

"There were tablets, a liquid mixture, and a placebo in the form of a colored liquid syrup."

"Was it Sir William who took charge of Lady Edith's taking this medication?"

"It was. And he was most assiduous in this responsibility. He said that he was 'taking his orders from me.' It was a little joke we had. You see, as a high-ranking military officer—"

"Dr. Watson and I understand the little joke, Doctor. Where did these medicines come from?"

"Why, from Rowan Styles' shop in High Street. He's the only chemist in town."

"Did Styles make up the prescriptions himself?"

"As far as I know, he did. Styles or his daughter. Adelaide may have seen to some of them. The prescription was one which could be repeated several times without an additional script from me."

"Good! And who made up the packets of arsenic that Sir William used to destroy his dandelion crop?"

"Oh, there would be no need of an expert to dispense a bulk chemical of that sort. It was part of the common stock. There was no mixing or fine measurement involved. So, I would say that such a job fell to Adelaide. You understand that the poison book was found to be in order at the time of the investigation. None of the poison was unaccounted for. Sir William was the only person in town to buy the arsenic in bulk. Each order was signed by the dispensing chemist. Sir William divided up the poison into separate packets when he returned home to Maryfield. He said that doses of about an ounce each served for each of his regular walks across the lawns. He would insert the end of his stick under the root of the offending weed and empty part of a packet's contents into the

hole. Then he would tread on the spot to flatten it. He was a martinet about weeds. He gave no quarter."

"You are a little premature in your use of the past tense, Doctor,
are you not?"

"You don't seriously think you can save him, do you, Mr.
Holmes?"

"Whether I can or cannot is not the point. Please don't rob the
poor fellow of the little time left to him." Holmes went on to more
questions without catching his breath. "Was gastritis a complaint of
Lady Edith's before she was committed, Doctor?"

"Lady Edith had a very susceptible stomach for as long as I knew
her."

"Is it your opinion that Sir William had been giving her small
doses of poison over a long period?"

"I have no way of determining that, sir. To test for prolonged
intoxication from a poison such as arsenic, one would need to split
a hair and measure the arsenic lodged there under a powerful microscope. No laboratory that I know of has such equipment, sir."

"And the Marsh test?" I asked.

"Of no use at all except for identifying the presence of an arsenic
compound in human organs."

"One last question, Doctor: can you advise me about Lady Edith's
life expectancy had the murderer not intervened?"

"You mean how long she might have lived?"

"Exactly."

"Well, Mr. Holmes, Lady Edith was not a well woman by any
stretch of the imagination. She had her gastritis, true, but I was
treating her for other things as well. In few, Mr. Holmes, even without the arsenic, Lady Edith was not destined to be among us for
long. She had at least two mortal ailments that contended for her
breath."

"Intriguing! I want to thank you for all the information you've
given me, Dr. Flanner. You have been most generous with your
time." We rose from our seats and walked the good doctor to the

hotel lobby. He saluted us with his raised hat and went down the steps to the door while putting on his gray gloves.

When he had gone, Holmes turned to me: "Would you like a stroll through the town to aid your digestion, Watson? Many interesting monuments hereabouts." There was that in his eye that made me suspicious. I consented with some apprehension.

"A sound digestion is the backbone of England," I observed.

"Very neat," said Holmes, "although anatomically confused." We walked the length of High Street, looking into the windows of the shops along the way. Holmes paid particular attention to a shop in the middle of the block we were treading: Rowan Styles, Chemist. Large glass flasks of colored water stood in the window, with a host of patent medicines, dentifrices, toothbrushes and perfumed soaps arrayed in between. Through the window, I could see the dispensing area, with shelves of porcelain jars with gold and black labels arranged within easy reach of the chemist.

About one hundred feet further along, we saw the law firms of Sir William Trotter—dark, dusty, with the sign hanging lopsided from its chain. There had been an attempt to remove handwritten graffiti from the window glass. The letters that remained were indecipherable, but still showed the original anger of the writer. Through the glass, the office resembled a diorama in a museum. It looked so very much like a law office of the mid-century, that it seemed unreal. Across the street, the office of "A. Cronin, Solicitor at Law" appeared to be the chambers of a successful solicitor of today. The furniture and office fittings one could see through the window were new. Even the briefs left unfiled on the desktops looked as though they involved law in its least dusty aspect. Perhaps my observation was meaningful, perhaps it only recorded the fact that Sir William bought out another lawyer who had been in practice for many years before Trotter arrived in town.

We continued to walk silently. I could feel Holmes trying to form and store an impression of the town. After some ten minutes or more of this, as I was about to complain, he turned into a side street and rapped with his stick on a black-painted door in the corner building. The word "Chambers" was carved into the lintel above the doorway in straightforward Roman capitals. After a moment or so, the door swung inward, and we were looking into the sallow face of a man of some sixty or sixty-five years. Whiskers valanced his face, chestnut whiskers that were frosted with silver. Lit by the oil lamp he carried, his face looked like a painting by a Dutch master. "Mr. Sherlock Holmes?" he asked.

"The same," my friend replied, removing his hat. "And this is my associate, Dr. John Watson." Holmes then turned to me: "May I present Mr. Evelyn Compton, Queen's Counsel. Mr. Compton has kindly stayed here in his chambers waiting for us. I apologize for our tardiness, Mr. Compton. Dr. Flanner held us like the Ancient Mariner of old. But *his* tale was well worth hearing I am glad to say." Mr. Compton led the way up a beautifully carved and well-proportioned stairway to a snug, book-and-brief-filled study overlooking the street.

"I received a telegram from Eunice Trotter telling me of your appearance in Shrewsbury, Mr. Holmes. I wish it were upon a happier occasion. Gentlemen?" He indicated seats near him as he sat in a comfortable chair in front of his desk. His manner was serious but informal. This inner sanctum was more than that of a man steeped in the law. I detected an interest in geography and natural history among the displayed possessions. He offered cigars from a mahogany humidor and we both accepted. While he was lighting mine, my friend explained: "Mr. Compton led the Crown's case against Sir William, Watson. My congratulations upon it, sir. I have seen a transcript. A most impeccable piece of work."

"Thank you, Mr. Holmes. Did you know that Sir William was a part-time clerk of the court? During his trial for murder, he showed the learned judge where pens and paper were kept, where the water jug was and once or twice repeated testimony the court recorder had missed. I'm sorry it ended this way. Sir William seems a most unlikely villain. A harmless sort of chap in spite of that military reputation. I still can't reconcile my picture of the man and what

I know of his character with the crimes the jury, quite justly, found him guilty of."

"I understand that after his wife's death he became something of a philanderer?"

"Oh, yes. But he handled it *so* badly. There are several well-known men in town who are cheating on their *living* wives. Poor Sir William was cheating, without much success or judgment, on his deceased wife. Not a capital crime in my view."

"Yes, I think that it was suggested in the transcript that another woman may have motivated Sir William in the matter of disposing of his nagging wife."

"Perhaps the jury may have taken that farther than I intended. But you know juries in small towns. *Sanitas sanitatum.* Sanctity of the home and all that."

"Yes. Mr. Compton, I should like to place an alternate case before you."

"Another case? But I thought—"

"I'll put it more precisely. I want you to examine the same case, but from a new and until now unspoken point of view."

"Are you being a trifle fanciful, Mr. Holmes?"

"Indulge me in my fancy for ten minutes, Mr. Compton." Compton, nodded, then suddenly rose from his chair, striding to the sideboard in three steps. He held a brandy bottle and poured three glasses to sustain us. Back in his seat, he steepled his fingers and prepared to listen.

"Whenever I am asked to examine a case," Holmes began, "I ask myself one small question: 'Who benefits?' Who benefits from the death on Monday morning of Field Marshal Sir William Trotter? Society at large? Perhaps, in a general way. His family? His daughters are distraught and at their wits end to know what to do. His wife's family? As far as I have been able to learn, they were glad when Sir William took Edith off their hands. There is no large fortune, as you know: the house, Maryfield, a few stocks and shares. Is that a fortune to risk one's neck for?"

"I'll agree for the sake of argument," said Compton. I nodded my agreement for the sake of avoiding argument. Holmes went on: "I've been told the town disliked Lady Edith. It resented the way she treated Sir William in public, the manner in which—"

"I can personally attest to that," Compton interrupted. "She was a noisy, detestable woman on her best day. We were all relieved when she was certified insane."

"And does Sir William share this view?"

"Well, uh, he was always a perfect gentleman. He did the right thing. He stood by her. He knew she was not popular with the ladies of Shrewsbury. He was always bringing her flowers and small presents."

"So, would you say that Sir William loved his wife?"

Mr. Compton thought for a minute before speaking. "Let me say this: Sir William was the only man who could stomach the woman."

"Then, we have to rule out the possibility that he murdered her to be rid of her once and for all."

"So it would seem. On the strength of what we have witnessed."

"Dr. Flanner told me that he was treating her for at least two terminal diseases."

"That is correct."

"Presumably, Sir William knew of this."

"I know right well he did."

"Then, since Lady Edith was a dying woman, why did he hurry her along with arsenic?"

"I— Surely, to make way for another, sir."

"What other? We know that he did some inexpert philandering after his wife's death. But where is the heiress apparent? Did she surface during the investigation? No! Trotter loved his wife and knew she was dying. The motive for her death could not have had anything to do with clearing a space in his life. Nor would anyone use arsenic to put a loved one out of her pain." Compton looked as though his queen and both bishops were pinned. Holmes continued: "I began by asking, 'Who benefits?' Would you still say that that person is Sir William, Mr. Compton?" He looked at Compton, who could not meet my friend's gaze. He went on: "No, I think you would not. All it has succeeded in doing is get him into a courtroom and very soon a grave that quite possibly has already been opened for him. Very well, let us assume that on Monday morning, Sir William takes that eight o'clock walk with the peripatetic Mr. Billington and his assistant. Sir William is no longer on the scene. What remains? The courts will find their own pens and paper without Sir William. The dandelions will thrive on the lawns of Maryfield, which will soon also display a sign advertizing that the house is for sale. Who in the neighborhood might want a house like that, Compton? With its history, it won't go at a high price, will it?"

"Mr. Holmes, I—"

"Humor me, Compton," Holmes said, leaning further back in his chair, looking at the stained wood beams above. "What about Sir William's law firm on High Street? What will happen to that? Will it gather more dust and graffiti for another six months? Will another solicitor come along to take Sir William's place? Perhaps eventually. Perhaps. Perhaps there is not work enough for two solicitors in Shrewsbury in this year of our Lord. Years from now, no doubt, the town will grow, burst its medieval seams and spread far beyond the river and its English and Welsh bridges. But now, Compton, what would a clever young solicitor do?"

Compton's cigar had gone cold in his hand. He was leaning toward my friend, his jaw almost slack. "You can't mean this, Holmes? You must know what you are suggesting?"

"Sir William was making a profitable living from his legal work, I believe, before this unpleasantness?"

"Yes."

"Young Cronin could buy up the business for a trifle of its real worth, I suspect?"

"Of course he could. 'Who benefits?' you said. Good God, how blind I've been!" For a moment the air seemed to go out of him, like a bicycle tire with a puncture. Then he straightened his back just as suddenly. "Hold on, Mr. Holmes. It's not quite that simple. I'll grant you that Cronin is an ambitious young fellow. I can see him wanting to get on. Damn me, I can *see* him succeeding. He has

the modern spirit, you know. I couldn't honestly say that Shrewsbury would be worse off with Cronin dispersing legal advice instead
of Trotter. But that is simply character and ambition. What about
opportunity? Cronin didn't carry packets of arsenic around with
him. Cronin didn't try to kill Sir William. It was the other way
around."

"Mr. Compton, this case appears to be reduced to a simple
deadly white powder: the poisonous mineral Donne speaks of: arsenic. Where did Sir William get his arsenic? From the chemist's.
Where did Lady Edith's medicines come from? From the chemist's.
The chemist's shop ties all of the little red tapes together. Don't
you see? When I ask 'Who benefits?' the answer lies inside that
shop. Cronin's business rival was Sir William's law practice. With
Sir William removed from the scene, the fortunes of the Cronins
begin a meteoric and sudden rise. Can you not see them happily
settled in Maryfield in a few years?"

"What are you saying, man? Cronin knows nothing of chemicals.
Sir William is the only person whom we know had daily access to
the poison."

"Rowan Styles had access. So did his daughter, Adelaide, Mrs.
Cronin," I prompted.

"But the poison book? The police went into that. No poison was
missing or unaccounted for."

"I should have a look at the chemicals themselves. The poison
arsenic, white arsenic, is an oxide. It is colorless, odorless and tasteless—tasteless in the extreme, one might say. No wonder they call
it 'inheritance or succession powder' throughout history right down
to modern times. I should think that a little sodium bicarbonate,
some other handy white chemical, or even ordinary white flour,
might replace missing amounts of poison. The chemist might also
give other customers short weights, or change the proportion of
indigo or soot that the law now insists be added to arsenic sold over
the counter. Another reason, Mr. Compton, why the poison Sir
William bought would prove awkward to administer either to

his wife or in a hot scone to his rival. What could poor Sir William do about the color? Where did he acquire his fine understanding of poisons? From another fanatical gardener, I suppose?"

"I'm truly confused now, Mr. Holmes. Come at last, for pity's sake, to the bottom of your brief. If it wasn't Sir William, then, who the devil was it in your view?"

"Let me exclude everyone we have been talking about with the exception of the chemist, Rowan Styles, his daughter, and his son-in-law, Alister Cronin. Cronin would gain in his business. Adelaide could boast of a successful husband, and Styles could rejoice in the success of the happy pair."

"You haven't fastened a noose yet, Mr. Holmes. And all of this is absurd. Why would Cronin poison himself? He could have lost his life."

"A chemist knows when enough is enough, sir, even when some physicians do not. And ambition could measure the risk against the prize."

"If Sir William didn't murder his wife to make way for a more pliable consort, or to remove an unpleasant, sickly, nagging scold, why was she murdered at all?"

"Her death was intended to attract attention to the fact that murder had been done. It was intended to put the rope around Trotter's neck. But it didn't work. Her unpopularity saw to that. There was no alarm sounded at her passing. A second scheme, another offensive had to be launched. That, of course, was the apparent attempt to murder Cronin."

"But, I *know* young Cronin. Quite frankly, I don't think he is clever enough to hit upon this scheme. He could never bring it off. I've known Rowan Styles for thirty years, Holmes. He is an honest man. We put our lives in his hands with every prescription he fills."

"You've left out Adelaide Styles Cronin. Was she capable of adding small amounts of poison to the potions Dr. Flanner ordered made up for Lady Edith? Could she determine how much poison would make her husband sick short of doing him lasting damage? I think she is capable. Damn it, Compton, I *know* she is capable. I believe her to be as cunning and clever a fiend as I have ever encountered."

"May I remind you, my dear Holmes," Compton interjected, "that we have no time for a conventional investigation."

"I think I know of a way," my friend said. Compton was caught in the act of refilling my glass. I held it firmly, but the bottle, with its distinctive Westhouse & Marbank label, trembled in his hand, so that he had to steady it with the other.

"Mr. Compton, should Maryfield come on the market, who in Shrewsbury is most likely to handle the transaction?" Somewhat restored, Compton completed replenishing my drink and straightened himself.

"Francis Grierson is the local man. He would advertize in the provincial papers, of course, and in the better London dailies."

"Watson, in the morning I want you to seek out Grierson and try to discover whether any inquiries have been made concerning the property."

"But, Holmes, I have no standing. Such information is confidential, surely."

"Make up something. Tell him you're from the National Office. Tell him you're a tax inspector. Tell him you're from Central Headquarters. You look like an honest man, ostentatiously honest, I might say. That stolid English face of yours will disarm the wiliest opponent. Meanwhile, *I* shall pay a visit to the chemist's." This statement caused a minor sensation. Compton and I exchanged glances and waited for Holmes to say more. "Compton, you know better than most that time is of the essence in this matter. Could you bring the chief constable to the chemist's tomorrow morning at eleven o'clock? I *know* you have influence there. Tell him to remain silent whatever I say. From you, I ask only that you support me as far as your conscience will allow."

"I can try, man, but I cannot promise," he said. "He is unusually busy."

"I am usually busy," said my friend. "But, for pity's sake remember the cost of failure."

We bade our host goodnight and made our way out into High Street once more. The night was hot, with moths destroying themselves in the glare of the gas lamps. A church bell sounded off somewhere a good distance away. As it echoed, the streets resumed a silence unheard in Baker Street for three hundred years. It seemed miles to the hotel along all but deserted streets.

In the morning, following a night of dreams of being under canvas in an overworked advance medical party, I made inquiries at the hotel where I quickly discovered Francis Grierson's address. He seemed to be a dabbler in several occupations, everything from title-searching to water-witching. After breakfast, Holmes vanished from my sight. I wasn't to see him again for some hours. Examining my face in the looking-glass over the water basin in my room, I told myself that I very well *might* be an inspector from Central Headquarters.

Francis Grierson, or Frank, as he was known universally he informed me, proved to be a cunning rogue, the town's agent for most of the real property on the market. I was surprised by what I heard myself telling him. I thought that no one could be benighted enough to believe me. But because of what I said or because of my bright blue eyes, he led me around the counter and into his private room. Here I learned that before Sir William bought it some years ago, Maryfield had been easily the most attractive property in the neighborhood. I had to interrupt him in his desire to tell me all about the murder case. It seemed to hurt his civic pride to learn that I was interested in neither the murder nor the coming execution. He appeared to be well-furnished with gossip about both. However I held him to giving me information about the property. Since the trial, there had been one inquiry about whether the house would be coming on the market again. That inquiry came from Adelaide Cronin. She had left a check on a London bank as deposit, in order to be the first to be informed about any intention to sell. Another motive, I thought, but deucedly hard to prove.

While I was so occupied, Holmes was engaged in a far more risky business, which he told me about in detail in the train on our way back to town. Let me try to set it down as he told it to me.

"On leaving the hotel, I went directly to a stationer's shop and found a few standard legal forms with black letter headings on good foolscap paper. I pinned them together with a blue triangular corner binding and brass fastener, folded them in half and placed what looked like a formidable brief in an inside pocket. At the writing desk in the hotel lobby, I scribbled in some words that came to me, my boy. You know them well. There was a passage from the first book of Newton's *Principia* and a part of an aphorism from Bacon's *Novum Organum.* I assure you, Watson, when I'd finished, it looked very legal and official. As you know, it was a short walk under a hot sun to Rowan Styles' shop. I knew that the chief strength of my plan resided in its audacity. It was a pretty little problem, as you might imagine. I was quite anxious to see how it would play out. I loitered outside until I saw Compton and the chief constable making their way to the door of the shop.

"Both Adelaide and her father were in the shop, behind the marble counter among the chemicals, retorts, mortars and pestles. I advanced toward Styles. He looked up, rather solemnly from his work and bade me, in the sober fashion of these parts, a good day.

" 'Are you Rowan Styles, proprietor of this chemist's shop?' I said in a stentorian manner. Cronin's wife stopped what she had been doing.

" 'I am.' Here I pulled out the sheaf of paper I had been carrying.

" 'I have an order for your arrest in the matter of the death of Edith Trotter and the attempted murder of Alister Cronin.' Here I made as though I intended to pass the paper to Styles, whose hands at that moment were incapable of movement. I did not look behind me to inspect the surprised expressions on Evelyn Compton's face or that of the police officer.

" 'Hold on!' said Styles when he had caught his breath. 'They've got their man. Sir William Trotter. It's all over and done with.'

" 'So it might seem to you, sir. But it was all part of the process of winkling out the true murderer.'

" 'Father!' Adelaide came closer. She abandoned the work she had been doing. Her face was a mask of concern and confusion.

" 'Hush, lass, this doesn't concern you!'

" 'You must accompany us to the station,' I said. 'You have a right to remain silent and to be represented by counsel, but anything you do say will be taken down in writing and may be produced at the trial. Come along peacefully, sir.'

" '*Trial?* What trial? There's already *been* a bloody trial!' Beads of moisture appeared on the man's forehead, my boy. He stammered incoherently.

" 'Let me see those papers,' demanded Adelaide. 'I'll be the judge of who is being arrested in this shop.' She reached toward my bogus handful of paper.

" 'Please do not interfere, Madam. You are not concerned in this.' I turned to the chief constable. 'Take charge of your prisoner!' I didn't know the name of the officer, but it was too late to inquire.

" 'Not *concerned?* What are you talking about? He's my *father!* He's never harmed a fly!'

" 'That is for a jury to determine. Come! We waste time!'

" 'You listen to me!' Adelaide Cronin was in tears now; her hair was coming down, 'You don't know what you're saying.'

" 'It is just my duty, Madam. Tell him it'll go better for him if he comes quietly.'

" 'But you'll *not* take my father!' She moved to his side like an avenging angel. 'You must explain yourself!'

" 'There has been a dispute at the Home Office about the evidence at the trial of Sir William,' I said.

" 'But there was no dispute at the time! *Now*, it's too late.'

" 'Your husband returned from having tea at Sir William's, and after a late supper, began complaining of stomach pains?'

" 'Yes, *yes*. I *told* all that. He was dangerously sick. I sent for the doctor. It was the poisoned scone. Why are you asking this again?'

" 'That's no concern of yours. He vomited, he was in great pain?'

" '*Yes*. When the doctor arrived, I gave him something. Dr. Flanner pumped his stomach.'

" 'What exactly did you administer, Mrs. Cronin?'

" 'I gave him ferric hydrate.'

" 'Excellent! It was freshly precipitated?'

" 'I did it myself as soon as his pains began.'

" 'You added ammonia to iron per-chloride?'

" 'Of course. I gave him the precipitate in water. His recovery began almost at once.'

" 'That's right,' her father added, 'it was near miraculous.'

" 'And how, pray, Mrs. Cronin, did you know to give him this antidote?'

" 'Why, it's the only thing in acute arsenic poisoning! Ask anyone.'

" 'When your husband became ill, you had every right to suspect that he had been poisoned, but, Mrs. Cronin, there are hundreds of toxic substances that could have caused him to collapse. Why could it not have been antimony or digitalis? Why not hyoscine or mercury, yellow phosphorous or morphine? Did you never consider his pains came from strychnine or any one of a dozen other common poisons?'

" 'But Sir William poisoned his wife with arsenic. I sold it to him. It's all in the book.'

" 'My dear lady, according to Dr. Flanner, it was only *after* your husband began to recuperate that you began to suspect poison in both his case and the case of Lady Edith. How did you know of a certainty that the poison causing your husband's upset was arsenic?'

" 'I had to do something to stop his pain!'

" 'One does not give ferric hydrate on a whim, Mrs. Cronin. You *knew* that it was arsenic. Further, I suggest to you that you had the antidote standing ready when your husband returned from tea at Sir William's.'

"Watson, all the color in her cheeks vanished. She stuttered, tried to explain, but each attempt broke off in fragments. She looked at all of us, hoping to find some explanation in our faces. Of course, she found none.

"Suddenly, she smashed a large flask and held the broken edge toward me in a threatening manner. The noise of the breaking glass startled me. 'You hear me? Take your paper and go away!'

" 'Keep the peace. I warn you, Ma'am!'

" 'Adelaide, please!' It was Compton speaking from behind my right shoulder. 'You can't help this way. We'll find the best counsel; we'll find bail.'

" 'You shut your mouth Evelyn Compton!'

" 'He knows why we've come,' I said. 'Look at his face. He's known all along. Do you have manacles for her wrists?'

"Here Adelaide let out a great cry that seemed to come from her very soul.

" 'You fools! You great fools!' she cried. Her face altered. An idea had struck her. 'Why?' she asked. 'Why? To save that old martinet?'

" 'Please, Madam, you're not going to help with violence.' For another minute, the woman held the jagged broken glass in my face. At last her father gently took in from her, allowing the constable to affix his handcuffs.

"On the way to the station, she made a defiant confession, which, I must say, is still ringing in my ears.

" 'I killed Lady Edith,' she said. 'I gave poison to Alister. I wanted him to get on. *I* wanted him to make something of himself. You think I want to die living above the shop? We're going to have Maryfield and be respected. I'm going to have fine things. We're going to be quality. We're . . .' She stopped in mid-sentence and caught her breath. 'Show *me* those papers,' she said in a raspy whisper. '*Give* them to me!' I held my Trojan horse where she could see it. She examined it carefully, then looked up at me, rolling the papers up in her pinioned hands.

" 'Perhaps I should introduce myself, Mrs. Cronin. My name is Sherlock Holmes. You must forgive me for the subterfuge, but, you see, there wasn't time to come about it another way. Thus the prop paper. Merely mise-en-scène, a theatrical expedient, which may prove to be the saving of a life. I was certain that your love for your father would put you off your guard and I was right.' "

Her father began to weep helplessly as she went toward the station quietly without a glance at Holmes and, according to the information we received later, was dictating a full statement within the hour. Compton and the chief constable eclipsed themselves, accompanying their prisoner, while Holmes and I retired to the hotel to pack our bags. When Compton met us in the saloon bar, later, he had made contact telegraphically with the Home Office and a stay of execution had been ordered and was in effect.

"Holmes, there are many aspects of this case I will have to quiz you about when I make my notes, but what I can't understand now is how Adelaide was able both to poison Lady Edith and dispense poison to Sir William without falsifying the poison book at the shop."

"Yes, a finite quantity of poison and it seemed to double itself," Holmes said almost smiling. "That puzzled me from the beginning. If the allotted arsenic went to Sir William, as the poison book states, from where did the poison in Lady Edith's medicine come? If Lady Edith received the required poison to kill her over a long period of time, was Mrs. Cronin giving Sir William short weights? What I think she did is this: she reserved half of Sir William's dandelion poison for use in Lady Edith's prescriptions and made up the difference in weight with sodium bicarbonate or some such stable white chemical. Had he been more astute, Sir William might have noticed that the arsenic was now only half as effective against his detested dandelions."

While we were waiting for the cab to take us to the station, Evelyn Compton remained to see us off. He was able to assure us, over some refreshment, that James Billington and his assistant had been sent packing. "For the moment at least," he added. Holmes, smiled at this. In the station's refreshment kiosk, he bought two-and-sixpence worth of assorted nuts for the journey back to town.

THE SIREN OF SENNEN COVE

Peter Tremayne

OF THE MANY adventures and curious hazards that I have shared with my good friend, Sherlock Holmes, the well-known consulting detective, there is one that still brings an icy chill to my bones and a tingle to the hairs on the nape of my neck. I can still recall the apprehension—nay, the unutterable fear—that gripped me when I saw the pale specter of that naked, dancing woman who had lured so many seamen to their watery deaths—and she no more than ten yards away from where Holmes and I huddled in an open dinghy on the tempestuous seas off the rocky granite coast of Cornwall.

Lest Holmes rebuke me for starting my account at the end rather than at the beginning, let me remind those of my readers who have followed my record of his adventures that in the spring of 1897, Dr. Moore Agar of Harley Street had prescribed to my friend a complete rest, should he wish to avoid a breakdown in his health. We had taken a small cottage near Poldhu Bay, near Mullion, on the Lizard Peninsula almost, but not quite, on the furthest extremity of Cornwall.

It was here that the ancient Cornish language had arrested Holmes' attention and he received a consignment of books on philology and set himself to writing a monograph on what he perceived as Chaldean roots in that branch of the Celtic languages.

Our idyll was rudely interrupted when, taking tea at the local vicarage with its incumbent Mr. Roundhay, we became involved with the strange case of Mortimer Tregennis, which I have recounted as "The Adventure of the Devil's Foot." It was a stimulating exercise in deduction but, as Holmes remarked at the end of it, he was pleased to get back to the study of the Cornish language.

Only three days elapsed before we had a visitor who would send us helter-skelter into a case which made the investigation of the death of Mortimer Tregennis seem a mere diversion in mental entertainment by comparison with the terrifying peril it presented.

It was just before noon. I was taking the sun in a garden chair outside our cottage, sipping a pre-prandial sherry. Although it was April, it was a warm day and not at all breezy. Holmes was enclosed in the room which we had set aside as his study, poring over a newly-acquired volume that had arrived by that morning's mail. It was *Some Observations on the Rev. R. Williams' Preface to his Lexicon Cornu-Britannicum*, written by no less a luminary than Prince Louis Lucien Bonaparte. That is why I recall it so well; the idea of one of the Bonaparte family becoming a philologist and an authority on the Cornish language was a matter which intrigued me.

Holmes had scooped up the book and disappeared into his study after breakfast promising faithfully to appear for luncheon because our daily help, Mrs. Chirgwin, was preparing it, and she did not take kindly to her meals being missed.

I was, therefore, sitting, reading the *Falmouth Packet* when I heard the sound of a carriage rattling along the track which led to our cottage. I reluctantly placed my sherry and newspaper aside and stood up, waiting to receive the unexpected visitor with some curiosity. We were so isolated that visitors were an unusual phenomenon.

It took a moment for the carriage to appear from behind a clump of trees and come to a halt before the garden gate. It was a sturdily built carriage, one more often seen in the country than in town. But it was clearly the vehicle of some well-to-do personage.

A tall, dark-faced coachman leaped down and opened the door. From the interior, a short, well-built man alighted and glanced about him. He had a shock of white hair, a red face and was well-dressed, bearing the hallmarks of a country squire. In fact, he seemed almost a caricature of one. He saw me and hailed even as he opened the gate and came toward me.

"Mr. Sherlock Holmes?"

"I am his colleague, Dr. Watson," I replied. "Can I be of assistance, sir?"

The man frowned impatiently.

"It is Mr. Holmes that I must see."

"I am afraid that he is busy at the moment. May I take your name, sir, and I will see . . . ?"

"It's all right, Watson," came Holmes' voice from behind me. He was leaning out of his study window, which he had opened. "I heard the carriage arriving. What can I do for you . . . ?"

The white haired man examined him for a moment with intense blue eyes; a keen examination which seemed to miss nothing.

"A moment of your time is what I require, sir. Perhaps some advice at the end of it. My name is Sir Jelbart Trevossow. It is a name not unknown in these parts."

Holmes stared at the man in amusement.

"That's as maybe, sir, yet, unfortunately, it is a name unknown to me," he replied amiably. "Nevertheless, I have a moment before luncheon. Watson, old fellow, bring Sir Jelbart into our little parlor and I will be there directly."

I smiled a little at the mortification on the country squire's face. He was apparently unused to people not recognizing him nor having his wishes obeyed instantly. I gestured to the door with a slight bow.

His mouth tightened but he moved inside to the room we had set aside as our common parlor. I followed him and closed the cottage door behind me.

"Now, sir," I said, "may I offer you some refreshment? Something to keep out the chill? A whiskey or a sherry, perhaps?"

"I do not agree with strong spirits, Doctor," Sir Jelbart snapped. "I am of the Wesleyan religion, sir. My views are firm on strong drink and tobacco . . ."

He sniffed suspiciously, for Holmes' noxious weed could be discerned all over our small cottage.

"Then be seated, sir," I invited. "Perhaps Mrs. Chirgwin might be prevailed upon to make you some tea?"

"I will have nothing, thank 'ee," he replied firmly, sitting down. His attitude was somewhat pugnacious.

Holmes entered at that moment and I was thankful for it, raising my eyes to the ceiling to indicate to him that our guest was of an awkward nature.

Holmes stretched himself at his ease in an armchair opposite our visitor and, undaunted by the look which would have sent others straight to the fires of hell, he took a pipe from his pocket and lit up.

"I do not agree with tobacco, sir," snapped our guest.

Holmes' good-natured expression did not change.

"Each to their own enjoyment, sir," he replied indifferently. "Myself, I think best over a pipe or two of shag tobacco. The coarser the better."

Sir Jelbart eyed Holmes for a moment and, when he saw that he was dealing with someone of an equal steel will, he suddenly relented. Holmes would have doubtless pointed out that by giving way so easily on the matter, Sir Jelbart's business must have been of considerable importance to him.

"Now, sir," smiled Holmes, "perhaps we can discuss the reason for this visit for I presume you have not come merely to pass the time of day with me on our respective likes and prejudices?"

Sir Jelbart Trevossow cleared his throat more in an expression of annoyance than to help him in his speech.

"I am not one to waste time, Mr. Holmes. I have business interests, sir. I was a stockholder in the company which owned the barque "Sophy Anderson." Ten years ago you investigated her loss, which could have bankrupted those who had financed her voyage. I was one of them."

Holmes leaned back for a moment, his eyes closed as he recalled the case.

"Exactly ten years ago," he agreed. He turned to me. "It is not a case that you have, as yet recorded, Watson, old fellow."

"I did mention it in passing when I was relating the case of 'The Five Orange Pips,' " I replied in defense. "I felt that it was too pedestrian a case to excite the temperament of readers of *The Strand Magazine*, Holmes. As I recall . . ."

Sir Jelbart cleared his throat again in annoyance.

Holmes smiled politely.

"Pray, proceed," he said, waving a hand.

"I came to you, Mr. Holmes, knowing that you have some dealings with the mysteries of the sea."

"A number of my cases have been concerned with the disappearance or foundering of ships. The cutter 'Alicia,' for example, and the 'Friesland,' on which Watson and I nearly lost our lives . . ."

"Mr. Holmes," interrupted Sir Jelbart, "do you know how many ships, and I mean ships of some tonnage not merely little coasters, have been lost on this coast alone during the last fifteen years?"

Holmes speculated.

"A half-dozen, a dozen, perhaps?"

"One hundred and eight," our guest informed us solemnly. "This, sir, is a wrecker's coast, always has been. The people scavenge from the sea."

Holmes pursed his lips.

"If memory serves me well, three years ago the new Merchant Shipping Act, especially part nine on the law of salvage and wrecks, should now prevent any lucrative business being made out of wrecking."

"Not at all, sir. My brother, Captain Silas Trevossow is the local Excise Officer. He will tell you that wrecking is still a virile business as ever it was."

"Most interesting, Sir Jelbart, but I cannot yet see what has brought you to my door."

"I come to you for assistance, Mr. Holmes. As soon as I learned that you were staying in the Duchy, I knew that you were the one man who could help."

"I am still waiting for your explanation."

"I live in Chy Trevescan, a house near Sennen Cove, at the far end of the Cornish peninsula. It is by Land's End. The area is gray granite place, and its village was once called the first and last on this island. It stands on an open, rocky tableland and to the west the land ends in granite cliffs facing the sea.

"Sennen Cove is about one and a quarter miles from the village and this is reached by a narrow road which drops down very steeply between the hills to the sea and then extends along the sea's edge into a long sandy beach which curves along the margin of Whitesand Bay, a mile or so of sandy beach. The people in the area usually live by pilchard fishing or lifting lobsters. Whitesand Bay appears a hospitable shoreline, but the Brisons Rocks are a mile offshore and in the distance is Cape Cornwall where the seas can smash a great ship to matchwood if it is unlucky enough to founder there. There is another group of rocks to the south, The Tribbens, of which the largest is Cowloe."

Sir Jelbart paused.

Holmes made no move, asked no question.

Our visitor decided to continue.

"During the last two weeks, three vessels have foundered on The Tribbens."

"Pray what is so singular about these three sinkings out of the hundred or so others you enumerate which causes you so much concern?" demanded Holmes.

Jelbart looked at him in surprise.

"I have not as yet said that there was anything singular about them. How did you . . . ?"

"Elementary," Holmes replied wearily. "You would not come

here, bear to sit in the proximity of my pipe, and refer to these three specific vessels out of the hundreds of sinkings if they were but simple additional statistics. Something must have caused you some great concern. Pray elucidate."

Sir Jelbart leaned forward.

"There were several survivors from the wrecks. They all recount a singular manifestation which was the cause of their ships foundering on the rocks."

"Which is?"

"They claim the ships were lured ashore by a siren."

"A siren?" Holmes smiled quickly. "I presume that you do not mean a signal device like a horn?"

"No sir, I do not!" spluttered our guest indignantly. "I mean a spirit, a seductress, an enchantress."

I could not control my amusement but Holmes calmly began to refill his pipe.

"I think that you had better clarify your statement, Sir Jelbart."

"These ships were heading for the Port of St. Ives. Coasters, they were. Many local captains cut across the mouth of Whitesand Bay instead of standing out to sea. They steer a course between the Carn Bras Longships, rocky islands to the west, and the inshore rocks in order to make up sea time. The wrecks have happened at night. Usually there are no problems for local skippers on this course, for there are lights at strategic points and the captains of these vessels know the waters well. All three captains of the wrecked coasters had run this course many times."

"How did this enchantress manifest herself?" I ventured.

"Each survivor says that she was a specter that appeared to the crew dancing on the rocks."

So serious was the man that I could not suppress a chuckle.

"But Holmes . . ." I began when I saw him silencing me with a disdainful glance.

"In what form did this specter manifest itself?" he repeated my question. "Some specifics, please."

"A woman. Gad sir, a naked woman, dancing on one of the rocks. But the figure was large and shimmered white. Indeed, many of the survivors said that they could see right through her."

"Did anyone hear anything?"

"Not at the time of the sinking but in the nights following some locals report that they have heard a heavy breathing from the direction of the rocks. So loud was it that it was heard ashore when the wind was in the right direction. A sound of hissing breath like some giant was hiding behind the rocks. The locals are in fear of The Tribbens, even though it was a favorite spot to lift lobsters."

"No music? No Pan pipes?" I smiled sarcastically.

Before the man could answer Holmes had cut in.

"Nothing else was seen around these rocks? Has anyone ventured to examine them?"

"No, sir. The survivors were scared out of their wits, sailors being so superstitious. The fear at the sight of the specter caused the crews to panic, the captains to lose control. It only takes a moment's distraction to put a vessel on those rocks. Some seventy-five men have perished, sir, and the news is abroad about the siren of Sennen Cove luring the men to their deaths."

"And you have come to me. Why?"

"Because, in spite of the merriment of your colleague," he glanced dourly at me, "I do not believe in ghosts, sir. I am a Methodist. A plain man raised in a plain religion. A man who believes in rationality. I think there is some mischief afoot, but I cannot find an explanation."

Holmes laid down his pipe for a moment, leaning back in his chair and placing his hands, fingertips together, and gave Sir Jelbart a careful scrutiny.

"I am sure that you have some explanation, Sir Jelbart. Some theory to propose to me?"

"I have made a study of shipwrecks along this coast, Mr. Holmes. That is why I know the statistics. I believe that wreckers are at work."

"From what you say, this Sennen Cove is not so far removed from civilization that a gang of wreckers could work with impunity," I intervened. "Unless it is a conspiracy of the entire local populace."

"On the contrary, Doctor," Sir Jelbart said, "the coastline is not the easiest place to police."

"But three vessels, sir . . . if what you say is correct . . . that would cause a more careful watch to be kept?"

"No, indeed. That's is the confounded point of the matter. The stories of the specter have scared off local people. Imagine, sir, tales of this siren, this seductress dancing naked on a rock whose sides are so sheer that no one could land on it let alone find a shelf on which to balance. And the size of her . . . they say the figure is at least twelve feet tall. No one in those parts will venture even to the shore after dark, not even Mr. Neal, our minister. He now goes around warning people to stay clear of the area unless they wish to see the enchantress and suffer the fate of Lot's wife when she turned back to look upon Sodom and Gomorrah."

"Does he now?" mused Holmes. "You say that your brother is in the Excise? Have you made your views known to him?"

"I have."

"And what does he say?"

"He does not share them."

"Why?"

"Because the ships founder and sink. Little wreckage, if any, is swept ashore. He argues that if wreckers are the cause, what happens to their spoils? They go straight to the bottom. There seems nothing to profit from. He believes, therefore, that we can rule wrecking out."

"It is a sound, logical deduction," agreed Holmes.

"Nevertheless, the alternative is preposterous. I must believe that the matter has a rational explanation. I refuse to believe that it is a siren luring passing ships onto the rocks. A specter? A ghost? This is why I have come to you, Mr. Holmes. You, I am sure, cannot believe in the supernatural."

"On the contrary," Holmes replied seriously. "What is the supernatural but nature which has not yet been explained? Tell me, Sir

Jelbart, in what condition was the weather when these ships foundered?"

"The weather?"

"Yes, was it a tempestuous night, was there a sea fog, were high seas running?"

Sir Jelbart shook his head.

"On the contrary. The wrecks occurred on fine nights. Good visibility and calm seas. That is why the captains of these doomed vessels took the passage so close to The Tribbens Rocks. In bad weather, a good seaman would have stood out to sea and given his ship plenty of sea room."

"Has your brother, Captain Trevossow, made an investigation of the area?"

"He intends to do so this very night. That is why I have been encouraged to come to you for I fear for his life. The Torrington Lass is sailing from Penzance overnight around the coast to St. Ives. She should pass The Tribbens at midnight. My brother intends to be aboard to inspect the rocks as they sail by."

"Isn't that dangerous in view of what has transpired to the previous ships?" I asked.

"It will be a clear night tonight with calm weather," he replied. "In normal circumstances, there should be no danger. However . . ." He ended with an eloquent shrug.

"Surely, your brother is a practical man?" Holmes said, "and would be prepared for any unusual occurrence?"

"He is not the skipper and crew," pointed out Sir Jelbart.

"You have piqued my curiosity, Sir Jelbart," Holmes said thoughtfully.

Just then Mrs. Chirgwin put her head around the parlor door and announced that the midday meal was ready and she would not be blamed if it was to get cold, gentleman caller or no. Holmes arose smiling.

"Pray, stay to lunch with us, Sir Jelbart and, afterward, we will accompany you back to this Sennen Cove. We will stay overnight if you can accommodate us. By the way, do you have access to a rowing boat and a competent seaman who would be prepared to row us out to these haunted rocks?"

Sir Jelbart rose and held out his hand.

"I do, indeed, sir. I am glad the instinct which brought me hither has been proved a good one."

The journey from Poldhu Bay around the great stretch of Mount's Bay, through the town of Penzance, along the inhospitable inland road, passing such strange unEnglish sounding places as Buryas, Trenuggo, Crows-an-Wra, Treave and Carn Towan, before reaching the village of Sennen, was longer than I had expected. We finally arrived at Sir Jelbart's house of Chy Trevescan in the early evening. It was this journey, through the desolate landscape, with standing stones and ancient crosses that illustrated, for me at least, that Cornwall was, indeed, 'the land beyond England.' A strange, ancient place, lost in time.

The sun was low in the sky, almost directly in our eyes, as we came along the road above Whitesand Bay heading south to Sennen. I saw a spectacular stretch of sandy beach about a mile long and curving. Sir Jelbart was full of local folklore. It was here, apparently that the Saxon King Athelstan landed during his attempt to conquer the Celts of Cornwall. It was here that the Pretender Perkin Warbeck came ashore from Ireland in his vain attempt to seize the English Crown. The sea was calm now but our guide told us that it usually came rolling shoreward in long breakers.

"There is a small craft out there by that point," observed Holmes. "It seems to have a curious engine fitted on its stern."

Sir Jelbart glanced toward it. It was anchored at the north end of the bay, the opposite end of the large bay to the location of Sennen Cove.

"That's Aire's Point." He screwed up his eyes to focus on the point. "Ah, that is young Harry Penwarne's boat."

"What's he doing?"

"No idea. He's a bit of an inventor. Amateur, of course. He once explained it all to me. The Penwarne place is just by Aire's Point at Tregriffian. Sad history."

"Why so?" asked Holmes.

"The Penwarnes are one of the old families in these parts but young Harry's father was a gambler. He lost most of the family fortune. Shot himself while young Harry was studying at the Sorbonne in Paris about ten years ago. Harry returned here and has tried to keep Tregriffian House going. Inventive young man. Full of all these modern technological ideas, but he worries too much. Frequently seen him with bloodshot eyes. Burning the midnight oil, what?"

Chy Trevescan was certainly a large house in anyone's estimation. But it was an ugly house. Squat and brooding, thickset, just like the granite countryside. As we drove up to the main door, we noticed that a small pony and trap stood outside. It was a single horse, two-wheeled affair. Standing on the step was a solemn-faced man whose black broadcloth proclaimed him as a minister.

"Sir Jelbart," the man greeted him even before he descended, "I do not approve of this enterprise. I have heard that your brother is sailing on the Torrington Lass tonight and I do not approve."

"Our local minister, Mr. Neal," explained Sir Jelbart under his breath. Then aloud: "I fail to see what business it is of yours, sir. You have abrogated your responsibility to your flock by not demonstrating that what is happening on The Tribbens Rocks is not the Devil's work. Now my brother and I must take matters into our own hands."

Mr. Neal's face was distorted in anger.

"As your minister, I forbid it. You have no right to interfere with matters of the otherworld. It is God's wish that these vessels be stricken down for their crews must be debauched. They are being punished for their sins otherwise God would intervene and save them from their doom! I tell you, it is God who drives those ships on The Tribbens Rocks! Their vines are vines of Sodom, grown on the terraces of Gomorrah; their grapes are poisonous, the clusters bitter to the taste . . ."

"Deuteronomy!" snapped Holmes suddenly, the sharpness of his voice causing the minister to stop, blinking. "But hardly appropriate. God would surely not waste his time organizing shipwrecks, Mr. Neal, in order to punish those souls who have met their fate on those rocks."

"I warn you, sir," cried the minister, "do not attempt to interfere or you, too, will be doomed—the way of the wicked is doomed. . . ."

"But the Lord watches over the way of the righteous," replied Holmes solemnly, quoting from the same Psalm.

The minister turned and climbed in his governess' cart. "You have been warned!" he cried as he climbed into his pony and trap and disappeared down the driveway.

Sir Jelbart bade us come inside for refreshment while he sent for the local fisherman whom he trusted. Holmes suggested that only he and myself, together with the boatman, need set out on the expedition to examine the rocks. The boatman's name was Noall Tresawna, a simple, thickset man. Holmes explained that what he wanted and the man made no demur. When Holmes asked him if he had heard about the supernatural phenomenon, Tresawna nodded.

"Are you not a little apprehensive, my friend?" asked Holmes. "We must rely on your nerve and experience in a little boat out there among the rocks."

"I do be a God fearing man, master," Tresawna replied. "I say my prayers and keep the commandmants and I place my fate in God's hands. For it is written in the Good Book:

> "Happy is the man
> who does not take the wicked for his guide
> nor walk the road that sinners tread
> nor take his seat among the scornful . . ."

Holmes broke in:

> ". . . the law of the Lord is his delight
> the law his mediation night and day."

Tresawna looked impressed.

"Aye, master, that do be so and thus I be not afear'd of specters."

Toward midnight, Tresawna met us at the kitchen door of the house and led us by the light of a storm lantern across fields to a cliff top, which was a point overlooking The Tribbens. The point was called Pedn-men-du, which Holmes afterward told me meant the head of black stone. A dangerous stair-like path descended to where he had moored his boat. The night was a dark blue velvet. Bright white stars winked in the sky and the moon was only in its first quarter and thus shedding little illumination.

Once inside the boat, Tresawna extinguished the lantern for he knew the seas around the coast better in what little natural light there was than by artificial means.

Holmes bent close to me as we sat in the stern.

"Have you brought your revolver as I requested, Watson?"

"I have. But do you expect me to shoot at a twelve-foot-high naked dancer?" I inquired sarcastically.

"Not quite, old fellow. I expect a more tangible, flesh and blood target to present itself."

The little boat rocked its way through the calm, dark seas along the tower cliffs of Pedn-men-du, out to a point where we could see the line of white surf breaking along the stretch of Whitesand Bay.

"There be The Tribbens now, sir," called our boatman, pointing toward the black shadows that were looming up ahead of us. We could hear the whispering seas sighing and crashing gently against them.

"They don't look so menacing," I ventured.

"Not to us in this small boat, sir," Noall Tresawna agreed. "But a large vessel with a lower keel could be ripped open by the hidden jagged rocks that be just a few feet below us."

"Is that what happened to the vessels that have been sunk here?" asked Holmes.

"That's about it, sir. A good skipper can take his vessel up between Tal-y-men and Kettle's Bottom to the west or between Kettle's Bottom and The Peal on the east. After that, it is a straight run between Shark's Fin and The Tribbens and out across the bay. But I hear tell from those who have survived that the curiosity to see the dancing lady caused them to steer too close to the rocks on their starboard and before they knew it, the ship's keels were sheared away, like a knife going through butter."

"Is it a deep bottom here?"

"Not too deep as happens but deep enough."

"What do you think is the cause of these vessels foundering? Do you think it is wreckers?"

"Not for me to say, sir. I wouldn't say so. If it were wreckers, why choose a place where the ships aren't driven ashore so that you could pick up the cargoes? That's what they did in the old days. But here, the ships go down and lay on the bottom. There's no currents to bring anything ashore."

The rocks were now closer. The one closest to the cliffs was almost an island in its size and this, Tresawna told us, was called Cowloe. Beyond these rocks were two other large pinnacles jutting from the sea.

Holmes glanced at his pocket watch.

"Nearly midnight. The Torrington Lass should be approaching here soon, if Sir Jelbart's timing of her sailing is correct."

Tresawna rested on his oars. Everything was silent except for the incessant whispering of the sea.

Then suddenly a curious white light seemed to illuminate the waters between the rocks.

A cold fear seized me such as I had never known.

I have been in some pretty tight spots, I can tell you. Not even when I received my wound at the battle of Maiwand, facing the hordes of Afghan tribesmen, thinking that I was about to breathe my last, did I feel such fear.

I gripped Holmes' arm in a vice.

"God, Holmes! Look there! Tell me that it is an illusion! Tell me that you don't see it?"

On the farthest rock, a cold white light bathed.

And in that white ethereal light stood the figure of a giant woman, nearly twelve feet high. It was a strange flickering; one which had a transparent quality for I could see the rock through the image. The figure was that of an attractive woman. Quite beautiful. She was naked. She moved in voluptuous contortions, dancing in such provocative poses that I have never seen before; seductive, alluring, moving as an enchantress to ensnare weak souls.

The hairs on the nape of my neck rose. I could not draw my attention away from the figure. I felt like a rabbit before a snake.

"Fascinating!" muttered Holmes at my side.

From a distance there came a sound of a ship's horn.

"Come, Watson, old fellow, get a grip of yourself." Holmes nudged me. "That's the Torrington Lass approaching."

I stared at him in bewilderment.

"But, Holmes, don't you see her . . . God help us, it is a phantom . . . !"

Holmes had turned sharply to Tresawna.

"Have you brought the rockets ready, as I asked?"

"I have, Mr. Holmes." The man had kept his gaze averted from the rocks while muttering some prayer.

"Then we must send them up at once. There is no time to get nearer the rocks before the Torrington Lass will be down upon them."

Tresawna had three rockets of the sort carried by ships as distress signals. He placed one in the bows and struck a match. Within moments it took off into the night sky.

About half-a-mile away we could see the lights of the steam packet heading in our direction.

Tresawna set off the remaining two rockets and eventually we saw the ship turn westward and move on its northerly course.

"Now," cried Holmes triumphantly, "make for the rocks."

Even as we turned and Tresawna began to row with all his might toward the rocks there came a crack much like a rifle shot. The ethereal white light suddenly vanished and all was dark and quiet.

" 'Vast rowing," snapped Holmes.

We sat in silence. There was no sound except the whispering sea again.

Holmes gave a deep sigh.

"I don't think there will be anything more we can do until daylight. We won't see anything more tonight. Best take us back to Chy Trevescan and meet us there again tomorrow as soon as it is light."

Holmes was in one of his infuriating moods, not answering any questions, not even when our host, Sir Jelbart demanded to know what adventure had befallen us.

The next morning we had just finished breakfast when a tall, naval officer arrived and was greeted familiarly by Sir Jelbart. He introduced the man as his brother Captain Silas Trevossow. The Captain had ridden over from St. Ives that morning. Holmes admitted responsibility for sending up the rockets to prevent the Torrington Lass being lured onto the rocks.

"Thank God, you did. The skipper and his crew were petrified. They froze like ice as a fear gripped the ship. Only when we saw your danger signals was the skipper brought back to his senses and he seized the wheel to alter course."

"You are in time to come with us, Captain," Holmes invited. "I think you might find this interesting and, I assure you, by this evening you will have apprehended the person behind these sinkings. A most evil genius."

An hour later found Holmes, Captain Trevossow, Noall Tresawna and myself out by the rocks again, though they seemed less menacing in daylight.

"That is the rock on which we saw the dancing woman," Holmes pointed. "Make for that."

We came close to the rock on which the giant woman had been dancing.

"Look!" I cried. "Look at the angle of the face of this rock. No physical entity could stand on it, much less dance. It is almost a forty-five-degree sheer angle."

"Close to sixty degrees, Watson," replied Holmes unmoved. "As smooth a rock face as ever you would see and look at the covering on it."

I frowned, examining it.

"Covering? That is only guano."

"Exactly, my medical friend. The long-accumulated dung of sea fowl, a yellow white substance as if the rock, that flat, almost vertical surface, has been whitewashed."

"I don't see how that concerns us."

Holmes merely shook his head sadly and glanced around.

"Now, Tresawna, head for that other rock there."

He indicated a large pinnacle raising itself above the water some fifteen yards away. This was easy to land on as the waves were not at all rough and Holmes insisted on climbing onto it while we held the boat steady. He took with him a small canvas bag, which he had brought from Sir Jelbart's house. He spent some time examining a particular area all the while glancing back to the first guano-covered rock as if taking measurements or alignments.

Eventually he turned to a third rock at an angle to both of these. He seemed to measure the distance to it. It was about another fifteen yards away, rising higher than the others and larger. Holmes scrambled back into the boat.

"What did you find, Mr. Holmes?" asked Captain Trevossow, for Holmes had put several items into a canvas bag. He handed it to the captain who glanced into it.

"Be careful," Holmes admonished. "They are sharp."

"Why, they are only fragments of glass."

"Only?" Holmes raised an eyebrow. "In fact, they are more than glass. They are fragments of a shattered concave mirror."

He answered no more questions but instructed Tresawna to row toward the third rock which he had indicated.

This pinnacle had a natural sea pool at the foot of it, making an excellent landing place and we could all climb out and follow a little circular path which went around the island-like rock to a small cave. It was no higher than four feet at its entrance.

Holmes gave a cry of elation as he beheld it. He immediately bent down and entered. There was only room for himself in the cave but we heard, almost at once, a further cry of exaltation. He re-emerged pushing a large square glass container with some metal pieces in it, zinc and some other substance. This seemed to have been discarded at the back of the cave. Holmes brought it forward. There was a chemical smell to it which I hazarded was ammonium chloride.

"What do you make of that?" he announced.

Captain Trevossow and I exchanged a bewildered glance and shrugged. Holmes sighed impatiently.

"This is a Leclanche cell, and a pretty strong one," he said irritably when he saw we were lost.

"An electric battery?" Captain Trevossow frowned. "What's that doing on this godforsaken rock?"

Holmes gave him one of his enigmatic looks.

"I am sure that we will be able to find the answer very soon."

He suddenly took his magnifying glass from his pocket and examined a flat-topped rock which was in the center of the entrance. He went down on his hands and knees and seemed to take a sighting from the rock gazing straight out across the sea to the smaller pinnacle on which he had found the mirror fragments.

"You'll notice the grooves here and the scraping of metal on this rock," he inquired of us.

We both nodded, still confused.

Holmes stood up with a smile of satisfaction.

"Excellent. I think that we will now pay a visit on Mr. Harry Penwarne at Tregriffian House."

It took some time to row back to the shore and collect Sir Jelbart from Chy Trevescan. Leaving Noall Tresawna to attend to his boat, Sir Jelbart and his brother, Holmes and myself, climbed into the carriage and made the journey through Sennen along the road above Whitesand Bay to Tregriffian House.

HARRY PENWARNE WAS no more than thirty-five. A young man whose boyish looks seemed to have a hardness to them. He smiled only with a movement of his facial muscles but he bade us welcome to his house. I thought his eyes held a suspicious look in them. Then I realized that they were quite bloodshot. His manservant was a muscular man also with dour looks, who appeared less like a servant and more like a soldier or sailor. He spoke little but I detected a French accent when he did.

"What can I do for you, Sir Jelbart?" he inquired. "What brings you and your friends to my house?"

Holmes intervened immediately.

"You'll forgive me," he said, "but when I saw your diving experiments the other day, I just had to come and meet you."

Penwarne's eyes narrowed. He glanced at Sir Jelbart, who was looking in astonishment at Holmes.

"I didn't know it was generally known that I was making such experiments."

Holmes smiled.

"My dear sir, I have been reading Kleingert of Breslau's experimentations with diving equipment, and it seemed obvious you were using a machine to send compressed air to the diver."

Harry Penwarne frowned.

"Are you involved in deep sea diving, Mr. Holmes?"

"I have a little knowledge," confessed Holmes. "Though I confess to being a mere amateur. I know that there are some new French inventions which have extended the time divers can remain underwater."

"You mean the new compressor modification by Laplace of the Sorbonne?" inquired Penwarne.

"Exactly so. I understand that you, also, were a student at the Sorbonne?"

"I graduated from there ten years ago."

"Pray what were you studying?"

"Marine engineering, of course."

"I think, at that time, Dr. Marey was experimenting at the Sorbonne with his new invention, wasn't he?"

"Dr. Marey? I do not know the gentleman." Penwarne shook his head. "I am not a medical man, Mr. Holmes."

Holmes looked at him sharply.

"I did not say that he was a doctor of medicine."

Penwarne's mouth tightened.

"However, you are right. He was a physician but his experiments were concerned with another discipline. Ten years ago, he invented the first motion pictures using a single camera."

"Is that supposed to be of interest to me?" asked Penwarne defensively. "My study is marine engineering, sir."

"You are possessed of a bright mind, Mr. Penwarne. You saw the potential of Marey's camera and started your own development of it. But two years ago, Auguste and Louis Lumiere patented their cinematograph in Paris. They produced a combined camera and projector operating at sixteen frames a second. You were devastated. You were working on a similar system, but they were first with the patent. Therefore, I believe that you have turned your invention to a more dreadful use."

"I have no idea what you mean," protested Penwarne, his face was white now. His nervousness was self-evident. For the first time, I began to see the direction in which Holmes was leading.

"Your father was impecunious. You needed desperately to restore the family fortune otherwise you were faced with selling Tregriffian House to pay his debts. So a new plan came to your mind, one that would make you a mass murderer but rich. Using your projector, and a piece of film, you lured three ships to their doom. You went into the wrecking business as many folks in these parts used to do over a hundred years ago."

"How do you claim that I managed to lure them?"

"With a film of some dancer which you probably made in Paris. Because of the angles involved to ensure the ships saw the image, you had to reflect your image via a third means. A concave mirror would bounce the image, which your projector shone onto it across to the large rock covered with guano. That almost whitewash substance made a suitable screen on which to project it."

"Rubbish," snorted the now trembling Harry Penwarne. "The ships went down off the rocks. If I were able to do such a thing, how could I have collected the salvage from those wrecks?"

"You went diving there at night, with your assistant. People heard the whining and gasping of your compressed air apparatus but being anchored behind the rocks, they did not see your boat. I presume that you went down looking only for the ship's safe and taking cash and jewels. Perhaps you planned to lift some of the less easily negotiable materials at a later day . . ."

Harry Penwarne half rose from his chair but his pale face and dark staring eyes were not on Holmes. They were staring past him.

"Jean-Claude!" he cried in French. "We can bluff it out. Don't give the game away . . . !"

I turned at once and saw Penwarne's manservant leveling a revolver at Holmes.

I confess that I was considered something of a crack shot when I was serving in the Northumberland Fusiliers, but at that instance I had never shot so well. I did so from my lap, for thus far only could I draw my revolver and let off a shot which impacted on the hand of Jean-Claude. He cried out in pain. The gun fell from his hand. Captain Trevossow leaped forward and scooped it up to cover the manservant.

I was now covering Harry Penwarne, but the shock of the discovery of his nefarious crimes sent the young man into a state of incapability. He collapsed back in his chair.

"I cannot believe it!" cried the astounded Sir Jelbart. "What made you suspect young Harry?"

"When I realized that he was using a compressed air machine on his boat, as I said. Also, when you told me about noticing his bloodshot eyes. It's a condition caused by breaking blood vessels in the eye, a hazard of deep sea diving that has not been overcome yet."

Sir Jelbart shook his head. "Astounding," he muttered.

"You were absolutely right in your theory, Sir Jelbart. The only problem I had was to discover how it was done. A search of the house will probably supply the evidence," Holmes said airily. "You will find cameras, projectors, the electrical batteries which he ferried out to the cave to work the projector, and above all the film of the young woman dancing."

"What was the meaning of the broken glass, Mr. Holmes?" asked Captain Trevossow. "Why was it broken?"

"Previously, no one had noticed the mirror that Penwarne had erected to reflect the image where it was needed, so that it could be seen from the ships. He was able to row to the rock and retrieve it at his leisure. Last night, however, he realized someone was near the rocks investigating. Our rockets gave us away. To destroy the evidence of the concave mirror, he used a rifle or pistol to shatter it to save time in rowing across from where he had the camera. He switched off his projector, dismantled it and hurried home in his boat with his accomplice, Jean-Claude. In his rush he forgot to take the used Leclanche battery."

As Holmes predicted, in a cellar of the old house an entire laboratory was discovered with Penwarne's experiments and models of cameras and projectors and various pieces of film which he had shot.

Holmes spent a long time examining them with intense interest.

"In many ways our friend Penwarne's development of the camera, projector and the film he used seems more advanced than Lumiere. The coated celluloid is inspirational. In other circumstances, Penwarne might have been a genius and pioneer of this new cinematography and made his fortune. Instead, like all twisted genius, he resorted to crime. Doubtless, he and his accomplice will make that early morning walk to meet the end of a hemp rope at Bodmin Moor. When all is said and done, he was stupid."

I frowned.

"Why stupid, Holmes?"

"Because the most successful criminal is one who does not draw attention to himself nor his crime. A naked siren dancing on a rock—why, that is enough to bring all manner of interested persons rushing to this isolated part of Cornwall. The supernatural always entices people like moths are enticed to a candle. Sooner or later, he would have been discovered."

"But you discovered him the sooner, Holmes," I pointed out.

"It required no great mental effort on my part, dear fellow. I fear that people will think the less of my powers of deduction if they perceive this as a case of which I am proud. Therefore, I entreat you not to publish any account of it until after I have shuffled off this mortal coil."

He gave a deep sigh.

"Now, I hope, we can return to our cottage and suffer no more interruptions. After all, I am down here to rest from such activities. Once again, my dear Watson, I think we may dismiss the matter from our mind, and go back with a clear conscience to the study of those Chaldean roots which are surely to be traced in the Cornish branch of the great Celtic speech."

THE CASE OF THE BLOODLESS SOCK

Anne Perry

THERE HAD BEEN no cases of any interest for some weeks, and my friend Sherlock Holmes was bored by the trivia that came his way. His temper showed it to the degree where I was happy to accept an invitation from an old friend, Robert Hunt, a widower who lived in the country, not far from the handsome city of Durham.

"By all means go, Watson," Holmes encouraged, except that that is far too joyful and heartening a word for the expression on his face that accompanied it. "Take the afternoon train," he added, scowling at the papers in front of him. "At this time of the year you will be in your village, wherever it is, before dark. Good-bye."

Thus was I dismissed. And I admit, I left without the pleasure I would have felt with a more sanguine farewell.

However the late summer journey northward from London toward the ever-widening countryside of Yorkshire, and then the climb to the dales, and the great, bare moors of County Durham, improved my spirits greatly. By the time I had taken the short, local journey to the village where Robert Hunt had his very fine house, I was smiling to myself, and fully sensitive to the peculiar beauty of that part of the world. There is nothing of the comfortable Home Counties about it, but rather a width, a great clarity of light, and rolling moorland where hill upon hill disappears into the distance, fading in subtle shades of blues and purples until the horizon melts into the sky. As I came over the high crest and looked down toward the village, it was as if I were on the roof of the world. I had almost a giddy feeling.

I had wired ahead to inform Hunt of my arrival. Imagine then, my dismay at finding no one to meet me at the deserted station, and being obliged to set out in the darkening air, chillier than I am accustomed to, being so much further north and at a considerable altitude, carrying my suitcase in my hand.

I had walked some four miles, and was worn out both from exertion and from temper, when an elderly man in a pony trap finally offered me a lift, which I accepted, and then arrived at Morton Grange tired, dusty and in far from my best humor.

I had barely set my feet upon the ground when a man I took to be a groom came running around the corner of the house, a wild hope lighting his face. "Have you found her?" he cried to me. From my bewilderment he understood immediately that I had not, and despair overtook him, the greater after his momentary surge of belief.

I was concerned for him and his obviously deep distress. "I regret I have not," I said. "Who is lost? Can I assist in your search?"

"Jenny!" he gasped. "Jenny Hunt, the master's daughter. She's only five years old! God knows where she is! She's been gone since four this afternoon, and it's near ten now. Whoever you are, sir, in pity's name, help me look—although where else there is to search I can't think."

I was appalled. How could a five-year-old child, and a girl at that, have wandered off and been gone for such a time? The light was fading rapidly and even if no harm had come to her already, soon she would be in danger from the cold, and surely terrified.

"Of course!" I said, dropping my case on the front step and starting toward him. "Where shall I begin?"

There followed one of the most dreadful hours I can remember.

My friend Robert Hunt acknowledged my presence, but was too distraught with fear for his only child to do more than thank me for my help, and then start once more to look again and again in every place we could think of. Servants had already gone to ask all the neighbors even though the closest was quarter of a mile away.

In the dark, lanterns were visible in every direction as more and more people joined in the search. We would not have given up had it taken all night. Not a man of us, nor a woman, for the female staff was all out too, even gave our comfort, our hunger or our weariness a thought.

Then at some time just after midnight there went up a great shout, and even at the distance I was, and unable to hear the words, the joy in it told me the child was found, and they believed her unhurt. I confess the overwhelming relief after such fear brought momentary tears to my eyes, and I was glad of the wind and the darkness to conceal them.

I ran toward the noise, and moments later I saw Hunt clasping in his arms a pale and frightened child who clung onto him frantically, but seemed in no way injured. A great cheer went up from all those who had turned out to search for her, and we all tramped back to the house where the cook poured out wine and spices into a great bowl, and the butler plunged a hot poker into it.

"Thanks be to God!" Hunt said, his voice shaking with emotion. "And to all of you, my dear friends." He looked around at us, shivering with cold still, hands numb, but face shining with happiness. We needed two hands each to hold the cups that were passed around, and the hot wine was like fire in our throats.

We quickly parted as relaxation took over, and the nursemaid, chattering with laughter and relief, took the child up to put her to bed.

It was not until the following morning, all of us having slept a trifle late, that Hunt and I were sitting over breakfast that he looked at me earnestly and spoke of the mystery that still lay unaddressed.

"I am very exercised in my mind, Watson, as to how to deal with the matter for the best. Jenny is devoted to Josephine, the nurse-maid. Yet how can I keep in my employ a servant who could allow a child of five to wander off and become lost? And yet if I dismiss her, Jenny will be desolated. The girl is all but a mother to her, and since her own mother died . . ." His voice broke for a moment and he required some effort to regain his composure. "Advise me, Watson!" he begged. "What can I do that will bring about the least harm? And yet be just . . . and not place Jenny in danger again?"

It was a problem that had already occurred to me, but I had not thought he would ask my counsel. I had observed for myself on the previous evening the nursemaid's care for the child, and the child's deep affection for her. Indeed after the first relief of being found, it was to her that she turned, even when her father still clung to her. It might well do her more hurt to part her from the only female companionship and care that she knew, than even the fear of being lost. She had already been bereaved once in her short life. In spite of last night's events I thought it a certain cruelty to dismiss the maid. Perhaps she would now be even more careful than any new employee would, and I am in the process of saying so, when the butler came in with a note for Hunt.

"This was just delivered, sir," he said grimly.

We had already received the post, and this had no stamp upon it, so obviously it had come by hand. Hunt tore it open, and as he read it I saw his face lose all its color and his hand shook as if he had a fever.

"What is it?" I cried, although it might well have been none of my affair.

Wordlessly he passed it across to me.

> Dear Mr. Hunt,
>
> Yesterday you lost your daughter, and last night at exactly twelve of the clock you received her back again. You may take any precautions you care to, but they will not prevent me from taking her again, any time I choose, and returning her when, and if I choose.

And if it is my mind not to, then you, will never see her again.

M.

I confess my own hand was shaking as I laid the piece of paper down. Suddenly everything was not the happy ending to a wretched mischance, it had become the beginning of a nightmare. Who was "M," but far more pressing than that, what did he want? He made no demand, it was simply a terrible threat, leaving us helpless to do anything about it, even to comply with his wishes, had that been possible. I looked across at my friend, and saw such fear in his face as I have only ever seen before when men faced death and had not the inner resolve prepared for it. But then a good man is always more vulnerable for those he loves than he is for himself.

Hunt rose from the table. "I must warn the servants," he said, gaining some control as he thought of action. "I have shotguns sufficient for all the outdoor staff, and we shall keep the doors locked and admit no one unknown to us. The windows have locks and I myself shall make the rounds every night to see that all is secure." He went to the door. "Excuse me, Watson, but I am sure you understand I must be about this matter with the utmost urgency."

"Of course," I agreed, rising also. My mind was racing. What would Sherlock Holmes do were he here? He would do more than defend, he would attack. He would discover all he could about the nature and identity of this creature who called himself "M." Hunt's mind was instantly concerned in doing all he could to protect the child, but I was free to apply my intelligence to the problem.

My medical experience has been with military men and the diseases and injuries of war, nevertheless I believe I may have a manner toward those who are frightened or ill which would set them at as much ease as possible. Therefore I determined to seek permission of the nursemaid, and see if I might speak with Jenny herself, and learn what she could tell me of her experience.

The maid was naturally deeply reluctant to pursue anything

which might distress the child, of whom she was extraordinarily fond. I judged her to be an honest and good-hearted young woman such as anyone might choose to care for an infant who had lost her own mother. However the fact that I was a guest in the house, and above all that I was a doctor, convinced her that my intentions and my skill were both acceptable.

I found Jenny sitting at her breakfast of bread and butter cut into fingers, and a soft-boiled egg. I waited until she had finished eating before addressing her. She seemed to be little worse for her kidnap, but then of course she had no idea that the threat of that again, and worse, awaited her.

She looked at me guardedly, but without alarm, as long as her nursemaid stayed close to her.

"Good morning, Dr. Watson," she replied when I had introduced myself. I sat down on one of the small nursery chairs, so as not to tower over her. She was a beautiful child with very fair hair and wide eyes of an unusually dark blue.

"Are you all right after your adventure, yesterday night?" I asked her.

"Yes, I don't need any medicine," she said quickly. It seemed that her last taste of medicine was not one she wished to repeat.

"Good," I agreed. "Did you sleep well?"

The question did not appear to have much meaning for her. I had forgotten in the face of her solemn composure just how very young she was.

"You did not have bad dreams?" I asked.

She shook her head.

"I'm glad. Can you tell me what happened?"

"I was in the garden," she said, her eyes downcast.

"What were you doing there?" I pressed her. It was important that I learn all I could.

"Picking flowers," she whispered, then looked up at me to see how I took that. I gathered that was something she was not supposed to do.

"I see." I dismissed the subject and she looked relieved. "And someone came and spoke to you? Someone you did not know?"

She nodded.

"What did he look like? Do you remember?"

"Yes. He was old. He had no hair at the front," she indicated her brow. "His face was white. He is very big, but thin, and he talked a funny way."

"Was his hair white?" What was her idea of old?

She shook her head.

"What did you call him?" That might give some clue.

"Fessa," she replied.

"Fessa?" What an odd name.

"No!" she said impatiently. "P'fessa!" This time she emphasized the little noise at the beginning.

"Professor?" I said aghast.

She nodded. A ridiculous and horrible thought began to form in my mind. "He was thin, and pale, with a high forehead. Did he have unusual eyes?" I asked.

She shivered, suddenly the remembered fear returned to her. The nursemaid took a step closer and put her arms around the child, giving me a glare, warning me to go no further. In that moment I became convinced within myself that it was indeed Professor Moriarty that we were dealing with, and why he had kidnapped a child and returned her with a fearful warning, would in time become only too apparent.

"Where did he take you?" I asked with more urgency in my tone than I had intended.

She looked at me with anxiety. "A house," she said very quietly. "A big room."

How could I get her to describe it for me, without suggesting her answers so they would be of no value?

"Did you ride in a carriage to get there?" I began.

She looked uncertain, as if she could have said yes, and then no.

"In something else?" I guessed.

"Yes. A little kind of carriage, not like ours. It was cold."

"Did you go very far?"

"No."

I realized after I had said it that it was a foolish question. What was far in a child's mind? Holmes would chastise me for such a pointless waste of time.

"Was it warm in the room? Was there a fire?"

"No."

"Who was there, besides the Professor? Did they give you anything to eat?"

"Yes. I had teacakes with lots of butter." She smiled as she said that, apparently the memory was not unpleasant. But how could I get her to tell me something that would help find the place where she had been taken, or anything whatever which would be of use in preventing Moriarty from succeeding in his vile plan? "Did you go upstairs?" I tried.

She nodded. "Lots," she answered, looking at me solemnly. "I could see for miles and miles and miles out of the window."

"Oh?" I had no need to feign my interest. "What did you see?"

She described an entire scene for me with much vividness. I had no doubt as to at least the general area in which she had been held. It was a tall house, from the stairs she climbed, at least three stories, and situated a little to the west of the nearby village of Hampden. I thanked her profoundly, told her she was very clever, which seemed to please her, and hastened away to tell my friend Hunt of our advance in information. However I did not mention that I believed our enemy to be the infamous Moriarty.

"I have reason to think that the matter is of great gravity," I said as we sat in his study, he still ashen-faced and so beset with anxiety he was unable to keep from fidgeting first with a paper knife, then with a quill, scribbling as if he had ink in it but merely damaging the nib.

"What does he want?" he burst out in desperation. "I cannot even comply! He asks for nothing!"

"I would like your permission to go into the village and send a wire to my friend Sherlock Holmes," I replied. "I think he would involve himself in this matter willingly, and I know of no better chance in the world to detect any matter than to have his help."

His face lit with hope. "Would he? So simple a thing as a child who has been taken, and returned, with no ransom asked? It is hardly a great crime."

"It is a great crime to cause such distress," I said quite genuinely. "And the fact that he has asked no price, and yet threatened to do it again, is a mystery which I believe will intrigue him."

"Then call him, Watson, I beg you. I will have the trap sent around to the front to take you immediately. Ask him to come as soon as he may. I will reward him any and every way in my power, if there is any reward he will accept."

But I knew, of course, that the name of Moriarty would be sufficient to bring him, and so it turned out. I received a return wire within a few hours, saying that he would be there by the late train that evening, if someone would be good enough to meet him at the station. I spent the rest of the afternoon searching in the village of Hampden until I was sure that I had found the house Jenny had described, but I was careful to appear merely to be passing by on my way somewhere else, so if any watcher saw me it would cause no alarm.

In the evening I went to meet the train, and the moment it drew in and stopped amid clouds of steam, one door flew open and I saw Holmes' lean figure striding along the platform toward me. He looked a different man from the miserable figure I had left behind me in Baker Street. He reached me and said the one word, as if it were some magic incantation, his eyes alight. "Moriarty!"

I was suddenly afraid that I had miscalculated the situation, perhaps been too quick to leap to a conclusion. He so often charged me with precisely that fault. "I believe so," I said somewhat cautiously.

He gave me a quick glance. "You are uncertain. What makes you doubt, Watson? What has happened since you wired me?"

"Nothing!" I said hastily. "Nothing whatever. It is simply a deduction, not a known fact that it was he who took the child."

"Has any demand been received yet?" There was still interest in his voice, but I thought I detected a note of disappointment all the same.

"Not yet," I answered as we reached the gate to the lane where the trap was waiting. He climbed in and I drove it in silence through the winding, steep banked roads, already shadowed in the sinking sun. I told him of my conversation with Jenny and all I had learned from it, also my location of the house, all of which he listened to without comment. I was certainly not going to apologize to him for having called him out on a matter which may not, after all, involve his archenemy. It involved the abduction of a child, which as far as I can see, is as important as any single case could be.

We were within quarter of a mile of the Grange when I saw in the dusk the gardener come running toward me, arms waving frantically. I pulled up, in case he should startle the pony and cause it to bolt. "Steady, man!" I shouted. "Whatever has happened?"

"She's gone again!" he cried while still some yards from me. He caught his breath in a sob. "She's gone!"

Instantly Holmes was all attention. He leaped out of the trap and strode to the wretched man. "I am Sherlock Holmes. Tell me precisely what has occurred. Omit no detail but tell me only what you have observed for yourself, or if someone has told you, give me their words as exactly as you can recall them."

The man made a mighty effort to regain control of himself, but his distress was palpable all the time he gasped out his story.

"The maid, Josephine, was with Jenny upstairs in the nursery. Jenny had been running around and had stubbed her toe quite badly. It was bleeding, so Josephine went to the cupboard in the dressing room where she keeps bandages and the like, and when she returned Jenny was gone. At first she was not concerned, because she had heard the hokey-pokey man outside the gates, and Jenny loves ice-cream, so she thought that she had run down for the kitchen maid to find him." He was so distraught he was gasping between his words. "But she wasn't there, and the kitchen maid said she hadn't seen her at all. We searched everywhere, upstairs and down . . ."

"But you did not find the child," Holmes finished for him, his own face grim.

"That's right! Please sir, in the name of heaven, if you can help us, do it! Find her for us! I know the master'll give that devil anything he wants, just so we get Jenny back again, an' not hurt."

"Where is the hokey-pokey man now?" Holmes asked.

"Percy? Why, he's right there with us, helping to look for her," the gardener replied.

"Is he local?"

"Yes. Known him most of my life. You're never thinking he would harm her? He wouldn't, but he couldn't either, because he's been here all the time."

"Then the answer lies elsewhere." Holmes climbed back into the trap. "Watson may know where she was taken the first time and we shall go there immediately. Tell your master what we have done, and continue your search in all other places. If it is indeed who we think, he will not be so obvious as to show us the place again, but we must look.

We drove with all speed to Hampden and I took Holmes to the street parallel with the one on which was the house. We searched it and found it empty. We had no time to lose in examining it closely, and only the carriage lantern with which to do it.

"She has not been here tonight," Holmes said bitterly, although we had not truly dared believe she would be. "We shall return in the morning to learn what we may."

We left to go back to the Grange to continue with any assistance we could. It was in turmoil as on the evening before, and as then, we joined the others seeking desperately for the child. Holmes questioned every one of the staff, both indoor and outdoor, and by nearly eleven o'clock we were exhausted and frantic with fear for her.

I found Holmes in the kitchen garden, having looked once again through the sheds and glass houses, holding a lantern up to see what the damp ground might tell him.

"This is a miserable business, Watson," he said, knowing my step and not bothering to raise the light to see. "There is something peculiarly vile about using a child to accomplish one's purposes. If it is in fact Moriarty, he has sunk very low indeed. But he must want something." He stared at me earnestly, the lamplight picking out the lines of his face, harsh with the anger inside him. I have never observed him show any special fondness for children, but the anguish caused to a parent had been only too clear for all to see. And Holmes despised a coward even more than he did a fool. Foolishness was more often than not an affliction of nature. Cowardice was a vice sprung from placing one's own safety before the love of truth, known as the safety and welfare of others. It is the essential selfishness, and as such he saw it as lying at the core of so much other sin.

"But he wants something, Watson. Moriarty never does anything simply because he has the power to do it. You say the child was returned last night, and this morning a note was delivered? There will be another note. He may choose to torture his victim by lengthening the process, until the poor man is so weak with the exhaustion of swinging from hope to despair and back, but sooner or later he will name his price. And you may be sure, the longer he waits, the higher the stakes he is playing for!

I tried to concentrate on what he was saying, but I was longing to take up my lantern again and renew my effort to find Jenny. After my conversation with her this morning she was no longer merely a lost child, she was a person for whom I had already grown a fondness, and I admit the thought of Moriarty using her in his plot nearly robbed me of sensible judgment. If I could have laid hands on him at that moment I might have beaten him to within an inch of his life—or closer even than that.

I walked what seemed to be miles, calling her name, stumbling over tussock and plowed field, scrambling through hedgerows and frightening birds and beasts in the little coppice of woodland. But I still returned to the house wretched and with no word of hope at all.

We were all gathered together in the kitchen, the indoor staff, the outdoor, Hunt, Holmes and myself. It was all but midnight. The cook brewed a hot, fresh pot of tea and the butler fetched the best brandy to strengthen it a little, when there was a faint sound in the passage beyond and the door swung open. As one person we turned to face it, and saw Jenny standing white-faced, one shoe off and her foot smeared with blood.

"Papa . . ." she started.

Hunt strode across the floor and picked her up. He held her so tightly she cried out with momentary pain, then buried her head on his shoulder and started to cry. She was not alone, every female servant in the place wept with her, and not a few of the men found a sudden need to blow their noses uncommonly fiercely, or to turn away for a moment and regain their composure.

HOLMES WAS UP before six and I found him in the hall pacing back and forth when I came down for breakfast just after half past seven. He swung around to face me. "Ah, at last," he said critically. "Go and question the child again," he commanded. "Learn anything you can, and pay particular attention to who took her and who brought her back."

"Surely you don't think one of the household staff is involved?" I dreaded the idea, and yet it had been done with such speed and efficiency I was obliged to entertain the possibility myself.

"I don't know, Watson. There is something about this that eludes me, something beyond the ordinary. It is Moriarty at his most fiendish, because it is at heart very simple."

"Simple!" I burst out. "The child has twice been taken, the second time in spite of all our attempts to safeguard her. If he has caused one of these people to betray their master in such a way, it is the work of the devil himself."

Holmes shook his head. "If so then it is co-incidental. It is very much his own work he is about. While you were asleep I buried myself learning something of Hunt's affairs. Apparently he is the main stockholder in the local mine, as well as owner of a large amount of land in the area, but he has no political aspirations or any apparent enemies. I cannot yet see why he interests Moriarty."

"Money!" I said bitterly. "Surely any man with wealth and a family, or friends he loves, can be threatened, and ultimately, by someone clever and ruthless enough, money may be extorted from him?"

"It is clumsy, Watson, and the police would pursue him for the rest of his life. Money can be traced, if the plans are carefully laid. No, such a kidnap has not the stamp of Moriarty upon it. It gives no satisfaction."

"I hope you are right," I said with little conviction. "The amount Hunt would pay to have his child safe from being taken again would be satisfaction to most thieves."

Holmes gave me a withering look, but perhaps he sensed my deep fear and anger in the matter, and instead of arguing with me, he again bade me go and question Jenny.

However I was obliged to wait until nine, and after much persuasion of the nursemaid, I found Jenny in the nursery, pale-faced but very composed for one who had had such a fearful experience not only once but twice. Perhaps she was too innocent to appreciate the danger in which she had been.

"Hello, Dr. Watson," she said, as if quite pleased to see me. "I haven't had breakfast yet. Have you?"

"No," I admitted. "I felt it more important to see how you were, after last night's adventure. How do you feel, Jenny?"

"I don't like it," she replied. "I don't want to go there again."

My heart ached that I was obliged to have her tell me of it, and I was terribly aware that a whole house full of men seemed unable to protect her. "I'm sorry. We are doing all we can to see that you never do," I told her. "But you must help me. I need to know all about it. Was it the same man again? The Professor?"

She nodded.

"And to the same place?"

"No," she shook her head. "It was a stable I think. There was a lot of straw, and a yellow horse. The straw prickled and there was nothing to do."

"How did the Professor take you from the nursery here?"

She thought for several minutes and I waited as patiently as I could.

"I don't 'member," she said at last.

"Did he carry you, or did you walk?" I tried to suggest something that might shake her memory.

"Don't 'member. I walked."

"Down the back stairs, where the servants go?" Why had no one seen her? Why had Moriarty dared such a brazen thing? Surely it had to be one of the servants in his pay? There was no other sane answer. It did not need Holmes to deduce that!

"Don't 'member," she said again.

Could she have been asleep? Could they have administered some drug to her? I looked at the face of the nursemaid and wondered if anything else lay behind her expression of love for the child.

I questioned Jenny about her return, but again to no avail. She said she did not remember, and Josephine would not allow me to press her any further. Which might have been fear I would discover something, but might equally easily have been concern that I not distress the child any more. In her place I would have forbidden it also.

I went down the stairs again expecting Holmes to be disappointed in my efforts and I felt fully deserving of his criticism. Instead he met me waving a note which had apparently just been delivered.

"This is the reason, Watson!" he said. "And in true Moriarty style. You were correct in your deduction." And he offered me the paper.

My Dear Hunt,

I see that you have called in Sherlock Holmes. How predictable Watson is! But it will avail you nothing. I can still take the child any time I choose, and you will be helpless to do anything about it.

However if you should choose to sell 90% of your shares in the Morton Mine, at whatever the current market price is—I believe you will find it to be £1.3.6d more or less, then I shall trouble you no further.

Moriarty.

I looked up at Holmes. "Why on earth should he wish Hunt to sell his shares?" I asked. "What good would that do Moriarty?"

"It would start a panic and plunge the value of the entire mine," Holmes replied. "Very probably of other mines in the area, in the fear that Hunt knew something damaging about his own mine which was likely to be true of all the others. Any denial he might make would only fuel speculation."

"Yes . . . yes, of course. And then Moriarty, or whoever he is acting for, would be able to buy them all at rock-bottom price."

"Exactly," Holmes agreed. "And not only that, but appear as a local hero as well, saving everyone's livelihood. This is the true Moriarty, Watson. This has his stamp upon it." There was a fire within him as he said it that I confess angered me. The thrill of the chase was nothing compared with the cost to Hunt, and above all to Jenny. "Now," he continued. "What have you learned from the child of how she left here?"

"Very little," I replied. "I fear she may somehow have been drugged." I repeated what little she had been able to tell me, and also a description of the stable, as far as she had been able to give one.

"We shall borrow the pony and trap and go back to the house in Hampden in daylight," he replied. "There may be something to learn from a fuller examination, and then seek the stable, although I have no doubt Moriarty has long left it now. But first I shall speak to Hunt, and persuade him to do nothing regarding the shares . . ."

I was appalled. "You cannot ask that of him! We have already proved that we are unable to protect Jenny. On two successive nights she has been taken from the house and returned to it, and we have never seen her go, nor seen her come back, and are helpless to prevent it happening again."

"It is not yet time to despair," Holmes said grimly. "I believe we have some hours." He pulled out his watch and looked at it. "It is only six minutes past ten. Let us give ourselves until two of the clock. That will still allow Hunt sufficient time to inform his stockbroker before close of business today, if that should be necessary, and Moriarty may be given proof of it, if the worst should befall."

"Do you see an end to it?" I asked, struggling to find some hope in the affair. It galled me bitterly to have to give in to any villain, but to Moriarty of all men. But we were too vulnerable, I had no strength to fight or to withstand any threat where the life of a child was concerned, and I know Hunt would sacrifice anything at all to save Jenny, and I said as much.

"Except his honor, Watson," Holmes replied very quickly. "It may tear at his very soul, but he will not plunge a thousand families into destitution, with their own children to feed and to care for, in order to save one, even though it is his own. But we have no time to stand here debating. Have the trap ready for us, and as soon as I have spoken with Hunt, I shall join you at the front door."

"What use is it going to Hampden, or the stable, if Moriarty has long left them?" I said miserably.

"Men leave traces of their acts, Watson," he replied, but I feared he was going only because we were desperate and had no better idea. "It might be to our advantage when we have so little time, if you were to bring a gardener or some other person who knows the area well," he continued, already striding away from me.

It was barely thirty minutes later that he returned just as the gardener drew the trap around, with me in the back ready to set out for the village. I had also questioned the gardener as to any local farms which might be vacant, and answer such slight description as Jenny had given me, or where the owner might either be unaware of such use of his stables, or be a willing accomplice.

"Did you persuade Hunt to delay action?" I asked as Holmes climbed in beside me and we set off at a brisk trot.

"Only until two," he said, tight-lipped. I know that he had had some agreement to achieve even that much time from the fact that he stepped forward in the seat and immediately engaged the gardener in conversation about every aspect of the nearby farms, their owners and any past relationship with Hunt, good or ill.

What he was told only served to make matters worse. Either the gardener, a pleasant chap of some fifty-odd years named Hodgkins, was more loyal than candid, or Hunt was generally liked in the region and had incurred a certain mild envy among one or two, but it was without malice. The death of his wife while Jenny was still an infant had brought great sympathy. Hunt was wealthy in real possessions, the house and land and the mine itself, but he had no great amount of ready money, and he lived well, but quite modestly for his station in life. He was generous to his staff, his tenants and to charity in general. Naturally he had faults, but they were such as are common to all people, a sometimes hasty tongue, a rash judgment here or there, too quick a loyalty to friends, and a certain blindness when it suited him.

Holmes grew more and more withdrawn as he listened to the catalog of praise. It told him nothing helpful, only added to the urgency that we not only find where Jenny had been taken, but far more challenging, we learn from it something of use.

We found the tall house again easily, and a few questions from neighbors elicited an excellent description of Moriarty.

We went inside and up again to the room that in the daylight answered Jenny's description in a way which startled me. It was indeed bright and airy. There was a red couch, but the grate was clean and cold, as if no fire had been lit in it recently. I saw a few crumbs on the floor, which I mentioned to Holmes as coming from the teacakes Jenny had been given.

"I do not doubt it," Holmes said with no satisfaction. "There is also a fine yellow hair on the cushion." He waved absently at the red couch while staring out of one of the many windows. "Come!" he said suddenly. "There is nothing else to be learned here. This is where he kept her, and he intended us to know it. He even left crumbs for us to find. Now why was that, do you suppose?"

"Carelessness," I replied, following him out of the door and down the stairs again, Hodgkins on his heels. "And arrogance."

"No, Watson, no! Moriarty is never careless. He has left them here for a reason. Let us find this stable. There is something . . . some clue, something done, or left undone, which will give me the key."

But I feared he was speaking more in hope than knowledge. He would not ever admit it, but there is a streak of kindness in him which does not always sit well with reason. Of course, I have never said so to him.

We got into the trap again and Hodgkins asked Holmes which direction he should drive. For several moments Holmes did not reply. I was about to repeat the question, for fear that he had not heard, when he sat very upright. "Which is the most obvious farm, from here?" he demanded. "That meets our requirements, that is?"

"Miller's," Hodgkins replied.

"How far?"

"Just under two miles. Shall I take you there?"

"No. Which is the second most obvious?"

Hodgkins thought for a moment or two. "I reckon the old Adams place, sir."

"Good. Then take us there, as fast as you may."

"Yes, sir!"

It proved to be some distance further than the first farm mentioned, and I admit I became anxious as the minutes passed and the time grew closer and closer to two. Holmes frequently kept me in the dark regarding his ideas, but I was very much afraid that in this instance he had no better notion of how to foil Moriarty than I did myself. Even if we found the farm, how was it going to help us? There was no reason to suppose he would be there now, or indeed ever again. I forbore from saying so perhaps out of cowardice. I did not want to hear that he had no solution, that he was as fallible and as frightened as I.

We reached the Adams' farm and the disused stable. Holmes opened the door wide to let in all the light he could, and examined the place as if he might read in the straw and dust some answers to all our needs. I thought it pointless. How could anyone find here a footprint of meaning, a child's hair, or indeed crumbs of anything? I watched him and fidgeted from one foot to the other, feeling helpless, and as if we were wasting precious moments.

"Holmes!" I burst out at last. "We . . ." I got no further. Triumphantly he held up a very small, grubby, white sock, such as might fit a child. He examined it quickly, and with growing amazement and delight.

"What?" I said angrily. "So it is Jenny's sock. She was here. How does that help us? He will still take her tonight, and you may be sure it will not be to this place!"

Holmes pulled his pocket watch out. "It is after one already!" he said with desperate urgency. "We have no time to lose at all. Hodgkins, take me back to the Grange as fast as the pony can go!"

It was a hectic journey. Hodgkins had more faith than I that there was some good reason for it, and he drove the animal as hard as he could short of cruelty, and I must say it gave of its best. It was a brave little creature and was lathered and blowing hard when we finally pulled in the drive at the front door and Holmes leaped out, waving the sock in his hand. "All will be well!" he shouted to Hodgkins. "Care for that excellent animal! Watson!" And he plunged into the hall, calling out for Hunt at the top of his voice.

I saw with dread that the long case clock by the foot of the stairs already said three minutes past two.

Hunt threw open his study door, his face pale, eyes wide with fear.

Holmes held up the sock. "Bloodless!" he said triumphantly. "Tell me, what time does the hokey-pokey man play?"

Hunt looked at him as if he had taken leave of his wits, and I admit the same thought had occurred to me. He stammered a blasphemy and turned on his heel, too overcome with emotion to form any answer.

Holmes strode after him, catching him by the shoulder, and Hunt swung around, his eyes blazing, his fist raised as if to strike.

"Believe me, sir, I am deadly earnest!" Holmes said grimly. "Your daughter will be perfectly safe until the ice-cream man comes . . ."

"The ice-cream man!" Hunt exploded. "You are mad, sir! I have known Percy Bradford all my life! He would no more . . ."

"With no intent," Holmes agreed, still clasping Hunt by the arm. "It is the tune he plays. Look!" He held up the small, grubby sock again. "You see, it has no blood on it! This was left where Moriarty wishes us to believe he held her last night, and that this sock somehow was left behind. But it is not so. It is no doubt her sock, but taken from the first kidnap when you were not guarding her, having no reason for concern."

"What difference does that make?" Hunt demanded, the raw edge of fear in his voice only too apparent.

"Send for the hokey-pokey man, and I will show you," Holmes replied. "Have him come to the gates as is his custom, but immediately, now in daylight, and play his tunes."

"Do it, my dear fellow!" I urged. I had seen this look of triumph in Holmes before, and now all my faith in him flooded back, although I still had no idea what he intended, or indeed what it was that he suddenly understood.

Hunt hesitated only moments, then like a man plunging into ice-cold water, he obeyed, his body clenched, his jaw so tight I was afraid he might break his teeth.

"Come!" Holmes ordered me. "I might need you, Watson. Your medical skill may be stretched to the limits." And without any explanation whatever of this extraordinary remark he started up the stairs. "Take me to the nursery!" he called over his shoulder. "Quickly, man!"

As it turned out we had some half-hour or more to wait while the ice-cream vendor was sent for and brought from his position at this hour in the village. Holmes paced the floor, every now and then going to the window and staring out until at last he saw what he wanted, and within moments we heard the happy, lilting sound of the barrel organ playing.

Holmes swiveled from the window to stare at the child. He held up one hand in command of silence, while in the same fashion forbidding me from moving.

Jenny sat perfectly still. The small woolen golliwog she had been holding fell from her fingers and, staring straight ahead of her, she rose to her feet and walked to the nursery door.

Josephine started up after her.

"No!" Holmes ordered with such fierceness that the poor girl froze.

"But . . ." she began in anguish as the child opened the door and walked through.

"No!" Holmes repeated. "Follow, but don't touch her. You may harm her if you do! Come . . ." And he set off after her himself, moving on tip-toe so that no noise should alarm her or let her know she was being followed, though indeed she seemed oblivious of everything around her.

In single file behind we pursued the child, who seemed to be walking as if in her sleep, along the corridor and up the attic stairs, narrow and winding, until she came to a stop beside a small cupboard in an angle of the combe. She opened it and crept inside, pulling a blanket over herself, and then closed the door.

Holmes turned to the maid. "When the nursery clock chimes eleven, I believe she will awaken and return to normal, confused but not physically injured. She will believe what she has been mesmerized to believe, that she was again taken by Professor Moriarty, as she was in truth the first time. No doubt he took her to at least three different places, and she will recall them in successive order, as he has told her. You will wait here so you can comfort her when she awakens and comes out, no doubt confused and frightened. Do not disturb her before that. Do you understand me?"

"Yes sir! I'll not move or speak, I swear," Josephine promised, her eyes wide with admiration and I think not a little relief.

"Good. Now we must find Hunt and assure him of Jenny's welfare. He must issue a statement denying any rumor that he might sell his holdings in the mine. In fact if he can raise the funds, a small purchase of more stock might be advantageous. We must not allow Moriarty to imagine that he has won anything, don't you agree?"

"I do!" I said vehemently. "Are you sure she will be all right, Holmes?"

"Of course, my dear Watson!" he said, allowing himself to smile at last. "She will have the most excellent medical attention possible, and a friend to assure her that she is well and strong, and that this will not occur again. Possibly eat as much ice-cream as she wishes, provided it is not accompanied by that particular tune."

"And a new pair of socks!" I agreed, wanting to laugh and cry at the same time. "You are brilliant, Holmes, quite brilliant! No resolution to a case has given me more pleasure."

"It was my good fortune she stubbed her toe," he said modestly. "And that you were wise enough to send immediately for me, of course!"

The Adventure
of the Anonymous Author

Edward D. Hoch

I T WAS A bleak April afternoon in 1902, ten days after our early
Easter and the first full year into King Edward's reign, and
Holmes and I had remained close to the fire. I was reading the
latest issue of *The Strand* magazine while he puttered in the next
room with one of his scientific experiments. It was Mrs. Hudson
who announced our visitors in her usual manner. "A man and a
boy to see Mr. Holmes on a business matter," she said after knock-
ing on the door and presenting him with a calling card.

Holmes frowned at the interruption but instructed her to send
the visitors up. He quickly slipped on his dressing gown to cover a
shirt stained with chemicals and said to me, "Well, Watson, this
appears to be an acquaintance of yours."

"Of mine?"

"Mr. Rutherford Wilson, a sub-editor of that magazine where
your literary agent has placed several of your flamboyant accounts
of my cases."

"You mean the Strand?" I asked, holding up the issue I was reading. But by then there was a second knock and the door opened
to admit a middle-aged man wearing pince-nez and an obvious tou-
pee. Accompanying him was a red-haired boy, perhaps ten or

eleven years of age, his hands almost hidden by the sleeves of a gray winter coat.

"Mr. Holmes," the man said, managing a nervous smile as he thrust the boy ahead of him into our parlor. "I hope you'll excuse my bringing Roddy along, but he so wanted to meet you. He's read about all of your early adventures in our magazine. Roddy, this is the famous Mr. Sherlock Holmes. And you must be Dr. Watson."

I acknowledged the fact and shook his hand. "I don't believe we've met, though I have lunched with my literary agent and Mr. Greenbough Smith on occasion at the Café Royal."

Rutherford Wilson quickly nodded. "I am a mere sub-editor at the Strand. Mr. Smith is our chief editor, as you know. He dearly wishes there would be more of your little stories, Doctor, now that Mr. Holmes is truly back among us."

"Perhaps there will be," I replied.

Ever since entering our rooms the boy had not taken his wide eyes off Holmes. He seemed at a loss for words so Holmes bent to shake his hand. "So good to meet you, Master Roddy. Might I offer you a cup of hot cocoa while your father and I talk?"

"Yes, sir. Thank you, sir."

Holmes smiled and rang for Mrs. Hudson. Then he addressed our visitor. "Your older son did not wish to accompany you?"

Wilson was taken aback. "Do you know of my family, Mr. Holmes?"

"No, but I observe that young Roddy's coat seems a bit long in the sleeves, the sort that would have been handed down by an older brother."

"And you are quite correct. Richard is thirteen and away at school, or I am sure he would have wanted to meet you too." He smiled in admiration. "Dr. Watson has not exaggerated your powers of observation, Mr. Holmes."

When Mrs. Hudson returned with the boy's hot cocoa, I gave him a picture book to look through while we talked with his father. "What brings you to us, Mr. Wilson?" Holmes asked.

"It is a matter of one of our authors at the Strand. If you read the magazine regularly—"

"I leave that for Watson," Holmes assured him.

"Well then, Dr. Watson," he said, turning to me with a bit of reluctance. "Perhaps you remember a long story, 'The Extra Passenger,' that appeared in our Christmas issue. It was almost novel length and was published anonymously. I have brought you a copy to read."

I remembered it vaguely. "A man on a train—"

"That's the one! You know some authors prefer to publish anonymously, for one reason or another. Your own literary agent, Dr. Doyle, published an anonymous story in *The Strand* many years ago."

"I never knew that."

"Oh, yes. Our problem now is that the story has proven so popular a publisher wants to bring it out in book form. But we have no idea as to the author's identity."

"How is that possible?" Holmes wanted to know. "Surely someone submitted the story. Surely someone was paid for it."

"The author gave the name Jane Austin, clearly a pseudonym. When I wrote to tell her we couldn't use that name on the story she said to publish it anonymously."

"Where did you send payment?"

"To a Miss Jane Austin in care of the Croydon post office. She collected her mail there, but when I visited them they knew nothing more about her. I realize this isn't a criminal matter but you're our last hope of finding her, Mr. Holmes. I thought you might discover some clue to her identity in reading the story. I've brought you a copy."

"Have you written her about the book offer?"

"Of course. Several times. I explained that the publisher wanted to issue it under her own name and that it would bring her a certain amount of fame as well as money. She replied that she wasn't interested in the offer, and since then she has simply ignored my letters."

Holmes considered that. "Tell me something. How soon after your first letter did this mysterious Jane Austin respond?"

"At once. The very next day."

"So she probably calls at the post office for her mail each day," he mused. Then, surprisingly, he turned to the boy. "Master Roddy, if you have read about some of my investigations as written up by the good doctor here, you are no doubt familiar with my Baker Street Irregulars."

He nodded at once. "They are local street urchins you sometimes recruit to search for clues. Their leader is young Wiggins."

Holmes allowed himself a smile. "Wiggins is grown to adulthood now, but the spirit of the Irregulars remains. Unfortunately their ungainly appearance makes them ill-suited to the working class borough of Croydon. Whereas you, Master Roddy, would be perfect."

"What . . . what would I have to do?" he asked uncertainly.

"We will send Miss Jane Austin a letter to her Croydon post office address. It will be some sort of bogus flyer in a brightly colored envelope that is easily recognized. If you can manage to linger at or near the post office and follow the woman who picks up the envelope, I believe we can locate your mysterious author with a minimum of effort. Dr. Watson can accompany you there, and see that you return safely."

"A brilliant plan!" Rutherford Wilson exclaimed. "You can follow her right to her lodgings, Roddy. Once we know her true name and address, I will make an effort to convince her that she should allow publication of the book."

THE LETTER WAS dispatched the following afternoon in a bright blue envelope, and on Friday morning I took a carriage with young Roddy to the borough of Croydon on the southern edge of the city. It was an area of factories with nearby houses for many of the workers and their families. The post office itself was located in a soot-stained brick building near an old cemetery. While I lingered in a tea shop across the road, the lad positioned himself near the door of the building. Luckily the weather had improved and London was experiencing a rare morning of April sunshine.

After a full hour of this I was prepared to give it up. A postman leaving in his red, blue and gold uniform, carrying a large sack of mail for delivery, gave Roddy a suspicious glance. Surely Holmes could not expect us to remain at our posts for the entire day, watching for a woman who might never come. I ordered another cup of tea and some biscuits, deciding to give it a half-hour more.

Then the lad seemed to disappear for a moment among some more postmen departing on their rounds. When I saw him again he was talking to a young girl who couldn't have been much older than him. Even as I watched, they set off together down the road. I paid my bill and hurried outside. What had happened to cause Roddy to desert his post and go off with a girl?

I fell into step about fifty yards behind them, feeling just a bit like a foolish uncle keeping track of his wayward nephew. Then I saw a sudden flash of blue and all became clear. Roddy had struck up a conversation with the girl because it was she who had called for the mail. She was carrying it now, protruding from the top of her small purse. I guessed correctly that she had not come far, and she turned in at the first house beyond the cemetery, giving a little good-bye wave to Roddy. The front door opened and I saw a young blond woman greet the child, keeping a wary eye on Roddy as he hurried away.

I kept walking, trying to seem inconspicuous, until both the lad and I had rounded the corner out of sight of the house. When he realized I was following he waited for me to catch up. "That girl picked up the mail," he told me excitedly. "Her name is Jenny and she lives with her big sister Catherine. I told her I'd just moved in down the road."

"You did very well," I assured him. "Holmes will be pleased."

I was able to gather some information of my own by speaking with a neighbor down the street who happened to be out in her yard. She eyed me with some suspicion at first, but finally informed me that Catherine Crider and her younger sister Jenny indeed lived in the house by the cemetery. Miss Crider was a teacher at a private school in the neighborhood.

ON SATURDAY MORNING when Rutherford Wilson paid a second visit to our lodgings, Holmes was able to tell the Strand editor everything we'd learned. "Roddy was a great help," he informed the boy's father. "I would welcome him into my small band of Irregulars at any time."

"I don't know how to thank you, sir! I will call upon Miss Catherine Crider this very afternoon."

While I had been out the previous day Holmes had surprised me by reading the magazine Wilson had brought for us. It was one of his rare ventures into popular fiction, and he said now, "Her tale of the man who appears and then disappears on a train to Rome is really a good mystery story. I would very much like to meet the author sometime."

Rutherford Wilson took up the suggestion at once. "Come with me now, Mr. Holmes. And Dr. Watson too! Perhaps the three of us together can convince her that 'The Other Passenger' deserves book publication under her own name."

Holmes pondered the suggestion and then to my surprise he agreed. In a moment he had donned his greatcoat and deerstalker against the chill April air and we were on our way to Croydon.

The blond young woman who answered the door to face three strange men was the one I'd glimpsed briefly the previous day, though her face seemed older when viewed close up. Wilson identified himself and asked to speak with her. She ushered us into a plain sitting room with some reluctance. "And these two men?" she asked, motioning toward us.

"This is Mr. Sherlock Holmes, the renowned private inquiry agent, and Dr. Watson. They were instrumental in locating you."

"Did you ever consider that I might not wish to be located, Mr. Wilson?"

"Your novel that we published at Christmastime engendered a good bit of praise, Miss Crider. A leading London publisher, John

Milne, is offering to bring it out in book form for a generous sum of money."

"But only if I allow it to be published under my own name."

"What is so wrong with that? Catherine Crider is a perfectly good name."

"So is Jane Austin."

"Please be reasonable."

"All right. Then let them publish it anonymously, as you did in the Strand."

Rutherford Wilson sighed. "Do you fear repercussions from the school where you teach?"

"No. I simply do not want my name on it."

Her sister Jenny came into the room then, carrying a textbook of English grammar. I guessed her age at about fourteen, with long blond hair and pretty blue eyes like her sister. "Cathy, can you help me with this?"

"Not now, Jenny. After our company has left."

"It must be quite a task looking after a growing sister," Holmes commented as the girl returned to the next room.

"Indeed it is! Our parents died when I was eleven and Jenny was but a year old. I have looked after her ever since."

"How long have you been teaching?"

"Three years. I try to help Jenny with her studies at home too."

"How old is she now? About fourteen?"

"She has just turned fifteen, a difficult age for any girl. I have tried to instill in her a love of music." She stood up and motioned for us to follow. In the parlor where Jenny studied there was an upright piano, its finish scarred and dented with use. "Will you play something for our guests?" she asked her sister.

Jenny smiled and went to the piano. She played a selection from the opera *Carmen* with surprising skill and when she'd finished we applauded. "That's very good!" I congratulated her.

Catherine Crider was pleased. "When I was very young my father took me to a concert by Bizet, the composer of *Carmen*. I never forgot it. But I do not have the gift for music that Jenny has."

When we returned to the sitting room Rutherford Wilson again urged her to permit book publication of the novel. "The money you earn could be used for your sister's music education," he argued.

For the first time his words seemed to have an effect on the woman. Perhaps she was considering her sister's future rather than her own. "I promise to give it some thought," she said. "If I decide to do it, there is something I would have to attend to first."

We departed soon after, and I could see that Wilson was encouraged by her words. "You have been a great help, Mr. Holmes," he said on the ride back to the central city.

"I did nothing," Holmes replied modestly. But I could see that something was troubling him.

THE MIDDLE OF the following week brought us troubling and unexpected news. We'd had a telephone for some four years and Baker Street even had its own telephone directory that I found useful at times. Holmes himself rarely used it, and on this day the ringing of the phone startled us both. Holmes answered it with some irritation, which gradually gave way to a concern that furrowed his brows.

"That was Rutherford Wilson at the Strand, Watson. There has been an unforeseen development. A man has been found murdered in the cemetery adjoining Miss Crider's house. She telephoned him from the Post Office and seemed quite disturbed. He's going out there now and requests that we join him."

"What can this mean, Holmes?"

"Perhaps nothing, an unrelated event." But he was already getting out his coat and I knew that he meant to pursue it.

We were back in Croydon within the hour. It had rained earlier and a morning mist still hung over the graveyard. We found one of the Scotland Yard men, Tobias Gregson, conducting the investigation. Holmes had always admired him, considering him the smartest of the Yarders. "What do we have here, Gregson?" he asked as we approached across the damp grass of the graveyard.

Gregson, a tall white-faced man with flaxen hair now turning white, seemed surprised to see us. "It's Mr. Holmes and Dr. Watson, isn't it? Been some years since you helped me on an investigation. Are you involved with this one?"

Holmes glanced over to where a pair of bobbies stood guard by a man's body. "I may be. Who is the victim?"

Gregson consulted his notebook. "Identification on him says his name is William Knox. He played in the orchestra at the Gaiety Music Hall, lived up in Islington."

"Far from home," my friend commented. "How did he die?"

"Knife wound to the stomach. It wasn't deep but he seems to have collapsed here and bled to death. He'd been dead for hours before a postman spotted the body back here."

Then I noticed Rutherford Wilson making his way in our direction from the street. The Strand editor had his arm around Catherine Crider's shoulders as if protecting her from the chill in the air. Holmes hurried over to intercept them before they reached the body. "What can you tell us about this, Miss Crider?" he asked.

Her face was pale and I could see now that she was trembling. "It . . . it happened just outside my house. The killer might still be in the neighborhood. The police said he stabbed that man. I felt I had to call someone."

"I'm glad you phoned me," Wilson said. "What do you think, Mr. Holmes?"

"I think we should get Miss Crider inside out of this damp air."

I told Gregson where we would be and the four of us went into the house. "Is your sister at home today?" I asked.

She shook her head. "She's at school. Thank God she'd already left the house before that postman discovered the body."

"You must calm down, Miss Crider, and tell us what you know."

"I know nothing," she insisted.

"Does the name William Knox mean anything to you?"

"No."

Before she could move Holmes shot out his hand and gripped her wrist, pushing back the sleeve of her dress to reveal a purple bruise. "Are there more bruises beside this one?"

"What is this, Holmes?" Wilson asked. "What are you getting at?"

"Tell him, Miss Crider, or I shall."

But she was sobbing uncontrollably now. "I didn't—," she managed. And then, "I didn't mean to kill him!"

"Kill him!" The color drained from Wilson's face. "You mean she stabbed a man she didn't even know?"

"Oh, she knew him, all right. William Knox was the father of her daughter Jenny."

"THERE IS NO way you could have known that," I insisted to Holmes later, after Catherine Crider had told her story to the authorities. "There is no way you could even have guessed it."

"You are wrong, Watson." He filled his pipe and lit it, in preparation for explaining the logic of his reasoning. "It seemed obvious from the beginning that Catherine Crider's insistence on a pseudonym was because she was hiding from someone—the police, her parents, a lover. In any event it had to be someone whom she feared might harm her, or separate her from Jenny."

"Jenny is her daughter?"

Holmes nodded. "Consider the mathematics, Watson. Jenny has just turned fifteen, and Catherine told us she had cared for her little sister since she was eleven and Jenny was one. If Jenny is fifteen, Catherine must be about twenty-five, born around 1876 or '77. She seemed older than that when seen up close, and I remembered her telling us her father took her to a Bizet concert when she was a child. But Bizet died in 1875, at least a year before she claimed to have been born. There would be no point in her making up such a story, so we are left with the likelihood that she is lying about her age. Instead of being about twenty-five, it seems she is closer to thirty-five."

"But why would she lie?"

"Exactly, Watson! Why? She is not an actress wanting to prolong her career, nor an heiress who must marry by a certain age. She is a middle-class teacher raising a younger sister. However if the truth of their age difference became known, that younger sister could easily be seen as her daughter. Our Victorian era did not pass with the death of Her Majesty, Watson. An unmarried woman with a child to raise is still an object of scorn."

"I understand it now, Holmes. She could not use her real name on her writings because the truth of her age might come out."

"More than that. She might be found by the person she most fears—Jenny's father."

"But he did find her, this morning. How was that possible?"

"Catherine made a terrible mistake. She'd always known where William Knox was because he played in an orchestra whose bookings were in the daily papers. Jenny's musical talent came from her father, not her mother. Over the weekend Catherine decided to allow publication of 'The Extra Passenger' under her own name, and rather than fret about Knox tracking her down she telephoned him at the Gaiety Music Hall and told him where she was. All this we heard today from her own lips. She never imagined he would turn up after the Music Hall closed, half drunk on cheap wine, and demand the child he'd never seen. They fought while Jenny slept in the room above. Knox hit her and she fought him off with a kitchen knife. He stumbled out of the house without Catherine realizing the seriousness of his wound. He wandered into the graveyard where he passed out and later died from loss of blood. She was horrified this morning when the body was found, and immediately called Rutherford Wilson for help. I believe she would have told the truth even if I hadn't deduced it."

"What will become of her now?" I asked.

"Wilson is arranging for a leading barrister to handle her defense. It seems likely the law will be lenient when the full facts are known, if only for Jenny's sake."

"Is there anyone to pay you for your efforts, Holmes?"

He waved away my question with a smile. "It was more a diversion than an effort. I only wish we could have arrived at a happier conclusion, before the untimely death of Mr. William Knox."

The Case of the Vampire's Mark

Bill Crider

I N GOING OVER my notes, I see that I have seldom commented upon the housekeeping abilities of my good friend Sherlock Holmes, except perhaps to criticize them. Even he, I believe, would confess to the truth of the statement that he is among the untidiest of men.

The sitting room of the residence we sometimes shared at 221B Baker Street was often filled with the noxious odors emanating from his chemistry experiments, and it was not unusual for retorts to be bubbling away at all hours. His fingers were commonly stained with chemicals or ink, and papers littered the floor. Cigars lay in the coal scuttle, and his unanswered correspondence was skewered to the center of the wooden mantelpiece with a jackknife.

But, to be fair, there are some domestic chores at which Holmes excelled. Cooking breakfast was one of these, breakfast being the only meal he truly enjoyed. So it was no surprise to me when I visited him early one warm summer's day in 1889 to see the table laden with a hearty English breakfast that he had prepared himself.

"Come in, Watson!" he called just as I raised my hand to knock at the door. "The door is unlocked."

I opened the door and went inside. Holmes was there, wearing his old mouse-colored dressing gown and seated at the table, having his breakfast.

"My dear Holmes," I said, "I know that you are skilled in deduction, but I did not know that you could see through a solid wooden door!"

"See?" said Holmes. "I hardly needed to see you, Watson. Have I not heard your tread on the stairs hundreds of times? I should hope that I could identify you, of all men, from the sound of your step."

"Of course," said I. "I should have known."

"Then put aside your hat and stick and have a bit of breakfast with me. You can tell me of your practice whilst you are at it."

"I could not presume so much on your hospitality," I protested.

"Nonsense," said Holmes with a laugh. "As you can see, I have prepared far too much for my own needs. That is what comes of cooking so seldom."

It was obvious that he was right. There were eggs and ham in plenty, and a bit of curried fowl to go with them, so I agreed to join him and we set to with a will. When we were done, Holmes fetched a pipe from the coal scuttle, where it had lain among the cigars, and filled it with shag from the Persian slipper where he kept his tobacco. His pre-breakfast pipe was always filled with the dottle of the previous day's pipes, preserved in a pile on the mantel, and he was now making his start toward accumulating this day's pile.

"Now, Watson," said he, when he had the pipe going satisfactorily, "tell me about yourself, as I know little of your life these days except that your wife is off visiting and that you stropped your razor this morning."

"By Jove, Holmes!" said I. "Your powers never cease to astonish me. There is no way that you could know these things, and yet it seems that you do. There is more to this than knowing the sound of my footstep on the stair."

"You know my methods better than anyone, Watson," said he. "Observation of trifles is chief among them."

I raised my hand to my jawline, where the skin was scraped a bit raw and touched my chin where there was a tiny scab from a razor nick.

"Yes," said Holmes. "I noticed the cut at once, and I do believe you have spotted your napkin. Mrs. Hudson will forgive you, however."

"Mrs. Hudson is not here to forgive me," said I. "Permit me to draw an inference of my own. You would not have made breakfast yourself had she been here, and I would not have had to let myself in downstairs. So I believe that I can safely say that Mrs. Hudson is away."

"Capital, Watson," said Holmes. "You have unplumbed depths, as I have more than once observed. Mrs. Hudson is indeed away on a visit."

"As is my wife," I replied. "But how did you know?"

"Your very presence here at this hour of the morning is proof enough. I now that she is not ill because you are clearly in a fine mood and able to enjoy your breakfast. Had she been at home, your wife surely would have made one for you. Obviously she did not, or you would not have been out and about at such an early hour. Therefore she is away, most likely on a visit."

"Now that you have explained your reasoning with regard to my wife, it seems a bit less remarkable," said I, "but how did you know that my wound was caused by a freshly-stropped razor?"

"And how else? There is hardly any other way to obtain a scraped jaw or those small nicks, unless possibly in a fight, and I know that you would never fight before breakfast."

I had to agree, and he smiled thinly, then puffed away on his pipe until his head was wreathed with the pungent smoke.

"And you, Holmes?" I said. "Have you had any interesting cases of late?"

My host's good humor faded. "Nothing, Watson. I spend my days in idleness. It seems that there is no need for a consulting detective these days, other than to find out unfaithful husbands or locate lost pets."

"But Holmes," said I, "surely you would never—"

Holmes waved his hand in front of his face, causing the smoke from his pipe to eddy around him.

"Correct, Watson," he said. "I would never interest myself in matters such as those. They are an insult to my abilities."

At that moment the bell at the door below began to jangle.

"Perhaps that is a client with an interesting tale to tell," I said.

"That may well be, Watson, and if we are to judge by the frantic tone of the bell, he is in quite a hurry to tell it. Would you be so kind as to greet him and conduct him here?"

Of course I was glad to be able to perform this humble service, which would have been Mrs. Hudson's job had she been at home. The man I met when I opened the door was of medium height, with short black hair parted on the side and a black beard. He wore a dark suit with a white shirt and tie and held a hat in his hands.

"Good morning," he said when I greeted him. "Do I have the honor of addressing Mr. Sherlock Holmes?"

I smiled and told him that Holmes was above. "I am merely his friend, Dr. Watson."

"Ah," the man said. "And I am Abraham Stoker. I have heard of you Dr. Watson, and of your friend, but it is he I have come seeking. Would it be possible for me to see him?"

"Of course," said I, and conducted Mr. Stoker upstairs, where Holmes had made a halfhearted effort to make the room presentable. It still smelled of breakfast and pipe smoke, but the dishes had somehow been made to vanish.

"Come in," said Holmes when he saw us in the doorway. He still wore the mouse-colored dressing gown.

We entered, and I introduced Mr. Stoker to Holmes, who said, "And how long has it been since you left Dublin, Mr. Stoker?"

"What?" said Stoker. "How did you know that I was from Dublin. I had thought that any trace of accent was gone from my voice by now."

"Not for one who has made a study of the different ways of speaking on our two islands," said Holmes. "And I would venture to say that you are an educated man, for your accent is not that of the working classes."

"Trinity College," Stoker said, "and I now begin to believe all that I have heard of you is true."

"Not all, perhaps," said Holmes, "but a goodly portion no doubt. What brought you to London?"

"The theatre," said Stoker.

He explained that he had been a theatre critic during his college days and that he was now the manager of the Lyceum Theatre and secretary to Sir Henry Irving, the owner and star of most of the theatre's productions.

"One of London's largest theatres," said Holmes, though I am sure he had never attended a play there.

"And Sir Henry is one of England's finest actors," said I, for I had seen him in Shakespeare's *Henry IV, Part I.*

"But you did not come here to talk of the theatre, I hope," said Holmes, his eyes alight at the prospect of investigating some despicable criminal act.

"No," said Stoker. "I came to talk about an occurrence so bizarre, so horrible, that I can hardly expect you to believe it. I can hardly believe it myself."

"Ah," exclaimed Holmes, his enthusiasm increasing. "Tell us what this occurrence might be."

"It is a bite," said Stoker. "Or bites, I should say. Bites on the neck of a child. The mark of a vampire!"

Holmes snorted, and the light in his eyes died. "Bah. The living dead? Nothing more than superstition of the basest sort. Irrational and completely impossible."

Stoker drew himself erect. "I am not talking of some sensational novel or play, sir. I know that such things have filled the stages of England and France for years, but this is real."

"No," said Holmes. "It is not. Human blood drinkers may have lived, it is true, and we can read of the likes of Countess Bathory, called the Blood Countess, and Vlad Tepes, called the Impaler, but there are no vampires."

"Countess Bathory? Vlad Tepes?" Stoker said. "And who are they?"

As I knew no more of the names Holmes had spoken, I could have asked the same question, and I am sure Holmes could have answered at length should he have chosen to do so. His ignorance of the world's great literature sometimes astounded me, but when it came to tales of sensational crimes and their perpetrators, his reading was both wide and deep.

"Bathory and Tepes are of no importance," Holmes said. "They were criminals on a grand scale, but they are long dead. They do not change themselves into bats and fly through the yellow fogs of London to gorge themselves on the blood of innocents."

"Nevertheless, someone—something—has done so," said Stoker. "The person who told me would not lie. You may see for yourself if you come with me. I am told that the most recent bite is still fresh."

"Very well," said Holmes, his interest somewhat rekindled. "It may well be that this case, though not what you think, does indeed require my talents. I will make myself ready, and Dr. Watson and I will accompany you."

"But Holmes," I protested, "I must—"

"Tut, Watson. Your wife is away and will not miss you. I, on the other hand, might very well find myself in need of your assistance. You have performed admirably in the past."

I admit to being pleased at Holmes' words. He was not a man to use flattery, so I knew that he meant what he had said.

"Yes, Dr. Watson," Stoker said. "Please do come. Your abilities as a physician may be of great help."

"Very well," said I, "I shall be glad to go with you. But where is it that we are going?"

"The countryside near Cobham, in Surrey," said Stoker. "Sir Henry's coach is awaiting us below."

"A pleasant countryside," I said, having visited the area in the past.

"And Surrey has an admirable beekeepers' association," Holmes added. "I have quite an interest in bees. Amazing creatures. However, that does not obviate the fact that the country is a place of far more evil than most people know, and crime often goes unpunished there for more reasons than one. We must be on our way, Watson, for the case may be far more urgent than I first had thought."

ON OUR COACH ride to Surrey, Mr. Stoker gave us more details of the affair that had caused him to fetch us in such a hurry. It seemed that Robin, the young son of Lily Montgomery, one of the finest actresses of the English stage and often Mr. Henry Irving's leading lady, had for some time been feeling unwell. He was nervous and irritable and could not bear the light of day. Often at night he became quite restless.

"He seemed to fear something that he could not name," Stoker said, "and at first his mother thought it was merely the result of some nightmare. But he grew less and less interested in his studies, and she summoned medical advice. It was the family doctor who discovered the horrible bites only at daybreak this morning."

"And what was the doctor's diagnosis?" asked Holmes. "That the boy had been bitten by a vampire?"

"Oh, no," said Stoker, "but he could think of no other explanation for the tooth marks."

"Then he is not a doctor that I should like to have call upon me," said Holmes. "Who identified the marks?"

"Mrs. Tedescu," Stoker replied.

"And who is Mrs. Tedescu?"

"She and her husband, Wladyslaw, are the family servants. They are from Transylvania, Romania, as is Mrs. Montgomery's husband."

"But her name," said I. "Surely it is not Romanian."

"It is Mrs. Montgomery's maiden name, which she adopted as her stage name to suit the English ear," said Stoker. "At any rate,

Mrs. Tedescu was the first to recognize the bite of the vampire and to give it a name. She is steeped in the legends of her country, I suppose."

"You said something of lessons," Holmes remarked. "Does young Robin attend the local school?"

"No. There is a tutor living with the family. His name is John Cabot."

"Is there anyone else living in the house?"

"No one," said Stoker.

"And the husband."

"Brasov is his name," said Stoker. "Nicholas Brasov. He lives there as well, of course."

"Yet we are in Mr. Irving's carriage," Holmes pointed out.

"Mr. Irving cares deeply for Mrs. Montgomery's welfare and for the welfare of her family, as do I," Stoker said stiffly. "He was glad to send his carriage for you when called upon. Mr. Brasov rode into town himself to ask for help. Of course he has now returned to Surrey, where he awaits us."

"Of course," said Holmes. "And does everyone in the house know of the bites?"

"Yes," Stoker replied. "It is a matter of utmost concern to all, for an immortal soul is at stake."

Holmes opened his mouth as if to speak, but he forbore. I said, "Has anyone suggested a remedy?"

"No," said Stoker, "though Mr. Irving says that preventatives have been mentioned."

"And what might those be?" asked Holmes.

"Garlic and crosses," Stoker replied. "Sir Henry tells me that Mr. Cabot has vowed to protect Robin from all harm. He says that he will stay in the boy's room, armed only with a crucifix, and defeat the vampire. Mrs. Montgomery feels he is quite brave."

"Bravery?" said Holmes. "It is foolery and nothing more. Crucifixes and garlic are worse than useless. Has anyone had a glimpse of this so-called vampire?"

"No one," said Stoker, "but the creatures are supposed to be able to change shape and enter a room as mist and fog."

"Let me hear no more of this," said Holmes. "It is all nothing and less than nothing. We will, I assure you, find some very human villain at work here."

"But the bites," said Stoker. "Such bites were never made by human teeth."

"You have seen them?" Holmes inquired.

"No. But I believe what I have heard. Mrs. Montgomery would never stoop to falsehood."

"She is a woman," said Holmes, whose disdain of the female sex knew no bounds. "And even the best of women cannot be trusted. But for now I will accept your word as to her veracity."

After that remark, we rode in silence save for the sound of the coach as it rolled over the road. The Surrey countryside soon came into view, and we saw the brilliant green willows that lined the river Mole. When we passed an old stone mill, the coach turned off the main road and onto a rougher path that led through the greensward and across a wooden bridge over a shallow stream of brackish water. We soon arrived at a rustic country house that appeared from the outside to have many commodious rooms. The flower beds were blooming with red and white, and I recognized the distinctive bell shape of the Lily of the Valley. I was reminded that Mrs. Montgomery's first name was that of the flower.

The coach stopped outside the door, and when we stepped down, Stoker said, "This is Mr. Brasov's country home. The boy is inside, along with the rest of the family."

"I should like to see the boy first," said Holmes, "in order to examine the bites."

"Very well," said Stoker, and made use of a bronze knocker on the door, which was almost at once pulled open by a wizened old man dressed all in black.

"Good morrow, Wladyslaw," said Stoker. "These men are Dr. Watson and Mr. Sherlock Holmes, here to see young Robin."

"Come in," croaked the old man, standing aside, and we entered the house, which was quite dark after the sunlight outside.

Wladyslaw Tedescu led us along a hallway to a large sitting room. In it were two women, one of whom was obviously Mrs. Montgomery. She was tall and regal, though her face was sad in the curtained gloom. The other woman was older and wore black. She was undoubtedly Mrs. Tedescu. Fidgeting in a wing chair was a young lad, who must be Robin, and standing behind him was an earnest-looking fellow that I took for the tutor, John Cabot, who was nervously rubbing his fingertips with his thumb.

"Bram!" Mrs. Montgomery said when she saw us. "Thank God. Is this Mr. Holmes?"

"Yes," said Stoker, smiling at her use of his familiar name, "and Dr. Watson is here as well. Mr. Holmes wishes to have a look at Robin."

Mrs. Montgomery crossed the room with such grace that it almost appeared she might be floating. She was very beautiful, with raven hair, blue eyes, and delicate skin. She pressed Holmes' hand, looked into his eyes, and said, "You must help us, Mr. Holmes. This is like some sort of horrible dream."

"It is no dream," Holmes said. "Yet horror is largely a product of the imagination."

He walked over to the chair where Robin sat and asked why the curtains were drawn.

"The light bothers me," Robin said sharply. "I cannot bear it."

"It is the blood of the vampire mingling with his," said Mrs. Tedescu hoarsely. Her accent was heavy, but she was easily understood. "Soon he will become one of the children of the night."

"Rubbish," said Holmes. "Utter nonsense." He then spoke to the man standing by the chair. "We must have light if I am to examine the bite. Are you Mr. Cabot?"

"Yes," said Cabot in a pleasant voice. "Shall I open the curtains?"

"Please do so," said Holmes, reaching into a pocket of his jacket for his magnifying glass.

Cabot pulled back the heavy curtains, and sunlight flooded the room. Robin flinched away, but Holmes gently turned the boy's face toward the window. Robin jerked his head back, but Holmes took a firm grip.

"You may close your eyes if the sun bothers you," said Holmes, as he scrutinized the boy's neck with the glass. He studied it for what seemed like quite a long time before he said, "Come here, Watson, and tell me what you make of this."

I walked across the room and took the glass. Through it I examined the bites, of which there seemed to be two, both made by the same set of teeth. Or fangs.

"Well?" said Holmes.

"One bite," said I, "seems almost fresh. The blood is still oozing, though the bite is supposed to have been incurred last night."

"That is the way of the vampire," Cabot said. He rubbed his thumb across his fingertips. "The creature's saliva mingles with the blood to infect the body and to keep the wound fresh for later feeding. This boy needs a man to stand between him and the forces of darkness, and if no one else is willing, I shall be glad to do so."

Mrs. Montgomery smiled at this, and Cabot preened a bit, but Stoker was not amused. He said, "Good Lord, man, have you no sensitivity?"

"I believe in speaking the truth," said Cabot. "I am sure that Mr. Holmes would agree that the truth is always better than a lie."

Holmes did not deign to reply. Instead, he said, "I would like to see the boy's room. How many people have visited it since the so-called vampire attack?"

"No one save for myself," said Mrs. Montgomery. "I heard Robin cry out early this morning and went to inquire about the cause. He was in such a state that I sent for the doctor, who discovered the bites."

Robin reached up to scratch his neck, but his mother stopped his hand. He yanked it away from her, but she took it again. After a brief struggle, the boy gave in.

"Don't touch those places, Robin. Please, don't touch them."

"They itch," said Robin. "I must scratch them!"

"No, you mustn't."

"Perhaps Dr. Watson can prescribe a remedy," said Holmes. "But first we must see the boy's room."

The butler, Mr. Tedescu, led Holmes and me upstairs to a room at the end of a hall. He opened the door, and we went inside. The room was dark, the curtains drawn.

"Walk around the wall and open the curtains, Watson," said Holmes. "Do not disturb anything in the room."

I did as he asked. When I pulled the curtains, the room was bright with the sun. The bed stood nearby, and beside it there was a small table that held nothing other than a glass of water.

"The window, Watson," said Holmes. "Examine it to see if it has been opened."

I looked at the window and then gave it a try. It seemed stuck in its position, and I told Holmes that I would wager it had not been opened in years.

"As I thought," said he. "Nothing has entered that way, not even a mist or fog."

With those words, Holmes wasted no time in beginning his minute inspection of the room. He got down on hands and knees and went over the floor, staring for quite some time at the edge of the carpet.

"Come have a look, Watson," he said after a time.

I knelt beside him, and he showed me what appeared to be a bit of dried mud. When I said as much, Holmes remarked that a small amount of dirt might tell much if it could talk, and almost as much if it remained mute. He picked the dirt up carefully and dropped it in a bag from his pocket.

"Feel the carpet here," said he, indicating a spot near where the dirt had lain.

I touched my fingers to the rug and felt the slightest bit of dampness.

"From the fog?" I asked.

"I said that there had been no fog. This is something more sinister than that." He turned to Tedescu, who had remained in the doorway. "What is the purpose of this glass of water?"

"That should have been removed," Tedescu said. His English was really quite good. "My wife must have been flustered and forgotten it. Each evening, Mr. Cabot reads to the young master, and he sometimes needs to refresh his voice. I shall take the glass away."

"No," said Holmes. "Leave it there. Well, Watson, I believe I am near the solution of the matter, though there is still more to be discovered."

"Near to the solution, Holmes?" said I in astonishment. "Surely you are joking."

"I seldom joke, Watson, and never about a matter as serious as this." He turned again to Mr. Tedescu and said, "Where is Mr. Brasov?"

"He is in the stables, sir. He has no groom, as he prefers to care for the horses himself."

"What is his relationship with is wife?"

The old man blinked. "I do not know what you mean, sir."

"I believe you do," said Holmes.

Tedescu lowered his eyes and said, "They get along as well as any man and woman."

Holmes looked at me as if to say that he knew what that meant.

"My wife and I get along famously," said I, "if that is what you are thinking."

"I am sure that it is as you say, Watson," said Holmes, "for you are the most amiable of men. But it may be that Brasov is not."

"He is a good man," said Tedescu. "And all men love my mistress."

"Of that I am certain," said Holmes. "Mr. Brasov is uncomfortable with the idea of the vampire, I take it."

"You cannot blame him for that," said Tedescu. "But he is no coward, no matter what you might think. All in our country know of the depredations of the night-flyers."

I expected Holmes to say something of the foolishness of such a belief, but instead he changed the subject.

"Does the boy eat with you in the kitchen?" he asked. "Or at the table with his parents?"

"Oh, at the table, sir. Only my wife and I eat in the kitchen."

"And your wife prepares the meals?"

"Yes, sir. She is an excellent cook, if I may say so."

"Indeed you may," Holmes responded. "Well, Watson, I believe we have learned enough for our purposes. Let us go down and join the others."

WHEN WE RETURNED to the parlor, it almost seemed if no time had passed, with everyone in approximately the same places as when we had left. Mr. Cabot, however, had moved next to Mrs. Montgomery to put a comforting arm about her shoulders.

"Have you discovered anything to thwart the vampire?" she asked anxiously.

"There is no vampire," Holmes replied. "Merely someone wanting others to believe that one exists."

"What do you mean?" said Cabot. "We have all seen the evidence."

"Seeing is one thing," said Holmes. "Interpretation is an entirely different matter."

"What do you mean?" asked Mrs. Montgomery.

"It is a matter of constructing a reasonable hypothesis from the evidence," said Holmes, "rather than an unreasonable one. For example, did anyone ask where a vampire might have come from or why it might attack your Robin?"

There was no reply, and Holmes continued. "Of course not, for there could be no logical answer, and the idea would at once have seemed ridiculous. But let us suppose that there is indeed a reason why someone would want it to *appear* that a vampire had come for a visit."

"But what could the reason be, Holmes?" I asked.

"There could be many reasons, but in this case, it was a woman," said Holmes. "It was Mrs. Montgomery."

"But I do not understand," she protested. "How could I have been the cause?"

"Women such as you inspire men to do stupid things from time to time," said Holmes. "Sir Henry Irving seems to have a tremendous admiration for you. He was willing to recommend my services and send his coach to fetch me."

Mrs. Montgomery blushed and said, "Anyone would do the same."

"Perhaps," Holmes said. "At any rate, it is not Sir Henry with whom we are concerned here."

"Who, then?" I asked.

"Mr. Cabot," said Holmes.

"You lie, sir," Cabot said.

Mrs. Montgomery moved away from him. She took her son's hands and drew him from the chair. They walked over to stand by Holmes.

"Please explain yourself," she said.

"Gladly," said Holmes. "As I did not believe in vampires from the first, I knew there must be some human agent involved. When I examined Robin's neck, I knew it. Did you not see it, Watson?"

"See what?" I asked, completely at a loss.

"The shape and size of the bites," said Holmes. "The *Y* shape of the larger one is indicative of a bloodsucker, true, but not a vampire. It is the mark of the three jaws of the leech. The leech typically attaches itself to its host by both ends of its body, but the sucker on the front end is invariably smaller than the one at the rear. The bite of the leech often bleeds for hours after the animal has been removed."

"Leeches might easily be obtained in the stream we passed over on the way here," said Stoker. "In fact I have seen them there."

"Thank you for the confirmation," said Holmes. "I was sure that was where they were found. I expect we can find one now in Mr. Cabot's quarters, contained in water."

Cabot started forward, but Stoker stepped in front of him and put a hand to his chest.

"You blackguard," said Stoker. "Stop there and allow Mr. Holmes to finish."

Holmes nodded. "The carpet in young Robin's room was slightly damp because of water spilled on it when Cabot removed the leech from its container, and there was a bit of dried mud from Mr. Cabot's shoe, mud that got there when he visited the stream."

"But the symptoms," Mrs. Montgomery said. "How can they be explained."

"Poison," said Holmes.

Mrs. Montgomery gasped.

"Not a lethal dose," Holmes assured her. "When we arrived here, I noticed the flowers growing in the beds. The Lily of the Valley can be quite dangerous. If the flowers are picked and put in a vase, even the water can become harmful. Robin cringes from the sun because of the dilation of his pupils caused by the dose he ingested from the water glass beside his bed."

"But that was Mr. Cabot's glass," said Mrs. Tedescu. "I took it to the room myself."

"But will Mr. Cabot drink from it now?" asked Holmes.

Cabot shook his head.

"I thought not," Holmes said. "Mr. Cabot slipped in a bit of Lily of the Valley, perhaps from the stem or leaves, and offered Robin a drink. Is that not so, Cabot?"

Cabot remained mute, but Robin said, "He asked if my mouth was dry. I took a drink."

"The effect of the drug would be enough for Cabot to apply and remove the leech undetected," said Holmes. "After he had read the boy to sleep, of course."

"But Holmes," said I, "how did you know it was Mr. Cabot?"

"His fingers," said Holmes. "Did you not see how he was rubbing the tips with his thumb?"

"Yes, but I made nothing of it."

"To get a leech to bite, sometimes one must give it a reason," said Holmes. "One way is to give it a bit of blood as an appetizer. Mr. Cabot pricked his own fingers to place blood drops on Robin's neck, and his fingers still itch as a result. Is it not so, Mr. Cabot?"

Again Cabot refused to speak.

Holmes shrugged. "No matter. If we inspect the fingertips, we will discover the truth."

Cabot put his hands in his pockets and balled them into fists.

Mrs. Montgomery said, "But why? Why do such a thing?"

"Because he loves you," said Holmes. "As do many men, I am sure. He hoped to prove his bravery and shame your husband."

"I am ashamed, indeed," said a voice from the doorway behind us.

We turned to see a tall man dressed in riding clothes. He had a chiseled face, and aquiline nose, and side-whiskers.

"I am Nicholas Brasov," he said, "and I stayed out of my own house because of superstitious fear. I see now how stupid I have been. I ask your forgiveness, Robin. And yours, Lily."

Mrs. Montgomery and Robin went to him and embraced him.

"You have no need to ask," said his wife. "For you have done nothing for which you need forgiveness. You are here now."

"And I am discharging you, Mr. Cabot," said Brasov. "Leave now, and never come near my house again."

Cabot's face was a mask of hate as he stalked from the room, but he said not a word.

"Mr. Holmes," said Mrs. Montgomery when Cabot was gone, "you have done our family a great service."

"Thank you, sir," said Robin. "I am glad to know that the vampire was not real."

"There are worse things than imaginary vampires," said Holmes. "I pray you never meet another."

"You are welcome here at any time," Brasov said. "I had heard of you, but I did not believe. Now I do."

"You must come to the theatre," said Mrs. Montgomery. "I am sure Sir Henry can arrange tickets for you."

"Thank you," said Holmes. "And now, Watson, I believe it is time for us to depart."

AS WE RODE back to town in Sir Henry Irving's coach, Stoker remained thoughtful and silent for the most part. I said to Holmes, "I am sorry that this case demanded so little of you. It can hardly have engaged your interest."

"You are mistaken, Watson," said Holmes. "It was most lucky that I was called upon. Someone else might have failed or, worse, even encouraged the idea of the vampire. In that case, something far more terrible might have happened. It is awful to see a tutor betray the trust of those who employ him. Such betrayals can result in horrors of a very human kind."

With those words, my friend turned his face from me and looked out the window at the passing countryside, though I doubt that he saw it. He said not another word until we reached London.

When we had been deposited at Baker Street, Stoker leaned out of the coach and said, "Mr. Watson, I have read and admired your accounts of Sherlock Holmes. You may not know that I, too, am a writer of sorts."

I confessed that I did not know.

"That is no surprise, as I write fiction of the wilder sort. However, I have an idea now that I believe will bring me greater recognition than I have attained heretofore."

"And what could that be?"

"A novel about a vampire," said he. "I shall read about those people you mentioned, Mr. Holmes, Tepes and Bathory, and I shall see what I can learn."

"There are no vampires," Holmes said, though it was plain he was still a bit distracted.

"Nevertheless," said Stoker, "after they read my book, they will believe."

As the coach clattered away, I said to Holmes, "Do you think he will succeed?"

"Perhaps," said my friend, "but the mind of man is more perverse than any horrors of the imagination." With that, he shook himself and appeared to brighten a bit. "But we have averted one disaster today, and that may be enough. Let us go in and see if Mrs. Hudson has returned. It may be that she can prepare us a decent dinner. It has been a long time since breakfast."

He turned to the door, and I followed him inside.

A Hansom for Mr. Holmes

Gillian Linscott

"**A** HANSOM FOR Mr. Holmes."

What they all wants to hear. Every hansom cabdriver in the whole suffering city. Every one of them, that is, with bran mash where his brains should be and hardly on the job long enough to get the corduroy on the seats of his pants worn smooth. Everyone under the age of thirty. Everyone who thinks magic beanstalks come sprouting out of window boxes, golden eggs get laid on the seats of old hansom cabs and the next fare you're hailed by will turn out to be the gent who'll make your fortune or the beautiful woman who'll take you home with her. Next time you're in Baker Street, you watch the empty cabs cruising up and down just waiting for the call. I'll take you for a sovereign that the driver up on the box will be as wet behind the ears as a puppy dog two hours old. Some of the youngsters driving hansoms these days, you wouldn't have trusted to strap on a nag's nosebag the right way up in the days when I started. Thirty years ago that is, come Christmas, and there are things about this city I know that they won't know if they go on driving twice as long as I have. Maybe I had my daft notions too, back then, but I can tell you I grew out of them pretty quick. If you come from the East End of London and work your way up to your own hansom cab—very own hansom cab, no part-owners and all paid for—you learn to look after yourself, your cab and your horse. Anything outside that, like families and so on, well that's up to you. Yourself, your horse, your cab. Everything else is either friend, foe or fare. Friends—well I've got a few of them, mostly from the times when we were boys stealing apples off stalls and dodging the peelers. I trust my friends and they trust me. Up to a point, which comes into this story I'm going to tell you. Foes, well enough of those too and mostly I know who they are and where they are and a fair bit of the time what they're up to. Put friends and foes together, that's maybe three or four dozen. No more, at any rate, than you could fit into a couple of omnibuses, inside and riding on top. All the rest of the world is fares. There's good fares, like Paddington Station to Knightsbridge, small bag, big tip and thank you kindly sir. There's gawd-awful fares like Liverpool Street to Lambeth on a foggy night, argument about whether you've taken the shortest route, no tip, dud sixpence and bleeding good night to you too sir. But mostly they're just fares that put cold beef and pickles on the plate, oats in the nosebag and no trouble. Trouble is what you don't want if you're a hansom driver with other things on your mind. And if trouble's what you don't want you certainly don't go driving up and down Baker Street waiting for some geezer to shout, "A hansom for Mr. Holmes." When I think how I came to be there, purely accidental, I could kick myself from here to Hammersmith and back.

MIND YOU, I did have an excuse. The excuse was black and white, about fourteen pounds in weight when in good fighting trim, which he was, curled up in the box under my driving seat and snoring so loud you could hear him above the noise of the traffic. Does the name Hector of Hackney mean anything to you? All right, we can't all be sporting gents so live and let live. If you knew anything about ratting, you'd know Hector's got a reputation for rat killing that if he'd happened to be born a horse instead of a terrier would have made him as famous as a Derby winner. I don't mean racehorses kill rats, of course. What I'm trying to explain to you is that Hector was at the time at the very top of his chosen sport. Hundreds if not thousands of guineas had changed hands among gentlemen of the fancy from Epsom to Epping Forest on how many rats he could kill with his teeth in a given time. I swear to you I've heard dukes yelling him on and seen the best friend of the Prince of Wales pick him up and kiss him—I mean actually kiss the poor little tyke—out of sheer gratitude and admiration. Altogether, Hector of Hackney was a dog anybody would be proud to own. Only we didn't, me and my friends, which was why I had other things on my mind that afternoon in the middle of July when I made a mistake and drove down flaming Baker Street.

Considering that all my friends and enemies know already what happened, I might as well tell you the truth. We'd got together a little betting syndicate too complicated for you to trouble yourself with, but what it all hinged on was an event that evening in the cellar of a public house in Camden Town where we'd bet more money than we could afford to lose on another terrier belonging to a friend of mine. Only the day before our terrier had gone on the sick list after an argument with a cat of a very nasty disposition he should have seen coming but didn't. So there we all were, bets on and no terrier up to scratch. One of us—might have been me, might not—came up with the idea that we might borrow Hector of Hackney for the evening, disguise him a bit and pass him off as ours. Only problem was, the syndicate that owned Hector weren't exactly on friendly terms with our syndicate and they'd sooner have loaned him out to Old Nick. So we came up with this idea. One of us with a bit of experience in these things crept into Hector's yard in the morning, with aniseed sprinkled on his cuffs to keep the dog interested, and fed him a nice piece of veal soaked in syrup of opium. Not enough to do him any harm, of course, just enough to keep him quiet and get him out of the yard to somewhere we could look after him till evening. The problem was, long before evening his owners would find out he was missing, put two and two together and come around all the places where we lived threatening ten different types of murder. So one of us says, "You've got a box under that driving seat of yours, haven't you Joe?" Which of course, I have. I usually keep a few things of my own there and a little bag of spare feed for the horse but that day what was in it was Hector. While he was out for the count we'd taken the opportunity to alter his appearance a bit, with a black patch in Indian ink over the left ear, then tucked him up nice and comfortable on an old blanket, with a couple of holes drilled in the box for air. The reason I was anywhere near Baker Street was I had to keep close to the park. Regents Park, that is, just up from Baker Street. You see, Hector wouldn't be much use killing rats for us that evening if we didn't get him nicely woken up and exercised during the day. My friend had worked out the dose nice and carefully and the idea was I should drive around in the ordinary way while he was still sleeping it off, picking up a fare or two in the process, then give him a run in the park in the afternoon chasing squirrels and so on to get his mind on the job. Up till then, it had worked like a charm. I'd got a fare or two in the Oxford Street area, driven around without anything to worry about apart from the snoring and was just on my way to the park to get him woken up, hardly even registering what street I was in to be honest when, would you believe, up goes that confounded call.

"A hansom. A hansom for Mr. Holmes."

THE ONE DOING the calling was a little middle-aged geezer dressed up to the nines—pearl gray frock coat, top hat, lilac waistcoat and matching cravat with pearl pin. Face as round as a penny bun and shiny like somebody had been overdoing the butter. He was hopping up and down with anxiety, flapping his little hand in its gray glove like a butterfly going around in circles.

"A hansom for Mr. Holmes." Voice squeaky but penetrating, with an edge to it like someone used to being obeyed. If it hadn't been for that I'd have pretended I didn't hear him and driven straight on, but something about that voice made me say to myself, "Look out, Joe, that's one of them natural-born complainers who'll have

your license if you put a foot out of line." And if you're plying for
hire and you don't stop when called, the authorities will have your
license soon as look at you. So I drew up by the curb, behind a
nice neat little brougham hitched to a showy bay with a driver in
livery on the box, hoping against hope that I'd misheard the name
and it would turn out to be Hope or Hayes or any other H you
cared to mention, but of course it wasn't. Soon as I stopped, there
he was, couldn't be any other. At least he wasn't wearing that bleeding silly hat with the earflaps, it being summer and a bowler the
town wear for a gentleman. But no mistaking him—six foot tall and
thin as pipe-cleaner, with a chin stretching from now to next Tues-
day. His doctor friend was with him as usual, dark suit and curly
brimmed bowler, worried look. The agitated little lilac gent had his
hand on my passenger door, trying to open it for them, before I
could vault down from the driving seat. I edged him aside, politely
as reasonable in the circumstances, and did the job.

"Where to, sir?"

In spite of it all, I was still hoping. After all, even Mr. Holmes
must have days when he goes on ordinary errands same as anybody
else does. If my luck was in it would be Marylebone station or some
club in Pall Mall, then back lickety-split to the park and look after
Hector.

"Celandine Square," says the lilac gent. "Just off Berkeley
Square." Now he didn't need to have told me that, knowing Mayfair
like I do. Small and very select Celandine Square is, place people
buy houses if they find Berkeley Square itself a touch common for
their liking. Nice little garden in the middle where they have parties
in summer. Still, the good news was that it wasn't much more than
ten minutes drive away in moderate traffic. But before I could start
feeling relieved on that score, three things happened. The first was,
I noticed as Mr. Holmes and the doctor got in that they both had
bulges in the right pockets of their jackets that looked too heavy
by a long chalk to be gents' handkerchiefs. The second was that
Hector, who'd been quiet for a bit, suddenly let off a snore from

under my driving seat that sounded like a flaming rhinoceros in a mud patch. They couldn't have helped hearing it and I saw Mr. Holmes raise his eyebrows. Thinking as quick as I could I said, "I'm sorry about that, sir. Somebody's been feeding the old horse too many carrots." The eyebrows went up another notch at that and thinking it over I couldn't blame him. Well, you think about the way a hansom cab's built. Driver perched up right at the back, covered carriage in front of him with the fare in it, then the footboard and shafts, then the back end of the horse. You don't have to be the greatest detective in the world to work out that you'd have to feed a nag a hell of a lot of carrots for the noise to come out from under the driver's seat. Anyway, Mr. Holmes gives me a long look and says nothing. They hadn't warned me about his eyes. If you can imagine chips of ice with a fire in them you could light a pipe with, you've got somewhere near it.

Then the third thing happened. He said something to me, right out of the blue, that knocked me sideways. "I see you're interested in cartography, cabbie."

"Beg your pardon, sir."

"The making of maps."

Well, the reason it knocked me sideways was it was about as wide of the mark as you could get. I've never in my entire life had anything to do with maps. Don't need them, having the whole of London in my head.

"No, sir. Nothing like that."

"Curious."

Meanwhile, I was closing the door on them in a hurry, wanting to start rolling before Hector ripped off one of his specials again. All the time this had been going on, the lilac gent had been fidgeting around trying to get a word in edgeways.

"Mr. Holmes, I really must impress on you the vital importance of confidentiality. All of Britain's influence in the region. . . ."

He got a look that would have stopped a steam-hammer.

"If the Foreign Office, sir, had been less concerned about protocol and more about the facts of the case, you wouldn't have had to call on my services at such inconveniently short notice. As it is, you must leave things entirely in my hands."

So I got up on the driving seat and we left the lilac gent gaping like a haddock on a slab. Before we turned the corner I looked back and saw him being driven off lickety-split in the brougham with the bay.

WHEN WE GOT near Celandine Square you could tell it was a big society occasion from the number of gray top hats and the amount of swearing going on. It was the cabbies and drivers doing the swearing, so many of them trying to get as close as they could to the garden in the middle of the square they'd blocked the street. Well, I thought, this is where I get my ticket of leave. I leaned forward and shouted so they could hear me inside, "Quicker to get out and walk from here, sir." But he wasn't having any. "Park right up against the railings, cabbie. There's an extra sovereign in it if you do." Well, since there was no getting out of it that way I thought I might as well earn the extra one and there was a bit of professional pride in it as well because I knew a little road that would get us into the square, avoiding the blighted circus at this end. So I turned the nag around (collecting a fair number of curses in the process) and in five minutes there we are up alongside the railings as requested. I jumps down, opens the door and waits for my money. Mr. Holmes gets out, cool as you please.

"Wait for us here, cabbie."

"Not bloody likely" was on the tip of my tongue, on account of I'd just heard a sound from under the seat that I didn't want to hear. Not a snore and not loud. A snuffle. The kind of snuffle a terrier might give when it's waking up after a long spell of shut-eye wondering what's happening to it. And terriers, especially Hector, don't stay wondering for long without saying something about it. Then I saw I had no choice in the matter. Two more hansoms and a phaeton had gone and followed my example and here I was, boxed in and couldn't move till they'd gone. So I thought, make the best of it. Wait till they've gone into the bun-fight in the square, then take the little tyke for a walk around Mayfair. Not what I'd planned but beggars can't be choosers. Then, gawd help us, Mr. Holmes suddenly goes as tense as a pointer dog on the scent and grabs the doctor by the arm. "Watson, that man over there with the green check neck-cloth—that's one of them."

We both of us followed his eyes, and sure enough there was a rough-looking geezer in a dark jacket and trousers disappearing behind a gaggle of ladies in party-going frocks, though moving so quick I didn't get more than a flicker of him, certainly not to see a neckcloth. Anyway, the great detective was certain.

"I noticed him and a tall man in a tartan cap just after we left Baker Street. They must have followed us here on foot."

I will admit that was just about possible given the weight of the traffic, though I didn't see how he could be so sure about it. Anyway, he grabbed the doctor by the elbow and took him off a yard or two so I couldn't hear what was being said. Not that I cared. All I wanted was to see the backs of both of them. When they'd finished their little chat though, it was disappointment time for me again.

"Cabbie, you strike me as a strong and resourceful man," says Mr. Holmes.

Well, I didn't like the sound of that. Terrible trouble I had with my back these days, I said, and as for my fallen arches. Didn't take a blind bit of notice.

"And I'm sure you have your country's interests at heart."

I liked the sound of that even less. Generally when anybody's sure you've got your country's interests at heart it means go out somewhere hot and unhealthy and be shot at for a bob a day payable to your widow. Still, it doesn't do to sound unpatriotic so I just nodded.

"The fact is, there may be some little danger here and I should be greatly obliged if you'd accompany me into the garden party and keep a keen eye out."

I looked at the doctor. "I thought that was usually supposed to be his job."

"In this case, Dr. Watson has other duties which will keep him outside the railings. I promise you, if things go as I hope you won't find me ungrateful."

"And what if they don't?" I felt like asking, but those eyes were on me again so I didn't, just pointed out that I couldn't leave my cab.

"I'm sure we can find a boy to look after it for us for a shilling."

And, of course, there was a boy idling around the railings and a shilling in the doctor's hand, so bang went my last excuse. Mr. Holmes put his hand on my arm said something to the flunkey on the gate and there we were inside the gardens in the middle of Celandine Square like Lord and Lady Muck, and me listening all the time for Hector to start telling the world what he thought about waking up under a cabdriver's seat in Mayfair when he was supposed to be safe at home in Hackney. Only after we'd gone a little way into the crowd of society ladies and gents I couldn't have heard him if he had, because on a platform in the middle of the gardens, beside a green-and-white-striped marquee with tables outside, there was a band kicking up enough noise to wake the seven sleepers and what with that and toff's voices braying in my ear and teacups clattering you wouldn't have heard a whole pack of terriers. So of course that was when Mr. Holmes, sticking as close to me as a long lost brother, decided to start explaining what was going on. Now, I couldn't have cared less, wanting only one thing out of all this, which was not to be there. But whether I wanted it or not he leaned down toward me so that I could hear and filled in the scorecard for me. I can still hear that voice of his, not sarcastic exactly, not sneering, but as if he could see without trouble into everybody's heads and found what was inside them amusing more or less, like a moderate evening at the music hall, but not that surprising.

"You and I, cabbie, are the victims of diplomats. This party has been set up to please an illustrious personage whose goodwill is considered essential by the Foreign Office. They hold it vital to our interests in Eastern Europe that he should be persuaded to sign a treaty with Great Britain during this visit to London. Ah, you can see him now."

The crowds around the marquee had parted for a moment and we got a view of a tubby little gent in court dress with a sash across his chest and more baubles than you'd see on the Queen's Christmas tree. Then the crowd closed in again and hid him.

"Some of those people around him are policemen in plainclothes," Mr. Holmes said, "as you can tell even at a distance by the awkward cut of their morning coats. The sartorial resources of Scotland Yard must be severely strained by this operation."

So are my bleeding nerves, I felt like telling him, but he was going on.

"They have their limitations, but I think we may take it that they are competent to guard His Highness against ordinary threats. It's the extraordinary ones with which we must occupy ourselves."

"Extraordinary threats?" I daresay I yelped it like a terrier myself because he gave me a pipe-down look.

"His Highness has a morbid fear of assassination. Anarchists have attempted to kill him twice in his own country and he was persuaded to visit London on assurances that it is the safest capital in Europe. If he believed himself seriously at risk here he'd be off straight back home with the treaty unsigned. As it happens, the Foreign Office has received information from a reliable source that there is to be an attempt to kill him at this garden party."

I started saying never mind His bleeding Highness, I had a morbid fear of getting killed as well, but Mr. Holmes' grip on my arm was like an ice-man's tongs.

"As usual, they sought my advice far too late. All I could promise was to attend the event and do anything in my power to frustrate an attack. But it is considered essential that His Highness should be unaware of the threat."

While he was speaking, he was working us nearer the center of things, where the band and marquee were. Apart from anything else, the music was blowing my eardrums right into my skull so I thought they'd meet in the middle. I couldn't help putting my free hand to my ear. Mr. Holmes laughed.

"Do I take it you have no liking for the modern school of German music? I admit I agree with you and, artistic preferences apart, it makes our task more difficult. It demands a larger orchestra than I'd anticipated."

I noticed that all the time he was working us closer to the center he kept glancing back over his shoulder, as if he was worried about something going on behind him. It didn't make me feel any better, I can tell you. But it wasn't until we got alongside the woman with the dishmop that things took another turn for the worse. She was a large party of middle age, well-upholstered with a lot of rubies and diamonds on a chest that had plenty of room for them. She must have been deaf or daft because she'd got herself up as close to the band as she could get and she was listening to it with a hypnotized kind of expression on her face, eyes closed and swaying from side to side a bit. And in her arms, snuggled up against all the diamonds and stuff, she was holding this here dishmop.

NOW, I KNOW a bit about dogs and I thought I'd seen most of the shapes and sizes God made, but it was some time before it dawned on me that was what the dishmop was supposed to be. I've seen rats bigger. It was a kind of beigy-pink in color, all long silky hair so the only way I could tell which end was which was when she opened her eyes and said something to it and it uncurled a tongue from somewhere under the face foliage and licked her nose, which I wouldn't have done to win a bet. You could see from the way Mr. Holmes was looking at it that he thought it out of the common as well. Anyway, it was time to bring him back to business.

"So somebody in this crowd," I says, "is going to take a potshot at His Highness and you don't know who he is or where he is or what he looks like. Is that the size of it?"

He started answering, but this time there was something going on the other side of the railings, back where we'd come from. It sounded like men's voices having a bit of a barney, then I heard someone shouting, "Catch him." Naturally I was worried thinking of my horse and cab back there with nothing but a boy to hold them, then in the next minute I got a lot more worried because from the same direction I heard a dog barking. Not just any dog either. That high yip, yip, yip like a concert tenor being punched in the breadbasket is a sound you get from terriers. And, having heard him in full cry before now, I'd have bet my last sovereign that what we were hearing was Hector of Hackney getting out and about. I thought "That bleeding boy's been poking around where he's not supposed to and gone and let him out." I'd fillet and smoke the little so-and-so and have him on toast for breakfast when I caught up with him. But before that, the first thing I had to do was catch up with Hector. I tore my arm away from Mr. Holmes and started trying to push my way back through the crowd but before I could get more than a few steps, the main attraction came to us. First a golden labrador dashing between the legs of the crowd, skittling people right and left like a fireball in a waxworks exhibition. Teacups went flying, top hats rolling and what with the screams from the ladies and the useless suggestions from the gentlemen you could hardly hear the band, which happened to have got to a quieter bit at that point. No more than two lengths behind the labrador and gaining ground with each stride well—you can guess, can't you? Even so, I might have saved the situation if it hadn't been for the bleeding dishmop. I was getting into a crouch, ready to dive at Hector, when dishmop lets out a kind of a squeal. Now if luck had been on my side, which it hadn't been all day, Hector wouldn't have paid any attention and gone on chasing the labrador. But as it was he looked up and saw it. Now I'm not making excuses for Hector, but you have to say this for him. He was a dog bred and brought up for killing rats and you could practically hear him saying to himself, "Well, it's a bit of a rum-looking one, but a rat's a rat for all that." So up he jumps, straight to where dishmop's sitting it out in the fat lady's arms.

*   *   *

NOW, I THOUGHT at the time that Mr. Holmes could have done a sight more to help. He was nearer the fat lady than I was. He's supposed to be the one who's quick-thinking and clearheaded after all. If he'd made a grab for the dishmop and hoisted it up as far as he could reach—which was pretty considerable—he wouldn't have got much worse than a few bites to the shins from Hector and it would have given me a chance to get the situation under control. But oh no. He looks on and does nothing like he's watching a play, dishmop panics and half jumps, half falls out of fat lady's arms onto the band platform and Hector goes through the little ornamental barrier that wasn't much more than matchwood and straight after him, straight through the bleeding band. Well, I don't know if you've ever heard a German band of the modern school going on trying to scrape and tootle through one of the quiet bits while the best ratting terrier in London goes hurtling through them, with the dishmop yelling and a fat lady screaming a few inches away from your ear and half of London society shouting the odds all around you, but if you haven't take it from me it doesn't make for peaceful contemplation. But all I could do was stand and watch, hoping Hector and I were still alive when it was all over and never mind the rest of them, especially Mr. Holmes who'd got me into this. He'd disappeared by this time of course. I didn't know where. As far as I was concerned if I never saw him again that would be once too often.

THE BAND GAVE up quite soon. German or not, they didn't have the stamina of one of your music hall pit bands that go on playing if the customers are breaking up the seats and throwing them. I suppose they had some excuse. Most of the music and music stands were scattered around the platform, a double bass had got smashed and two or three of the tubas had dents in them that probably weren't there when they started the day. But most of the other players, the flute and piccolo tooters and the violin scrapers had taken their instruments with them and formed a huddle around their conductor. From the sounds coming out of the huddle in two or three different languages, they weren't happy. Over by the striped marquee, the men in the morning suits had formed a different huddle around His Highness and you could see they weren't happy either. The other guests were just milling around in a disorganized sort of way asking each other what had happened and saying wasn't it dreadful. There, at any rate, they had my vote too. Dreadful didn't begin to describe it. No words I could think of that wouldn't get me up before the magistrate if I used them would come within a mile of describing it. Because there was no sign of Hector. Not a yap, not a hair, not a footprint. Over the next ten minutes or so I went all around the gardens, looking behind stone urns and under bushes in case he'd killed the dishmop and taken it away to eat it. No result. So feeling as down as I'd felt in a long time I went back toward the band platform and what do I see there? I see Mr. Greatest Detective in the World hunting around among the music stands and tubas as if he'd lost his bleeding handkerchief.

"Well, you won't find him there," I said, letting him see I was annoyed. "He was there ten minutes ago but as plain as the nose on your face he ain't there now."

(If I hadn't been so angry I might not have made that remark about the nose. His isn't one of the smallest.) Anyway, he doesn't seem to take offense but the look he gives me is faraway somewhere. Then he says, "Oh, the terrier" as if he thought I was looking for a bleeding polar bear.

"Yes," I says, "the best ratting terrier in London, only he's probably got as far as Buckinghamshire by now and if you hadn't dragged me on this wild-goose chase it would never have happened."

He doesn't take any notice. Blow me if he hasn't picked up a violin left on one of the chairs and is staring at it like it was the most fascinating fiddle in the world, though it looked just like any other one to me.

"Do you happen to play the violin, cabbie?"

Well, I fair exploded at that and can you blame me? "No, Mr. Holmes," I said. "I don't play the violin and I don't draw maps and I don't do fancy embroidery on muslin either. What I do is drive a cab and put a few bets on ratting events and after what you've got me into I'll be lucky if I go on doing either of those much longer."

I was thinking of the syndicate that owned Hector, and what they'd do when they caught up with me. Again, he took no notice and went on staring at the fiddle.

"So you don't observe anything odd about this one? Remember the orchestra has been playing vigorously for some time."

I said, sick at heart and not caring either way, "I suppose you're going to tell me it's fixed up as a gun inside, all ready to shoot His Highness."

"Not at all," he said. "It's a perfectly ordinary violin."

He put it back down on the chair and turned to me, all smiles suddenly. "You didn't happen to notice Lady Cookham's little dog when you were looking, around, did you. She is most distressed at its loss. In fact, she was carried off to her carriage in a faint."

No I didn't, I said, being glad at any rate it wasn't me had to do the carrying. By then the band was coming past us back onto the platform. Mr. Holmes remarked that it looked as if the music would be starting again soon and he'd be back in a few minutes and strolled off toward the marquee, cool as you please.

SO THE BAND started playing again and the teacups got refilled and they all went on with the party. I waited there by the band platform, much where we'd been before, in no hurry to go anywhere now because all I could see waiting for me anywhere was more trouble. His Nibs wasn't back in a few minutes but something else happened, something you wouldn't even have noticed unless you'd been standing where I was standing, wanting anything to distract you from what you were thinking. Two blokes in dark suits and black bowlers stepped over the barrier at the back of the platform, weaved in and out of the musicians without making too much fuss about it and put their hands on the shoulders of a bloke playing the fiddle at the end of the second row from the back. Little dark bloke with a mustache, quite young. When they brought him back over the barrier I could see they'd got his arms twisted up behind his back, so if he didn't like it he couldn't do much about it anyway. And away the three of them went, toward the gate. A little after that, back comes Mr. Holmes.

"His Highness is about to leave. If you'd care to come over to the marquee there are a few gentlemen who'd like to meet you."

Well, it was no news there were people who'd like to meet me— not that I'd call them gentlemen—but even Hector's syndicate wasn't likely to get in here, so I followed him over. And sure enough, there was His Highness shaking hands and being bowed to right and left. Seemed he'd enjoyed the music, though goodness knows why, and they must have got a glass or two of champagne inside him because he looked in a high good humor, the spot of trouble with the dogs all forgotten. If they kept him in that mood they'd probably get a dozen treaties out of him for a guinea with a little one thrown in for luck. Anyway, away he went too with his attendant flunkies, the band stopped playing at last, which was one relief, and the ladies and gents started moving away to their carriages. Which left a little group of us outside the marquee, the men from Scotland Yard in the morning suits, a few blokes with Civil Servant written all over them, Mr. Holmes and me. Plus the lilac geezer, the one who'd started it all by hailing me back in Baker Street. He was beaming all over his face, shaking hands with Mr. Holmes, practically bouncing up and down with excitement.

"Mr. Holmes, we are forever in your debt. You have entirely exceeded our wildest expectations." Mr. Holmes took it coolly enough, but I could see he was pleased. Lilac let go of his hand but went burbling on. "You have your methods, I know, but if you could be kind enough to give us some hint what put you onto his trail. . . ."

I thought Mr. Holmes might say "elementary" but he didn't, probably because the doctor still hadn't joined us. But it came to the same thing.

"It was hardly difficult. You yourself had told me that His Highness had a great liking for music. So there was a strong possibility that his potential assassin would choose to conceal himself among the orchestra."

"But such a large orchestra."

"Indeed, and I admit that was an aspect of the case that I initially found disconcerting. But luckily I had made a plan and put it into effect. The object was to get a closer look at the orchestral platform without alerting His Highness to a possible threat to his life. I therefore organized a small disturbance to give me the opportunity I needed."

By then I'd managed to get my hand around a glass of champagne and I nearly choked on it. My terrier (more or less) and my life probably and he talked about organizing a small disturbance. Lilac gasped.

"The dogs were your idea?" Holmes gave him a nod. "But even so, how could you tell from an empty band platform which one was the assassin?"

"Two things. You may have heard that I am, in my way, a modest amateur violinist."

Respectful nods all around. *Modest*, I thought, that's good.

"But even a modest violinist," he goes on, "respects his instrument. I have heard of men going into burning houses to save their violins. For a professional musician, his violin is his life. In any dangerous or disturbing circumstances, his first thought would be to take it with him. He certainly wouldn't abandon it on a chair in a mere dogfight."

Lilac said, "I see. You simply had to see which chair had the violin on it and tell the officers to arrest that man."

He got a frown for that "simply."

"No, I found something much more convincing than that. You will be aware, gentlemen, that a violinist applies a resinous powder to his bow every day before he plays, to prevent the bow sliding from the strings. When he plays, particularly if he plays energetically for a long period, a white coating of the resinous powder transfers itself from his bow to the surface of the violin, just above the bridge. The violin abandoned on the chair had no such resinous powder on it. Therefore its owner had not been playing, he had merely been pretending to play. Once I knew that, it was an easy matter to point him out to the officers from Scotland Yard."

"He had a loaded revolver in his pocket," one of the civil service types murmured.

Lilac was babbling on about seeing that Mr. Holmes was suitably rewarded. He held up his hand to stop him.

"If the Foreign Office is in the business of rewarding people, then I suggest it consider some recompense for this gentleman."

And gawd help us, he was pointing that chin of his at me. They all turned in my direction just as I was getting a good gulp of champagne down me. More choking.

"Isn't that the cabdriver?"

Not a lot of gratitude in Lilac's tone of voice.

"Indeed, but quite apart from cab driving, his services today have been invaluable. In fact I may honestly say that I could scarcely have managed without him."

Well, that more or less broke up our little party. Lilac wasn't grateful enough to put his hand in his pocket, so after a bit more chat about how indebted they all were to Mr. Holmes there we were walking to the gate side by side, the way we'd come in. Outside the gate the doctor was waiting for us. When he saw Mr. Holmes he gave a little nod as if to say "job done." Well, I thought, whatever your job was, I'll bet you got the soft option compared to me.

My horse and cab were still waiting there with the boy, thank gawd for small mercies, so then it was a case of driving them back to Baker Street in time for dinner. When we arrived I got down off the driving seat and opened the door for them, wondering whether to ask Mr. Holmes, sarcastic-like, if he'd take on the case when my headless corpse was found floating in the Thames but by then his hand was in his pocket, rattling coins, and a tip's a tip however you look at it. Then he says, looking at a handful of sovereigns and sounding quite casual-like, "Do you know a Mr. Bert Fleet?"

Well, my blood ran cold. Slogger Fleet's the leader of the syndicate who owns Hector, the one who'd be first in there with the cosh or the knife, depending on his mood.

"I might do," I said. "Why?"

"He asked me to tell you how grateful he was to you for getting his terrier back."

"He what!" I nearly fell over flat on my back on the pavement and I hadn't even had a full glass of champagne. "Slogger *thanked* me?"

"Indeed. I have to admit he was under a misapprehension at first, but luckily Dr. Watson and I were able to explain things entirely to his satisfaction."

"What kind of a misapprehension?" I said.

"He seemed to have got it into his head that you'd kidnapped the dog. He was the man in the green check neckcloth who followed your cab from Baker Street. When we explained that you'd found it wandering in the street in a dazed state and picked it up to return it to him, he naturally changed his opinion."

"Slogger believed *that*?"

Mr. Holmes smiled, a smile much like anyone else's with no ice in it. "Let's say I was able to offer him some inducement to believe it. I don't think you'll have any trouble from that quarter. My writ runs in the East End."

And fair's fair, I have to say that he was as good as his word. Whether he knew some things to Slogger's discredit (not difficult) or whether he bought him off I'll never know but from that day to this I've had no trouble from Slogger.

"But how did you find Hector to give him back?"

"On my suggestion, Dr. Watson was waiting on the far side of the square. We admittedly hadn't anticipated the effect of Lady Cookham's lapdog, but when you put a terrier and another dog into a crowd you can predict that they'll come out on the other side."

I admit I was crushed by then. What with all that had happened and the noise and the worry and finding that I'd been led by the nose after all I could hardly get out a word. In the end I managed just four. "How did you know?"

"About the terrier under your driving seat? When you first opened the cab door for us I noticed that you had Indian ink stains on your thumb and index finger. They might possibly be explained by map drawing or some kinds of artistic activity, but you said you had no interest in maps and you did not strike me as an artistic type. So I asked myself for what other purposes a man might use Indian ink. That noise from the back of your cab provided my answer. So, once I knew we had a dog with us, I decided to borrow him for my purposes. I trust it hasn't inconvenienced you too severely. Good day, and thank you."

And he handed over quite a few sovereigns—enough to pay for the hire all afternoon and a good bit over—and he and the doctor walked across the pavement to their doorstep. Then just before going inside he turned. "You might like to have a look under your driving seat. I'm sure Lady Cookham would be overjoyed to have Bijou restored to her. She lives in Belgrave Square."

And there, in the space under the seat where Hector had been, was the dishmop. It bit me twice, once when I lifted it out of the box and again when I was standing on her ladyship's doorstep. When she'd finished kissing it and crying over it she tipped me five quid and looked as if she'd kiss me as well, only I moved quick. So what with her five quid, and Mr. Holmes' sovereigns, the undying gratitude of the Foreign Office (I don't think), a Sherlock Holmes story of my own to tell, plus not getting my head pulled off by Slogger, you might say I'd come out of it quite well all things considered. But that's not counting the nervous wear or tear, or what my own syndicate said to me when they found out they hadn't got a dog after all, or the quiver that comes over me when anybody says "Baker Street." So I don't drive down it when I don't have to, and if I have to I make sure I've got a fare in the cab already. Because if Mr. Holmes wants a hansom again as far as I'm concerned he can whistle for it. He can just whistle.

THE ADVENTURE
OF THE ARABIAN KNIGHT

Loren D. Estleman

"STAND ASIDE, HOLMES!" said I, gripping my stick in the defensive position familiar to my service in India and Afghanistan. "Here is a proper cut-throat."

Sherlock Holmes and I were returning from a constitutional which I as his physician had prescribed to counter the evil effects of a fortnight during which my friend and fellow-lodger had not ventured outside our smoke-filled digs, even to breathe the comparatively less sinister air of greater London. His confinement comprised an investigation into the mysterious death of Edmond Warworthy, Bart., whose solution was eventually discovered in an entry made some thirty years previously in his journals, which ran to fifty-six volumes dated between 1 January 1832 and 11 August 1888, the day upon which he died.

The evening now under examination was a balmy one in early September of that year. A trade wind had extended summer whilst removing the noxious yellow fog that is so typical of autumn in our metropolis, and a sunset of staggering beauty was in full cry over Middlesex, painting even the blackest chimneys the color of claret. However, it is a fair wind indeed that blows nobody bad, for a pleasant climate and creeping shadows provide a hunting ground for two-legged predators after complacent strollers with fat purses. I was, therefore, on the lookout for just such creatures as the fellow shamming sleep in the darkness beyond the fanlight above the entrance to our home at 221B Baker Street.

In appearance he was of a type not uncommon in that cosmopolitan city: swarthy and bearded, dark as hickory, and swathed in the robes and hooded mantle, called a *burnoose*, which are affected by the Muslims of the Near East. Huddled as he was in this voluminous raiment, seated on his haunches against the wall of our building, he might have been taken for a bundle of discarded bedclothes but for the way the whites of his eyes glistened as he observed our approach. I knew too well from my experience of war just how quickly so ignoble an element of the scenery could spring upon the passing transient, pressing a razor-edged dirk against the wretch's throat and demanding *baksheesh* or blood. Holmes, however, steadied me with his iron grasp about my wrist.

"Calm yourself, old fellow," said he. "This may be a client. You, there, *Haji*! Kindly oblige a pair of *infidels* and join us in the light."

For the space of thirty seconds the man in the shadows did not stir, although he continued to watch us like some beast on the edge of a campfire. Then, slowly and with queer dignity, he arose with a rustle and stepped forward until he stood before us in full view. I tightened my hold on the old Penang lawyer; for he was a particularly wicked-looking specimen of Arab. Standing slightly over the medium height, he wore a coal-black beard only a shade darker than his burnished flesh, against which those startling eye-whites shone like scaled pearls, their nut-colored irises glaring balefully. As if to put the fine point on a countenance that was altogether devilish, the brigand displayed a vicious scar on either cheek, sunken with age and puckered at the edges, the less noticeable of the pair fully as long as a man's hand is wide. The obvious conclusion, that he had been transfixed by some savage blade, made me shudder as if I had witnessed the event at firsthand. The silken sash he had tied about his waist, red once but now faded, like the scars, suggested the ideal girdle for a weapon which was not in evidence, although its presence posed the uneasy likelihood that he had one concealed upon his person. I daresay that in that sprawling city of four millions there was not one who inspired greater dread.

"A hundred thousand pardons, *effendim*. These ancient eyes are no longer what once they were. The low cur who owns them could not be certain he was in the presence of the great *sahib* detective until he was near enough to smell the breath of the camel."

This fulsome speech, delivered in faultless English, was nonetheless heavy with the guttural but not unmusical accent of the deserts and oases of popular romance. Of his age, at least, he spoke the truth. The folds and creases in his leathery hide were at the lowest estimate sixty years in the creation. I thought it not unlikely the vain old fellow dyed his whiskers with lampblack.

"I am Sherlock Holmes, in the event there is more than one great *sahib* detective living on this street. This is Dr. Watson, upon whose discretion you may rely as surely as the Bank of England. Whom have I the honor of addressing?"

The fellow bowed whilst performing the pretty *salaam* gesture with his right hand. "Most certainly, respected one, the honor belongs to me. I am called Sheik Abdullah."

"Sheik, if you will allow me the impertinence." Holmes extended a hand and, to my surprise, grasped the Arab's chin and gently turned his face to this side and that, exposing each of the man's scars to the light. "The left is the more pronounced. Would you concur, Doctor, that this is the exit wound?"

"I would. Most tissue damage occurs on the way out."

"Torn palate, Sheik?"

"Yes, *effendim*. And four back teeth for Allah."

"The entry is as clean as an incision. The projectile, then, passed through on the instant, which is seldom the case with anything as long as a conventional spear or as clumsy as a sword or saber. A javelin, perhaps. Somali?"

"Wonderful, respected sir! I was chief of bearers on *safari*. Savages attacked us for our goods. Through the grace of the Prophet, blessings and peace be upon him, I fought my way to safety. Alas, others were not so favored."

The oily obsequiousness of this response made me distrust the stranger all the more, for I had seen surprise, admiration, and suspicion succeed one another in his eyes as Holmes deduced the details of his injury. I found myself wondering if he was not himself the savage behind the attack of which he spoke.

"In any case, the affair is years in the past," said Holmes. "It can hardly be the reason for your visit."

"It is not. I have come to consult you upon a matter of grave importance."

"Then let us continue this conversation upstairs. A London street is not the marketplace in Cairo."

"Is it wise, Holmes?" I could not help whispering. "We know nothing of this fellow's reputation."

Grim amusement stirred my friend's spare features. "I might venture to say that were we to know very much more, we would think it even less wise."

With this cryptic remark, he led the way up the well-trodden steps to the cluttered sitting-room whence so many adventures had been launched.

Wordlessly, and with (it seemed to me) a disregard for invitation that ran counter to the humility he sought to express, Sheik Abdullah embarked upon a self-guided tour of the many curious items which were placed rather carelessly upon exhibit in our homely parlor. His interest in some things, at the expense of others, was odd. The dagger of Danish manufacture that had featured prominently in the Blackwell murder case received only cursory attention, whilst the shabby Persian slipper in which Holmes kept his coarse tobacco became an object of some five minutes' close scrutiny. He studied the weave of the hanging basket chair at length, but ignored completely the Borgia ring, for which Holmes had declined a princely offer from the British Museum only the month before. Throughout, Holmes retained his bemused expression. His offer of a libation prompted a request for plain water, which was accepted with effusive gratitude, and he watched from beneath heavy lids as our singular guest went through the elaborate ritual of thanks to the powers of Islam before imbibing. At last Holmes said:

"Now that you've partaken of our hospitality, Sir Richard, perhaps you will provide an explanation for this show of false colors."

The man in Arabian garb choked, coughed, and lowered the glass, using the loose sleeve of his robe to sponge the water from his beard. He stared at Holmes. Then a sinister smile appeared. "I see that I am not misled as to your abilities after all," said he, in a deep voice in which there was now no trace of the Orient. "Perhaps, for my own edification, you'll tell me just where I erred. In another time and place, the intelligence may save my life."

"I suspected the truth when I examined your scars. They are more famous than you realize, having spent so much time in the far reaches of the Empire. When I accurately assigned them to a Somali javelin and observed your reaction, I was emboldened further, but withheld certainty until you committed the blunder of accepting and drinking from a vessel with your left hand. No Muslim worthy of his faith would do that."

"Blast! Too many years have passed since I immersed myself last in the Koran. I've grown rusty as well as fat. I should have been placed on my guard when my girdle would not tie in the old place. A careless mistake. I no longer trust the public journals, and so am guilty of forming an opinion of your talents in reverse ratio to the notices you've received in the press. I beg you to accept the apologies of a retired officer."

Hereupon, impatient and disgruntled, I interposed myself. "I confess I'm at sea, Holmes. Who is this fellow, of whose famous scars I was ignorant only moments ago?"

"Really, Watson, it amazes me when fellow members of a species fail to recognize one another. An old adventurer-journalist such as yourself must be aware of Captain Sir Richard Francis Burton, author of *The Arabian Nights* and discoverer of the source of the River Nile."

"Flattering, but inaccurate upon both counts," protested the other. "The Nile is John Speke's, may his troubled soul find rest, and I merely translated the chronicle of the thousand-and-one nights, whose actual authors are dust these seven hundred years. I will own to Lake Tanganyika, and two volumes upon my experiences during a pilgrimage to Mecca, among other trifles. My disguise upon that occasion was superior, I'm bound to say."

As he spoke, our guest removed his hood, exposing gray hair cropped close to his skull and a band of unstained skin at the hairline. It was a singular head, with advanced frontal development, fierce brows, and those sinister scars, which were even more pronounced without the distraction of the burnoose.

"Great Scott! I have followed each installment of the *Nights* as it has appeared. Remarkable." I grasped the hand he'd extended, only to break the grip when a fresh and disturbing association presented itself. "But, did you not translate also—" I left off, blushing to pronounce the disreputable title.

"The *Kama Sutra*." Burton's smile was wicked. "I may as well own to it. It cost me a club membership."

"The authentic explorer acknowledges no forbidden frontiers," Holmes said. "Now, Sir Richard, there is the siphon, and there the basket chair you admired. Make free with both and tell us the reason for your fancy dress."

Burton declined the whiskey, explaining that as long as he wore Muslim garments he would not blaspheme the faith, but curled himself into the chair in the same anti-Occidental fashion that my friend was wont to adopt. The old adventurer was exceptionally supple for a man nearing his threescore and ten.

"You will find, Holmes, as you continue to acquire notoriety, that people do not always conduct themselves in your presence as they would under most circumstances," he began. "It's an intolerable nuisance, as it slows the process of judging character. An incognito visit seemed the best way to save time. As things turned out, I was right. You are the man for the job I have in mind."

Holmes, seated in his favorite armchair, lit his pipe and said nothing. I noted with interest that he had selected the old black clay he preferred when in a contemplative humor.

"I am at present only a temporary resident of London," Burton continued. "My leave expires next month, when I return to my post at the British Consulate in Trieste. Meanwhile I am engaged in a number of projects, one of which is the translation of documents which came into my hands while I was on the Ivory Coast in 1860. That is to say, I was until four weeks ago; but I shall come to that. How much do you know, Holmes, about ancient culture in Egypt?"

"Rather less than I do about modern criminal enterprise in Brixton. Do the subjects intersect?"

"Possibly, although I'm uncertain about Brixton. The document that commanded my attention until late is a transcription in Second Century Aramaic from a hieroglyphic scroll that was burned in the great fire that consumed Alexandria. I translated just enough of it into English to form the conclusion that it provides explicit directions to the tomb of a Pharaoh who ruled during the Eighteenth Dynasty."

At this point Holmes, to my chagrin and Burton's amazement, yawned.

"Forgive me, Sir Richard, but unless the Pharaoh was done to death I confess little interest in the affair thus far. The good doctor can enlighten you upon the futility of instructing me in anything not related to the science of deduction."

"Just so," said our guest; but it was plain he regretted denying himself the reinforcement of strong spirits. "As to the nature of the king's demise, I am without illumination. He expired before his twentieth year, but beyond that I know nothing save that he was a son of Akhenaton, the Sun King. The boy's name was Tutankhamen."

"It rings no bells."

"Nor should it. It does not appear in any of the royal lists which have come down to us. As a matter of fact, the extent to which he was stricken from history emboldens me to hope that his burial vault is undefiled. It will come as no surprise to you that grave-robbing was not invented by Burke and Hare. To date, not one tomb in the Valley of the Kings has been unearthed which was not stripped of its treasures centuries before Christ."

The detective's lids drooped further, a sure sign that his interest was awakened at last. "Pray continue, Sir Richard. But please confine your narrative to the present century. What became of the document?"

Burton nodded curtly. "I knew you would surmise it was missing. No other circumstance would have driven me to leave off the task before it was complete. It was stolen, Holmes; spirited away by my assistant while I was out, under my wife's very nose. I am as certain James Patterson is the thief as I am that polygamy is the instinctive law of nature."

"Not the son of Colonel Henry Patterson!" I exclaimed.

"The same, Doctor. No acorn ever rolled farther from the oak than the scion of the hero of Roarke's Drift. More fool I, knowing the little bounder's reputation; but mine is scarcely better, and I thought if some stalwart had lent me a hand up when it counted, I might have found a better billet in my decrepitude than a third-rate consulate on the Adriatic. I've paid dearly for my charity. The day after tomorrow marks a month since he walked out on me, with King Tutankhamen under his coat."

With the economy of language typical of his writing style, our prospective client described those events which had brought him to our door. Immediately upon renting the house he shared with his wife, Isabel, he had unpacked a trunk he'd kept in storage nearly forty years, containing papers he'd collected and almost forgotten. The importance of the Tutankhamen manuscript was instantly apparent, and he had engaged young Patterson to perform errands which would otherwise distract him from his work. Colonel Patterson had disinherited his son upon learning that he'd been stealing from him to repay gambling debts, after which the jack-anape had managed to bar himself from every club in London as a card and billiards cheat. He'd spent a month in Reading Gaol for petty theft, and when he came to Burton with his tale of woe was living in Spitalfields with a woman of unsavory reputation. For reasons already explained, Burton agreed to take him on in consideration for room and board and a small wage.

Straightaway the adventurer realized he'd accepted one challenge too many. Daily the fellow vanished before his work was done, stayed out all night, and could not be roused to begin his duties on the morrow until the day was half gone, whereupon the cycle would repeat itself. There was a brief period, when Patterson spent his first week's pay to obtain a Kodak camera, during which Burton thought he might be showing an interest in something constructive, but the novelty of the purchase soon faded, and the camera languished upon a shelf in Burton's study while the assistant returned to his dissolute habits.

Finally, after a day spent researching in the Reading Room of the British Museum, Burton returned home determined to dismiss Patterson. There he was told by Lady Isabel that the young man had given notice and left. When an inspection revealed that the Egyptian document was missing, Burton interrogated his wife, who reported that Patterson had left the study empty-handed, gone up to his quarters to pack his meager belongings, and left carrying only the worn portmanteau with which he had arrived. She swore he did not return to the study where the papers were kept. Moreover, she had seen them spread out on the desk only a quarter-hour before, and had spent the intervening time writing letters in the little anteroom which separated the study from the stairs. Had he gone out or come in again during that period, she would have seen him.

"Is the manuscript fairly compact?" asked Holmes at this point in the narrative.

"Certainly not. With my notes, which vanished with it, it is as thick as a city directory. The original parchment is brittle and leaves a trail of brown flakes whenever it is moved."

"Then it is unlikely he carried it out beneath his coat."

"Impossible. I was merely employing a figure of speech."

"Is there a possibility he sneaked back in later, or that some anonymous thief gained entry between the time Patterson departed and you arrived?"

"There is not. Isabel was in the anteroom the entire time. There is no other entrance to the study save the window, which has been nailed shut since we moved in."

"Have you been in contact with Patterson?"

"He returned straightaway to the woman he resided with formerly in Spitalfields. When I went there and confronted him, he did not take the trouble to deny the theft. A police search of his quarters failed to uncover the papers, and no amount of threats on my part would persuade him to confess what he had done with them. He has me over a barrel, Holmes. The authorities won't jail him without evidence. The insolent creature as much as challenged me to take action. Ten years ago I would have called him out. I still would, if I thought it would serve any useful purpose." Impotent rage colored the old knight's features under his artificial pigment.

"Do you think he intends to loot the tomb himself?"

"Hardly. He is not an archaeologist, and the work is heartbreaking even if one has the wherewithal to finance an expedition. He is as lazy as Ludlam's dog and as poor as a leper. His only hope for profit would be to sell the manuscript, but since I have alerted the Royal Geographical Society to that possibility, his only recourse would be to ransom it back to me. I let four weeks pass to allow him to reach that conclusion. But he has made no contact, and Isabel suggested I consult you."

"You have had him watched, no doubt."

"I've surrounded his house with private inquiry agents around the clock. The farthest he has traveled is to the corner post office and back. The agents' fees are ruinous, and I am a poor man. The situation cannot continue. The key to the greatest historical find in a generation lies in the hands of a common thief. You are my court of last resort."

"I think of having a placard lettered to that effect." Holmes pulled at his pipe. "I should like to visit your study, if you will have me."

"Certainly, although I fail to see what the visit will achieve. The layout is as I described."

"I do not think otherwise. However, as you well know, the source of the Nile remained invisible to those who lived next to it for ten thousand years. It took a stranger to identify it. A cab, if you please, Watson. Tutankhamen awaits."

A brief ride in a four-wheeler deposited we three before an unprepossessing house in Westminster, where Sir Richard presented us to his wife, a woman of serene dignity at whose throat reposed a gold crucifix, in the heart of Protestant England; an adventurer, she, every bit as much as her husband penetrating the African interior, Mecca, India, and the Country of the Saints. She greeted us graciously, adding, "I hope, Mr. Holmes, you can help Richard find his pagan shrine. It has the virtue at least of being less dubious than some of his other projects."

"Isabel still has hopes of civilizing her barbarian," our host confided.

"Would that Jimmy Patterson had absconded with *The Perfumed Garden.*" With this Parthian shot—delivered, it seemed to me, without trace of irony—she left us to our exploration.

As anticipated, Burton's private study was an exhibition hall of Orientalia: beaded curtains, scimitars, an Indian hookah, blowguns of various lengths, and at least one shrunken head, interspersed among no fewer than five writing-desks, each cluttered with papers related to a different literary enterprise. Sir Richard, reappearing after a brief absence in a proper European turnout of shirt, shoes, waistcoat, and trousers, with most of the stain scrubbed from his skin, assured us that in years past there had been twice as many, but the diplomatic service had forced him to limit his extracurricular activities. The information passed without comment from Holmes, who was engaged in his examination of the crime theater of the moment. His intense gray eyes scanned the books and *objets d'art* upon the shelves, peered inside the kneeholes of desks, and passed without scholarly interest across the scattered sheets containing dense notations in Burton's nervous hand, while his fingers busied themselves with such oddly domestic actions as prodding the smoking ashes of a recent fire in the hearth with a poker that had begun life as a Sepoy lance.

Suddenly, he dropped the lance, knelt before the grate, and picked up a tiny object from the leopardskin hearth-rug. As he fished out his pocket lens to study it more closely, he asked how often there was a fire in the room.

"Every day, even in summer," came the reply. "All those years in the tropics have ruined me for the English climate."

"Tell me, Sir Richard, if you recognize this."

Burton accepted the proffered object, which was smaller than a child's fingernail. He then borrowed the lens, through which he scrutinized it for a few seconds only. "Parchment, without a doubt, and ancient." He paled. "Good Lord, Holmes! You can't suppose—"

"I never suppose. I only propose. Burning would be one explanation as to how the document left this room; meaning, of course, that it never left it at all."

"Then the man is a vandal, which is worse than a thief, and a madman besides. He has acted entirely without purpose, depriving posterity of the key to the riddle of Tutankhamen's tomb."

"Let us hope that this is not the case. Where there is no reason, deductive reasoning is futile, and I am not prepared to surrender the point. Your vandal theory does not cover the second disappearance which has taken place."

"There is nothing else missing."

"Where, then, is the Kodak camera you said young Patterson abandoned to a shelf in the study?"

The explorer directed his gaze toward a space between books and exotic bric-a-brac on a shelf which reposed upon the wall above one of the disheveled desks.

"I hadn't noticed," said he. "I'm certain it isn't in his old quarters, either. I searched the room thoroughly. But certainly Isabel would have seen him removing it."

"Possibly not. Apart from its simplicity, portability is the Kodak's chief advantage. He could have hidden it under his coat, as you first surmised. The simplest and earliest answer is often the best."

"But if the blackguard photographed the papers, why have I not received his demand for ransom? I am convinced he has approached no one else to offer them for sale."

"For the answer to that, we must wait for morning," said Holmes. "Will your purse enable you to maintain your watch upon his movements one more night?"

"Just that. I fail to see—"

"Failure to see is the driving force behind exploration. If the fellow attempts to fly tonight, he will have Tutankhamen on his person, and presently you will have him upon yours. Tomorrow, or the next day at the very latest, the Pharaoh will without doubt be comfortably ensconced in Westminster. Should it be the latter, Dr. Watson and I shall stand the watch through tomorrow night. By then, one month will have passed since the deed was done, a wizard measure of time. My faith in the efficiency of our government institutions encourages me to expect success."

My friend's certainty had an effect upon the chronic cynicism of our host, whose fierceness of feature had abated to some extent. "I shall be in your debt, quite literally. It goes without saying that history will be as well."

"History can look to its own account. Yours, Sir Richard, will be discharged if we can prevail upon you to put us up tonight at least. Should Patterson take flight, it is best we learn of the fact simultaneously with you. Action must be taken in concert and at once."

Burton accepted Holmes' terms without hesitation. His major-domo, a Mameluke whose British livery did not subtract from his ferocious countenance, was sent around to our quarters with a note to Mrs. Hudson to pack two overnight cases. By the time he returned, we had dined with Sir Richard and his lady upon curried lamb such as I had not tasted since my Indian service, paradoxically prepared by their stoic Scottish cook, and been shown to our room, which contained two camp beds and various items of arcania which had spilled into it from the master's overladen study. There we slept through the night, with no alarum having been given that our game had flown.

The following morning, Holmes with some difficulty persuaded Burton to stay home rather than resume his Arab disguise and accompany us upon our mission ("Your illustrious scars, and Patterson's familiarity, place the odds overmuch in his favor"), after which my friend and I repaired to Spitalfields. We wore our simplest garb and alighted from the hansom several squares ahead of our destination so as to avoid calling attention to our affluence in a neighborhood of day-laborers, common loafers, and strangers to prosperity.

Holmes, armed with Patterson's description, inquired at the post office on his street, and satisfied himself that our quarry had not been in yet that day. We thereupon took up our vigil outside the entrance. There a group of unfortunates in motley attire waited glumly upon the steps and pavement, hoping to earn a shilling by helping the odd postal customer carry his or her parcels. At Holmes' insistence, I pretended not to notice the black looks we received from our supposed rivals, whilst fingering the revolver in my coat pocket. There were evil faces in that crew, some of whom (I had no doubt) were described in detail in police bulletins posted inside the building.

The day wore on, and people of every description, although few thriving in appearance, came and went; fewer still succumbing to our companions' ministrations to relieve them of their burdens upon exiting. Lady Isabel had provided us with cold mutton sandwiches, which we unwrapped at mid-day, and earned some grudging approval from the others when we shared them with two of those present who had not sufficient provisions at home to supply themselves with luncheon.

Throughout this surveillance, we did not converse, other than to comment upon the occasional anomaly in low voices which would not reach the ears of eavesdroppers. Upon my part, curious though I was to learn what we were about, I had learned from experience the folly of attempting to draw Holmes out on the subject of his plans. Upon Holmes' part, I suspected he was reluctant to make my inability to ape the accents of the East End known to the neighborhood.

Toward late afternoon, I was aroused from my stupefaction and weariness of standing in one place by an exclamation beneath Holmes' breath and his warning grip upon my near wrist. Belatedly, I noted the approach of a youngish man in need of a haircut and wearing a shabby overcoat, but whose bearing betrayed a breeding not indicative of a lifetime among the squalid conditions of our present surroundings. His fair coloring and blue eyes, shot through at that early hour with the ensanguination of strong drink, had been described to us by Burton as those of James Patterson, the disinherited son of the hero of Roarke's Drift.

I tightened my grip upon my pistol, but was prevented from drawing it out by a quick squeeze of Holmes' hand. Thus we stood unmoving as Burton's late assistant climbed the steps and entered the post office.

Leaning close, Holmes whispered in my ear. "If he should emerge carrying a parcel, we shall follow him until we are clear of these other fellows. He may have friends among them. Be prepared upon my signal to step in close and press your revolver against his ribs. Discreetly, I pray you; a day at the Assizes to answer a charge of robbery by a passing patrolman may undo a lifetime of respectable behavior."

An eternity seemed to pass before Patterson reappeared. In truth it was not quite five minutes, and then he sauntered down the steps, considerably lighter on his heels than he had seemed on the way up. Beneath his right arm, clutched as tightly as if it contained the treasures of the Tower, was a brown paper-wrapped parcel no larger than an officer's toilet kit.

As directed, I fell in beside Holmes and we trailed the young man at a distance of perhaps fifty yards until we were well quit of the crowd outside the post office. Then we picked up our pace, and an instant before I was sure the sound of our approaching footsteps must alert Patterson to our presence, Holmes cried, "Now, Watson! Sharp!"

I stepped in with alacrity, thrusting my weapon's muzzle through the material of my coat pocket against Patterson's side just as he turned. He seemed to recognize the feel of the tempered steel, for he tensed, but took no action which might compel me to compress my finger upon the trigger. At that same instant, the detective circled around in front of him. His eyes were bright.

"Your game is done, Patterson!" Holmes announced. "My friend is no stranger to the hazardous life, and will not hesitate to fire if you offer him no choice. The parcel, if you please." He held out a hand.

From my angle I could not see the action, but I was close enough to hear the young man wet his lips. "Is it a hold-up, then?" asked he, loudly.

"Were I you, I would not seek to summon police help, however clumsily. It would be the word of a disgraced son against a knight of the realm." Holmes' tone was withering in its contempt.

The tension went out of Patterson like wind from a torn sail. He surrendered the parcel.

Instinctively I stepped back a pace, widening my field of fire whilst watching Holmes tear away the coarse brown paper. Within seconds he had exposed a box covered in black fabric, with a round opening upon one side encircled by shining steel.

"A marvelous invention, the Kodak," said he, extricating a square brown envelope from the wrapping. "It makes every man a Louis Daguerre, without the expense of maintaining a processing laboratory. One has but to snap away until the rolled film is exposed, then send the camera to the company headquarters in America, where it is opened, the film is developed, and camera and pictures are returned by the next post. With the aid of Mr. Fulton's equally marvelous steamship, a British subject can expect to view the results within a month."

As he spoke, Holmes drew a sheaf of glossy photographic paper from the envelope, and there on that scrofulous street in modern London, we three gazed upon page after page of writing which few men had laid eyes on since before the fall of Rome.

SIR RICHARD BURTON, seated at one of the desks in his study in a worn fez and an equally ancient dressing-gown of heavy Chinese silk, shuffled through the photographs like some old seer reading the Tarot. His predatory eyes were bright. "The bounder's a passing good photographer, thank the Lord for that," said he. "Shot ten pages at a time, and with some enlargement and the help of a good glass, I should be able to read them all. How in thunder did you work it out?"

"Your mentioning his brief interest in the Kodak stood out against the indolent portrait you painted," Holmes said. "When you referred to his trips to the corner post office, the thing was fairly settled for me. What interest can a disinherited man, recently dismissed and without prospects, have in the post? I withheld my suspicions until I could examine the vicinity of the theft. The scrap of parchment near the hearth and the missing camera eliminated any other theory which might have proposed itself."

"You have rescued history."

"Hardly that. I have merely saved you the price of Patterson's extortion. He would almost certainly have approached you with the pictures, as you surmised. In any case, the credit is as much Watson's as mine. You'd have done well to have such a fast-moving companion with you in Africa."

"If I'd had you both, I'd have tracked the blasted Nile to its cradle," he grumbled. "You let Patterson go?"

"I thought it better the record of Tutankhamen's tomb remain with you than in the evidence room at Scotland Yard. I did him no service. Eventually he will commit a crime from which no one can or will absolve him."

Burton studied each photograph in turn a second time. At last he set them down and rose, offering Holmes his hand. "I wish I'd known you in '60."

"You would not have found my company diverting, Sir Richard. I was six years old."

THE CASE WHICH I have indulged myself so far as to call "The Adventure of the Arabian Knight" has proven more valuable in enlightening the public upon the singular methods of Sherlock Holmes than the details of the undefiled resting-place of an Egyptian pharaoh. Twenty-six months after the events hereinfore described, Sir Richard Burton died, a victim of a combination of ailments he had contracted during his many explorations into places which before him were unknown to white society. In order to protect her late husband's reputation from malicious gossip connected to some manuscripts she thought morally objectionable, Lady Isabel Burton burned most of his voluminous papers; among which, it must be concluded, since nothing has since been heard of them, the photographs James Patterson took of the Egyptian document and any notes Burton may have made subsequent to their recovery. In view of this calamity, it seems likely that King Tutankhamen's tomb will remain forever buried beneath the sand of many centuries.

John H. Watson, M.D.
10 May 1904

THE ADVENTURE
OF THE CHESHIRE CHEESE

Jon L. Breen

"**W**ATSON," SAID SHERLOCK Holmes, "I believe you have been known to frequent the Cheshire Cheese from time to time. Perhaps you can enlighten our American friend as to the reason for his reception there."

Holmes' deference to me was a mixed blessing, surprising, gratifying, and unnerving all at once. He had already regaled our unexpected late-evening visitor to the Baker Street rooms with his usual string of remarkable observations—that Mr. Calvin Broadbent was an American, that he had arrived in England three days earlier and had been troubled on his crossing by seasickness, that his comfortable financial status had suffered recent reverses, and that he had just come from a disturbing experience at the venerable Fleet Street tavern most famous for its association with the Great Lexicographer, Dr. Samuel Johnson. Of course, Holmes had explained his deductions with the usual exasperating offhandedness. Some of the points seemed elementary in retrospect (that four-day-old New York newspaper in our guest's coat pocket, the fraying at the cuffs of his expensive jacket, his obvious air of agitation) and others remarkably lucky guesswork (that stain on his waistcoat and the sawdust clinging to his shoes). Now my friend was offering me the chance to contribute more to the elucidation of our visitor's problem than admiring cries of "Amazing, my dear fellow." Fortunately I would not disgrace myself completely.

Mr. Broadbent was an energetic, well-spoken, tastefully dressed young man of less than thirty. His manner was respectful and polite, with only the lightest seasoning of that brashness we often associate with his countrymen. The story he had told us, delivered in meticulously crafted sentences in a surprisingly pleasant and cultured American accent, was a remarkable one indeed.

"I'm a member of the Ichabod Crane Club in New York," he began. "Oh, I'm sure you've never heard of it, but it's a pretty long-established literary society. The somewhat whimsical name came from a character in the works of Washington Irving."

"*The Legend of Sleepy Hollow*, I believe," Holmes remarked. "A schoolmaster bedeviled by the Headless Horseman, was he not?"

"Why, yes, that's right." The young man appeared surprised and impressed. I had long since ceased to marvel at the arcane knowledge at my friend's command.

"We are a club of intellectuals, you might say, mostly but not entirely writers and journalists, certainly appreciators of the finer things in life. We gather every six weeks or so in a good Manhattan restaurant to share a meal and a fine vintage and listen to a lecture that is improving or entertaining or, at the best of times, both. How many members turn out depends upon the lecturer, and we've found to bring out the full membership, there's nothing like a visiting Englishman. Charles Dickens was a great success—that, I hasten to say, was well before my time—and so was Oscar Wilde a few years back. So when his tour managers offered us a chance to hear Algernon Fordyce, naturally we jumped at the chance."

Holmes and I glanced at each other meaningfully but said nothing. The old Fleet Street hack Fordyce was hardly in a class with Dickens or Wilde.

"As chairman of the program committee, I had the duty and honor of playing host to the guest lecturer and his wife in my home during his stay in New York. My circumstances have given me a unique ability to offer this hospitality. I am a bachelor and enjoy a small private income, though as you rightly observed, Mr. Holmes, recent reversals in the stock market have somewhat reduced it.

"Unfortunately, the morning after Mr. Fordyce spoke to our society—and he was a great speaker, let me tell you, well worth the fee his agency charged us—he was stricken with a sudden and mysterious illness. At first, we thought it would pass after a few days' rest, but it did not. Mr. Fordyce was my invalid houseguest for three weeks, with all manner of medical specialists in and out. Try as they might, they could do nothing for him, and one tragic morning Mr. Fordyce passed away."

"We read of his death in the *Times*," I said. "A sad event."

"It was indeed. Of course, I did my best to comfort his widow and help her with what arrangements needed to be made."

"What was determined to be the cause of death?" Holmes asked.

"There was disagreement on that point among the medical men. The death certificate listed heart failure as the cause, and I have no reason to doubt it."

"Nor do I," said Holmes dryly. "But what caused the heart to fail? I seem to remember that poisoning was suspected." Clearly, I reflected, Holmes had been reading about the case in papers other than the *Times*.

"It's true that one of the doctors was convinced Fordyce had been poisoned, but I assure you there was no basis for that. Who would have poisoned him? His wife loved him, was prostrate with grief. My servants I can vouch for entirely, and they would have had no motive. No one else, save his doctors and a highly respectable nurse, came near the man during his stay in my house. I'm sure the cause of his death was natural."

"As I recall," said Holmes, "Mrs. Fordyce is some years younger than her husband."

"Yes, that is true, but completely devoted to him. You could not possibly be around them in those last sad days of his life and doubt that. Now, in order for you to understand my problem, I must speak of my own relationship with Fordyce. In those waning days of his life, we became great friends. Though he grew steadily weaker day by day, his mind remained clear, and the discussions we had of literature and sports and art and politics served to take his mind off his affliction. He had come to America not only to lecture but to write of his experiences. He hadn't the strength to produce those articles about America his London editors had contracted for, but he did continue writing verse in an increasingly unsteady scrawl to the very end.

"One day as I sat by his bedside—his exhausted wife was sleeping at the time, the poor dear—we came to talk of our clubs. I told him about the Ichabod Crane and the few other Manhattan clubs of which I'm privileged to be a member. Fordyce belonged to several in London, but the one he mentioned with the most fondness was called the 1457 Club, or simply the Fourteen Club for short. This club, he told me, met every month at one of his favorite London haunts, an old tavern called the Cheshire Cheese. Do either of you gentlemen know of the 1457 Club?"

While I could think of several clubs that had their meetings at the Cheese—St. Dunstan's, the Johnson Club, the Rhymers' Club, the amusingly named Soakers' Club—I obviously did not know them all, and the 1457 or Fourteen Club was unfamiliar.

"Can't say that I do," I replied. I glanced toward Holmes, who remained impassive.

Broadbent went on, "He told me more about the meeting place than he did the club, if truth be told. He said the Cheshire Cheese was a famous tavern that dated back hundreds of years and had long been a gathering place for journalists and writers and barristers. I remember he called it 'a storied inn where Dr. Johnson is still a living presence.' But I was much more curious about the oddly named 1457 Club. I asked him many questions about it, and it seemed to amuse him to keep me in the dark. What, I wondered, did the 1457 signify? Was it part of a street address?"

"Rather a high number for a street address," I said. "Don't you think so, Holmes?" My friend did not answer. "More likely to be a year, I should think."

"That's what I decided," Broadbent said. "I wondered what had happened in the year 1457 that could be the basis for a club. It was not an especially eventful year, and the possibilities I suggested only made Fordyce laugh. I found it frustrating, but after all, he was dying, not I, so let him take what pleasure he could. As he grew more and more ill, he began to realize that he would never again enter Wine Office Court and share drink and good fellowship with his friends. To staunch his melancholia, he wrote in those last days of his life one final poem, a sonnet in tribute to the Cheshire Cheese. He asked me to deliver the sonnet in person to a meeting of the Fourteen Club in the event he could not do so himself. I, of course, reassured him that he would recover, but by that time I was certain he would not."

"You've come all the way to London for a sentimental gesture, Mr. Broadbent?" Holmes inquired.

Broadbent smiled ruefully. "Not entirely. He told me something else about the club, not what it was devoted to or what the 1457 meant, oh, no, not that, but something that would be of more practical importance. Fordyce said that several members of the Club owed him large sums of money, which in the event of his death he wanted me to collect for the welfare of his widow. That there were no written records of these debts seemed to me most odd, but he assured me his debtors were honorable men who would surely volunteer them to me once they were assured by my reading of the sonnet that I had appeared as his posthumous representative."

"That would be honorable indeed," Holmes murmured, "to insist on paying an unrecorded debt to a dead man. And where is Mrs. Fordyce now? No doubt she has returned to England?"

Broadbent seemed a bit uncomfortable as he said, "She has remained in New York."

"That seems odd, doesn't it?" I ventured. "Surely she would want to be with friends and family at such a time."

"Ah, she has little family left, I fear, and she quite likes America. I assured her I would collect the moneys owed and bring them back to her."

"Thus your visit tonight to the Cheshire Cheese," Holmes prompted.

"Yes. Fordyce told me when the Fourteen Club would be holding its regular meeting and assured me that I would be made welcome once I mentioned his name. I must confess when I entered, I was subject to some disconcerting stares, not impolite precisely but— well, I gather the crowd is mostly made up of regulars."

"It's a conservative place," I told him, "mindful of tradition and the old ways of doing things. The clientele is suspicious of strangers and resistant to change, any kind of change. I remember when they imported a lemon-squeezing machine from your country, Mr. Broadbent. The controversy was enormous. It was intended to be a simple labor-saving device, but you should have heard some of the cries of outrage."

"They were a bit more friendly when they realized I was an American. Someone shouted out, 'He'll want a serviette then!' I can't imagine what that meant."

"What you would call a napkin, Mr. Broadbent," Holmes explained. "Provision of such luxuries is not automatic in London eating houses as I understand it is in your country."

"I see. They thought I'd want to see Dr. Johnson's table, the right hand table in the left hand room, just after the entry. They showed me a copy of Joshua Reynolds' portrait of Johnson and a picture depicting Johnson saving Oliver Goldsmith from his landlady. They pointed out to me the portraits of past waiters that were the most prominent non-Johnson paintings on the walls— honoring waiters in that way seems to me a most civilized custom, and I said so, but I was struggling to control my impatience to complete my business. Finally, after my guided tour of the ground floor, I asked where I might find the Fourteen Club and was directed to the upstairs room where they were meeting. There are so many little rooms in that place, a stranger could easily find himself lost. Once I found the Club and told them why this foreign stranger was in their midst, they were most hospitable. I described to them Fordyce's last days in my house, tried to express how much the Cheshire Cheese and the Fourteen Club meant to him, and told them Fordyce had insisted that I read them his final sonnet. They of course were eager to hear it." Broadbent probed in his coat pocket and pulled out a crumpled sheet of paper. "This is a fair copy of the sonnet, made by me from Fordyce's original, which was barely legible."

Holmes glanced at the poem for a moment and passed it over to me. This is what I read:

> "The weary trav'ler back from foreign port
> Up Fleet Street strolls full up with memories
> Of jolly times at Ye Olde Cheshire Cheese,
> Down dark and narrow old Wine Office Court.
> No Great Fire singed the treasured seat
> Upon which good Will Shakespeare came to sit
> Or scorched that storied bar even a bit
> From which Boswell his source of fame would greet.
> End your meal with pudding; have some more,
> Remembering the chops that went before,
> And how Scotch, Irish, claret, port, or gin
> Unlock tongues the more you let them in.
> Oh, Fourteen Club, declare loud if you please
> Your love of golf at Ye Olde Cheshire Cheese."

"As I read the first four lines," Broadbent declared, "I was certain I saw tears in the eyes of some of the club members. They seemed truly moved by Fordyce's reverence for their meeting place. But as I read on, their expressions began to harden. They looked at each other in consternation, even anger. And when I was finished, I was denounced as an impostor and summarily asked to leave the premises. My demands for an explanation fell on deaf ears. Such was their outrage, I feared some of them, one very large person in particular, might do physical damage to me if I did not flee at once. I had not even had dinner. Mr. Holmes, your reputation as an elucidator of mysteries is well known all over the world. Can you tell me where I went wrong, how I offended these clubmen? And can you make any suggestion how I might collect Algernon Fordyce's unwritten debts for the benefit of his brave widow?"

Holmes looked at our visitor with a somewhat unsympathetic expression. He appeared about to say something but held his tongue. It was then he referred to my sometime patronage of the Cheshire Cheese and passed the torch to me.

"Mr. Broadbent," I said gently, "at least the reference to golf tells you to what pastime this club is apparently devoted. But the sonnet has a few errors in it, I fear."

"Errors? What do you mean?"

"To begin with, the Great Fire of 1666 *did* destroy Ye Olde Cheshire Cheese, and it was rebuilt the following year. Legend has it that Shakespeare and Ben Jonson frequented the place in earlier years, but no seat the Bard of Avon sat upon can have survived. Secondly, the pudding for which the Cheshire Cheese is famous is not a sweet that comes at the end of the meal but rather a meal in itself. They serve it on Wednesdays and Saturdays, and its size ranges from fifty to eighty pounds. Under its flaky crust you'll find rump steak, kidneys, oysters, larks, mushrooms. It's a lovely dish, makes me hungry just talking about it. When it's cooking on a breezy day, they say you can savor its aroma as far away as the Stock Exchange."

"Spare us your raptures, Watson," Holmes said.

"Quite so. The point, Mr. Broadbent, is that you would not follow a chop with that pudding, no, indeed. It is by no means a dessert as the sonnet implies." I cleared my throat. "I must point out some other problems of nomenclature. No patron of the Cheshire Cheese would refer to Scotch, Irish, or gin."

"Why on earth not?" Broadbent cried in seeming outrage. "The place is a tavern, is it not?"

"Yes, but if you want Scotch, you simply ask for whiskey; if you want Irish whiskey, you must ask for Cork; and gin is never referred to as anything but rack."

"How on earth would I be expected to know that?" Broadbent demanded.

"You wouldn't," said Holmes, "but Algernon Fordyce certainly would. Do you have any more observations, Watson?"

"Ah, no, I believe that's all." And quite enough, I would have thought.

"I have only a couple of points to add. What was Boswell doing at the Cheese?"

"Holmes," I remonstrated, "surely Dr. Johnson would not have gone to the Cheese without Boswell."

"Ah, good old Watson, you are my Boswell, and a better one no man could hope for. But history is against you on this point. Boswell knew Johnson in his old age, years after he lived nearby the Cheese. Boswell makes no mention of the place in his life of Johnson, and as far as anyone knows, he never went there. And the reference to golf in the sonnet may suggest the meaning of the club's name."

"Fourteen Club," I cried. "Could it be named after the fourteenth hole on some golf course?"

"What then do you do with the 57?"

I thought about it for a moment, reluctant to abandon my theory. "Someone could have a total of 57 strokes through 14 holes, could he not?"

"A remarkable round," Broadbent murmured.

"No," said Holmes, "the reference is, as you thought, to a year. And one thing happened in the year 1457 that is significant in the history of golf. James II of Scotland issued an edict banning the game on the grounds that it was distracting men from the improvement of their archery, which was vital for military purposes. Knowing this, who would form an organization called the 1457 Club? Keen golfers? I think not. More likely those who hate the game of golf."

"But, Holmes," I objected, "surely the name could have been adopted ironically by lovers of golf."

"Could have been, yes, but since everything else in Algernon Fordyce's poem appears designed to embarrass the man he asked to deliver it, I shall stay with my first hypothesis. Declaring love of golf in that sonnet would be the final insult to the membership of a golf haters' club, the one most certain to bring about the banishment of Mr. Broadbent."

"I don't understand this," Broadbent cried. "Why would Fordyce perpetrate this hoax on someone who only tried to help him?"

"He would not," Holmes replied sharply.

Ignoring Holmes' implication, our visitor said, "And how can I hope to collect those debts?"

"Don't you see? Those supposed unwritten debts are a fiction. Tell me one thing, Mr. Broadbent."

"Yes?"

"Who was administering the poison that slowly drained the life from Algernon Fordyce. Was it you? Was it his wife? Or did you take the duty in turn?"

"Mr. Holmes," our visitor cried, "that is a monstrous suggestion."

"It was a monstrous act. What poison precisely did you use? Any of several might have achieved the desired effect of misleading the physicians. Oh, you needn't answer. It's merely professional curiosity. Probably you covered your tracks sufficiently to ensure that my 'monstrous suggestion' will never be made in an American law court."

Despite this pessimistic assertion, Holmes would cable his conclusions to Wilson Hargreave, his friend on the New York Police Bureau, shortly after Broadbent departed 221B.

"When Fordyce realized what was happening," Holmes continued, "that his young wife had fallen in love with a much younger man, that he was being slowly poisoned, he realized it was too late to get help from the outside world as a captive in your house. But he at least managed one very good joke on you, sending you across the Atlantic on a wild-goose chase."

"You presume a lot from just a poem, Mr. Holmes," Broadbent said, "however inaccurate."

"Ah, but there's that one final clue in the poem."

"Another clue, Holmes?" I said.

"It's staring us all in the face, and you needn't be a habitué of the Cheshire Cheese to interpret it. Look at the first letter of each line of the poem. Do they spell out anything?"

Broadbent and I both looked.

"T, U, O, D, N," I read.

"That spells nothing!" our visitor said.

"Try reading from the bottom," Holmes snapped. "Do you see it now, Broadbent? You are found out!"

Darkest Gold

L. B. Greenwood

"**B**AKER STREET, CABBIE," I called. "Number 221."

The reasons for my changed order were mixed. I had finished my morning rounds, had no claim on my time until afternoon surgery, was already bored with my paper, and hadn't seen Holmes for nearly two months. Nor, I realized as I rang the bell that always seemed to remember my hand, had I heard much of him of late.

"Good morning, Mrs. Hudson. How is your esteemed lodger?"

"You'll find him changed, Doctor," was her enigmatic reply, made with raised eyebrows and pursed mouth. Whatever these alterations, they didn't meet with her approval.

Nor with mine. I found Holmes clad in a safari jacket and shorts, with a pith helmet on his head, sprouting a particularly ridiculous short beard, and busily striking foppish poses in front of the standing glass that had been brought from his bedroom.

"Dr. Livingstone, I presume," I remarked, setting my bag down and tossing my hat onto the stand. "Going to a fancy dress ball, are you?"

Holmes had fixed a gilded monocle in his right eye in order to survey my reflection in the mirror. "Your deduction is admirable, Watson. Unfortunately, the case in which I am currently involved—

deeply enough to require this horrendous beard—is beyond that kind of logic. How," turning to face me, "do I look?"

"Like a fool," I answered frankly, eyeing his decidedly knobby knees.

"Then perhaps I will pass. The challenge, you understand is to hit precisely the correct note of idiocy, for much may depend upon it. Would you accept me as the mentally negligible and illegitimate scion of a noble house, brother to a much honored member of society?"

"With no difficulty whatsoever. Whom are you impersonating? And why?"

"*Creating* would be the more accurate word, Doctor, since Lord Ashley has no brother from either side of the blanket."

"Lord Ashley!" I exclaimed. "Why, he's mentioned in the morning press; something about a gold discovery in the Congo." I dug my newspaper out from my inner coat pocket. "Whatever is the matter, Holmes?"

For he had fairly snatched the paper from my hands, and, after a glance at the front page, had groaned aloud. "That's torn it!" he cried, and flung the paper from him. "We shall have to leave at once.

"Not you, Watson." He was answering my open mouth: I had been about to observe that I would have a hard push to leave my practice at such short notice. I admit to feeling a trifle hurt to hear that this would be unnecessary. "This is one time when your considerable abilities cannot be of use to me. What do you know of John, fourth duke of Ashley?"

"A fine English gentleman in every respect," I said promptly. "Made the usual continental tours after his university days, found them boring, drifted on to Africa, ended up among the Pygmy people of the Congo, and became their champion."

"You are remarkably well informed, Doctor. Have you met Lord Ashley?"

I shook my head. "Mary may have, for she is very active in the anti-slavery movement, and so I believe is Lady Ashley."

"That foul trade is precisely what has brought on the present crisis. The Pygmies are a peculiarly defenseless people, you know. They're very small, of course, by nature gentle and kindly, and live in familiary organized villages deep in the Congo forest."

"Their own Garden of Eden," I suggested. I fear that I spoke with the smile that comes too readily to our faces at such moments of imagined superiority. I would not do so now.

"If so, we can name the serpent: Karl Barker."

"That foulmouthed, foul-tempered—"

"Exploring entrepreneur whose ethics and morals were left in the Lost Luggage department of life very early in his career? Exactly. He was involved several months ago in a particularly filthy bit of business. He seized a Pygmy girl who was bartering a basket of nuts in a grassland village, and sold her as a particularly exotic piece of goods to the Berber slave trade."

"Abominable, Holmes!"

"All of that, and what followed is worse: The girl's father and brothers tracked Barker right to his camp. The Pygmies possess no more than the simplest stone weapons, and these men had too much sense to try to attack. Instead, they bought the girl back."

I was beginning to understand the importance of what I had read in my morning paper. "They bought the girl back with gold?"

"With two nuggets of gold, of precisely the kind and quality that have long been rumored to lie somewhere in the Congo, though no one has ever before seen any direct evidence."

"I wonder Barker didn't track the men and girl back to their village, no matter how deep in the forest."

"He tried, and failed. Lord Ashley says that Barker is an excellent bushman, but that the Pygmies are far better."

"So Barker hotfoot it home, and is putting together an expedition to find the Pygmies and steal the gold?"

"At any cost, in our kind of coin and Pygmy suffering: Some of the dirtiest money in London is involved. At the first hint Lord Ashley began arranging to go to warn his little friends of their danger, but he has also been heavily involved in trying to persuade our government to take the lead in banning all mining exploration in the Congo forests. As you can imagine, that is a terribly slow business, and we hoped that we had longer than this. But if Barker is on the move, we'll have to be so too."

"Lord Ashley's interest I can understand," I said. "What, though, of yours?"

"Lord Ashley believes that he will be attacked, and quite probably killed, by Barker. I agree with him."

"Bodyguards of a particularly thuggish quality Lord Ashley may need," I retorted. "I fail to see what use you can be. The Congo is, after all, hardly your purview."

Holmes gave a small smile at my blunt vehemence. "When it comes to rough behavior, Lord Ashley can probably take care of himself. What he fears is that he will be struck down somewhere in the African wild, with his killers officially unknown and never caught—he'll be traveling virtually alone. Except for me: the eyewitness, with some skills of his own and—if I may say so—impeccable reputation."

"And you intend traveling incognito as Lord Ashley's nonexistent and illegitimate brother? The latter touch no doubt concocted to explain why this figure has not been seen in society before. Really, Holmes!" I was highly alarmed, and disguising it with annoyance. "You are far from an unknown or inconspicuous figure yourself."

"It's not as fanciful a plan as it sounds. Certainly Lord Ashley cannot hope to travel far unrecognized, but he has never before had any kind of contact with me. Therefore a fop of a brother may be overlooked as a nonentity. Hence," he gave a wry smile, "this beard. It's quite remarkably awful, is it not?"

"It is," I agreed heartily. "I do understand why you're attempting this, Holmes. I do indeed."

I spoke truly. What I didn't say, what was equally true, was that my mind had been filled with a vision of a jungle scene, with one man sprawling dead, the other collapsed beside him, badly injured, abandoned without supplies or help. From that moment I was determined to go with Holmes, somehow.

MY FIRST STEP was to confide in Mary: Had she objected, I could not have gone, even for Holmes. Though her lip briefly trembled, she instantly agreed that someone had to try to stop Barker from starting a gold rush that would bring devastation to those helpless little people, that Lord Ashley and Holmes had the best chance of accomplishing this, and that it was foolhardy in the highest degree to go on such a mission without a doctor. (What a wife she is!)

Next, I sought out a semi-retired medical acquaintance, who agreed to assist Anstruther in taking care of my patients. I told both that I had come down with a sudden and severe form of gout, and that I was going to a continental spa. That Anstruther at least had his own opinion was evident by his wry comment: "I trust that Mr. Holmes also benefits from taking the waters."

I had also to do what is usually labeled "putting one's affairs in order," for of course what I was attempting to do would be dangerous. Even without the attentions of Barker and his hoodlums, malaria and sleeping sickness would see to that, not to mention the other myriad of diseases that lurk in the depths of Africa. I made my preparations, and stocked a small travel kit with emergency aids.

Then I had to choose a disguise. This of course I couldn't maintain once Holmes and I were in one another's presence. All I could hope for was to be unrecognized until discovery was inevitable and the way back too long to be contemplated.

I decided to appear as a self-made man, the kind who would refer complacently to his "tidy pile." It was Mary who named me Mr. Josiah Watkins so that I could keep my own initials and laundry markings, and decided that I would have traveled "in" casket fittings, surely as dull an occupation as could be contrived, and one guaranteed to be distasteful to my fellows. Some of my own attire I could use. Some I found in slop shops, some garments were bought blazingly new.

During these days I also paid many short visits to Holmes, and thus learned Lord Ashley's basic itinerary. He and Holmes were to sail on the *Queen's Star*, the latest and fastest of the new liners, to North Africa; from there it would be a succession of trains to Leopoldville. Holmes would say nothing of the plans past that point. "You need know no more, Doctor," was his sole comment. I would have to make what arrangements I could when that became necessary.

Naturally I kept my distance while on board the *Star*, not difficult since Lord Ashley and Holmes were in first class, and Mr. Josiah Watkins in second. Since much of the lower decks were visible from above, I took the added precaution of not venturing out until after dusk.

Even so, one evening I had a close call. I was as usual "quarter-decking" in the dark, enjoying my evening pipe, when from directly above me I heard Holmes' quite unforgettable normal voice. "That wire confirmed our route, Lord Ashley?"

"It did. Nawga will collect our heavy baggage at Turka and see it started on the way to Kabkow. That is an immense relief to my mind."

"This Nawga *is* reliable? Honest?"

"Both, absolutely. He has helped me many times."

"Ah. Still no sign of Barker?"

"None. We may actually have stolen the march on him by moving so promptly. What do you say to a drink before we turn in, Holmes?"

"A capital idea." Receding footsteps sounded from above.

I could hardly believe my good fortune. The most serious problem for my following Lord Ashley and my friend had been solved! Of how I was to find transport first to Turka and then to Kabkow I had no idea, but I did at least now know that that was where I had to head.

Before I could take myself off an all too familiar female voice trilled in my ear. "What a delicious aroma your pipe has!" And a hand gloved in purple kid slipped possessively through my arm.

Later events make me feel quite at liberty to say that Mrs. Hiram Jones from Liverpool, traveling—she said—to try to overcome her grief at the recent loss of her husband, was a pest, an undiluted pest. We had hardly left England before she was making it abundantly clear that she believed that her best antidote to sorrow was a marital replacement, and that she had decided that one Mr. Josiah Watkins would do admirably.

I know that this sounds laughable now, but it was a confounded complication then. Nor was she easy to discourage, for behind the veils and feather—and paint—gleamed a pair of intelligent and determined gray eyes. Such a woman could all too easily trip me into saying something that would fit ill with my assumed persona, and I strove mightily to avoid her. You might as well have tried to keep dry in a downpour.

She tipped with a generosity that was close to bribery, and so had contrived to have the seat next to me at every meal. From that vantage point she trailed her draperies across my knee at breakfast, offered to share her luncheon with me while begging for tidbits from mine, and bobbed her well corsetted cleavage at me at dinner. Nor was she in any way a woman with whom any gentleman would wish to be seen: Her clothes were gaudy, her jewelry massive, and her perfume unbelievably potent.

Now I escorted Mrs. Jones to the lower deck lounge, and there firmly excused myself.

"I do believe you're going to visit the upper deck," she exclaimed archly, "so you can hobnob with the swells!"

I assured her that that was the last of my intentions, and left.

FROM OUR NORTH African docking we traveled to Leopoldville by a series of increasingly uncomfortable trains (which gave Mrs. Jones marvelous opportunity for megrims and pleas of assistance). At the capital of the Congo I had the immense pleasure of parting with my incubus, for she was journeying on to visit an old nurse farther down the coast. She bade me such an affectionate farewell at the station that I was forced to step back onto the train to avoid the embarrassment of a public embrace. She was an utterly *terrible* woman!

Lord Ashley and Holmes, and therefore I, had now to travel east, heading into the true depths of the continent. An irregular though frequent service of various wheeled vehicles headed in that direction, and thus I was able still to keep myself separate on the way to Turka.

No doubt this is a common enough kind of town for the area; I found it quite awful. Not large, and yet always noisy, dirty beyond what I had ever experienced in my military life, and awash with men of distasteful manners and hidden nationality; all engaged in what was tactfully labeled trade.

If you wanted strange liquor and secret potions, or flimsy cottons mixed in with the occasional section of startlingly fine silk, or carved ivory that was supposed to come from China and might even have done so, the Turka bazaar was the place to be. I saw shrunken heads that I could only hope were from monkies, and enough cowed women to fear that something very like a slave trade could be found in the smelly shadows.

By the time I arrived Lord Ashley and Holmes had taken rooms at the one even partially respectable hotel. The porter there directed me to his brother's house, where a little English was spoken and I could have a room. (Little more; a cot and a bench.) Unfortunately the only cafe that would not prove disastrous for white men was that of the hotel, and so I was forced to take my dinner there.

I had made sure that neither Lord Ashley nor Holmes was even in the hotel before I entered, but before my meal had even arrived I heard their voices behind me. All I could do was to take refuge behind a newspaper that had been left on my table.

So I learned that our time in this wretched town might be considerably longer than originally planned. The heavy baggage that was to have been collected and sent on by Nawga had not only not arrived, it seemed to have vanished altogether, and the unfortunate Nawga was in bed with a broken leg.

Lord Ashley and Holmes were deep in discussion of this serious problem when Holmes suddenly drew a deep breath. "That fellow who has just entered. Isn't he Barker?"

"You're right," Lord Ashley replied grimly. "He's on our trail already."

I lowered a corner of my newspaper in order to see the devil who had tried to sell a Pygmy girl into slavery. He was not particularly tall though massively wide with muscle, dressed in well-worn khaki and light boots. It was his eyes that told his story: small and mean and constantly shifting.

As they reached the vicinity of my table, from somewhere behind me Holmes raised a shrill voice: He was in his role as the foppish brother.

"I say, Ash," he ejaculated. "Isn't that chappy by the door that awful cad, Barker? What's he doing here, d'you think? Let's get going to this Kabkow place *instanter*!"

"Be quiet, Reggie!" Lord Ashley snapped, and, to judge by the slight scuffling sounds and the reiterated "I say, Ash!", was hauling his "brother" away.

Meanwhile a young native lad had come from the back of the cafe to attend to Barker. With many bows and gestures, the boy was offering to show him to a table. Barker, gazing thoughtfully after Lord Ashley and Holmes, paid no attention. The lad ventured to touch his arm, and received a backhand that sent him sprawling.

I would have given much to have been able to accost Barker. All I could do was to leave at once, aware that I was favored by a contemptuous bark of laughter as I retired.

Next morning I went to the cafe very early, and chose a table behind some potted greenery. I had hardly seated myself when Holmes and Lord Ashley came in. "Reggie" at once surveyed the room (I was very glad of my protective greenery) through his monocle, and expressed his pleasure that "that bounder" wasn't present.

"Hasn't gone, has he?" he asked the waiter.

And the waiter nodded! "He be gone, seer. Star time, he go. Go d'rection Kabkow."

I hurried to my room to ask my native host to find out if this startling news was indeed true. He didn't need to find out, he promptly replied. All the bazaar knew that the "loud English" had left sometime in the night, taking the men who had come with him, on the road to Kabkow.

Well, what else could have been expected? I thought resignedly. Holmes had overplayed his "Reggie" and fairly shrieked out the name of Lord Ashley's immediate destination. Of course Barker and his doubtless foul entourage had set out at once. Lord Ashley and Holmes would be very soon on the way too, probably hoping to outdistance their opponent, and all I could do was to follow as soon as I could.

I accordingly began the infinitely frustrating task of trying to find transport without being able to speak a word of any native tongue. I was rapidly fuming myself into a fever when, at a curio shop where I had been misleadingly directed, a soft voice spoke from the shadows: the native boy from the cafe, bowing low as if to hide the bruise on his cheek.

"Meester?" he said. "You want go too, meester?"

"Meester" had never wanted anything more. "You can arrange it?" I asked eagerly. "To follow my two . . . friends and those others to Kabkow?" At the boy's nod, I had begun to pull out my purse when he placed a restraining hand on my arm.

"No, no," he murmured urgently. "Not show money, not here. Don't worry, meester, I see to. You be here, dusk. Small baggage, only small." With which he had gone.

I could do nothing except trust him and make what preparations I could. I reduced my effects to a single pack (I am, after all, an old campaigner), and, with my canteen full and my pockets stuffed with a few chocolate bars I had bought at the hotel and some nuts from the market, at dusk I set out.

At the curio shop I discovered that I was joining a couple of rough-looking fellows on horseback, and that the native boy had enlisted himself as my attendant. I had a balky gelding, the boy a thin mare.

As we left the town, I caught the name of Banto tossed between the men, complete with gestures that suggested a destination. I quickly turned to the boy. "Not Banto," I said urgently. "The others have gone to Kabkow, and so must I."

"Yes, yes, meester," he assured me. "Not listen to these rough ones, they talk of other things. We go to Kabkow as meester wishes."

I had to trust him, for, behind the map knowledge that Kabkow lay to the east, I knew nothing of where we should go, much less of where the winding path across the grassland was actually headed. We set off at a brisk trot and continued so as long as the moon was up. As soon as we had made a simple camp, I was asleep.

All too shortly the boy was shaking me awake, offering a bowl of rice flavored with bits of fresh meat and a most blessed mug of tea. Dawn was filling the sky with glory, and I was sleepily admiring it when the boy cried out.

Our villainous escort, who had been packing up, had now swung into their saddles and were reaching for the ropes of our horses. The boy was trying to pull one of these free when the larger man leaned from his saddle and, with a filthy leer, cupped his dirty fingers around what was all too clearly a female breast.

I understood little except that this was intolerable. "Stop that!" I roared, flinging myself forward.

The men only galloped off, laughing uproariously. They had left little behind except our personal baggage.

The girl had pulled herself into a sitting position, and was now looking up at me. "I owe you an apology, Dr. Watson," she said, as calmly as if we were in Regent's Park. "I have behaved abominably, I know."

"Mrs. Jones!" I exclaimed, with abrupt insight. Admittedly there was little in this slim shape and pale bruised face to suggest the buxom and froward matron, yet if you subtracted all that padding and paint could do. . . . Certainly the eyes were the same intelligent and determined gray. "You *are* Mrs. Jones, aren't you?"

"In a way, yes. I am Julia, Lady Ashley."

I more collapsed than sat down on the hard earth.

"You see, I could think of no other way of following my husband."

"But I saw you off at Leopoldville!"

"Oh, I bribed the conductor to let me off as soon as you'd gone. I've done quite a bit of bribing, really. The owner of that hotel to let me act the part of a native service lad, and his wife to cut my hair. And those thieves who have stranded us here."

"You have doubtless been very clever, Lady Ashley," I agreed. "But what on earth are we to do now?"

My reply was ritualistic, her reply quite the reverse. "With the horses, we have traveled much faster than my husband and Mr. Holmes. I caught a glimpse of them last night from that hill, remember it? I'm sure they're not far ahead of us."

" 'Not far' is hardly enough, Lady Julia. Not situated as we are."

"We will make it do," she said simply. From some inside pocket she brought forth a dainty little revolver, with pearl handle and gleaming gold-tinted barrel.

"I asked Johnny to give me this as a wedding present," she went on, "and he did. He has never refused me anything that he can buy. I thought that possessing this little toy—and learning to use it too—would help convince him that I could safely accompany him sometimes. But he has never been interested in that. By the way, Dr. Watson, we're headed toward Banto. Johnny made Barker think that he was going to Kabkow, but that was only a blind."

"He told Holmes the same thing," I protested. "On board the ship. I heard him."

"Then that too was a blind," she replied. "I have read all Johnny's travel diaries, you see. Not what was published, the whole diaries in his own writing. There he always says that the easiest way from Turka to the forest is through Kabkow, but that the quickest route is on foot and toward Banto. That's what he's doing now, what he always intended."

"But the heavy baggage—"

"There never was any heavy baggage. Only an excuse to linger at Turka until Barker could be set off on a false trail." Pointing her little revolver to the sky, she pulled the trigger. The explosion was surprisingly large, with a distinctly sharp *pop* to it.

"There!" Lady Julia said matter-of-factly into the cacophonous outburst of a myriad of startled birds. "Johnny will recognize that sound: There's nothing other quite like it. Perhaps we can finish our breakfast while we wait."

And, utterly astonishing as it was to me, that was what we were doing when Lord Ashley burst through the light brush into our camp, closely followed by Holmes.

"Julia!" Lord Ashley yelled, scarlet in the face. "What madness has brought you here?"

"Since you have never cared to discuss anything with me, Johnny, I had to make up my own mind. I decided to follow you. To be part of your life for once. Good morning, Mr. Holmes. Would you care for a mug of tea?"

Lord Ashley was standing over her now, glaring down. "Have you any idea how dangerous this . . . gallivant of yours will almost surely be?"

"I know only what I have read in the newspapers. And from your actions. Never from what you tell me, for that is always nothing."

"You at least know that the Pygmies are as kind, generous and unprotected a people as exist—"

"If you recall, I have attended all of your lectures."

"Then do you just happen to understand the fate that your being here will bring down upon them?"

"I cannot see that my presence has anything to do with that," she replied with spirit. "If my gathering of the scraps of information concerning this expedition of yours is correct, you have come to warn the Pygmies about Barker and his greed for gold. You can still do that—I shan't stop you."

"Your very existence here does that. Speed was the only advantage I had. Now we will have to tiptoe along at the pace you can endure."

"I can travel as quickly as you, Johnny."

"You can't," he snapped. He drew a long breath, and a frightening change came over his face. All the color drained away, leaving a cold and distant mask set on the rage and frustration now within his iron control.

He sat down beside his wife and said, "I think I would like that mug of tea you offered, my dear."

From then on this was the attitude he maintained toward her: courtesy so icy that it must have hurt far more than the blow that Barker had landed on her cheek. That was healing, this could only fester.

Of course Lord Ashley was correct in his blunt assessment: Lady Julia couldn't keep up the ferocious pace that he set. *I* had to use every ounce of determination I could muster, and even Holmes showed signs of deep weariness.

When we had made camp at the end of that first night, I drew Holmes aside. "You didn't recognize Lady Julia in her boy's disguise at the hotel cafe?"

"I had never met the lady, and in the cafe I had only a glimpse of a small figure sprawling on the floor."

"You didn't recognize me, either, did you?" I asked confidently. In fact, I felt rather proud of myself. "In the cafe or on the boat or train?"

Holmes gave the kind of tolerant smile with which he has often favored me in Baker Street. "My dear Doctor, of course I recognized you. To begin with, I was expecting you, for I had seen your face when I told you that you weren't to come."

No doubt I looked quite crestfallen, for Holmes laid a gentle hand on my shoulder. "Never attempt the part of a character whose soul remains closed to you," he said. "Never could Dr. Watson have worn that check suit, or sported that massive signet ring. I trust it was purchased at a pawn shop?"

"It was. For a shilling."

"Wouldn't Mr. Josiah Watkins have bought something just as ugly, but from Bond Street and costing five guineas?"

I knew at once that Holmes was right. Mr. Josiah Watkins would have been trying to show off his money, not save it.

"And your footware," Holmes went on. "Shoes and boots and no doubt slippers. Those that I saw were all your own."

This too I had to admit. "I couldn't stand anything else on my feet."

"Exactly, and a dead giveaway. Then there's the tobacco you smoke: A most amazing coincidence that Dr. Watson and Mr. Watkins should prefer the same brand. As for Lady Julia, in her earlier incarnation, was she the buxom widow who was so touchingly attached to you? Mrs. Watson will be highly amused."

"She will be, I wasn't."

"No doubt. That the lady was playing a part to the hilt was certainly obvious even in the brief moments that I saw her. An adventuress, I thought, and that was all. Of course I knew no more of Lord Ashley's domestic affairs than that he had a wife. He never spoke of her."

"That indeed touches the heart of their problem. As to what will happen now. . . ."

"Sleep," Holmes replied. As we stretched out, he murmured, "I won't deny that I'm glad to see you, Watson. Even though I would give much to know you were safe in London."

"I am where I chose to be," I replied. "I and Mary."

The next day Lady Julia once more insisted that she carry her own pack. Again Lord Ashley replied, in tones of utter indifference, "Whatever you wish, my dear," and so we set off.

Before the sun was overhead, she stumbled over a root and fell heavily. Without a word, Lord Ashley pulled her up, neatly removed her pack, slung it over his shoulder with his own, and continued on.

I offered her my arm, but the grim lady would have none of it. She continued at her husband's heels until early in the afternoon, when she quite simply collapsed.

Without either comment or a glance, Lord Ashley said, "We will camp here," and, dropping both packs, set off into the first outcroppings of the forest.

Up to then we had had to be very careful with our water. Now as we approached the forest we were accompanied by a tiny stream.

While our sole pot heated for tea, Holmes and I retired behind some bushes, and there both bathed and scrubbed our sweat-soaked clothes, emerging mightily refreshed.

When I took Lady Julia a mug of tea, I urged her to do the same. She only looked up at me with shadow-smudged eyes. If she wished, I offered, Holmes and I would remain where she could see us, with backs turned. Still there was no response: She was too far gone in exhaustion. I held the mug to her lips, and she drank, eagerly once she had tasted the hot sweetness.

"We must save the little sugar we have for her tea," I said to Holmes. "It seems the only sweetness the poor lady will have."

At that moment Lord Ashley returned, tossing down the small rabbit that he had shot and skinned.

While Holmes began preparing the meat for the fire, I told Lord Ashley what had happened.

"Thank you, Doctor," he said distantly, and walked over to where his wife lay, eyes shut, in the shade. Without a word he picked her up bodily and impersonally, placed her neatly in the stream, and left her there. I think she would have thanked him if he had remained to hear her; he did not.

By the time the rabbit was cooked, Lady Julia had returned to her blankets. We men ate heartily, she not a bite. She can't go on much longer, I thought helplessly. I thought of the medications in my bag, and discarded the idea: There was nothing there for exhaustion better than sweet tea, and nothing at all for a broken heart.

For the next couple of days our travel time was little over three or four hours, even that done with a slow pace and frequent stops. As soon as Lady Julia could go no farther without assistance (and she still would accept none), Lord Ashley would leave Holmes and me to make camp and would vanish into the now thickening trees.

On the third evening he returned with a bird of some kind, still warm in the leaf wrappings in which it had been cooked. He cut off a wing and breast and put it in front of his wife. Whether it was because it was food that he had not provided, or only the succulent aroma it gave off, she took the meat into her fingers and began to eat eagerly.

While we dined so sumptuously, Lord Ashley told us his news. He had made contact with some of his little friends, impressing upon them the danger of Barker and any who followed him. They assured Lord Ashley that they knew that the "forest-hated one" (so they named Barker) was not far away and moving fast.

"Then you have succeeded!" I exclaimed. "You have reached them first and warned them."

Lord Ashley shook his head. "It's not quite that simple," he said sadly. "You see, whatever the Pygmies were once, for a long time they have been becoming increasingly dependent on their larger neighbors. They trade fowl such as this, nuts and berries, fish from the river for the grain that they can't grow. For tools, for other things too.

"They can forgo such bartering for a time, no more. All Barker has to do is wait, wait until he can grab another of them at the forest's edge, and then do some trading of his own: That one's freedom—or quick death—in return for the secret of the Congo gold."

The little color there had been in Lady Julia's face drained away, leaving the healing bruise on her cheek a still livid mark. Holmes had gone rigid, and I swore. Yes, even in the presence of Lady Julia, who I'm sure at that moment was not even aware of my presence.

"What did you intend doing?" she asked her husband in a low voice. "If you had arrived earlier?"

"Get them well supplied first, and then off into the depths of the forest. And so bribe the neighboring tribes that they would shun Barker. He could have been starved out."

After that we all remained silent for many moments. Indeed, there seemed nothing to say.

Then Lady Julia made one of those lightning changes that had frozen Lord Ashley. She sat up very straight as if perched daintily on a parlor chair, wiped her slender hands on her much-stained handkerchief, and spoke in the pure tones of the drawing-room hostess. "I must call on your little friends," she said to her husband. "They have made me the gift of this excellent fowl, and I must thank them."

I could feel Holmes, sitting beside me, jerk with shock. I'm sure I had done the same, for to me this performance was perilously close to insanity.

"Very well," Lord Ashley replied, as if from the Arctic. "I will take you there in the morning."

"I would prefer going now."

Ever since I have wondered what would have happened if we had set out then and there. It was only late afternoon; we could have made the journey and remained with the Pygmies overnight.

All this is, of course, beside the point, which was the bitter struggle going on between those two. To him, his African life had always been all; for her, she had discovered that her husband had entered on an expedition of particular danger to him, and that he had done so without a word to her. Therefore, with that incalculable firmness of women, she had decided that she would make him *aware of her*, if only for once and only at the last. She would die to achieve that.

I had to end this. "I would very much like to see the Pygmies myself," I said, which was true. "But I feel that I am too weary to make the attempt today," which was not.

"Dr. Watson is weary," Lord Ashley said to his wife, his voice at its most reasonable. "Had we not better wait until morning?"

"Of course," Lady Julia replied at once, giving me the most gracious of little smiles.

So we had mugs of tea and rested, and set out shortly before dawn.

The forest in its depths was all that I had imagined. I felt alien, moving through unknown forces, all of which wore shades of green, gray and brown. The growth thickened until I realized that I could no longer see any sign of the sun, except in the luxuriant growth that enclosed us.

I could make progress only by keeping close to Lady Julia, and she only because of the grasp on her wrist of her husband's firm hand. As for Holmes, he was revealing more of his amazing resources. He maintained a varied pace, often being right behind me, often beside Lady Julia, and even at times a few steps ahead of Lord Ashley, apparently able to discern to me the invisible path that lay under our feet.

I later asked him how he had been able to do this. "By the feeling," he replied. "By the feeling of the forest."

That there certainly was. There were the cries of birds, scurryings of small creatures, now and then the glimpse of something wiggling over a root. But it was far more than this, was formed of all the life that existed there, that had existed there for eons beyond man's very existence, white or black, large or small.

We were soon forced to bend nearly double in order to duck below the branches and vines that would otherwise have brought us to a quick and entangled halt. Then abruptly Lord Ashley straightened and stepped forward, pulling Lady Julia after him.

We were in a clearing, with small conical huts of woven mats set all around the outer edge, each with a single opening facing inward. In the center of the clearing, stones held a handful of glowing coals—glowing only, with not a wisp of smoke rising. In every space that was not otherwise needed, the natural vegetation had been left undisturbed so that the huts and even the fire appeared to be nestled into beds of waving green. A jungle garden of Eden it indeed appeared.

Waiting for us were the residents of this green paradise, from half a dozen babies and children to an aged grandmother who was obviously the heart core of them all. She was brought forward to greet Lady Julia, and an instant mutual fascination resulted. Quickly Lady Julia was kneeling like a girl, and the old woman was stroking her face with her wrinkled old fingers.

What, I am often asked, were the Pygmies like?

Small, certainly, the tallest man nearly a foot shorter than I, and any of the women able to fit under my outstretched arm. Their skin was a dark golden brown, of a hue not unlike our own when deeply tanned. Their hair was black and somewhat coarse so that it held firmly the ornaments pushed into it, feathers, seeds, bit of vegetation. (No gold anywhere, none.) One child sported something like a tiny pink orchid above one perfect ear. None wore clothing except for a sort of short skirt of woven grass and bark, of so many different styles that the design was obviously a matter of individual taste.

Smiles there were everywhere, as we were escorted from hut to hut on an inspection tour, as we were invited to share a meal. Logs were placed for us to sit on—they sat on the ground, with a grace that we could never imitate—and the earth around was carefully patted to make sure that nothing was there that would imperil our gigantic feet. They were *tender* of us, all of them.

Did they understand the danger in which they lay? Even after the seizure and rescue of the girl, did they understand how their little patches of refuge were threatened? Looking at the children clustered before Lady Julia, who was playing patty-cake with them, I doubted it. Looking at the women absorbed in pulling roasted nuts out of the fire, I doubted it. Looking at the men bowing to us as they offered their food, I very much doubted it.

And I have never been more wrong.

The meal was delicious, though also alarming: The main dish was a kind of porridge, flavored with herbs I had never before tasted, and cooked in a large ceramic pot. Neither grain nor pottery was part of Pygmy culture, I knew; these they had obtained by the trade that kept them in steady contact with their neighbors, that took them steadily outside the security of their forest. Could even Lord Ashley make them understand, and that very quickly, that they must flee into the green depths, and remain there?

When the time came for our leaving, when the last child had been plucked from our persons by their laughing parents, we were led to a path different from that that had brought us here. Even

Lord Ashley didn't then understand the reason for this; it was simply what the Pygmies wished. Indeed, we had little choice, for, while they clustered around us, holding back branches and pushing aside vines to make our passage easy, they were also gently and inexorably bumping us forward.

I did notice that, while I and the Ashleys were laughing with our hosts, enjoying these last moments of green peace, Holmes was unexpectedly tense. His keen eyes never stopped probing the growth all around us, and he kept close to Lady Julia.

We had moved along the new path for perhaps fifty feet when, from somewhere, he burst among us: Karl Barker.

Whatever entourage he might have started with, he was alone now, and worn far past our own battered state, his hair and beard a tangled mass of twigs and dirt, his clothes in tatters. But there was nothing wrong with the rifle on his shoulder, or the knife that gleamed at his waist. He had launched himself right at Lady Julia, and already his massive hands had closed on her.

What, I remember distractedly thinking in those seconds, what would Lord Ashley pay for his wife's safety? All he had, I was sure, all he had of material goods. Would he also pay with betrayal of his little friends? For that would be Barker's price, of that I was instantly sure.

My wild thoughts had taken no account of Holmes. Alone of us he had been alert to all around, and even as Barker's grasp fastened on Lady Julia's shoulders, Holmes' steel fingers had enclosed her waist. With a mighty lift he swung her free and into Lord Ashley's arms.

With a roar of fury, Barker turned and coiled to spring back at the attack. His very movement made the ground collapse around him, and, with a shriek, he plunged out of our sight.

The pit into which he had fallen seemed incredibly deep, and in truth it was all of ten feet and probably equally wide at the bottom; at the top it was no more than half that, for the sides had been most perfectly, most cruelly inversely slanted. More, these sides bristled from top to bottom with sharpened stakes whose hard points gleamed wetly.

"Poison," I heard myself whisper.

"From some kind of viper, I should think," Holmes answered as softly.

"The Pygmies make such a thing?"

Holmes gave a small shrug. "They trade, remember, for what they need."

All this while, Barker had been screaming. Not the roaring yell of surprise he had emitted as his feet had plunged into space. This was the high scream of enormous and unending pain.

His huge shape rolled and jerked in and out of our sight, his face contorted so that the frantic mouth was torn at the corners, the eyes bulged sightless, blood streamed from the ruptured ears. His limbs were twisting so that the joints must have been bursting; at one second he was bent double, at the next flung straight up.

Certainly his rifle was down there somewhere with him, also his knife. Neither could aid him in the slightest, for even when he landed on that deep earth he had been past the muscular control needed to use either. He screamed; on and on he screamed. All that was left to him was to scream, to suffer and to scream.

Lord Ashley barked a few words to one of the Pygmies, clustered still and watchful around the edge of the pit, and was answered. "He says that it will take some hours for Barker to die."

"Can't we. . . ." I began and then stopped, for even if the Pygmies would permit us, we could do nothing. We couldn't climb down past those poisoned bayonet-like points, nor could Barker climb up even with a rope. If I threw down the package of opium that I had in my medical box, he would neither understand its use nor be able to swallow the contents. There was nothing that we could do.

Except what Lady Julia did. From within the shelter of her husband's arms, she somehow slipped out her little revolver, leveled it and fired, down, into the pit.

With a single wet choke, the screams abruptly ceased.

"I cannot stand suffering," Lady Julia said, as if in apology. She was looking at the Pygmies, and they—they understood something that made them incline their heads to her.

WE WERE ESCORTED safely to the edge of the forest, our packs filled with food. When we left, the little girl took the pink flower from her hair and pressed it into Lady Julia's short locks, and the old grandmother blessed her.

Later, after we had made camp and Lord Ashley had stretched out beside his wife, much closer than had yet occurred on this fateful journey, she asked, "What did the old woman say?"

"She said," he replied, "that they would hold a feast 'to rejoice the forest' because of what you did. They don't like suffering either, you see, but thought that in this case the forest required that they inflict it."

At that Julia gave a soft little sound that made Holmes and I move our blankets to a tactful distance.

UPON OUR ARRIVAL back in England, Lord Ashley began giving so many accounts of his latest trip to Africa, in all saying that he had seen no sign of any gold, that interest in the subject quickly subsided. Never had the man's integrity been put to better use: If he told only partial truth, he did that most convincingly.

Some six months later the papers reported that Karl Barker seemed to have gone missing somewhere in the Congo. The general opinion was that this was good riddance to some very bad rubbish, and that was that.

Within the following year two more items appeared. The first said that Lord Ashley was planning another expedition to the Congo, and that Lady Julia would accompany him. (This made quite a stir among the lady columnists, and Lady Julia was commissioned to write innumerable articles.)

The second paragraph of news was that this same lady had edited a full edition of her husband's travel diaries, and that they would soon be published. A reserve list for the first copies was already nearly full.

So much had been gained by that horrendous journey.

Not to forget that Lady Julia and Mary have become close friends, and that Mrs. Jones is a topic of unceasing amusement to them both.

THE REMARKABLE WORM

Carolyn Wheat

"THINK OF IT, Holmes!" I cried, lifting my eyes from the single sheet of vellum. "Immortalized in wax!" My chest puffed out like a pouter pigeon and my voice betrayed a not, I think, unpardonable pride.

Who among us has not whiled away an afternoon gazing at the famous and the infamous? Who has not thrilled to the sight of the Prince of Wales, mounted upon his elephant, leveling his shotgun at the crouching tiger, poised to spring? Who has not escorted a lady to the evening musical promenade, or paid the extra sixpence to visit "the special room" in that vast establishment in the Marylebone Road?

Who, in short, has not visited Madame Tussaud's Museum of Waxworks? And who would not be flattered to be included among the parade of notables London offers to the provincial visitor?

The letter in question was from none other than Mr. John Tussaud, and it contained an invitation to visit the museum as his guest so that he might discuss the prospect of Holmes sitting for a wax simalcrum commemorating the sensational Blackfriars affair.

"Immortalized in wax," Sherlock Holmes repeated in a derisive tone, yet the hint of a smile told me he was not unmoved by the request. "A poor sort of immortality, to be sure. One candle held too close by a careless servant and I shall melt like butter in the sun. An ephemeral monument at best, my dear Watson."

"But, Holmes, think of the honor." I leaned forward in my chair, the newspaper I had been reading scattered at my feet. The fire blazed nicely, driving off the early spring chill. A wan sunlight struggled to make its way through thick, yellow fog. "Think of the people who will see, at last, tangible proof of the efficacy of your method of scientific detection."

A twitch of smile around the lips, a flash of humor in the cold gray eyes, a lift of the eyebrow and a single, barked "Ha!" greeted my words. "So the vast unwashed public will finally grasp the seriousness of my work by virtue of my statue appearing in a wax museum?" He illustrated his words with a wave of his slender hand, its fingers stained with chemicals. He had been up all night experimenting with a new test for metallic poisons, and the sitting-room reeked of some unholy brew.

"I had thought my photograph on the front page of the *Daily Fishwrapper* conveyed all the notoriety a man could want, but apparently I was mistaken. Fresh heights await. I suppose that upon my death, I shall be stuffed and mounted like the unfortunate elephant upon which the Prince of Wales rides in his tableau."

"Surely Mr. Tussaud's desire to include you in the Blackfriars exhibit is a tribute to your contribution in that unfortunate matter, and will be a lesson to all criminals that when Sherlock Holmes enters the case, all hope is lost."

My friend raised a single eyebrow. "Do you think many criminals visit the museum?" He lay supine on the sofa, clad in his most disreputable dressing-gown, completely spent by his night of debauchery among the test tubes. Another smile lurked around the edges of his mouth, and then disappeared as quickly as it had formed.

"As to that, I cannot say." I smiled in return, convinced now that Holmes meant to avail himself of the invitation. "I do have it on good authority that their relations visit rather often. I remember a young female patient of mine at Bart's telling me that her family took her to the museum every month, as a special treat, to visit her uncle Bertram." I raised my voice in imitation. " 'And natural as life 'e looked, too, even if 'e did 'ave the 'angman's rope round 'is neck.' "

Holmes did me the honor of another barked laugh. "Well, at least I shall be spared that indignity," he said, "although I do have reservations about being portrayed on all fours with a magnifying glass in my hand."

"But, Holmes," I protested, "that is precisely the way you solved the case. Had it not been for the single scarlet thread you discovered on the Turkey carpet, that monster should have escaped unpunished. The tangled skein that was the Blackfriars affair would never have been, er, untangled." I forbore to mention my own small part in the solution of those bizarre and tragic events which began with a misdelivered box of chocolates and ended with three deaths. I had rather hoped that if any such invitation ever arrived from the wax museum that I should be included in the display, but apparently, this was not to be.

"Very well, Watson," my friend said, raising himself from his supine position and speaking as if offering a treat to a child, "let us stroll around the corner and visit Mr. Tussaud's exhibition."

A quarter of an hour later, Holmes having dressed in haste, we stepped into a still, thick blur of fog, making our way slowly, handkerchiefs over our mouths, hands outstretched ahead of us to warn oncoming pedestrians. It was like walking through yards of cotton wool. Had our destination been further away. I should have begged Holmes to put off the appointment. Only the sounds of slow-moving horses told us when we approached a street-corner, for we could see neither carriages nor cabs, just hazy blurs clip-clopping past us in the wan sunlight.

When we reached the museum Holmes gave our names to the uniformed doorman who bowed and admitted us. "Mr. Flintridge has arranged to meet you in the Hall of Kings. On your left at the top of the stairs, gentlemen."

We shed our topcoats and handed them to an attendant, climbed the great marble staircase, and stepped into the cavernous hall where royalty deigned to appear for the delectation of commoners. There was our Prince of Wales, his elephant, and his tiger. There was our Queen, dressed all in black, a tiny figure that radiated a powerful personality despite being made of wax. I could have remained for hours, but Holmes strode into the next room without so much as a glance at the resplendent tableaux.

The next chamber was devoted to world statesmen, great thinkers, inventors and captains of industry. There stood Voltaire, wearing long curls, an ornately embroidered waistcoat, and a sardonic smile. Lord Beaconsfield, his famous curl centered on his broad forehead, stood facing Mr. Gladstone, each looking more pleased to be in the other's company than either would have been in life.

A small man with a broad moon face and an obsequious smile stepped toward us. "Cecil Flintridge, at your service," he said with a low bow. "Twenty-six years I've been with the Madame, sir, twenty-six years. I shall be most pleased to show you where you'll be standing, so to speak, and then to lead you to the workroom where you'll sit for your portrait."

"Who is that gentleman carrying handcuffs?" I asked, pointing to a figure whose breeches and powdered wig proclaimed him a man of the last century. "Shouldn't he be in the Chamber of Horrors?"

"Oh, no, Doctor Watson," our host replied with a smile. "That's Abraham Darby, the ironmaster who built the bridge at Coalbrookdale."

"He made handcuffs as well," Holmes pointed out. "*Put the darbies on him*, say the police officers, though I doubt many of them know why they say it."

"Of course," I said. "I should have known. And is that Malachi Westover next to him?" I gestured at the figure of a man with a beaked nose, long fair hair streaked with gray, and pince-nez glasses suspended from a ribbon around his neck. "Surprised he sat for a wax image at all, given his reputation as a recluse."

"Mr. Westover was right as rain when he sat for us," Flintridge replied. "It was only later that he began turning a bit"—the little man lowered his voice and leaned in so close I could smell the tobacco smoke on his breath—"odd."

"From what I've read," I continued, "he's more than just odd. Moved out of his manor house into a crofter's cottage. Won't let anyone in to see him, not the directors of his firm or members of his family. He's as afraid of poison as a Roman emperor."

"A man of his immense wealth must always fear that someone will cheat him of it," Holmes replied.

Our guide led us to the Chamber of Horrors, where Holmes' replica was to stand. He signaled the ticket-taker that we were to be allowed in without paying the extra sixpence.

"And here, gentlemen," the little man said with a bow and a flourish, "you will see the wickedest villains in the annals of crime." He spoke with a pronounced lisp, spraying his words through a servile smile, obviously relishing his role as master of ceremonies.

The murderers stood in a row, each holding his particular instrument of death, like medieval martyrs embracing the means of their martyrdom. There stood Charlie Peace, the most infamous villain of old London. Next to him, Burke and Hare, shovels in hand, plied their awful grave-robbing trade.

"Taken from life, they were," Flintridge said in a whisper. "Death masks made just after the hangman finished with them."

I could not name the others in the room, but Holmes, whose large brain contained its own Chamber of Horrors, greeted them like old friends.

"The woman over there," he said, pointing to a stout party in a drab gray dress, "is Mary Ann Cotton. She murdered twenty people, but was convicted of only six."

"Poison, I suppose?" Holmes and Flintridge both nodded. "A woman's weapon," I remarked.

"And a doctor's as well," my companion replied, pointing to a well-dressed figure carrying a medical bag. "Dr. Palmer used strychnine to dispatch his victims."

Holmes was a walking calendar of crime, but he met his match in Cecil Flintridge. The little man recited chapter and verse of every murderer in the Black Room and the two were soon comparing notes like connoisseurs discussing vintage wines.

Colored glass mantles shielded the gas-lamps, which were placed low so as to throw lurid shadows upon the faces of the wax figures. The flickering light wavered across the deadly instruments, creating almost the illusion of movement. Then one of the figures leaned toward me, polished ax in hand, and I jumped backward with a grunt I heartily wished I could have repressed.

"Not to worry, sir," Cecil Flintridge said with his smarmy smile. "It's only the Underground, sir. Comes through every twenty minutes, and gives a bit of a shake to the Murderers' Row. Gives one a proper start, though, don't it?"

A shiver ran down my spine. Holmes saw it and said in a crisp, decisive tone, "Yes, Watson, you are right. It is exceedingly cold in here. Let us repair to the workroom and begin the tedious business of sitting."

Little Mr. Flintridge looked crestfallen, as if we had failed to properly appreciate the treat he had offered us. He led us to the workroom on the ground floor, stopping at the refreshment room to order a pot of tea and a plate of sandwiches.

The unadorned room was as extraordinary a sight as anything on display in the public rooms, for on shelves lining the walls sat arms, legs, hands, and heads awaiting joining into whole figures. Wigs of every color and style rested upon the heads, and in the corner sat several clay molds drying under cheesecloth covers.

The sculptor wiped his hands on his apron and stepped forward. "My name is John Tussaud," he said with a smile.

"You are a descendant of the late Madame Tussaud, I take it?" Holmes inquired.

"Great-grandson, Mr. Holmes. And let me say what a pleasure it is to welcome you to the museum. We shall be honored to present you to the public."

The sitting proved to be as tedious as any such sedentary activity must be. Holmes was asked to turn his head this way and that, to stand and walk and hold his hand steady while John Tussaud sketched in charcoal and sculpted a rough clay head.

"The clay is a mold," he explained, "which will be filled with wax. After the wax has solidified, the face will be painted, the glass eyes put in place, and a wig affixed. Then it will be set upon the body and you will be a whole man, Mr. Holmes."

Try as I might, I could not rid myself of an unworthy disappointment at not being made part of the tableau. I firmly pushed all such considerations out of my mind and asked Mr. Tussaud if the rumor I'd heard regarding Mr. Gladstone was correct. "Did he really ask for a copy of his head so that he might have it cast as a bust?"

"Yes, indeed," Mr. Tussaud replied, "although it was my father, not I, who did the sculpting. He's all but retired now. It is a source of pride to the family that some of our sitters have requested to be given their heads, as it were. Mr. Gladstone is not the only man to have made such a request."

"When will the exhibit be unveiled?"

"The tableau will be completed in March," Tussaud said. "That is, it will be if Harald Blackfriars is executed as scheduled. We like to take a death mask of the deceased so as to render the exhibit as accurate as possible."

"I am delighted that my replica will not be quite as accurate as his," Holmes remarked.

As we passed through yet another chamber of notables on our way to the exit, an old man with a rich Yorkshire accent lifted his cane at the figure of Pitt the Younger and, in the overloud voice of the deaf, said, "And wot did that feller do?"

"Nothing, Grandfather," a harried-looking young man in a tweed coat shouted into the old man's ear. "He was Prime Minister, don't you remember?"

Apparently under the impression that all denizens of the museum were criminals of one stripe or another, the old countryman cried, "Yes, but 'oo'd 'e kill, lad? 'Ood 'e kill?"

The fog had lifted a bit; our walk back around the corner to Baker Street required no handkerchief over the face or outstretched hand. As we neared our rooms, I stopped to buy a paper from a sharp-faced newsboy.

The irony contained in the lead story overwhelmed me and I stood motionless for a moment, oblivious to the sights and sounds around me.

"What is it, Watson?" Holmes inquired.

"You remember my talking of Malachi Westover, the industrialist?"

Holmes glanced at the newspaper, noted the headline WESTOVER DEAD IN KENT and remarked, "He was an old man. His death must have been expected."

"But it is not he who has died." I pointed to the small print in the body of the article. "His son George, who has headed the firm these past seven years, is dead."

"Is there any mention of foul play?" Holmes' keen eyes studied my face for a response.

I shook my head. "The local doctor says it was gastric fever."

Holmes made no reply. We returned home in silence, but I was aware that my companion had made a mental note of the sudden death, in case any question of murder should arise. As was his custom, he would cut the article from the newspaper and keep it in his commonplace book in the event that his services were required.

It was nearly a month later that the name Westover was once again brought to our attention. George Westover's death, while plunging his company into disarray and causing a momentary panic in the City, was not declared murder and the matter soon ceased to occupy either of our minds.

Holmes had made several trips back to Madame Tussaud's since our visit. After one such session, he remarked, "It is given to few men to view their legs in one place, their arms in another, and their head duplicated twice over. I am told I shall soon be in one piece, but the effect, if I may say so, is rather disconcerting."

The door opened and Mrs. Hudson, our landlady, stepped into the room. "Mr. Holmes," she said, a touch of hauteur in her usually even tones, "there is a young person asking to see you. I told her to wait while I inquired whether you were at home."

"By all means admit her, Mrs. Hudson," Holmes replied. "I make no distinction in my work between master and servant, mistress and maid, and if this young domestic seeks my help, she shall have it."

The young woman who entered the room upon Mrs. Hudson's invitation wore a violet walking dress with a matching hat whose dyed ostrich feather danced up and down. She stepped into the room with a shy smile and stood at attention, as if waiting for permission to speak.

"Pray take a seat," Holmes said with an expansive gesture toward the chair nearest the fire. "Other than the fact that you are a house parlormaid-in-training, that you have come up from Kent on your day out, and that you were engaged to be married, I know nothing."

"My day out? And who told you I was here on my day out?" The girl, who looked barely eighteen, placed her hands on her hips and stood facing Holmes, challenge in her dark eyes and set mouth. "Who told you I was from Kent, come to that?"

"Why, you yourself have told me everything I need to know," my companion replied. He tossed his cigarette into the fire and continued, "You are a young woman, yet I heard you ascending the stairs slowly and painfully. You suffer from a condition known as housemaid's knee, caused by long hours spent kneeling on hard, cold surfaces.

"The rest is shown by your hands." Holmes glanced down at the girl's ungloved hands; she blushed and hid them behind her back. "They are finer than the hands of a housemaid; you do not immerse them in hot water."

He reached out before she could protest, grasped her right hand, and turned it over. "I see three separate burn marks, made at different times, on three different fingers. You shall have to improve your skill at hairdressing if you want to move up the domestic ladder. Ladies are wary of a maid who burns herself with the curling iron."

"Well, my lady's happy for me to learn," the girl replied, a stubborn frown on her pert little face.

"So long as you burn your own fingers and not her head, I suppose," Holmes replied. "Do, please, take a seat, miss, and enlighten us as to why you are here."

"Kent." The girl thrust her chin out at Holmes. "Tell me how you know I came up from Kent."

"I could discuss the color of the mud upon your new boots," he said in a languid tone, "or I might remark upon your delightful accent, but the truth is, I can see a ticket from Tunbridge Wells poking out of your reticule."

"Oh, well, anyone could have seen that," she said with a toss of her dusky curls.

"If you have so little faith in my deductive ability," Holmes replied, "why have you come to see me?"

"Because I can't stand it no more, Mr. Holmes." The dark eyes filled with tears. "I've served the family these twelve years, since I was a child, and I've stood it all, old Mr. Malachi's odd ways, and poor little Daniel's illness, and now Mr. George's death, but I just can't go on! I love Miss Sophie, but I can't keep quiet anymore. For her sake, for everyone's sake, you must help us!"

Holmes turned away in disgust and motioned to me to see to the girl. Any outpouring of feminine emotion brought out the worst in him. It was his fond belief that I knew how to handle women, so I guided her to the chair, handed her a handkerchief, and fetched a glass of water.

"My name," the little maid said after recovering herself, "is Cherry Jones, short for Charity because I was a charity girl. Miss Sophie's mother brought me to Westerleigh Grange when I was a slip of a girl, and I was that pleased to leave the workhouse and learn a trade and live in such a fine house. The family was so happy then, Mr. Holmes, you can't imagine."

"Mr. Malachi Westover still resided in the main house at that time, I presume," Holmes said.

"Oh, yes, sir. He was lord of the manor then, dressed as fine as any man in the county. Went to the City on weekdays and gave fine parties and balls on the weekends. Had any number of house-parties, him and his missus. She was a fine lady, was old Mrs. West-over, and it was her death that started him going mad." She blushed slightly and lowered her eyes. "We servants aren't supposed to speak of him as mad, but madness is as madness does, and when you hear how Mr. Malachi chooses to live, I think you'll agree that he's mad as a hatter, Mr. Holmes."

"I have heard a few tales about him myself," I said. "One of the gentlemen who frequents the Turkish bath on Northumberland Street is a banker, and he has visited Westerleigh Grange on several occasions to have documents signed."

"Then you know Mr. Malachi no longer lives in his own house," the maid said. "He moved into a cottage after his wife died. Lives there all by himself, won't allow any servants inside, not to clean or cook. Someone brings him his meals on a tray; he eats the food and leaves the tray outside when he's done."

"And is this what you mean when you say you can't stand it any longer?" Holmes asked, raising a single eyebrow. "Are you the one who brings his meals? Has he behaved badly toward you?"

"Oh, no, Mr. Holmes." The girl shook her head and the ostrich feather danced. "I've nothing to do with old Mr. Malachi. It's Muriel who brings his food, Muriel and only Muriel. He won't allow anyone else to come close, though Muriel's as slow and stupid as a cow. He takes fancies like that, does Mr. Malachi."

The color rose in her cheeks and she turned away for a moment, then gave Holmes a direct stare. "He took a fancy against my Jem. That's the young man I was engaged to, though I still don't know how you knew that. Mr. Malachi had him sacked just for walking near his cottage, and I know Jem never looked inside, never snooped around. Knew it would cost him his place if he did. He was just walking back to the barn with Miss Sophie's horse, and he passed too close to the cottage. Next thing I knew, he was sacked and my engagement broken because how could he support a wife when he'd been let go without a character?"

Holmes frowned. "You say that Malachi Westover 'had him sacked.' Do you mean that he discharged the young man in person?"

"No, sir," the little maid replied. "Mr. Malachi does everything by notes. He puts a light in the window when he wants Muriel, and she goes to the cottage. Then he slips a note under the door, which she picks up and brings to the main house. When Mr. George was alive, he read the notes and did what his father wanted. When he died so sudden-like, it was Mrs. Halloway, the housekeeper, who carried out the orders in the note."

"What is the situation at Westerleigh Grange at present?" Holmes inquired.

"Mrs. Elizabeth is prostrate with grief, sir. She loved Mr. George, and with him gone, she don't seem to have a reason to live. My Miss Sophie is so upset she's made herself ill. Can't eat anything, and can't keep down what little she does eat. Nothing's the same as it was, sir, and it's all because Mr. Malachi's running mad."

"What you say is highly suggestive, Miss Jones," Holmes said, steepling his fingers and staring at her with intense gray eyes. "But I believe you are holding something back, something I must hear from your own lips."

The girl's face flamed; she lowered her eyes and murmured something I had to bend low to hear. "I think Mr. Malachi killed his own son," she said. "I don't know how, but I do know that my Jem saw him out of his cottage the night Mr. George died, and he was coming from the kitchen."

"That is what I wanted to hear," Holmes replied. "Gastric fever is what the local doctor called it, but the death was so sudden, so unexpected, that poison must be suspected. Thank you for confirming what I had already come to believe."

"Then you'll help me, Mr. Holmes?" The little maid's simple, honest faith in Holmes was something I dearly hoped he could live up to.

"I shall leave at once," he replied. "We must pursue all avenues of inquiry to reach the bottom of these mysterious events."

The game was afoot.

THE KENTISH WEALD was tinged with early spring green, welcome after months of dreary London winter. Tufts of white cloud wandered across a sky the color of a robin's egg. Now and then we passed sheep grazing on grass made greener by recent rains. Oast houses made of brick, their tall cylindrical roofs pointing to the sky, dotted the landscape and I thought longingly of fresh, home-brewed ale, the most popular product of the county. As Holmes had little appreciation either of nature or of beer, I said nothing until the train came to a halt at the Tunbridge Wells station, which stood opposite the Calverley grounds on Mt. Pleasant Road.

Holmes and I stepped out of our compartment and commandeered a cart to take us to the Mount Ephraim Hotel, which despite its imposing name, turned out to constitute little more than rooms over the pub.

"Fear not, Watson," my companion said in a hearty tone, "the beer will be far better than we would receive at a more ostentatious hostelry, and when one is in Kent, one must by all means sample the local product."

"Ah, you won't do better'n the Rabbit, and that's a plain fact, gents," the hack driver agreed, giving the bays a flick of the reins. "Best stout in the county, even if I do say it as shouldn't, since me old dad taps the kegs."

After a short drive along muddy cart-tracks, he pulled up to a tavern with the sign HARE AND HOUNDS swinging in front of a small door. A larger door to the side beckoned the visitor into the hotel portion of the building. The man unloaded our cases and pocketed a coin with a grin and a tip of his cap, then drove off in a clatter of hoofbeats on cobblestones.

"But, Holmes," I said in protest, "I have never known you to drink ale of any kind."

"A country pub is the center of local gossip, Watson," Holmes said as we entered the smaller door. "If we are discreet in our inquiries, we should come away from our visit with a complete picture of life at Westerleigh Grange, upstairs and downstairs alike. We shall know better how to evaluate little Cherry's suspicions."

The pub was redolent of malt. Four tap-handles stood like soldiers along a plain mahogany bar backed by a simple mirror. No London frills such as etched glass or carved wood enhanced the sturdy, plain look of the place, yet I suspected the nectar that flowed from the several taps would outshine anything I had drunk in the capital.

"I have heard the stout praised highly," I said to the landlord, who resembled our hack driver to a marked extent. "Pray let me sample a glass."

"Ah, well, sir," the white-haired man behind the bar said in a country accent even thicker than his son's, "my lad claims high for our brew, but I can't say he claims too high, especially if he's talking to Londoners. No beer there at all, sir, no beer at all."

The hint of a smile crossed Holmes' face. He requested a pint of bitter and asked our host, "And how do you know we are from London, and that we talked to your son?"

"As to London, sir," the white-haired man replied, "why the eleven-ten from Charing Cross stopped a scant fifteen minutes ago, and fifteen minutes is what it takes for the dog-cart to reach the Rabbit from the station. And the amount of mud you gents have on your legs is exactly what Bob's horses will kick up on a fine spring day such as this."

"Watson, I have met my match!" Holmes cried, lifting the glass of bitter to his lips and draining half of it in a single pull. "And I have drunk the finest ale I have ever sampled as well," he added, wiping suds from his lips.

"Thankee, sir," the barkeep answered with a smile that failed to reach his bright blue eyes, "but now, perhaps, you will do me the honor of explaining what a first-class detective from London is doing in my pub."

Holmes glanced at the two men sitting at the end of the bar and the three others gracing a table near the window. He leaned in close to our host and said in a low voice, "I have heard that things are not as they should be at Westerleigh Grange."

"Ah, so little Cherry's been to see you, has she?" The landlord smiled again, and this time the blue eyes twinkled. "She's a caution, isn't she?"

"Our host appears to be the Sherlock Holmes of Tunbridge Wells," I murmured.

"Is the girl correct?" Holmes asked, his voice sharp. "Is there something amiss at the Grange?"

"Old Malachi Westover had two sons, George and Charles," the landlord began, settling in to tell a tale as only a country barkeep can. "As alike as two peas, they was, and as different as night and day. Mr. George was the younger, and he was everything the old man could have wanted in an heir. Took a First at Cambridge and then followed his father into the business."

"The ironworks, you mean?" Holmes interjected. The barkeep nodded.

"Many a son with his education would have refused, but Mr. George knew what was due his father. Mr. Charles, though—" He shook his head sadly and lifted his glass to his lips. "Broke his father's heart. Never did anything to make his old dad proud. Drank and gambled and got sent down from school. Ran off with a woman and was never heard from again. Mr. Malachi was that angry, he cut his elder son out of his will. Told the world he was leaving it all to Mr. George."

"And George took over the family business, married, raised a family, did all that was expected of him?" Holmes asked. I noticed that after his first effusive praise, he did not touch the glass in front of him.

"Indeed he did, Mr. Holmes. Until he died just three weeks ago. Tragic."

"Who signed the death certificate?" Holmes inquired.

"Dr. Marshall of East Grimstead," the landlord replied.

Holmes thanked and paid the landlord. We left the pub and stepped out into the spring day. A stable nearby supplied us with an open carriage, and we drove along the muddy Mount Ephraim Road in companionable silence. I caught glimpses of apple trees in early bloom and my heart lifted at the thought of spring at last.

Westerleigh Grange was an imposing country house in the classical mode. Parkland and walled gardens surrounded the main house, which was made of softly colored brick with large white-trimmed windows. Black crepe hung across the doorway and a black wreath on the front door informed the world that this was a house of mourning.

A butler admitted us and led us to a fine drawing-room. In one corner sat a spinet with music propped upon a stand. In another sat a welcoming trio of chairs covered in chintz, next to a potted palm with fan-shaped leaves. Six framed photographs sat upon a desk, pictures of a young married couple and their small children. It seemed unbearably sad to think that two of these were dead: the handsome man who stood by the side of his bride, and the little boy sitting in his dog-cart.

A woman in a dress of dark gray wool entered the room on the silent feet of a well-trained servant. She wore no ornament save a large brass chatelaine that hung from her waist.

"May I ask what it is you gentlemen wish?" The words were non-committal, but the underlying tone was significantly unfriendly. "I hope you realize that my mistress is not to be disturbed on any trivial account."

"I assure you, we are here on no trivial matter," Holmes replied. "Indeed, it may well be a matter of life and death. I understand that the young mistress of this house is unwell?"

"Miss Sophie is being treated by her own doctor," the woman replied. She glanced at my doctor's bag and said, "I've not been told that London specialists were to be called in."

"I am not here in my medical capacity," I began, but then realized that if I could examine the young woman, we would be much closer to proving or disproving the question of poison. It did not require the intelligence of Holmes to realize that if the late George Westover had indeed been poisoned, his daughter's illness might be caused by the same agency.

Before the housekeeper could reply, her mistress entered the room. Elizabeth Westover was a tall, slender woman with chestnut hair piled high upon her head. She was dressed all in black, and her pale face showed evidence of the sorrow she had not yet learned to forget.

Holmes began with profuse sympathies for her loss, introduced himself, and proceeded to the business at hand. Without mentioning Cherry Jones, he informed her that questions had arisen regarding her husband's death.

"I do not know what you mean," the widow said, but her eyes were alarmed. "Dr. Marshall examined my husband and said that it was a natural death, and not entirely unexpected due to his lifetime of stomach complaints."

"I would like to talk with Dr. Marshall," I said.

"You shall do so. He is upstairs with my daughter as we speak."

"May we have leave to speak with one of your servants as well?" Holmes asked. The housekeeper visibly bristled, but kept her silence. "I refer to Muriel, the maid who waits upon your father-in-law."

"Mr. Holmes, I dearly loved my husband and I will do anything to see my daughter safe, but I cannot believe that there is anything here but hereditary illness. Pray conduct your inquiry as quickly and discreetly as you can, and then leave us in peace to mourn our dead."

She instructed Mrs. Holloway to bring Muriel to the drawing-room. A small man with snow-white hair and the bright bulbous nose of a habitual drinker descended the staircase and beckoned to Mrs. Westover. She spoke to him for a moment and then walked up the steps to see to her daughter.

Dr. Marshall proved to be one of those village doctors with old-fashioned views regarding illness. "Gastric fever's what I said at the time, sir. Gastric fever's what I wrote on the death certificate, and gastric fever's what I'll go to my grave believing," he pronounced. Mention of poison only brought on a long harangue about the difficulties of dealing with a wealthy madman and the venality of London detectives who made a point of seeing murder where no murder existed.

"Why, it was hereditary weakness of the stomach," the man grumbled. "Killed poor little Daniel when the boy was only sixteen. Look at the way Sophie's reacted to her father's death. Same symptoms as her father, only not as violent. Some people just have weak stomachs and that's all there is to it."

"Have you consulted an alienist regarding Malachi Westover's odd behavior?" I asked. "I know a very good man in Mayfair who specializes in such cases."

"Of course," the doctor replied with an impatient twitch of his white mustache. "No expense spared. Doctors from Harley Street, doctors from France, doctors from Germany. All agreed on one point—the man's mad as a March hare. No agreement at all on what to do about it. 'Give him his head' was my advice. He's not harming anyone, living like a hermit in his little cottage. Bring him his meals, keep the servants away from the cottage."

"Did you not consider performing a post-mortem examination of George Westover's body?" Holmes inquired. "It is usual in cases of sudden death from unexplained causes."

The old doctor shook his head. "No need for it," he replied. "I'd treated his dicky stomach for years. Knew what killed him. Bleeding ulcers. No need to cut him into pieces to see that."

"What would you say, Doctor, if I told you the man had been poisoned?"

"I'd say you were mistaken, or worse."

He stamped out of the house in an angry huff. Mrs. Holloway, who had apparently stood outside the double door with her charge, entered the moment he was gone. With her was a maid in her mid-twenties, blonde and pockmarked, with the large protruding blue eyes of a thyroid case.

"This is Muriel, gentlemen," she said. "I shall remain while you question her."

"Very well," Holmes replied. He turned his attention to the girl, who bit her lip nervously and twisted her red raw hands.

"You are the servant who waits upon Mr. Malachi, is that correct?"

"It is, sir. I am, sir. I don't know why, sir. He asks for me and I goes to him, but I never sees him, sir, not to talk to. I bring the dinner and I takes away the dishes, but I never has two words with him, nor one neither, and I don't know nothing about Mr. George's death, truly I don't."

Then she burst into tears.

Mrs. Holloway, her words polite but the look on her face one of barely controlled anger, showed us the door.

"That doctor should be stricken from the rolls," I said indignantly as we made our way back toward Tunbridge Wells. The sun was low in the sky and the air as chill as if winter had returned. "He's an old fool, and he's no more competent to practice medicine than young Cherry."

"I agree, Watson, but the absence of a post-mortem is most suggestive, is it not?"

"The death certainly sounds like poison," I agreed.

"Only a post-mortem will tell," Holmes said, his tone grim. "And there is no likelihood of obtaining permission from the Home Office. There is only one thing for it, and that is to exhume the body ourselves."

"Holmes!" I was driving; I pulled the reins so tight the horses bucked in protest. "We should be no better than Burke and Hare if we were to dig up dead bodies without official permission. I would be risking my medical license and your reputation would never recover if it came out that we did such a reckless thing."

"Watson, a young woman may be dying as we speak," my companion replied. His hawklike visage had never seemed more determined. "We can let her die, or we can obtain the evidence which will allow us to save her."

Put that way, there was only one answer I could make. At two o'clock that morning, two figures crept out of the Mount Ephraim Hotel, shovels in hand, and made their way slowly and silently toward the churchyard. One had a lantern in his hand, the other carried a glass jar and a scalpel.

We dug in silence. Six feet into the ground, I caught a glimpse of what looked like straw.

"Earth to earth," Holmes said with a groan. "Watson, we are too late."

"What do you mean?" I lifted more dirt and realized I was looking at a coffin made of wicker. I had never seen such a thing; most families chose to bury their dead in the sturdiest box they could afford.

"There is a school of thought abroad in the land that seeks to return a deceased corpse to the earth from which it sprang in the most efficacious way possible. This sect rails against embalming and chooses a coffin made of the least impenetrable material it can find. They want the corpse to decay."

The wicker had degraded to the point where open holes revealed the dead man's clothing. Under the clothing I saw the glint of bone in the flickering lantern light. The body of George Westover was a skeleton.

"They have succeeded in that ambition," I said, turning my eyes away from the moving clothing, knowing what it portended and not wishing to see the agents of decay at work.

"Perhaps," Holmes said, leaning closer to the body, "perhaps there is hope after all."

"What do you mean? We cannot test bones for traces of poison, and there is no tissue left."

Holmes donned his gloves and plunged his hands into the coffin. He emerged with maggots hanging from them like buds on a shrub.

I understood. I choked back my disgust and did what I realized had to be done. I held the open jar under his gloves and collected the writing worms. When the jar was half-full, I closed the lid on it. Holmes dropped the gloves directly into the coffin, closed it up, and we began to re-bury the body.

We returned to London by the ten-fifteen train, Holmes carrying the precious jar wrapped in a scarf so as not to alarm or disgust our fellow passengers.

London's noise and bustle presented a forcible contrast to the bucolic beauty of the country. Coal dust dulled the natural color of the building-stones, and everywhere there was the sound of carriages clattering along the pavement, workmen shouting as they unloaded barrels and boxes, and street vendors crying their wares.

We caught a hansom cab and set off for Baker Street, where the old deal-table, already acid-stained from previous experiments, came out of its closet and did duty again. Retorts sat on stands, bunsen burners glowed bright blue, and test tubes gave off noxious fumes, while the clinking of glass was heard. Mutterings like "aconite, aconite—could it be aconite?" or "gastric fever—they said it was gastric fever. Sounds like antimony. Let me try Marsh's test" came to my ears. The old brass microscope I had used as a medical student sat on the table; Holmes sliced bits of maggot, placed them carefully under glass slides, and peered through the double eye-pieces, then shook his head and went back to the test tubes.

I finally took myself to the Turkish bath on Northumberland Avenue for a quiet afternoon of steaming and smoking.

When I returned, Holmes lay on the sofa, exhausted and pale, his eyes glittering with the effects of the seven percent solution I tried so hard to discourage him from using. His fingers made arabesques in the air, as if he heard celestial music, but the room was silent.

"What have you found out?" I asked eagerly, for it seemed clear that he had obtained good results from his afternoon's work.

"George Westover died of acute poisoning. The maggots were riddled with arsenic; fatal to him, but innocuous to them."

"Then the old man has gone mad," I said sadly. "His fears have led him to murder his own son. Horrible."

"Perhaps," Holmes replied, "but I have set in motion other inquiries which I hope will shed light upon this dark matter. Tomorrow I take further steps. Only when all is clear shall I return to Westerleigh Grange and acquaint the family with the truth."

"Do you think they will listen to the truth?" I asked as I made my way to the cabinet and poured myself a brandy.

"I shall make them listen!"

SPRING HAD COME to the Kentish countryside and the train ride from Charing Cross was a pleasant blur of greens and pinks. We hired a cab at the Tunbridge Wells station and drove directly to Westerleigh Grange, passing through a magnificent column of elm trees in full bloom. The cadaverous butler bowed and admitted us, and I gathered that we were expected.

"Step this way, gentlemen," he said in his lugubrious voice. "Mrs. Westover and her brother, Colonel Phillips, await you in the drawing-room."

The colonel stood beside the mantelpiece, his heavy brows knitted, a black cigar in his hand. He frowned as we entered, as if he should like nothing more than to show us the door. His sister, whose black bombazine dress made her pale face look even more wan and drawn, sat on a chair next to the blazing fire. By her side, knitting in her lap, eyes discreetly downcast, sat the housekeeper, Mrs. Holloway.

"I have done what you asked," Elizabeth Westover said, offering Holmes her hand. "I have barred everyone from my daughter's room with the exception of Cherry Jones. I have made certain that she ate nothing that was not also sampled by someone else. Dr. Marshall assures me that she is indeed getting better, but I am still in the dark. Why were these precautions necessary, Mr. Holmes, and what do they mean?"

"This is a deep business," the detective replied. "I have news that will distress you greatly, Mrs. Westover, but it is information that you must hear."

"See here, Mr. Holmes," the colonel said in a belligerent tone,

"I won't have you alarming my sister like this. She has suffered a great loss in the death of her husband, and she needs rest and quiet, not detectives from London barging around, asking questions and disrupting her life."

"Hush, Robert," the lady of the house replied. She lay her hand upon her brother's sleeve. He nodded curtly and sat in a leather chair opposite his sister. "Very well," he said with ill grace, "pray tell us this distressing news if you must."

Holmes took a piece of paper out of his pocket. "Permit me," he said, addressing his words to Mrs. Westover, "to acquaint you with the last will and testament of Malachi Westover."

"What's the point of that?" Colonel Phillips burst out, a puzzled expression on his outdoorsman's face. "Malachi Westover is alive. What significance can his will have?"

"Patience, Colonel," Holmes said, raising an admonishing finger. "All will be revealed in due time."

"Malachi Westover's will," Holmes continued, "leaves everything to the testator's son George and nothing at all to his firstborn son, Charles, for reasons known to everyone in this room. If George predeceased his father, which was unfortunately the case, 'the heirs of George's body' inherit. The provision was meant to ensure that a Westover son would always own the business, but your son Daniel died two years ago, leaving your daughter as the sole heir of George's body."

Mrs. Westover, pale but composed, nodded. "And you think someone tried to poison my daughter."

"Precisely." Holmes fixed the company with his piercing gray eyes.

"But that makes no sense, man," Colonel Phillips interjected, his face red. "Who benefits if Sophie dies? No one, that's who. All this talk of poison is nonsense, based on a madman's ravings. I'm sorry, Elizabeth," he said, turning to his sister, "but Sophie's been ill, not poisoned, and George died of a stomach ailment. Nothing more."

"What would happen," Holmes went on, ignoring the outburst,

"to the Westover fortune if Sophie were to predecease her grand-father?"

"The entire estate would escheat to the government," Colonel Phillips replied. "Dashed waste, if you ask me, but that's the law."

"No, Colonel, the estate would not escheat," announced Holmes. "There is another living heir, and that heir is the murderer of your brother-in-law, your nephew, and the would-be murderer of your niece."

"How can that be?" Mrs. Westover cried, placing her hand over her mouth.

"The last will and testament of Malachi Westover contains a contingent remainder clause, worded as follows." He raised his voice. " 'In the event that the issue of George Westover does not survive me, I hereby give and bequeath the residue of any property of which I die possessed, whether real or personal, tangible or intangible, of whatever nature, to any and all heirs of the body who shall survive me, per stirpes.' "

"Legal mumbo jumbo," the colonel complained. "It means nothing. There is no other heir."

Holmes fixed the soldier with his keen gray eyes. "Nothing in that clause, sir, prevents a descendant of Mr. *Charles* Westover from inheriting."

"But old Malachi wrote Charles out of his will," protested the colonel.

"It is clear that the testator did not want Charles himself to inherit, nor did he make provision for any issue of Charles in the granting clauses." Holmes agreed, "but when it comes to residuary legatees, many a testator prefers to cast the net wide rather than allow the family fortune to escheat to the state."

"But no one knows who the heirs of Charles might be," Mrs. Westover said in a puzzled voice. "The brothers were estranged, and none of the family has had any contact with Charles' family."

"No such heir would even know the provisions of old Malachi's will," the colonel agreed.

"There is where you are wrong, Colonel." My friend was grave as he tamped the residue of his pipe into the fire grate. "I believe Charles Westover's heir knew perfectly well what her ancestor's will provided, and I believe she set in motion the events which would clear the way for her to inherit her great-grandfather's fortune."

"Why, who can you be talking about?" The widow frowned. "I have never heard what happened to Charles after he left home."

"He married a woman named Margaret Spencer," Holmes replied. "She bore him one child, a daughter. The daughter married a Peter Holloway in a civil ceremony in Frome some twelve years ago."

The housekeeper rose to her feet, her face red and her eyes blazing. "I know what you mean to insinuate, Mr. Holmes," she said in a belligerent tone, "but you can prove nothing."

"You think not?" Holmes was at his most dangerous, his voice soft and cold, his manner inflexible. "Under the terms of Malachi Westover's will, you stand to inherit his entire fortune if all George's heirs predecease him."

"What if I am Charles' daughter?" Defiance and fear mingled in her face. "I have done nothing!"

"You have done a great deal, Madame, all of it evil," Holmes replied. "But the cleverest ruse of all is the one you continue to maintain and will maintain until you have succeeded in murdering Miss Sophie."

"What are you talking about? You are a madman, Mr. Holmes."

"I am talking about the fact that Malachi Westover is dead. He has been dead for a month. He died the day before you murdered his son, and you have maintained the fiction that he is alive because your inheritance depends upon Sophie Westover predeceasing her grandfather."

"If he is dead, who eats his food?"

"You do, Mrs. Holloway. You made certain that his meals were delivered by a housemaid with the poor eyesight of one who suffers from thyroid imbalance."

"This is preposterous," the colonel shouted. "Old Malachi dead? Impossible!"

"Who has seen him face-to-face?" Holmes faced the military man. "No one. He ceased to admit members of the family the day before his son became ill. He communicated by notes, written in the shaky hand of the elderly. It is a hand easily imitated."

"My father-in-law was seen at night, pacing in his cottage," Mrs. Westover protested.

"That was Mrs. Holloway as well," Holmes replied. "She dressed in her grandfather's night-shirt and cap, then walked about the cottage late at night with the lights blazing."

"But I am certain there were nights when I saw Mrs. Holloway in the house," the widow said. "How could she be in two places at once?"

"I have had dealings of late with Madame Tussaud's Wax Museum," Holmes said. "I made an inquiry of Mr. John Tussaud and discovered that Malachi Westover owns a bust of himself cast in wax. I believe that wax figure aided Mrs. Holloway in her deception. On nights when she was required at the Grange, she dressed the wax figure in the same clothes and placed it in a chair."

Holmes turned his attention to the woman in the drab dress. "You were on your way back from burying the old man, dressed as a coachman, when a curious young groom saw you. Even though you'd taken precautions, putting the wax effigy of Malachi Westover inside the carriage with you, you had him discharged from service."

"Did she kill my son as well as my husband?" Mrs. Westover fingered the miniature she wore on her breast; it contained the portrait of a blond boy and a lock of wheat-colored hair.

"You can't prove anything," Mrs. Holloway asserted, but there was a cloud of doubt on her face.

"Oh, but I can," Holmes replied with a triumphant smile. "With the help of a most remarkable worm."

The remarkable worm was the talk of London for several days. Even the ordinary death of a man so celebrated as Malachi Westover was bound to dominate the headlines, and the old man's death had been anything but ordinary. Tales of his eccentricity could only be enhanced by the bizarre manner of his demise and his impersonation by a granddaughter moved by greed. The exhumation of George Westover, the discovery of poison in the maggots that fed upon his corpse, added a morbid touch to the story and, I am told, led to a greater acceptance of the practice of embalming prior to burial.

Sophie Westover gradually recovered her health, inherited her grandfather's enormous fortune, and re-hired young Jem as coachman on the condition that he marry Charity Jones at once. To this he readily, even eagerly, agreed, and the young couple set up housekeeping in a small cottage near the coach-yard, the bride continuing her training as lady's maid.

One fact conspicuously absent from the newspapers was the use made by Margaret Spencer of her grandfather's waxen bust. Holmes quietly returned the figure to the museum and said nothing to the press, reasoning that he had no desire to see others of a criminal bent misuse the effigies and tarnish the name of the great London institution.

At last the day arrived when Holmes' alter ego was to be on display for the first time. An engraved invitation offered us a private preview one hour before the exhibit was to open to the public. To Holmes, I professed nothing but the most hearty congratulations, but in truth, I was still a bit miffed at being left out of the display.

Spring had arrived in earnest by now, and as we walked along the Marylebone road to the wax museum, we were treated to delicate breezes and the scent of flowers.

We were met at the door by Mr. Joseph Tussaud, his son John, and little Mr. Flintridge. We marched in a body through the halls of kings and presidents to the Chamber of Horrors, where the tableau of the Blackfriars case awaited us.

It was an eerie sight. There stood Holmes, deerstalker cap on his head, piercing gray eyes staring through a magnifying glass at a thread held between finger and waxen thumb. There stood Harald

Blackfriar, a study in guilt, his staring eyes fixed on the thread, knowledge of his inevitable execution marked on his countenance. And there, standing next to Holmes with a medical bag in his hand, looking with interest at the red thread, stood Dr. John H. Watson.

My throat constricted and my chest swelled with pride. "You didn't tell me they wanted both of us," I said in a low voice, meant for Holmes' ears only.

"Your friend thought it would be a splendid surprise," John Tussaud explained. "The day you both came for a sitting, I was sketching you, Doctor, not Mr. Holmes. He returned for his own sitting after the conclusion of the Westover matter."

The older man said, "How do you like our display, Mr. Holmes?"

"I should not, Mr. Tussaud," the detective said, "be so gauche as to wear my hat indoors."

The elder Mr. Tussaud smiled. "Yes, of course, Mr. Holmes," he replied, "but how is your public to recognize you without your distinctive headgear?"

Little Mr. Flintridge spoke up. Pointing to the wax figure of the famous murderer, he remarked. "Here is a place where one can truly rest with Peace."

As if gratified by the jest, Charlie Peace stared at us with glass blue eyes.

I gave a long sigh of satisfaction. The moment seemed to me to sum up my extraordinary friendship with Sherlock Holmes. Together we had stood in many a drawing-room, many a library, and in our own rooms in Baker Street, examining evidence, discussing the significance of trifles, sifting through the debris of shattered lives, searching for truth and justice. And now all London, all England, all the world, would come to Madame Tussaud's and see the importance of our work.

"Nothing else remains," I said in a low voice. "This—this is Fame!"

SIDELIGHTS ON SHERLOCK HOLMES

Sir Arthur Conan Doyle

I MAY AS well interrupt my narrative here in order to say what may interest my readers about my most notorious character.

The impression that Holmes was a real person of flesh and blood may have been intensified by his frequent appearance upon the stage. After the withdrawal of my dramatization of "Rodney Stone" from a theatre upon which I held a six months' lease, I determined to play a bold and energetic game, for an empty theatre spells ruin. When I saw the course that things were taking I shut myself up and devoted my whole mind to making a sensational Sherlock Holmes drama. I wrote it in a week and called it "The Speckled Band" after the short story of that name. I do not think that I exaggerate if I say that within a fortnight of the one play shutting down I had a company working upon the rehearsals of a second one, which had been written in the interval. It was a considerable success. Lyn Harding, as the half epileptic and wholly formidable Doctor Grimesby Rylott, was most masterful, while Saintsbury as Sherlock Holmes was also very good. Before the end of the run I had cleared off all that I had lost upon the other play, and I had created a permanent property of some value. It became a stock piece and is even now touring the country. We had a fine rock boa to play the title-rôle, a snake which was the pride of my heart, so one can imagine my disgust when I saw that one critic ended his disparaging review by the words "The crisis of the play was produced by the appearance of a palpably artificial serpent." I was inclined to offer him a goodly sum if he would undertake to go to bed with it. We had several snakes at different times, but they were none of them born actors and they were all inclined either to hang down from the hole in the wall like inanimate bell-pulls, or else to turn back through the hole and get even with the stage carpenter who pinched their tails in order to make them more lively. Finally we used artificial snakes, and every one, including the stage carpenter, agreed that it was more satisfactory.

This was the second Sherlock Holmes play. I should have spoken about the first, which was produced very much earlier, in fact at the time of the African war. It was written and most wonderfully acted by William Gillette, the famous American. Since he used my characters and to some extent my plots; he naturally gave me a share in the undertaking, which proved to be very successful. "May I marry Holmes?" was one cable which I received from him when in the throes of composition. "You may marry or murder or do what you like with him," was my heartless reply. I was charmed both with the play, the acting and the pecuniary result. I think that every man with a drop of artistic blood in his veins would agree that the latter consideration, though very welcome when it does arrive, is still the last of which he thinks.

Sir James Barrie paid his respects to Sherlock Holmes in a rollicking parody. It was really a gay gesture of resignation over the failure which we had encountered with a comic opera for which he undertook to write the libretto. I collaborated with him on this, but in spite of our joint efforts, the piece fell flat. Whereupon Barrie sent me a parody on Holmes, written on the fly leaves of one of his books. It ran thus:—

THE ADVENTURE OF THE TWO COLLABORATORS

In bringing to a close the adventures of my friend Sherlock Holmes I am perforce reminded that he never, save on the occasion which, as you will now hear, brought his singular career to an end, consented to act in any mystery which was concerned with persons who made a livelihood by their pen. "I am not particular about the people I mix among for business purposes," he would say, "but at literary characters I draw the line."

We were in our rooms in Baker Street one evening. I was (I remember) by the centre table writing out "The Adventure of the Man without a Cork Leg" (which had so puzzled the Royal Society and all the other scientific bodies of Europe), and Holmes was amusing himself with a little revolver practice. It was his custom of a summer evening to fire round my head, just shaving my face, until he had made a photograph of me on the opposite wall, and it is a slight proof of his skill that many of these portraits in pistol shots are considered admirable likenesses.

I happened to look out of the window, and perceiving two gentlemen advancing rapidly along Baker Street asked him who they were. He immediately lit his pipe, and, twisting himself on a chair into the figure 8, replied:

"They are two collaborators in comic opera, and their play has not been a triumph."

I sprang from my chair to the ceiling in amazement, and he then explained:

"My dear Watson, they are obviously men who follow some low calling. That much even you should be able to read in their faces. Those little pieces of blue paper which they fling angrily from them are Durrant's Press Notices. Of these they have obviously hundreds about their person (see how their pockets bulge). They would not dance on them if they were pleasant reading."

I again sprang to the ceiling (which is much dented), and shouted: "Amazing! but they may be mere authors."

"No," said Holmes, "for mere authors only get one press notice a week. Only criminals, dramatists and actors get them by the hundred."

"Then they may be actors."

"No, actors would come in a carriage."

"Can you tell me anything else about them?"

"A great deal. From the mud on the boots of the tall one I perceive that he comes from South Norwood. The other is as obviously a Scotch author."

"How can you tell that?"

"He is carrying in his pocket a book called (I clearly see) 'Auld Licht Something.' Would any one but the author be likely to carry about a book with such a title?"

I had to confess that this was improbable.

It was now evident that the two men (if such they can be called) were seeking our lodgings. I have said (often) that my friend Holmes seldom gave way to emotion of any kind, but he now turned livid with passion. Presently this gave place to a strange look of triumph.

"Watson," he said, "that big fellow has for years taken the credit for my most remarkable doings, but at last I have him—at last!"

Up I went to the ceiling, and when I returned the strangers were in the room.

"I perceive, gentlemen," said Mr. Sherlock Holmes, "that you are at present afflicted by an extraordinary novelty."

The handsomer of our visitors asked in amazement how he knew this, but the big one only scowled.

"You forget that you wear a ring on your fourth finger," replied Mr. Holmes calmly.

I was about to jump to the ceiling when the big brute interposed.

"That Tommy-rot is all very well for the public, Holmes," said he, "but you can drop it before me. And, Watson, if you go up to the ceiling again I shall make you stay there."

Here I observed a curious phenomenon. My friend Sherlock Holmes *shrank*. He became small before my eyes. I looked longingly at the ceiling, but dared not.

"Let us cut the first four pages," said the big man, "and proceed to business. I want to know why—"

"Allow me," said Mr. Holmes, with some of his old courage. "You want to know why the public does not go to your opera."

"Exactly," said the other ironically, "as you perceive by my shirt stud." He added more gravely, "And as you can only find out in one way I must insist on your witnessing an entire performance of the piece."

It was an anxious moment for me. I shuddered, for I knew that if Holmes went I should have to go with him. But my friend had a heart of gold. "Never," he cried fiercely, "I will do anything for you save that."

"Your continued existence depends on it," said the big man menacingly.

"I would rather melt into air," replied Holmes, proudly taking another chair. "But I can tell you why the public don't go to your piece without sitting the thing out myself."

"Why?"

"Because," replied Holmes calmly, "they prefer to stay away."

A dead silence followed that extraordinary remark. For a moment the two intruders gazed with awe upon the man who had unravelled their mystery so wonderfully. Then drawing their knives—

Holmes grew less and less, until nothing was left save a ring of smoke which slowly circled to the ceiling.

The last words of great men are often noteworthy. These were the last words of Sherlock Holmes: "Fool, fool! I have kept you in luxury for years. By my help you have ridden extensively in cabs, where no author was ever seen before. *Henceforth you will ride in buses!*"

The brute sunk into a chair aghast.

The other author did not turn a hair.

To A. Conan Doyle,
from his friend
J. M. Barrie.

This parody, the best of all the numerous parodies, may be taken as an example not only of the author's wit but of his debonnaire courage, for it was written immediately after our joint failure which at the moment was a bitter thought for both of us. There is indeed nothing more miserable than a theatrical failure, for you feel how many others who have backed you have been affected by it. It was, I am glad to say, my only experience of it, and I have no doubt that Barrie could say the same.

Before I leave the subject of the many impersonations of Holmes I may say that all of them, and all the drawings, are very unlike my own original idea of the man. I saw him as very tall—"over 6 feet, but so excessively lean that he seemed considerably taller," said "A Study in Scarlet." He had, as I imagined him, a thin razor-like face, with a great hawks-bill of a nose, and two small eyes, set close together on either side of it. Such was my conception. It chanced, however, that poor Sidney Paget who, before his premature death, drew all the original pictures, had a younger brother whose name, I think, was Walter, who served him as a model. The handsome Walter took the place of the more powerful but uglier Sherlock, and perhaps from the point of view of my lady readers it was as well. The stage has followed the type set up by the pictures.

Films of course were unknown when the stories appeared, and when these rights were finally discussed and a small sum offered for them by a French Company it seemed treasure trove and I was very glad to accept. Afterwards I had to buy them back again at exactly ten times what I had received, so the deal was a disastrous one. But now they have been done by the Stoll Company with Eille Norwood as Holmes, and it was worth all the expense to get so fine a production. Norwood has since played the part on the stage and won the approbation of the London public. He has that rare quality which can only be described as glamour, which compels you to watch an actor eagerly even when he is doing nothing. He has the brooding eye which excites expectation and he has also a quite unrivalled power of disguise. My only criticism of the films is that they introduce telephones, motor cars and other luxuries of which the Victorian Holmes never dreamed.

People have often asked me whether I knew the end of a Holmes story before I started it. Of course I do. One could not possibly steer a course if one did not know one's destination. The first thing is to get your idea. Having got that key idea one's next task is to conceal it and lay emphasis upon everything which can make for a different explanation. Holmes, however, can see all the fallacies of the alternatives, and arrives more or less dramatically at the true solution by steps which he can describe and justify. He shows his powers by what the South Americans now call "Sherlockholmitos," which means clever little deductions, which often have nothing to do with the matter in hand, but impress the reader with a general sense of power. The same effect is gained by his offhand allusion to other cases. Heaven knows how many titles I have thrown about in a casual way, and how many readers have begged me to satisfy their curiosity as to "Rigoletto and his abominable wife," "The Adventure of the Tired Captain," or "The Curious Experience of the Patterson Family in the Island of Uffa." Once or twice, as in "The Adventure of the Second Stain," which in my judgment is one of the neatest of the stories, I did actually use the title years before I wrote a story to correspond.

There are some questions concerned with particular stories which turn up periodically from every quarter of the globe. In "The Adventure of the Priory School" Holmes remarks in his offhand way that by looking at a bicycle track on a damp moor one can say which way it was heading. I had so many remonstrances upon this point, varying from pity to anger, that I took out my bicycle and tried. I had imagined that the observations of the way in which the track of the hind wheel overlaid the track of the front one when the machine was not running dead straight would show the direction. I found that my correspondents were right and I was wrong, for this would be the same whichever way the cycle was moving. On the other hand the real solution was much simpler, for on an undulating moor the wheels make a much deeper impression uphill and a more shallow one downhill, so Holmes was justified of his wisdom after all.

Sometimes I have got upon dangerous ground where I have taken risks through my own want of knowledge of the correct atmosphere. I have, for example, never been a racing man, and yet I ventured to write "Silver Blaze," in which the mystery depends upon the laws of training and racing. The story is all right, and Holmes may have been at the top of his form, but my ignorance cries aloud to heaven. I read an excellent and very damaging criticism of the story in some sporting paper, written clearly by a man who *did* know, in which he explained the exact penalties which would have come upon every one concerned if they had acted as I described. Half would have been in jail and the other half warned off the turf for ever. However, I have never been nervous about details, and one must be masterful sometimes. When an alarmed Editor wrote to me once: "There is no second line of rails at that point," I answered, "I make one." On the other hand, there are cases where accuracy is essential.

I do not wish to be ungrateful to Holmes, who has been a good friend to me in many ways. If I have sometimes been inclined to weary of him it is because his character admits of no light or shade. He is a calculating machine, and anything you add to that simply weakens the effect. Thus the variety of the stories must depend upon the romance and compact handling of the plots. I would say a word for Watson also, who in the course of seven volumes never shows one gleam of humour or makes one single joke. To make a real character one must sacrifice everything to consistency and remember Goldsmith's criticism of Johnson that "he would make the little fishes talk like whales."

I do not think that I ever realized what a living actual personality Holmes had become to the more guileless readers, until I heard of the very pleasing story of the char-à-banc of French schoolboys who, when asked what they wanted to see first in London, replied unanimously that they wanted to see Mr. Holmes' lodgings in Baker Street. Many have asked me which house it is, but that is a point which for excellent reasons I will not decide.

There are certain Sherlock Holmes stories, apocryphal I need not say, which go round and round the press and turn up at fixed intervals with the regularity of a comet.

One is the story of the cabman who is supposed to have taken me to an hotel in Paris. "Dr. Doyle," he cried, gazing at me fixedly, "I perceive from your appearance that you have been recently at Constantinople. I have reason to think also that you have been at Buda, and I perceive some indication that you were not far from Milan." "Wonderful. Five francs for the secret of how you did it?" "I looked at the labels pasted on your trunk," said the astute cabby.

Another perennial is of the woman who is said to have consulted Sherlock. "I am greatly puzzled, sir. In one week I have lost a motor horn, a brush, a box of golf balls, a dictionary and a bootjack. Can you explain it?" "Nothing simpler, madame," said Sherlock. "It is clear that your neighbour keeps a goat."

There was a third about how Sherlock entered heaven, and by virtue of his power of observation at once greeted Adam, but the point is perhaps too anatomical for further discussion.

I suppose that every author receives a good many curious letters. Certainly I have done so. Quite a number of these have been from Russia. When they have been in the vernacular I have been compelled to take them as read, but when they have been in English they have been among the most curious in my collection.

There was one young lady who began all her epistles with the words "Good Lord." Another had a large amount of guile underlying her simplicity. Writing from Warsaw, she stated that she had been bedridden for two years, and that my novels had been her only, etc., etc. So touched was I by this flattering statement that I at once prepared an autographed parcel of them to complete the fair invalid's collection. By good luck, however, I met a brother author on the same day to whom I recounted the touching incident. With a cynical smile, he drew an identical letter from his pocket. His novels had also been for two years her only, etc., etc. I do not know how many more the lady had written to; but if, as I imagine, her correspondence had extended to several countries, she must have amassed a rather interesting library.

The young Russian's habit of addressing me as "Good Lord" had an even stranger parallel at home which links it up with the subject of this article. Shortly after I received a knighthood, I had a bill from a tradesman which was quite correct and businesslike in every detail save that it was made out to Sir Sherlock Holmes. I hope that I can stand a joke as well as my neighbours, but this particular piece of humour seemed rather misapplied and I wrote sharply upon the subject.

In response to my letter there arrived at my hotel a very repentant clerk, who expressed his sorrow at the incident, but kept on repeating the phrase, "I assure you, sir, that it was bonâ fide."

"What do you mean by bonâ fide?" I asked.

"Well, sir," he replied, "my mates in the shop told me that you had been knighted, and that when a man was knighted he changed his name, and that you had taken that one."

I need not say that my annoyance vanished, and that I laughed as heartily as his pals were probably doing round the corner.

A few of the problems which have come my way have been very similar to some which I had invented for the exhibition of the reasoning of Mr. Holmes. I might perhaps quote one in which that gentleman's method of thought was copied with complete success. The case was as follows: A gentleman had disappeared. He had drawn a bank balance of £40 which was known to be on him. It was feared that he had been murdered for the sake of the money. He had last been heard of stopping at a large hotel in London, having come from the country that day. In the evening he went to a music-hall performance, came out of it about ten o'clock, returned to his hotel, changed his evening clothes, which were found in his room next day, and disappeared utterly. No one saw him leave the hotel, but a man occupying a neighbouring room declared that he had heard him moving during the night. A week had elapsed at the time that I was consulted, but the police had discovered nothing. Where was the man?

These were the whole of the facts as communicated to me by his relatives in the country. Endeavouring to see the matter through the eyes of Mr. Holmes, I answered by return mail that he was evidently either in Glasgow or in Edinburgh. It proved later that he had, as a fact, gone to Edinburgh, though in the week that had passed he had moved to another part of Scotland.

There I should leave the matter, for, as Dr. Watson has often shown, a solution explained is a mystery spoiled. At this stage the reader can lay down the book and show how simple it all is by working out the problem for himself. He has all the data which were ever given to me. For the sake of those, however, who have no turn for such conundrums, I will try to indicate the links which make the chain. The one advantage which I possessed was that I was familiar with the routine of London hotels—though I fancy it differs little from that of hotels elsewhere.

The first thing was to look at the facts and separate what was certain from what was conjecture. It was *all* certain except the statement of the person who heard the missing man in the night. How could he tell such a sound from any other sound in a large hotel? That point could be disregarded, if it traversed the general conclusions.

The first clear deduction was that the man had meant to disappear. Why else should he draw all his money? He had got out of the hotel during the night. But there is a night porter in all hotels, and it is impossible to get out without his knowledge when the door is once shut. The door is shut after the theatre-goers return—say at twelve o'clock. Therefore, the man left the hotel before twelve o'clock. He had come from the music-hall at ten, had changed his clothes, and had departed with his bag. No one had seen him do so. The inference is that he had done it at the moment when the hall was full of the returning guests, which is from eleven to eleven-thirty. After that hour, even if the door were still open, there are few people coming and going so that he with his bag would certainly have been seen.

Having got so far upon firm ground, we now ask ourselves why a man who desires to hide himself should go out at such an hour. If he intended to conceal himself in London he need never have gone to the hotel at all. Clearly then he was going to catch a train which would carry him away. But a man who is deposited by a train in any provincial station during the night is likely to be noticed, and he might be sure that when the alarm was raised and his description given, some guard or porter would remember him. Therefore, his destination would be some large town which he would reach as a terminus where all his fellow passengers would disembark and where he would lose himself in the crowd. When one turns up the time table and sees that the great Scotch expresses bound for Edinburgh and Glasgow start about midnight, the goal is reached. As for his dress-suit, the fact that he abandoned it proved that he intended to adopt a line of life where there were no social amenities. This deduction also proved to be correct.

I quote such a case in order to show that the general lines of reasoning advocated by Holmes have a real practical application to life. In another case, where a girl had become engaged to a young foreigner who suddenly disappeared, I was able, by a similar process of deduction, to show her very clearly both whither he had gone and how unworthy he was of her affections.

On the other hand, these semi-scientific methods are occasionally laboured and slow as compared with the results of the rough-and-ready, practical man. Lest I should seem to have been throwing bouquets either to myself or to Mr. Holmes, let me state that on the occasion of a burglary of the village inn, within a stone-throw of my house, the village constable, with no theories at all, had seized the culprit while I had got no further than that he was a left-handed man with nails in his boots.

The unusual or dramatic effects which lead to the invocation of Mr. Holmes in fiction are, of course, great aids to him in reaching a conclusion. It is the case where there is nothing to get hold of which is the deadly one. I heard of such a one in America which would certainly have presented a formidable problem. A gentleman of blameless life starting off for a Sunday evening walk with his family, suddenly observed that he had forgotten something. He went back into the house, the door of which was still open, and he left his people waiting for him outside. He never reappeared, and from that day to this there has been no clue as to what befell him. This was certainly one of the strangest cases of which I have ever heard in real life.

Another very singular case came within my own observation. It was sent to me by an eminent London publisher. This gentleman had in his employment a head of department whose name we shall take as Musgrave. He was a hard-working person, with no special feature in his character. Mr. Musgrave died, and several years after his death a letter was received addressed to him, in the care of his employers. It bore the postmark of a tourist resort in the west of Canada, and had the note "Conflfilms" upon the outside of the envelope, with the words "Report Sy" in one corner.

The publishers naturally opened the envelope as they had no note of the dead man's relatives. Inside were two blank sheets of paper. The letter, I may add, was registered. The publisher, being unable to make anything of this, sent it on to me, and I submitted the blank sheets to every possible chemical and heat test, with no result whatever. Beyond the fact that the writing appeared to be that of a woman there is nothing to add to this account. The matter was, and remains, an insoluble mystery. How the correspondent could have something so secret to say to Mr. Musgrave and yet not be aware that this person had been dead for several years is very hard to understand—or why blank sheets should be so carefully registered through the mail. I may add that I did not trust the sheets to my own chemical tests, but had the best expert advice without getting any result. Considered as a case it was a failure—and a very tantalizing one.

Mr. Sherlock Holmes has always been a fair mark for practical jokers, and I have had numerous bogus cases of various degrees of ingenuity, marked cards, mysterious warnings, cypher messages, and other curious communications. It is astonishing the amount of trouble which some people will take with no object save a mystification. Upon one occasion, as I was entering the hall to take part in an amateur billiard competition, I was handed by the attendant a small packet which had been left for me. Upon opening it I found a piece of ordinary green chalk such as is used in billiards. I was amused by the incident, and I put the chalk into my waistcoat pocket and used it during the game. Afterward, I continued to use it until one day, some months later, as I rubbed the tip of my cue the face of the chalk crumbled in, and I found it was hollow. From the recess thus exposed I drew out a small slip of paper with the words "From Arsene Lupin to Sherlock Holmes."

Imagine the state of mind of the joker who took such trouble to accomplish such a result.

One of the mysteries submitted to Mr. Holmes was rather upon the psychic plane and therefore beyond his powers. The facts as alleged are most remarkable, though I have no proof of their truth save that the lady wrote earnestly and gave both her name and address. The person, whom we will call Mrs. Seagrave, had been given a curious secondhand ring, snake-shaped, and dull gold. This she took from her finger at night. One night she slept with it on and had a fearsome dream in which she seemed to be pushing off some furious creature which fastened its teeth into her arm. On awakening, the pain in the arm continued, and next day the imprint of a double set of teeth appeared upon the arm, with one tooth of the lower jaw missing. The marks were in the shape of blue-black bruises which had not broken the skin.

"I do not know," says my correspondent, "what made me think the ring had anything to do with the matter, but I took a dislike to the thing and did not wear it for some months, when, being on a visit, I took to wearing it again." To make a long story short, the same thing happened, and the lady settled the matter forever by dropping her ring into the hottest corner of the kitchen range. This curious story, which I believe to be genuine, may not be as supernatural as it seems. It is well known that in some subjects a strong mental impression does produce a physical effect. Thus a very vivid nightmare dream with the impression of a bite might conceivably produce the mark of a bite. Such cases are well attested in medical annals. The second incident would, of course, arise by unconscious suggestion from the first. None the less, it is a very interesting little problem, whether psychic or material.

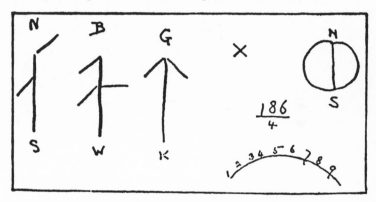

Buried treasures are naturally among the problems which have come to Mr. Holmes. One genuine case was accompanied by a diagram here reproduced. It refers to an Indiaman which was wrecked upon the South African coast in the year 1782. If I were a younger man, I should be seriously inclined to go personally and look into the matter.

The ship contained a remarkable treasure, including, I believe, the old crown regalia of Delhi. It is surmised that they buried these near the coast, and that this chart is a note of the spot. Each Indiaman in those days had its own semaphore code, and it is conjectured that the three marks upon the left are signals from a three-armed semaphore. Some record of their meaning might perhaps even now be found in the old papers of the India Office. The circle upon the right gives the compass bearings. The larger semicircle may be the curved edge of a reef or of a rock. The figures above are the indications how to reach the X which marks the treasure. Possibly they may give the bearings as 186 feet from the

4 upon the semi-circle. The scene of the wreck is a lonely part of the country, but I shall be surprised if sooner or later, some one does not seriously set to work to solve the mystery—indeed at the present moment (1923) there is a small company working to that end.

I must now apologise for this digressive chapter and return to the orderly sequence of my career.

100 YEARS OF SHERLOCK HOLMES

Lloyd Rose

ROUGHLY TWENTY MINUTES into *A Scandal in Bohemia* the first of the Granada TV dramatizations Jeremy Brett laughs. The laugh isn't exactly uncalled for—Holmes' client, the King of Bohemia, is making a fool of himself—but it's not quite appropriate to the situation either. It's abrupt and too loud. Brett throws his head back, his teeth show. Earlier, being lectured by Watson on the dangers of cocaine, Holmes has let out a twitchy, disturbing little snigger, but this laugh breaks everything into the open. As a mystery-buff friend of mine said to me the next day "He's great, isn't he? He's crazy."

Sherlock Holmes has been around now for a century and has been put, by his various admirers and detractors, to a lot of uses: advertising everything from Scotch to Postum; popping up as a point of reference in dozens of mystery novels; filling out a couplet for Vladimir Nabokov in *Pale Fire;* and appearing in hundreds of plays, films, and television shows. To some extent, Holmes' history in what, even though he first emerged in the Victorian era, can only be called pop culture, is the history of the actors who have played him. William Gillette contributed the curved meerschaum pipe, one of the major elements to the three-part Holmes iconography of magnifying glass, pipe, and deerstalker, when he found it impossible to deliver lines and still keep any other type clenched in his teeth. The deerstalker was supplied by Sidney Paget. Only the magnifying glass comes directly from Conan Doyle. Gillette inspired Frederick Dorr Steele, who based some of his drawings on photographs of him, with the result that his Holmes is disconcertingly square-faced: a strong-jawed, piercing-eyed sort, like the hero of some silent film melodrama. Steele had a strong graphic sense and his illustrations are formally quite pretty, but Holmes—stern, athletic, and with something of the go-getter in his stance—is all too obviously an American. The drawings don't really fit the stories, and when moviemakers started taking a serious interest in Holmes in the 1920s, the actors and atmosphere suggested Paget rather than Steele.

Sidney Paget, technically speaking was not the artist Steele was: his pictures aren't nearly as well-designed. He was also at the mercy of his several engravers, some of whom clumsily coarsened or distorted his work. But what his drawings lack in purely artistic terms they make up for in the way he captures the hominess and humor of the stories, and the vitality and eccentricity of their central character. His Holmes slouches in his armchair or throws himself on the ground with a lens, lights his pipe with a coal held in the fire tongs, leans back and closes his eyes to listen to music, a half-smile on his lips. He lies curled on a chaise-lounge and contemplates a battered hat hanging on the back of a chair, seeing in it information that will elude and foil his companion Watson, who is also in the picture, bending on the hat an earnest gaze quite at odds with Holmes' detached thoughtfulness. Like Conan Doyle's Holmes, Paget's is restless and sharp-minded, gentlemanly but impatient, and not above regarding a foolish client or dull-witted police detective with polite but ill-concealed irony.

Paget used his brother Walter as his model, creating a figure more handsome than Conan Doyle intended, but far less of a matinee-idol than Steele's clean-cut hero. From Paget we get the picture of Holmes as hollow-cheeked and high-foreheaded, with a receding hairline and sharp, prominent nose. We get, in short, a

model for Basil Rathbone, who recreated Holmes for the generations born too late to have seen Gillette, and who, because he
starred in the most successful series of Holmes films, is most people's idea of the character to this day.

The movies Rathbone starred in don't have much to do with the
stories Conan Doyle wrote. For one thing, after the first two they're
all set durng the Second World War. Holmes runs around in a
fedora and fights Nazis. They also take their plot cues from the
melodrama of movie serials—Holmes is regularly threatened, tied
up, or put in physical peril. This is completely unlike Conan Doyle,
who pretty much confined the violence to the crimes committed
and almost always had it happen before Holmes arrives on the
scene. Holmes occasionally claps a pistol to a villain's head, is engaged twice in a fistfight, is once attacked with a knife, and is once
beaten up by hired ruffians, but these are about the extent of his
brushes with danger. He *does* go over the Reichenbach to his supposed death, locked in mortal combat with Moriarty, but Conan
Doyle was giving Holmes a showy send-off and rather exerting himself for the occasion.

The action in the stories is mental, and though it might seem
logical for the movies, with their need for action, to turn to melo-
dramatic formulas out of necessity, the best moments in the films
are mental too, when Rathbone turns to his obtuse Watson and
rattles off a series of near-incomprehensible deductions to explain
how he has solved the crime. Rathbone is a prim, almost prissy
Holmes, but he's terrific in these scenes, clipping off his syllables
and zinging them at poor Watson like so many machine-gun bullets.
This is the great Holmes joke, a joke written into the stories.
Holmes is so smart he's funny. It's not really possible to take those
rapid-fire strings of deductions seriously, but it's not really possible
not to be surprised and delighted by them either. They come
breathtakingly out of left field and tumble our expectations
around—they're playful. There's a faintly surreal quality to them
too, as if Holmes had stepped out of the pages not of Conan Doyle's
mysteries but of *Alice in Wonderland* (in which it's possible to imag-

ine him quite at home, chatting with the Caterpillar perhaps). He makes sense of the world with the rapidity, wit, and weirdness with which Carroll's characters make nonsense of it; the comic style is the same.

Holmes eludes his satirists. He's already the subject of his creator's joke, and no one's come up with a better one. He *is* susceptible to affectionate parody; Nicol Williamson's coke-freak Holmes in *The Seven Percent Solution* succeeds because he plays into Conan Doyle's joke and one-ups it. Holmes is so damn smart because he's speeding. It was Conan Doyle himself who made Holmes a cocaine-user. He didn't make him a fool, a smug bully, a bisexual, or a soft-hearted liberal, and attempts to play him as any of these, by Peter Cook, Frank Langella, Robert Stevens, and Christopher Plummer respectively, fall flat. They're not offensive, they're just beside the point. The actors involved don't seem to *get* it. As a character, Holmes is very precisely defined; an actor approaching the role plays it successfully only if he plays it by Conan Doyle's rules. Peter Cushing, in most respects, is all wrong for the part (though it's his likeness that currently graces the sign for the Sherlock Holmes Pub in London), captured its fantastical elements perfectly, bounding up in the middle of conversations to chase after his own bolting thoughts. In *The Crucifer of Blood*, Paxton Whitehead played Holmes the moralist, a skeptic who nonetheless stood for Queen and Empire. Loping through a hodgepodge of boys' book Victoriana in *The Young Sherlock Holmes*, Nicholas Rowe, tall and lean with still, watchful eyes, suggested Holmes' intellectual isolation and loneliness. Rowe's approach was romantic, as was John Woods' in the Royal Shakespeare Company revival of Gillette's *Sherlock Holmes*. Praising him, critics used phrases like "haunted and steely." This isn't at all out-of-line with what Gillette wrote. When Watson gives the inevitable lecture about the dangers of cocaine, strongly implying it will mean Holmes' death, Holmes doesn't care. Life bores him. It's a *reductio ad absurdum* of Conan Doyle: Holmes is, finally, too smart to live. Of course, this was Gillette the ham giving himself a chance to play existential ennui. But he had Conan Doyle's input on the script (to what extent is unknown), and he wasn't exactly out-of-line with what Conan Doyle wrote either.

Conan Doyle's notes for *A Study in Scarlet* refer to Holmes as "Sherrinford Holmes" and the name is followed by these phrases "The Laws of Evidence. . . . Reserved. . . . Sleepy-eyed young man— Philosopher—collector of rare Violins . . . An Amati. . . . Chemical laboratory . . . I have four hundred a year . . . I am a Consulting detective," "the only one in the world," Holmes will claim to Watson, referring to the last phrase, but he isn't, in *A Study in Scarlet*, quite the man he becomes in *The Sign of the Four* and remains throughout the short stories. He's callower, and although his knowledge is impressive, he's not yet convincingly a genius: he's more like a smart, slightly obnoxious kid making fun of his parents, the official police. (Conan Doyle was twenty-seven when he wrote the novel, and Holmes seems about the same age.) Conan Doyle hadn't gotten the feel of showing Holmes through Watson's eyes; in order to convey him to us, Watson is reduced to making lists of his accomplishments and physical characteristics. Holmes isn't really grounded, as he is later, by the myriad homey behavioral details that give him such an oddly compelling reality. Without the weight, and the ordinariness of these details, his deductions are showy and not very convincing, a writer's sleight-of-hand rather than a character's peculiar brilliance. Even his famous initial greeting to Watson, "You have been in Afghanistan, I perceive," comes off a bit like a parlor trick.

There is one point, however, at which Conan Doyle has Watson focus on Holmes with the camera-like clarity he was to use to such effect later:

> Nothing could exceed his energy when the working fit was upon him; but now and again a reaction would seize him, and for days on end he would lie upon the sofa in the sitting room, hardly uttering a word or moving a muscle from morning to night. On these occasions, I have noticed such a dreamy, vacant

expression in his eyes, that I might have suspected him of being addicted to some narcotic, had not the temperance and cleanliness of his whole life forbidden such a notion.

As every reader of the stories knows, Watson was, as usual, wrong. Three years later, *The Sign of the Four* opens with:

> Sherlock Holmes took his bottle from the corner of the mantelpiece, and his hypodermic syringe from its neat morocco case. With his long, white, nervous fingers he adjusted the delicate needle, and rolled back his left shirt-cuff. For some little time his eyes rested thoughtfully upon the sinewy forearm and wrist, all dotted and scarred with innumerable puncture-marks. Finally, he thrust the sharp point home, pressed down the tiny piston, and sank back into the velvet-lined arm-chair with a long sigh of satisfaction.

With this injection, Holmes the literary legend—drug-addict, genius, bohemian: vain, arrogant, humorous, cold-blooded, deeply moral, continually one-up on all lesser mortals—arrives on the scene. Conan Doyle's writing here is marvelously assured and almost hypnotically visual, like the opening of a film. (This cinematic quality is perhaps his greatest strength as a writer, and all the more remarkable for his having developed it well before film itself could accomplish anything like a close-up.) Making Holmes a drug addict seems to have given Conan Doyle the clue as to how to inhabit him. There's no further development; he is complete. It's impossible to say why some time between 1886 and 1890 Conan Doyle hit on the idea of having Holmes use cocaine. The extreme contrasts between Holmes' lassitude and energy, which Conan Doyle presents as inherent rather than drug-induced in *A Study in Scarlet*, become a central part of his character. But even after *The Sign of the Four*, Conan Doyle doesn't always connect them with cocaine. In "The Red-Headed League," he has Holmes relax at a concert ". . . his dreamy, languid eyes were as unlike those of Holmes the sleuthhound, Holmes the relentless, keen-witted, ready-handed criminal agent, as it was possible to conceive. In his singular character, the dual nature alternately asserted itself, and his extreme exactness and astuteness represented, as I have often thought, the reaction against the poetic and contemplative mood which occasionally predominated in him." This sounds like so much naive 19th-century psychologizing. Holmes' defense of his drug habit is much more believable (and briskly written). "My mind rebels at stagnations. Give me problems, give me work, give me the most abstruse cryptogram, or the most intricate analysis, and I am in my own proper atmosphere. I can dispense then with artificial stimulents. But I abhor the dull routine of existence. I crave for mental exaltation." This is the romantic Holmes of Gillette's characterization, so brilliant he needs drugs to protect him from the soul-sapping horror of the everyday. But it's Conan Doyle's Holmes too, and, reading the stories one hundred years later, it's possible to wonder whether he made him a drug addict because he didn't otherwise know how to deal with the fact that he'd created a character with all the symptoms of what we recognize today as manic-depressive psychosis.

Conan Doyle's attitude toward Holmes is strange, hard to pin down and harder to understand. Feeling trapped by his creation's success, he threw him over a waterfall and let him rest there for eight years until, after using him in *The Hound of the Baskervilles*, he resurrected him and went on writing about him for another twenty-five years. He chaffed considerably at the attention paid his detective stories above his other work. "I believe that if I had never touched Holmes, who has tended to obscure my higher work, my position in literature would at the present moment be a more commanding one," he wrote in 1923. And of his 1889 historical novel, *The White Company*, he stated, "I knew in my heart that the book would live, and that it would illuminate our national traditions." Though it passed through fifty printings in Conan Doyle's lifetime, *The White Company* lives today only when readers of his mysteries decide, to their almost inevitable disappointment (Anthony Burgess is a notable exception), to try some of his historical novels. They find them creaky, pedestrian, sentimental, dated: exactly, in fact, what the Holmes stories are if you take Holmes out of them.

It's baffling, almost disorienting, to read Conan Doyle discussing these stories in terms not of their detective hero but of their *plots*: "If I have sometimes been inclined to weary of him [Holmes], it is because his character admits of no light or shade. He is a calculating machine, and anything you add to that simply weakens the effect. Thus the variety of the stories must depend on the romance and compact handling of the plots." But the plots, with occasional exceptions (the whimsical "Red-Headed League" or the Gothic *The Hound of the Baskervilles*, not originally conceived as a Holmes story at all) are Conan Doyle's weakest elements. "Conan Doyle made mistakes which completely invalidated some of his stories," Raymond Chandler wrote in *The Simple Art of Murder*, "but he was a pioneer, and Sherlock Holmes after all is mostly an attitude and a few dozen lines of unforgettable dialogue." Chandler, whose own plots are so tangled you could strangle in them, was being condescending, but essentially he was right. What is memorable about the Holmes stories is Holmes. The plots serve about the same purpose as they do in an Astaire movie; they're there to let the hero show what he can do. Years after one reads the stories, they blend in memory into one generic series of scenes: Holmes curled in his armchair in front of the fire, pipe in mouth, Watson across from him, while acrid yellow fog presses against the windows; Holmes stretched languidly on the sofa with the day's papers; Holmes on a case, lens in hand, pacing, bending, lying prone; Holmes shooting up; Holmes playing the violin; Holmes making sardonic remarks to the dogged but dim Inspector Lestrade; Holmes sternly confronting a criminal. The plots are as hazy as the seemingly ever-present fog; only Holmes burns away that haze and remains clear. Reading the stories is something like watching a silent film with a great actor in it—Gish, say, or Chaplin—and marveling how, in the midst of their old-fashioned, sometimes ludicrous surroundings, they seem modern and immediate, with us now.

Holmes' vividness is easy to explain. Conan Doyle pays more attention to him than to anyone else in the stories, and his attention is very specific. That passage that opens *The Sign of the Four* isn't an exception; throughout the stories Conan Doyle turns his camera-eye on Holmes:

> "You have erred, perhaps," he observed, taking up a glowing cinder with the tongs, and lighting with it the long cherrywood pipe which was wont to replace his clay when he was in a disputatious rather than a meditative mood. . . .

or:

> It was soon evident to me that he was now preparing for an all-night sitting. He took off his coat and waistcoat, put on a large blue dressing-gown, and then wandered about the room collecting pillows from his bed, and cushions from the sofa and arm-chairs. With these he constructed a sort of Eastern divan, upon which he perched himself cross-legged, with an ounce of shag tobacco and a box of matches laid out in front of him. In the dim light of the lamp I saw him sitting there, an old briar pipe between his lips, his eyes fixed vacantly upon the corner of the ceiling, the blue smoke curling up from him, silent, motionless, with the light shining upon his strong-set aquiline features. So he sat as I dropped off to sleep, and so he sat when a sudden ejaculation caused me to wake up, and I found the summer sun shining into the apartment. The pipe was still between his lips, the smoke still curled upwards, and the room was full of a dense tobacco haze, but nothing remained of the heap of shag which I had seen upon the previous night.

He does a superb job with Holmes' domestic habits as well, specifically in the well-known passage from "The Musgrave Ritual" in which Watson decries his roomate's untidiness

Not that I am in the least conventional in that respect myself. . . . But with me there is a limit, and when I find a man
who keeps his cigars in the coal-scuttle, his tobacco in the toe-
end of a Persian slipper, and his unanswered correspondence
transfixed by a jack-knife into the very centre of his wooden
mantelpiece, then I begin to give myself certain virtuous airs.
I have always held, too, that pistol practice should distinctly be
an open-air pastime; and when Holmes in one of his queer
humours would sit in an arm-chair, with his hair-trigger and a
hundred Boxer cartridges, and proceed to adorn the opposite
wall with a patriotic V.R. done in bullet-pocks, I felt strongly
that neither the atmosphere nor the appearance of our room
was improved by it.

Our chambers were always full of chemicals and of criminal
relics, which had a way of wandering into unlikely positions,
and or turning up in the butter-dish, or in even less desirable
places. . . . He had a horror of destroying documents, especially
those which were connected with his past cases, and yet it was
only once in every year or two that he would muster energy to
docket and arrange them . . . Thus month after month his papers accumulated, until every corner of the room was stacked
with bundles of manuscript which were on no account to be
burned, and which could not be put away save by their owner.

Nowhere else is Conan Doyle this lively and detailed, though he
comes close with a few other characters: the fiercely red-haired but
dull-witted Jabez Wilson of "The Red-headed League"; the pale
spectacled lepidopterist villain Stapleton in *The Hound of the Baskervilles*, corpulent, slow-moving Mycroft, Holmes' brother, who goes
nowhere except his home, club, and office, and in some mysterious
fashion *is* the British government. Most exceptionally, there is Professor Moriarty, the Napoleon of Crime, with his face "for ever
slowly oscillating from side to side in a curiously reptilian manner."
As Mary Shelley's Frankenstein is the progenitor of one hundred
and sixty-odd years of mad scientists, so Moriarty is the first of the

modern criminal masterminds, the ruler of a netherworld of vice that flows like a sewer beneath the placid bourgeois surface of Victorian English society. He appears directly in only one story and is an off-scene agent in two more: Conan Doyle clearly invented him just to bump Holmes off. Yet for most readers of the stories he's the second most memorable character, the evil genius who shadows the good one. He's a very potent figure to have put together in just a few paragraphs, an example of what Conan Doyle can do when he's really engaged by what he's writing. Whatever his disclaimers, it's difficult to read him without feeling that the decent victimized seekers of Holmes' aid—the honorable, stiff-upper-lipped gentlemen and delicately distressed maidens—and their predicaments bore Conan Doyle, that it's eccentricity that intrigues him (and brings his prose to life), and that he is having the most fun and writing at his best when he deals with his hero, an eccentric of near Dickensian magnificence.

Conan Doyle's own life, except for his embrace of Spiritualism toward the end of it, was not eccentric. It wasn't particularly easy either. He had an alcoholic father who ended up in an institution. His first wife died of tuberculosis after a thirteen-year illness, the last ten years of which Conan Doyle spent in chaste love with the woman who became his second wife. He lost a son in the World War. None of these trials, nor the money difficulties he endured until Holmes brought him financial reward in his thirties, undid him. He didn't turn to drink or have a nervous breakdown or mistreat his family. "I have often been asked whether I had myself the qualities which I depicted, or whether I was merely the Watson that I look," he once wrote and though he acknowledged that "a man cannot spin a character out of his own inner consciousness and make it really lifelike unless he has some of that character within him" (and a few times solved cases brought to him by Holmesian methods and with Holmesian brilliance), he lived the life of the Watson that he looked. Even his involvement with Spiritualism he pursued and defended in as levelheaded a manner as such a pursuit is possible. He was a good British bourgeois, a solid citizen, a "stout fellow," and from accounts of his children, a warmhearted and generous family man. Only occasionally in his writing is there a faint, strange current of something that isn't bourgeois and solid, an odd amoral little shock, and it shows up most clearly in his treatment of women.

Much has been made of Holmes' misogyny, mostly by members of all-male Sherlockian societies who, with a scriptural reverence for the texts, use Holmes' anti-feminism to keep women out of their clubs. Conan Doyle is certainly straightforward about Holmes' attitude: "He disliked and distrusted the sex." But, he has Watson add, "he was always a chivalrous opponent." Indeed, Holmes is so chivalrous that it becomes hard to figure out exactly in what ways he does dislike women; it's certainly an attitude that never leads anywhere. Watson explains at one point that for Holmes, the perfect reasoning machine, love would be akin to "grit in a sensitive instrument." A much funnier explanation for Holmes' prejudices can be gathered from his complaint about one female client. "You must have observed, Watson, how she maneuvered to have the light at her back. She did not wish us to read her expression. . . . And yet the motives of women are so inscrutable. You remember the woman at Margate whom I suspected for the same reason. No powder on her nose—that proved to be the correct solution. How can one build on such a quicksand?" This is about as actively misogynistic as Holmes ever gets, and it's difficult not to sympathize with him, reduced from his customary omnipotence to the lowly common status of the baffled male.

Whatever the exact nature of Holmes' feelings about women, they are clearly not Conan Doyle's. In contrast to Raymond Chandler, who shared his detective Philip Marlowe's dislike of women enough to make them the criminals in six of his seven novels, Conan Doyle created few female villains, and they are often sympathetically motivated. They are not the fair English flowers who usually grace Holmes' consulting-room, but more exotic blooms: South American, generally, or perhaps Greek or Jewish. These women, "tropical by birth and tropical by nature," are foreshadowed in "The Mystery of Uncle Jeremy's Household," a story Conan Doyle wrote for *Boy's Own Paper* in 1887. Here the villain is a mysterious governess with "a feline grace about her every movement" that the smitten narrator has never seen before "in any woman." This "dark handsome" creature turns out to be an Indian princess *and* a priestess of Thugee who has, against the ordinary order of things, become the first female leader of the cult. She orders one of her followers to kill a man who is blackmailing her, which seems fair enough. However, she has also previously murdered two of her charges as sacrifices, one a young woman and the other a little girl. Yet the narrator, far from being repulsed, continues to find her fascinating and even refers to her as an "unfortunate woman." This gives the story a peculiar moral tone, to say the least, and contrasted Conan Doyle's usual Victorian propriety is almost shocking. He lets her get away with it, too; she flees to London and escapes. The narrator here is both lover and detective. With Holmes, Conan Doyle cut the lover out (giving the role briefly to Watson in *The Sign of the Four*). But in his first Holmes short story, "A Scandal in Bohemia," he introduced, as the only woman Holmes might have loved, an American "adventuress" who has been a prince's mistress, not at all the sort of nice girl Holmes usually protects or whom, in the figure of Mary Morstan, Watson shyly woos then marries.

Conan Doyle was capable of imagining conditions under which swooning before the power of a femme fatale might be, however horrible, compelling if not actually pleasurable. Two of his non-Holmes tales are about men who fall into the clutches of evil, irresistable women (one of whom is not only plain but lame). One of the victims is destroyed; the other escapes only when the woman (rather too conveniently for the story to work) dies. The eponymous hero of the first, "John Barrington Cowles," is described as dreamy and languid, except when a subject that interests him is raised, when he becomes "all animation in a moment." He is "passionately attached to art in every form, and a pleasing chord in music or a delicate effect upon canvas would give exquisite pleasure to his highly-strung nature." In the second, *The Parasite*, the professor of physiology who narrates his own frightening experience with a female mesmerist writes in his diary: "A departure from pure reason affects me like an evil smell or a musical discord." In each case, Conan Doyle could be describing Holmes. There is a hint of sexual squeamishness in that "evil smell," and both stories are warnings about the sensual power of women. Perhaps this was one enemy Conan Doyle felt it wise never to let his invincible detective go up against.

Whatever Conan Doyle's motives, he succeeded in making Holmes perhaps the most confirmed bachelor in all of literature. Jokes have been made for years about Holmes having a homosexual relationship with Watson, but it's actually pretty hard to imagine him as a lover of either sex. He seems as beyond ordinary human sexuality as he is beyond ordinary human mentality, and it's appropriate that his two most obvious pop culture descendants—*Star Trek*'s Mr. Spock (with his twin Watsons, the admiring Kirk and the skeptical McCoy), and Tom Baker's Doctor Who—are both aliens, with no sexuality understandable in human terms.

Holmes' decision to live a life without women was a Victorian option that men mostly achieved by choosing a military career. In Holmes' case, it is a mark of his civilian bohemianism. By having no active sexual nature, he manages to evade the usual responsibilities of the good bourgeois. He may defend the values of home and hearth, but he has nothing to do with them in his own life. Though Baker Street is always depicted as domestically cozy—the fire burning warmly, its reflections glinting on the test-tubes of the sitting-room laboratory, two armchairs pulled up close, the genius in one, his biographer in the other, the former brooding brilliantly upon a case, the latter reading one of Clark Russell's sea stories— the fact is that a little of this goes a long way with Holmes. Too much of it and he is pacing and snarling, complaining about the dearth of criminals in London, commenting that it's a good thing for society *he* isn't a criminal, and finally, his mind rebelling at stagnation, turning to cocaine. Watson isn't much use to him at times like this, and in a sobering passage at the beginning of one of the last stories, "The Creeping Man," Conan Doyle has this to say about the famous friendship

> The relations between us in those latter days were peculiar. He was a man of habits, narrow and concentrated habits, and I had become one of them. As an institution I was like the violin, the shag tobacco, the old black pipe, the index books, and others perhaps less excusable. When it was a case of active work and a comrade was needed upon whose nerve he could place some reliance, my role was obvious. But apart from this I had uses. I was a whetstone for his mind. I stimulated him. He liked to think aloud in my presence. His remarks could hardly be said to be made to me—many of them would have been as appropriately addressed to his bedstead—but nonetheless, having formed the habit, it had become in some way helpful that I should register and interject. If I irritated him by a certain methodical slowness in my mentality, that irritation served only to make his flame-like intuitions and impressions flash up the more vividly and swiftly. Such was my humble role in our alliance.

This casually brutal passage is an example of Conan Doyle's most attractive quality in the Holmes stories, his almost total lack of sentimentality toward his hero. His attitude is appreciative but dry, and this is surely one of the things that accounts for the enormous amount of affection readers give to Holmes: Conan Doyle isn't in our way, pointing out what we ought to respond to, doing it all for us. We're free to discover Holmes ourselves, and to come under the spell of his charm and brilliance.

Conan Doyle is unique in this respect among the creators of great detectives. Dorothy L. Sayers, Raymond Chandler, and John le Carre all fell for their heroes. Chandler, who actually created a biography and detailed personal description of Philip Marlow and wrote about him that classic of he-man mawkishness that begins "Down these mean streets a man must go . . ." is perhaps the most besotted, but he's also, fortunately, the funniest, and Marlowe's wisecracks kept things from getting too cloying until the final couple of novels when Chandler was wearing out and his admiration for Marlowe's nobility got gooey. Sayers, whose Pygmalion-like infatuation with her own creation, Lord Peter Wimsey, has often been remarked on, practically acknowledged the problem by having him viewed in four of her novels by Harriet Vane, a woman both exasperated by and in love with him. By the end of *The Honorable Schoolboy*, le Carre's dumpy, diffident George Smiley had taken on the burden of being practically the only uncorrupted man in the whole Secret Service, and even at the end of *Smiley's People*, when he thinks himself no better than his Soviet rival, there is something heroic in his honesty and shame.

It never occurs to Holmes to wonder whether he is morally superior to Moriarty: the question is whether he's smarter. It's the contest he cares about, and once Moriarty is dead he is capable of sighing for the bad old days, bored with the new banality of English crime. It's precisely this heartless individualism that makes him so much fun, and so much easier to take than the lone knights Marlow and Smiley, or Peter Wimsey consulting a priest because he is worried about the unexpected and deadly consequences an apparently "good" act may lead to. Their morality weighs them down. Holmes is carried buoyantly along by his, confident in the belief (and this is Conan Doyle's advantage over his successors) that his society is basically decent and just, and that it is in the usual order of things for good to win over evil. In such a secure world, Holmes' blithe irresponsibility is easily contained. We know that in the end he will always rally round, that though when hearing of a young man accused of a murder he did not commit, he may respond "this is really most grati—most interesting," he will, of course, clear the poor fellow. Conan Doyle is having it both ways; we can enjoy Holmes' anti-social impulses without being threatened by them. He's a very tame rebel. The limit of his destructive behavior is putting bulletholes in his landlady's wall.

And yet, he isn't quite safe. Conan Doyle makes sure that

Holmes' high-mindedness and sense of duty always outweigh his darker tendencies, but he doesn't deny that the tendencies are there. He doesn't make them a set of cute affectations; he acknowledges their force. "Pray forgive me, Ma'am," Conan Doyle once wrote to the mother to whom he was devoted all his life, "if I have ever seemed petulant or argumentative—it is all nerves, of which I possess more than most people know." He lived his life according to a strict Victorian code of ethics, and he knew something about the price that virtue can exact from the personality. Holmes' amoral streak, depressions, nervous collapses, drug abuse, and peculiar solitariness are as real as anything else about him, more real perhaps to us today than they were to his first readers.

"Sherlock Holmes was a drug addict without a single amiable trait," wrote Bernard Shaw, and at times Jeremy Brett appeared to have taken this statement as his approach to the role. He said in interviews that he disliked Holmes, that he wouldn't cross the street to meet him, and yet the whole flamboyant and unsettling performance is an example of an actor going the whole distance to meet the character he is playing. Gaunt, nervous, and elegant, handsome in profile and almost ugly full-face, Brett seems to have sprung from Paget's pen as much as Conan Doyle's. (Periodically, the series takes its images directly from Paget, and the result is haunting, as if a dream had mysteriously reformed itself in the waking world.) At the beginning of each show, he stands in a front window of 221B gazing out into Baker Street. He turns slightly toward us, and his expression is hard to read. Is he meditating on the mysteries implicit in the crowds below, or is he merely arrogantly pleased that he has been given all of London for his mental playing field?

There is something spidery and unwholesome about Brett's Holmes. He doesn't look good, for one thing—pasty and unhealthy from too much tobacco and cocaine and too little sun. In one of the adventures, Watson returns from a few days away (bearing, in a nice touch, golf clubs) and finds the sitting-room a mess of papers and half-eaten food, with an unshaven Holmes lounging in drugged depression in his nightshirt and dressing gown. Fortunately, Watson has brought with him a case to be solved. David Burke (later replaced by Edward Hardwicke) is a sensible, sandy-haired Watson, not at all disposed to indulge his brilliant companion but very protective of his brittle fragility. He looks after him with a matter-of-fact tenderness that is if not exactly maternal at least familial; he's like a good-hearted younger brother watching out for the older brother he admires without quite understanding. Playing him as high-strung to the point of neurasthenia, Brett gives the unnerving impression that Holmes is in some fundamental way damaged. His need for Watson has a desperate edge, as if his friend's sanity were a buffer against his own loneliness and inner demons. Brett doesn't define these demons but they seem linked somehow to Holmes' held-in sensuality. At one point, he reaches out and very lightly strokes a beautiful young woman client's thick red hair. It isn't even clear whether he's aware he's done it.

This is an extreme interpretation of a sentimentally beloved character, and there are admirers of the stories who find Brett unendurable—mannered, nasty, effeminate. It's true that he took the shadow of the character and played it as if it were the soul, but though this may distort what we're used to in Holmes, it doesn't betray him—or Conan Doyle. It's all adumbrated in what Conan Doyle wrote, and by the times in which he wrote. Holmes' enduring vitality is certainly due in part to the way in which he makes flesh of the complex vision we have of the 19th century the sunny, triumphant rationalism with a canker of madness at its core.

AND NOW, A WORD FROM ARTHUR CONAN DOYLE

Jon L. Lellenberg

ACCORDING TO THE editors of the Oxford English Dictionary, more than 400 new words enter the English language every year—proof of remarkable vigor in both our tongue and the world's English-speaking community. Compare our situation with that of France, for example, where the venerable Academie Française works hard to keep new words *out* of the French language, especially ones with unseemly Anglo-Saxon origins.

For over seventy years, the Oxford English Dictionary has been the definitive authority on English vocabulary, illustrating historical and contemporary usages with some two million literary and journalistic quotations. The Dictionary's first section of the letter A appeared in 1884, and the final section was eventually published in 1928: twelve massive volumes, a marvel of lexicography thousands of pages long, recording, defining, and documenting the English language. Subsequent to that, five equally massive supplements were also published, recording the continuing growth and development of the language. The OED's first *Supplement and Bibliography* was published in 1933, later to be superseded by a modern four-volume *Supplement* appearing between 1972 and 1986. In considering what to add to their record of English words and usages, the OED's editors kept constantly before them "the opposing concepts of permanence and ephemerality, retaining vocabulary that seemed likely to be of interest now and to future generations."

I

Arthur Conan Doyle, be it noted, did his part to enrich the English language. Researching this was an intriguing challenge. The 15,385 pages of entries in the OED proper are enough to daunt Jabez Wilson, the dupe in the Sherlock Holmes story "The Red-Headed League" who was set to copying out the *Encyclopedia Britannica* by hand. But releasing it on CD-ROM made running down all the entry-words from Conan Doyle's works possible. And a long list it is: over 400, from 21 Conan Doyle books, six of them from the Sherlock Holmes Canon: *A Study in Scarlet; The Sign of the Four; The Adventures of Sherlock Holmes; The Memoirs; The Return;* and *His Last Bow.*

The seventy-four entry-words from the Canon are sometimes hard to pick out from the entire list. Conan Doyle's OED-worthy use of **thumbless** does not come from "The Engineer's Thumb," and his use of **thumb-mark** comes from his historical novel *Micah Clarke,* though its line "it is impossible to get the thumb-marks of any two men to be alike" was surely perspicacious for 1887, when the novel was written, anticipating Sherlock Holmes' exchange on fingerprints with the police in "The Norwood Builder" by sixteen years.

(It was disappointing to find that the OED did not draw upon Conan Doyle to illustrate the various meanings of the word **detective**—not even **consulting detective**, though Sherlock Holmes claimed to be the world's first. Later, however, the OED's modern *Supplement* added a new definition for the word **consultant**: "a person qualified to give professional advice or services; also spec. a private detective," justifying this definition with a quotation from "Silver Blaze": "I am rather disappointed in our London consultant." **Consulting-room,** as "a room in which a consultation takes place; esp. the room in which a doctor examines his patients," goes back to 1843, but Conan Doyle got partial credit for both the canonical "Two men had come from Paddington and were waiting in the consulting room," in "The Engineer's Thumb," and the non-canonical "If you will wait here in the consulting-room I have no doubt that I shall be able to send the doctor in to you," from *Round the Red Lamp*, a collection of medical stories. Only the former was retained by the modern *Supplement* from the 1933 *Supplement and Bibliography*.)

But some canonical entry-words are Sherlockian bell-ringers, such as **tantalus** and **dottle**. Some are British slang such as **fiver** and **ripping**, or American slang such as **deader** and **woozy**. A few are foreign words, such as **Lunkah** and **Trichinopoly**. Some betray medicine's influence in Dr. Conan Doyle's writing; when Dr. Watson spoke of Holmes adorning the wall of 221B "with a patriotic V.R. done in bullet-pocks," for example, the OED says he made a fresh use of the medical term meaning "a spot or mark like a pustule." Other examples show the equally strong influence of Conan Doyle's love of sports, such as *A Study in Scarlet's* "I told you that, whatever happened, Lestrade and Gregson would be sure to **score**."

Few words were actually coined by Conan Doyle, of course. Mostly he created new and original uses of existing words. The OED has a "third class carriage on the **Underground**" in *A Study in Scarlet* as that term's earliest recorded reference to London's Metropolitan Railway, for example (though Michael Harrison, in *London by Gaslight*, tells us that Londoners were already calling it that when its first line was still under construction in 1860). Another term for which Conan Doyle gets first credit is **snackle**, defined as "to secure, to make fast." The vengeful fugitive Jefferson Hope uses it toward the end of *A Study in Scarlet*: "This young man here had the bracelets on my wrists, and as neatly snackled as ever I saw in my life." In fact Conan Doyle gets sole credit, for the OED records no other use before or since his, and says that the word is "of obscure origin." Perhaps **snackled** was Conan Doyle's attempt at the sound of American slang, but it may have been simply a misprint for **shackled** that survived from *Beeton's Christmas Annual* for 1887, where *A Study in Scarlet* first appeared, into all subsequent editions of the first Sherlock Holmes tale. Since the manuscript is lost, probably we shall never know for sure.

A more likely example of Doylean originality is the modest word **snick**. The OED knows no earlier use of it to mean "a sharp noise, a click," than "The Naval Treaty": "suddenly there came from the window a sharp metallic snick." Often the possible borrowings are thought-provoking. In "The Stockbroker's Clerk," for example, the villainous Beddington brothers are seeking "a young, pushing man with plenty of **snap** about him." That 1893 use is interesting, because the term, in its meaning of "alertness, energy, vigor, 'go,' " is American in origin, the OED says. The only earlier use that the OED records is from 1872: "I like to see a man who has got snap in every part of him." The person who wrote that was the Rev. Henry Ward Beecher, and it is not too difficult to imagine that Beecher's book once lay on Conan Doyle's desk, even before Watson displayed Beecher's portrait ("The Cardboard Box" tells us) at 221B Baker Street.

II

The name Sherlock Holmes appears in only one OED quotation from 1928, from a December 9, 1899, London *Daily News* item, found under the entry **thought-reading**: "Do you think your thought-reading gift could be turned to practical service in detective work—a thought-reading Sherlock Holmes?" But when the OED's *Supplement and Bibliography* was published in 1933, **Sherlock Holmes** had become sufficiently permanent a term in the English language to merit its own entry, with the following definition:

> **SHERLOCK HOLMES.** The name of the amateur detective who is the chief figure in the detective stories of A. Conan Doyle, collected under the titles *Adventures of Sherlock Holmes,*

etc; used typically for a person who indulges in investigating and solving mysteries. Hence SHERLOCK (HOLMES) *v. intr.*, to play the detective.

Five examples of the use of the term **Sherlock Holmes** were given in that historic 1933 entry, the earliest from a long-forgotten 1899 *Introduction to Science*: "a coincidence that would hardly be devised in the fertile brain of a Sherlock Holmes." Not "of Sherlock Holmes," mind, but "of *a* Sherlock Holmes"—that was the OED's point about the term **Sherlock Holmes** having penetrated the language. George Bernard Shaw followed in 1903, calling a feminine character in *Man and Superman* "a regular Sherlock Holmes"; and a 1929 novel called *Roper's Row*, by G. W. Deeping, supposedly coined a pleasant turn of phrase with the passage: "Let's do a little Sherlock Holmesing."

We don't often see that particular expression these days. To my ear, it has a pleasant old-fashioned sound. It seems to have been fairly common usage once, and 1929, it turned out later, was not the first time that it appeared in print. When the final volume of the OED *Supplement* appeared in 1986, its continuing entry for **Sherlock Holmes** noted several more uses and permutations of "Sherlock Holmesing," beginning in 1922 with James Joyce's *Ulysses*, no less: "He had been meantime taking stock of the individual in front of him and Sherlock-holmesing him up."

By 1896, in fact, the Master actually rated two entries in the OED *Supplement*, one under **Sherlock Holmes**, and an even longer one under **Sherlock** alone. No big surprise to find **Sherlock** used as a noun or verb by such writers as Dorothy L. Sayers, in 1928, or even Rudyard Kipling, in 1932: "We aren't exactly first-class Sherlocks," he wrote in *Limits & Renewals*. No great surprise either to find Sherlockian scholars like Howard Haycraft and William S. Baring-Gould contributing new usages of their hero's name. Stronger evidence of the universality of the great detective was provided by less likely creators of usages, writers as diverse as John Galsworthy, in his 1920 play *Foundations* ("Don't call the police! Let me do the

Sherlocking for you!"), and Jack Kerouac, in 1957's beat epic *On the Road* ("They tried some amateur Sherlocking by asking the same question twice.")

Sherlockians have occasionally wondered when and what the first use of the term **Sherlockian** was. I once contended that it was at the turn of the century in *The Bookman*, that wonderful literary journal for a more literary age, but I was bluffing. I was unsure when the term was first used, or even why I thought it had been there. But happily the OED *Supplement* agrees, citing a comment in *The Bookman* in 1903: "If you decipher this you are a real Sherlockian." **Sherlockiana** made its debut much later, in 1942, says the OED, in *Murder for Pleasure*, Howard Haycraft's history of the detective story, when Haycraft referred to "Vincent Starrett's *Private Life of Sherlock Holmes* with its valuable appended bibliography of Sherlockiana." Tempting as it is to accept this, Haycraft commenting on Starrett, I find it difficult to believe that there are no earlier uses of the term **Sherlockiana**. Perhaps the OED needs a Sherlockian among its army of volunteer readers.

Or a Holmesian. **Holmesian** is an entry in the OED *Supplement* too, defined as: "A. *adj.* Of, pertaining to, or in the manner of Sherlock Holmes. B. *sb.* A devotee of Sherlock Holmes." The earliest use of which the OED's editors are aware occurs in the 1929 novel *Man in Queue* by "G. Daviot"—actually Josephine Tey's first novel, *The Man in the Queue*: "Grant disclaimed any such Holmesian qualities." Other examples in the OED introduce us to supposedly first references to Holmesian scholars, the Holmesian saga, Holmesian costume, etc., including, in 1972, the felicitous observation of the *Times Literary Supplement* that "the great Holmesian game trundles along with unabated vigor." Overlooked, though, to the pain of Baker Street Irregulars, is the term's use in 1930 by the BSI's founder, Christopher Morley—"Holmesians and Doyleites"— in his foreword to first American *Complete Sherlock Holmes*, still in print today.

Watson finds a place in the OED today as well, identified as "the name of the doctor who was the stolid, faithful assistant and foil" of Sherlock Holmes—not to mention being "used allusively of one who acts similarly as a stooge or audience, esp. for a detective." The earliest example given is from the 1927 mystery novel *The Three Taps* by Ronald A. Knox, who as an undergraduate at Oxford in 1912 wrote a paper called "Studies in the Literature of Sherlock Holmes" which defined what the *Times Literary Supplement* called the great Holmesian game. "Watson-work," wrote Knox in 1927, "meant that Angela tried to suggest new ideas to her husband under a mask of carefully assumed stupidity." Poor Watson, libeled even by the father of our own Higher Criticism! Other usages of **Watson** followed Knox's, by Dorothy L. Sayers, P. G. Wodehouse, Agatha Christie, and some others less obviously owing homage to the creator of Sherlock Holmes.

Watsonian is a separate entry in the OED's *Supplement* ("a. Of, pertaining to, or characteristic of someone called Watson"), though our Watson has to share the entry with the American behavioral psychologist J. B. Watson. The earliest **Watsonian** reference to *our* Watson is a 1940 comment, in mystery writer E. C. Bentley's reminiscences, *Those Days*, about "Watsonian chronology" being discussed at the dinners of London's Sherlock Holmes Society in the 1930s. Among several other examples, there is a strange one from a 1966 issue of the British magazine *Encounter.* "Just one more case of Watsonian blackmail." What could *Encounter*—a political journal for Tory intellectuals—have meant by that?

III

But these are mere permutations of the proper names of literary heroes, whom we and countless writers have celebrated in print for more than a century now. I must report some failures by devoted Sherlockians regarding the English language, at least as enshrined by the OED. In 1933, one OED definition of **Canon** was "the collection of books of the Bible accepted by the Christian Church as genuine and inspired; also, any set of sacred books." When in 1972 the OED *Supplement* extended the definition to include "those writings of a secular author accepted as authentic," the examples given could, and should, have included Sherlock Holmes as well as Plato and Shakespeare. They did not. Baker Street Irregularity, moreover, Irregularity with a capital I, is still unrecognized by the OED. And while the abbreviation **BSI** *is* recognized by the OED, its editors know it only as indicating the "British Standards Institution"! Obviously the BSI has work ahead of itself in its self-appointed task of thoroughly confusing the archaeologists of the future.

Perhaps the most egregious omission from the OED is the memorable expression known as the "Sherlockismus." A hypothetical (and incomplete) entry for "Sherlockismus" might go as follows:

> **SHERLOCKISMUS.** *n.* **Also Sherlockism.** Any of several kinds of memorable quotations or turns of phrase attributed to, or characteristic of, Sherlock Holmes (Arthur Conan Doyle's detective). 1. A memorable interlocutory exchange between Holmes and any second party in which Holmes retains the investigational upper hand. 1912: "There is a special kind of epigram, known as the Sherlockismus, of which the indefatigable Ratzegger has collected no less than 173 instances." Ronald A. Knox, "Studies in the Literature of Sherlock Holmes," *Gryphon* (Oxford University). 2. An enigmatic clue, described by Holmes to Watson (his foil) in the form of an ambage. 1949: "Call this 'Sherlockismus'; call it any other fancy name; the fact remains that it is a clue, and a thundering good one at that." John Dickson Carr, *The Life of Sir Arthur Conan Doyle.* 3. Any other memorable statement (whether by Holmes or one of his imitators), in the form of a maxim, hyperbole, meiosis, or antithesis, that is typical of Sherlock Holmes. 1988: "In other words, a Sherlockism is something said by Sherlock Holmes that is unique to Holmes." George Scheetz, "The Sherlockismus Revisited," *Baker Street Journal.*

Somewhere, I believe, the mystery writer and critic Anthony Boucher coined the alternative term "Sherlocution" for the memorable and uniquely Sherlockian statement, but I have not yet located the reference.

IV

Finally, what about words or expressions *created* by Conan Doyle? Are there any from the Canon? Yes, there are: several at least.

However, the first, **grimpen**, was probably included in the OED a trifle facetiously (however unlikely it may seem that the august Oxford English Dictionary would jest with the pure scholarly aspirations of its readers). The OED defines **grimpen** as "? A marshy area," with that diffident question mark compounded by a comment that the word's etymology is uncertain. That's putting it mildly—though there is a strong Old English sound to it; Grendel might well live in a grimpen. The OED cites Watson's marvelous passage in *The Hound of the Baskervilles* as the word's first known use in English literature: "Life has become like that great Grimpen Mire, with little green patches everywhere into which one may sink and with no guide to point the track." But I suspect **grimpen** would have gone unrecognized by the OED, had it not been picked up by no less a poet than that Old Possum of closet Sherlockians, T. S. Eliot, whose 1940 poem *East Coker* includes the lines:

> We are only undeceived
> Of that which, deceiving, could no longer harm.
> In the middle, not only in the middle of the way
> But all the way, in a dark wood, in a bramble,
> On the edge of a grimpen, where there is no secure foothold,
> And menaced by monsters, fancy lights,
> Risking enchantment.

For surely Conan Doyle meant Grimpen (Mire) as a proper place name—and the OED lets us know that it is in on the joke with its final example: William S. Baring-Gould's prosaically factual comment in his 1967 *Annotated Sherlock Holmes* that, "as is well known, Watson's 'Great Grimpen Mire' is Grimspound Bog, three miles to the north and east of Widecombe-in-the-Moor" on Dartmoor.

Whenever the OED brings its record of the English language up to date again, it can add some further usages of **grimpen**. They come this time from the February 27, 1988, issue of *The Blood-Horse*, a magazine for the horsey set. Its editors do not take equine matters lightly. After a garbled summary of the OED's exposition of the word **grimpen**, they launch into a heated discussion of what a pedestrian like myself would call "horse-doping," referring along the way to (a) the need to extend the definition of **grimpen** "to include onslaughts of emotional verbiage 'into which one may sink' "; (b) lemmings following one another into the great Grimpen Mire (an outré sight denied us by the author of *The Hound of the Baskervilles*); and (c) preventing the humane treatment of racehorses from sinking out of sight "in the great Grimpen Mire of rhetoric, theory, and off-target idealism."

One wishes the OED's editors luck.

More familiar today is the term "smoking gun" or "smoking pistol." It came into common use during Watergate, to mean (the OED *Supplement* says) "a piece of incontrovertible incriminating evidence." The OED *Supplement* cites a 1974 *New Yorker* article, though that quotation implies that the term was already in use by then to mean "the definitive piece of evidence that the President committed a crime." Curiously, the OED entry for **smoking gun/pistol** calls it a specifically American term—failing to link its origin to a canonical passage actually cited in the OED proper as the term's first use. **Smoking** is defined there as "emitting or giving out smoke"; the usages illustrating that definition begin with a 1374 quotation from Chaucer, and the ninth, with which we are concerned here, comes from a Sherlock Holmes story narrated by Holmes himself, "The 'Gloria Scott' ": "The chaplain stood with a smoking pistol in his hand." (While the OED failed to make the connection, the Watergate expression's origin was traced back to Sherlock Holmes by William Safire in his 1979 *New York Times* article "Sweet Land of

Euphemism," and specifically to "The 'Gloria Scott,' " with the help of BSI Peter E. Blau, in Safire's book *On Language* the following year.)

The OED's modern four-volume *Supplement* also listed, among half a dozen more Conan Doyle titles, *The Valley of Fear*. Browsing through it one day, I thought perhaps the term **brain-wave** might be an instance of Doylean originality: "One more coruscation, my dear Watson," says Holmes: "Yet another brain-wave." Wrong. **Brain-wave** was in use as early as 1869. So much for *my* brain-wave. I do have one last example of Doylean originality to offer, however, from *The Case-Book of Sherlock Holmes*. That volume of the Canon was not even mentioned in the OED's bibliographies, and yet this particular Doylean expression may be his least likely contribution of all to our language. The Oxford English Dictionary gives Arthur Conan Doyle credit for inventing the term—wait for it: **wonder-woman**—of all things! The term was used by Sherlock Holmes, readers will recall, to describe Miss Violet de Merville in "The Adventure of the Illustrious Client": "a wonder-woman in every way."

Who would have thought it? **Wonder-woman**—from the same writer who in another Sherlock Holmes story, "His Last Bow," called suffragettes "window-breaking Furies," and blamed them on German agitators! That's pretty wondrous in its own right. The creator of Sherlock Holmes never loses his ability to surprise us.

CONTRIBUTORS

Daniel Stashower is the author of the Edgar-winning *Teller of Tales: The Life of Arthur Conan Doyle*, and a member of the Baker Street Irregulars.

Stuart M. Kaminsky is the author of more than 50 published books and 35 short stories. His books include novels, 4 biographies, and books on film history, filmmaking and scriptwriting. His novels, which have been translated into 12 languages, include the Inspector Porfiry Petrovich Rostnikov books, one of which, *A Cold Red Sunrise*, won the Edgar Award of the Mystery Writers of America for best mystery novel of 1989. The novel also won the Prix Du Roman D'Aventure for the best mystery novel published in France in 1990. He also writes the popular Toby Peters mysteries set primarily in Los Angeles in the 1940s. There have been 20 Toby Peters novels, and his 1991 Toby Peters novel *Poor Butterfly* was nominated for a Shamus Award.

He is a past (1998) President of the Mystery Writers of America. He has had six M. W. A. Edgar nominations, three for best short story, two for best paperback and one for best novel.

He holds a B.S. in Journalism and Communications and an M.A. in English Literature from the University of Illinois and a Ph.D. in

Speech (Film-Television-Theater) from Northwestern University where he taught in and chaired the Department of Radio/Television/Film before coming to Florida State University where he was a Professor of Motion Picture, Television and Recording Arts. He has retired from teaching and is now writing full time in Sarasota, Florida where he lives with his family.

Howard Engel is best known for his Benny Cooperman series, about a hapless yet persistent Yiddish detective who lives and works in Canada. Before turning to writing full time, he was a freelance radio broadcaster, executive producer, and a literary editor. He is a co-founder of the Crime Writers of Canada organization, and a member of the Mystery Writers of America as well as the International Association of Crime Writers. He has also written non-fiction, notably a book about executioners, as well as edited an anthology of short mystery fiction by Canadian authors.

Peter Tremayne is the pseudonym of Peter Berresford Ellis, a Celtic scholar who lives in London, England. He conceived the idea for Sister Fidelma, a 7th Century Celtic lawyer, to demonstrate that women could be legal advocates under the Irish system of law. Sister Fidelma has since appeared in eight novels, the most recent being *The Monk Who Vanished*, and many short stories which have been collected in the anthology *Hemlock at Vespers and other Sister Fidelma Mysteries*. He has also written, under his own name, more than 25 books on history, biography, and Irish and Celtic mythology, including *Celtic Women: Women in Celtic Society and Literature* and *Celt and Greek: Celts in the Hellenic World*.

Anne Perry writes, "I was born in Blackheath, London in 1938. From an early age, I enjoyed reading and two of my favorite authors were Lewis Carroll and Charles Kingsley. It was always my desire to write, but it took 20 years before I produced a book which was accepted for publication. That was *The Cater Street Hangman*, which came out in 1979. I chose the Victorian era by accident, but I am happy to stay with it, because it was a remarkable time in British history, full of extremes, of poverty and wealth, social change, expansion of empire, and challenging ideas. In all levels of society there were the good and the bad, the happy and the miserable."

Edward D. Hoch is a past president of Mystery Writers of America and a winner of its 2001 Grand Master award and its Edgar award for the best short story of 1968. He has published nearly 850 stories as well as anthologies, collections and novels. He has been Guest of Honor at the annual Bouchercon mystery convention and received its Anthony Award for best short story. In 2001 he will receive the convention's Lifetime Achievement Award. In 2000 he received The Eye, the life achievement award of the Private Eye Writers of America. He resides in Rochester, NY, with his wife Patricia.

Bill Crider is the author of the Sheriff Dan Rhodes series, the first book of which won the Anthony Award in 1987. Crider's short stories have appeared in numerous anthologies, including *Holmes For The Holidays* and all the books in the celebrated Cat Crimes series.

Gillian Linscott is best known for her series of nine crime novels featuring the suffragette detective, Nell Bray. One of the most recent, Absent Friends, was awarded both the Crime Writers' Association Ellis Peters Historical Dagger in the UK and the Herodotus Best International Historical Mystery Award in the USA. She is a former journalist and lives in Herefordshire, England.

Loren D. Estleman is the author of nearly fifty books, including the Amos Walker detective series, several westerns, and the Detroit historical mystery series, including *Whiskey River, Motown, King of the Corner*, and *Edsel.* His first Sherlock Holmes pastiche, *Sherlock Holmes vs. Dracula*, has been in print for twenty-three years.

Jon L. Breen is the author of six novels, more than eighty short stories, and two Edgar Award winning critical volumes. His most recent books are *The Drowning Icecube and Other Stories* (Five Star), the second edition of *Novel Verdicts: A Guide to Courtroom Fiction* (Scarecrow), and the anthology *Sleuths of the Century* (Carroll & Graf), edited with Ed Gorman. He contributes "The Jury Box" review column in *Ellery Queen's Mystery Magazine*.

L. B. Greenwood's fiction has appeared in *Malice Domestic, Malice Domestic III*, and *Malice Domestic IV*. She is also one of the few women to take up the mantle of Sherlock Holmes in novel form. Her pastiches include *Sherlock Holmes and the Case of the Raleigh Legacy* and *Sherlock Holmes and the Thistle of Scotland*. She lives in British Columbia, Canada.

Carolyn Wheat is known for her series of legal mysteries involving Cass Jameson, although recently she has turned her hand to editing short story collections, including the recent *Women Before the Bench*. She has taught mystery writing at the New School in New York City, and legal writing at the Brooklyn Law School. An Adventuress of Sherlock Holmes, her investiture is The Penang Lawyer (Hound).

Sir Arthur Conan Doyle (1859–1930) was the creator of the most popular detective of all time. Sherlock Holmes' exploits took on a life of their own to thousands of mystery readers around the world and still resonate with a large audience today. His creator studied medicine at the University of Edinburgh, served as a senior physician at a South African field hospital during the Boer War, and was knighted in 1902. His writing career had been well established by then, with the tales of Holmes and his chronicler and companion John Watson passing from literature into legend.

Lloyd Rose is the theater critic of the *Washington Post*, and a member of the Baker Street Irregulars. She is the author of the Doctor Who novel *The City of the Dead* and of an episode of *Homicide: Life on the Street*.

Jon L. Lellenberg is the Baker Street Irregulars historian, and the U.S agent for the Estate of Dame Jean Conan Doyle.